FATED BLIGHT
THE SUM OF AGES: BOOK 1

Benjamin Schwarting

Williams & Rose Publishing LLC

Books by Benjamin Schwarting

The Sum of Ages

Fated Blight

Tainted Vessels

Harrowing Echoes

Waning Haven

Daughters of the Storm

Kindred Straits

Razed Harbor (*coming soon*)

Vows of the Void

The Gutter Prince (*coming soon*)

To my brilliant, talented, longsuffering wife. You slogged through endless, terrible drafts, you encouraged me when I was ready to quit, and, most importantly, you taught me empathy.

Thank you, Kalee.

TABLE OF CONTENTS

Great Sea
Centile
Dawns Harbor
Zhu Long
Shin Hai
Shan Zhong
Ka Jiya
West Muban
Sotay
Wharf
Lunsod sa Dagat

To enjoy good health, to bring true happiness to one's family, to bring peace to all, one must first discipline and control one's own mind. If a man can control his mind he can find the way to Enlightenment, and all wisdom and virtue will naturally come to him.

Just as treasures are uncovered from the earth, so virtue appears from good deeds, and wisdom appears from a pure and peaceful mind. To walk safely through the maze of human life, one needs the light of wisdom and the guidance of virtue.

Bukkyo Dendo Kyokai–The Teachings of Buddha

PROLOGUE
AN INCLEMENT FORECAST

TAKODA COULDN'T LOSE THIS HARVEST. THE HAY was all he had. So, with the whip of fear at his back, he moved too quickly through dawn's meager glow. He didn't bother to pace himself against his thumpy, bumpy heart, he didn't stop to wipe the grit and sweat out of his eyes…

…and he didn't notice the dark things creeping through the shadows beyond his field.

Takoda had lost a harvest once before to marauders, but that was *way*, way back. Back when his clubbed tail had barely finished blooming to spikes. He had been a younger, stronger man back then, with them quick little fingers and a real slippery tongue. He could probably find a way to get by if things came to that this season, but he was so close to market, you know? *Thunder and hail*, he was so close… Having to go back to picking pockets and smooth-talking wallies after a harvest this fine?

Well, that would be a real ugly thing indeed.

Dawn of the first harvest was *always* a bad morning, but today was downright urgent. It was them nasty weather predictions. He'd been talking with some of the other farmers, and they were all just as skiddy, diddy scared as him, you know? From what the outlanders could tell, the storm's front looked bad. *Real* bad. Like a bad batch of potatoes bad. The day before had been sweaty, and the evening that followed had been calm as a cold knife. That meant the chilly morning breeze against Takoda's itchy neck was just going to keep getting worse and worse. Black gales, thrashing sands, and a shredded, scattered, useless harvest.

Like so many outlander farmers, Takoda had poured the entirety of his savings into this year's crop. So, with that fear still cracking at his back, Takoda did what his mama always told him to do when life got bleak.

He sang.

"The sun was playing with her hair, when that wallie
 Vallin made me swear
"That I would always love her till I died."
"He said son the world's right bitter cold, and when
 you both are getting old,
"Just keep love's sunshine singing on inside."
"But storms they came with hail and snow. I cried to
 him where we gon' go?
"So Vallin built that wall for us to hide behind,
"Yeah, Vallin built a wallie place to hide."

Takoda smiled at the sad, lazy tune. It was a wallie song, for sure, but it was still a goodie, you know? Especially after he'd gone and spruced it up a bit. There was just something special about that silly, wallie legend. It made his insides get all soft and fluttery. And you didn't even need a drum or nothing to sing the song! But singing songs without drums?

Or dancing?

Or roaring fires?

Takoda shivered at the thought.

What would his poor mama think? It was another one of them bad, Centile habits he'd picked up after he'd left his village. Maybe that was why his luck had been so rotten lately…

Maybe he was starting to turn wallie on the *inside* too…

He glanced up at the pearly, peeking gleam coming through the eastern mountains as he scooped another great armful of hay into his wooden cart. Were those clouds getting faster, or was he getting slower? He *had* been up most of the night already. Just watching, cutting, packing, waiting, stressing, and yet there was still so much to do, you know?

Mi cola, there was still so much to do…

So, Takoda kept on singing.

> *"And when my love was sick abed, I called for Vallin*
> *and he done said:*
> *"He'd find a way to cure her of her ill."*
> *"He ran the whole world round, and then, he went and*
> *ran it all again,*
> *"And like the wind his feet went blurry, whirly shrill."*
> *"With thunder, yeah, his voice was filled, and from his*
> *fingers lightning spilled,*
> *"But in the end, he healed her with his will,*
> *"Yeah, that wallie healed my true love with his will."*

Takoda snorted. "Feet like the wind, yeah?" he muttered. "Wouldn't that be something…" He couldn't help the icky, sticky bitter feelings bubbling up in his empty stomach as he thought about it. The plains of Centile were not a forgiving place to farm. Water was scarce, the heat was intense, and the winds could wipe out a year's worth of labor in a matter of hours. Sometimes minutes.

Poof. Nothing left. Just a sad farmer.

Each season was a gamble. Some outlander farmers would be rich as inner-district wallies one year and then down-in-the-ditch-destitute the next. So much depended on luck, weather, and the will of the wallies that year.

Takoda didn't take no chances on trendy crops or fancy fields. He was perfectly fine sticking to hay: simple, stable, sellable hay. And he always cultivated it on his bitsy two-acre field. No money wasted on hired hands. No seasonal help. Just enough space to feed himself and reap a profit. And, with no family to support, Takoda was truly free to fend for himself. Free as the wind, you know? Yes sir, free as the plains! It was how a telak was *supposed* to live!

But all that sparkly freedom sort of lost its appeal on mornings like this…

So, with nothing else to fill the lonely, Takoda's smoky voice rattled out the third verse.

> *"Them years went by and I had no bread, and Vallin*
>   *came to my tent and said,*
> *"Take this seed and toss it on the plains."*
> *"So, I took it from his shiny hand and in an instant,*
>   *poof! All the land*
> *"Was filled with fruit and golden corn and grain."*
> *"And from that rocky, grouchy soil, without no plow or*
>   *sweat or toil,*
> *"He harvested the fields without the sun or rain,*
> *"Yeah, he harvested them fields without no rains."*

And as if on cue, a little spritzy, speckling of rain dotted his dusty cheeks.

Takoda plopped his load into the cart and gave the sky the grumpiest look he had. He picked a couple of straws out of the buttons of his worn, cloth shirt and bent down again, compressing all four knees of his two double-buckling legs to take the strain off his crackly back.

He had time. Rain or no rain, he had time.

If he kept this pace he would be on the road before midday. Maybe even at the southern gate. He just had to keep pushing, you know? Keep distracting himself from the storm and the fear and the achy, shaky feeling in his bones.

So, he kept on singing… Kept on distracting himself…

"And when that dark stuff gathered in, and all that's good was lost to sin,
"Dear Vallin... Vallin... something, something... dire?"

"Bah!" Takoda swore and spat. Thunder and hail, he could never remember that last verse. It was a weird one anyway, and he didn't have no time for wallie nonsense right now. He wiped his brow, grabbed another armful, and stuffed it into the cart.

* * *

THE SUN WAS UP NOW, AND THE PLAINS STRETCHED OUT like a sleepy cyove to meet it. More importantly, Takoda's cart was finally loaded. He yanked against the last end of twine and cinched it down as hard as he could around a bent nail in the wooden side. He was tired, filthy, itchy, sweaty, and more than a wee bit stinky, but at least he wasn't too cold no more. That was something, right?

Got to look on them *bright sides* every once in a while.

The chill of early morning work was the hardest part of farming. Takoda was quite certain. Telaks needed sun, you know? He stepped back from his cart and let the morning's first rays flutter over his wrinkled, leathery face. The dawn hadn't burnt off the clouds, though, and his grumbly, mumbly gut knew they would keep on building in the distance...

No time to rest yet.

He checked the bridles on his two lahartos one last time. He bundled up his cloth tarp and stakes on the seat of his cart, just in case. Then he checked the bridles on his lahartos one *last*, last time. The burly lizards stood cold and still on their pillar-like legs. They were grumpy and lumpy and rumbly about the drizzly rain, but they were good boys. Their faces were wide-mouthed and round, with blunt teeth, blunter snouts, dull yellow eyes, and stubby tails. Takoda patted one of the brutes and pulled his jacket over his tan, hay-scratched arms. The cold-blooded lahartos looked downright miserable about life, but Takoda had no sympathy for their whimpers. They'd warm up before long.

He gripped the back of his cart and hoisted himself up onto the seat, carefully swiveling his tail around to his thigh. He picked out a stray piece of hay caught between the four load-bearing toes of his left foot using the toes of his right, then he flicked it away with a grouch and a snort. He flipped up his hood, guiding his long, pointed ears through their slits in the cloth, and pulled the reins up to his lap with a practiced snap.

The grimy, grumbly red beasts snorted their guttural protests, but they obeyed. The cart jerked forward and pulled away from Takoda's homestead. He winced at the blinding glare of the rising sun and glanced back at his cabin. It wasn't much: porous stones, weathered beams, and cracked clay, but it was all he needed, you know? It took him too long to learn that.

All them wasted years trying to live in the city…

But that was in the past. He'd finally come to his senses and went crawling back home to Mama Mountains and Papa Plains. He couldn't stomach all the wallie politics in Centile, you know? His name alone made most of them stuck-up Centileans clutch their purses and glance around for the nearest guard. And, they usually did it *before* he'd even picked any pockets! The nerve. Far better to trust the land than them brillo bigots under the shield.

Takoda's cart pulled up over the hill at the edge of his field. The rising sun was so bright he could barely see the dirt path in front of him. It made the world look dark and colorless, like it wasn't quite real. He pulled down on the brow of his hood, squinted through the glare, and felt his icky gut finally start to settle. There were figures moving just over the next ridge. That *had* to be the caravan gathering on the main road. He'd actually made it!

Takoda's heart let out a big old sigh, relieved he wouldn't have to deal with the gates all by himself. A single farmer could count on getting stopped by the city guard, but it was hard to bully two hundred outlanders rushing the sentries at once, you know?

The smell alone was usually enough to make them brillos back off a pace or two.

Takoda chuckled at the thought. Served them over-stuffed wallies right. It wasn't like the farmers were going to do nothing once they got inside. They never stayed more than a night, just long enough to keep their wares safe under that sparkly shield of theirs. They'd sleep in the streets until the storm passed, trying their best to keep to themselves. After that, it would be off to the markets outside the city center, or to go restock the silos along the outer wall, or maybe to–

Something shot across Takoda's path, making him jump right out of his toes and tail.

He straightened his back and swiveled his ears forward. The sun's light had been too bright to see it clearly, and it had moved just under the glare cast off the ridge ahead. He wiped his eyes and brow. Maybe it was just some sweat blurring his vision. Maybe he was just seeing stuff. He *had* been up for a real long time, you know?

Jumpy, jumpy, jumpy... he scolded himself. Maybe his tired eyes needed–

It moved again, much quicker this time.

Takoda yelped. It couldn't have been a blur. Not twice in the same place. He strained his eyes, but it was gone now, whatever it was... Poof. Just a squeaky quick flash against the shadows. Takoda closed his mouth to keep his teeth from getting all chittery. He was used to seeing small, burrowing things hopping and scurrying across the plains, but that one had been *so big...*

A cyove perhaps?

No. He cast the thought aside. It had been roughly their size, and on all fours too, but it had been thinner than the big canines. And hairless. Its slender arms and round head had looked almost like a telak's...

Memories of marauders smacked him like a club-tailed toddler with a stick. Could there really be a raiding party out here? This was too close to Centile for a pandilla, wasn't it? Even the nastiest, gutsiest bandits wouldn't strike along the city's main patrol routes, would they? He snapped his reins three quick times, trying to rush the lahartos up over the ridge. Whatever it was, he didn't want to meet it out of line of sight of the caravan.

Just as it began to pick up speed, Takoda's cart jerked to a complete stop.

He felt the wood lurch beneath him as something real heavy pressed against the back of the cart, pulling hard on his lahartos, and harder on his buzzing heartstrings. The lizards grunted but settled quickly, too cold to protest with any passion.

Takoda raised himself up on his palms, craning his neck to see over the mound of hay behind him. The spiked tip of his tail twitched like a pine in the wind. The bandits would probably let him go if he surrendered the cart without a fight. He could even run ahead to the caravan and warn the others. They might be so thankful they'd give him some money to cover the loss. It was worth a shot, you know?

But only if he could avoid a slit throat…

Wood creaked and popped as a tremendous load hefted itself onto the bed of his cart. Takoda was too trippy, dippy scared to be confused or curious. He stood quietly, his long toes curled around the front of the cart like a bird gripping a branch, ready to spring off into a sprint at any instant. He didn't think he'd be able to get one of the lahartos free in time, but if he ran now he could probably avoid a fight…

Or he'd take an arrow to the back…

Stick. Splat. Plop.

Was it worth the risk? Maybe if he waited a—

His thoughts stilled as something terrible came into view.

First, he saw only a face: hard and chipped and ashen, like sun-bleached bone on the plains. Then, he saw a body: grey and wiry, like the fetid limbs of a skinned corpse. Takoda watched in horror as the wretched thing slowly climbed onto the seat beside him. It moved with drawn, deliberate steps, like a prairie cat slinking low in a patch of grass. It crawled forward on all fours: stretched wrists leading to two massive fingers on each hand. It walked on its knuckles, with bulbous, barbed talons curled tight against its greasy, black palms. Takoda stepped away gently, staring into what looked like the lifeless eye sockets of an empty skull.

In a frantic spasm, he turned to run, only to find another creature silently waiting on the seat beside him. With an empty yelp, Takoda felt the beast wrench his helpless body down, slamming him against the back of the cart like he didn't weigh nothing at all. The barbs on its fingers pierced his flesh and Takoda felt an immediate, burning pain as the creature's venom stung his nerves and poisoned his blood. He tried to scream, but the beast's claws closed around his throat, choking out the sound before it split his lips. The burning sensation scorched across his neck and he clenched his teeth in agony. It felt like his throat was swelling shut, closing up as he struggled for breath.

The rancid thing brought its face close to Takoda's, stretching out its lower jaw and letting a long, black tongue slide out between chipped, brittle teeth. It slipped the putrid appendage across his face before silently glancing to the other. The second beast reached for the cloth tarp at Takoda's side, delicately pulling it open and exposing the pile of rusty stakes within.

In one perfectly coordinated motion, the first creature lifted a stake to Takoda's chest while the other pounded its skull against it. In two hits, Takoda felt the stake drive through his skin and flesh and lungs, pinning his body to the wooden back of the cart. He choked but didn't scream, feeling hot blood bubble up into his throat. He looked up in shock at the monstrosity before him. The creature's forehead was dented and spiderwebbed with a hundred tiny fractures, yet the beast showed no signs of pain. Takoda looked into the monster's empty eyes and saw a faint, white gleam.

It somehow looked more alive, now that Takoda felt his own life seeping out his chest.

The cart thrashed and heaved as something shifted its weight in the back. Takoda watched the spike slip in and out of his chest with the sudden movement.

Surprisingly, it didn't hurt.

Nothing hurt.

He felt completely cold. Perfectly numb. With mild curiosity, Takoda watched as his murderers meticulously placed the reins back in his hands and gently draped them over his lap. With nimble claws, they then adjusted his shirt, carefully pulling the cloth to cover the stake.

I guess I'm going to the other side today... he thought, and his poisoned mind couldn't feel sad or scared or... nothing. His limbs hung cold and limp from his torso, and he felt his flesh fail all around him as his eyes slid closed for the last time.

* * *

BEYOND THE RIDGE, THE CARAVAN WAS GATHERING. A slow trickle of farmers converged in sleepy streams, each cart slipping smoothly into their midst. Takoda's lahartos knew the way. They pulled the cart along the familiar path and joined the others. Instantly forgotten, and instantly hidden. Together, the caravan meandered forward, steadily making its way to the city in the sun. Steadily approaching one of four stone gates that were the only path under Centile's flowing canopy of golden light.

The road advanced through the sky's sheltering glare, while shifting winds played along the endless grass of the Centilean Plain. Hills as soft as memory rose and fell along a seared skyline, hiding the cracks and seams and jagged cliffs of a forgotten chaos. They sat as topographical mementos: tokens of the global ataxia from a long-dormant caustic age. It was an age that few telaks acknowledged anymore. An age that none who lived could remember.

But it was also an age that was destined to be repeated.

Repeated, because it never truly ended.

PART ONE

THAT WHICH WAS LOST

CHAPTER 1

AN ISLAND WITH NO NAME

THE ONLY LIGHT GUIDING OLENKA'S STEPS CAME from the sour, yellow glow of fish oil lanterns clinging to the warped lintels she passed. The storm's crashing torrents were so relentless around her that they almost felt peaceful. It was an island that couldn't be found on most maps, just a collection of shanties and taverns far from the trade routes used by most sirena and siokoy. In fact, it was a place that was actively avoided by all but the most unsavory of crews. Still, Olenka stepped with poise and precision in the gloom, her long, webbed feet lighting over the water as it streamed across the rusty nails and splintering beams.

Her slight ankles stayed almost a hand's breadth off the ground as she walked, aligning perfectly with her calves. It gave Olenka's supple joints a high, exaggerated gait that seemed impractically elegant. In the water, however, the full length of her legs was employed in powerful kicks that rippled in fluid thrusts from the sockets of her hips all the way to the tips of her pointed, middle toes.

Her people, the Bantay Tubig, were built for life on the Great Sea. Not just their feet, but everything about them was streamlined for an aquatic existence. Their skin was thick and smooth, keeping them warm in the dark of the deep and swift against adverse currents. Their bodies were completely bald, save for the hair on their heads, which they often shaved or kept contained in tight, fish-skin hoods.

Their complexions were light and pearly across the face, torso, and inner thighs but faded at the ribs to a stark cobalt that painted their backs and shoulders as dark as the sea. The colors blended smoothly together except for an intricate pattern formed along the forehead.

This kudori mark was the only real distinction between the four castes of the Bantay Tubig: the pampered kataw hiding away in their perfect city beneath the waves, the warrior sirena and siokoy braving the dangers of the sea, and the vast villages of farming, peddling ugkoy supporting them all. Each were fixed into their castes by their kudori, like the moon driving the tides where it pleased.

Olenka's kudori had haunted her all her life.

She rounded a corner and marched deeper into the shanties, leaving the jagged edge of the boardwalk that jutted out over the sea. The seclusion made her uneasy. It was a unique claustrophobia she had acquired from three years sailing on a banca.

Just visible through the curtains of fat raindrops, an old ugkoy woman sat smoking an elaborate ivory pipe in the corner of an alley while the relentless torrent pounded a taut, cloth canopy above her. She watched Olenka closely through grey, shallow irises, the coils of smoke curling up from her nostrils. Olenka didn't make eye contact with her. There was only one person on this whole soggy rock she wanted to talk to. The rest were distractions at best and a slit throat at worst.

The walkway snaked to the left, coming full circle around the island's craggy wall. The entire landmass was little more than a fang of rock erupting from the tide. The collection of buildings was constructed on a series of wobbly beams fitted into drilled holes in the structure. They skirted the titanic slab like a siokoy's shark tooth necklace, just brushing the hightide line and creaking miserably whenever the water pulled away beneath it. Olenka kept her eyes on the tavern signs. There were no words or names, useless as they were to the illiterate crews that lurked under their doors. Instead they bore simple images. She passed a crab and a scallop shell before she found the one she was looking for.

The fire-fish sign swung in the breeze, the squeal of its iron hinges eclipsed by a million drops colliding with the ocean beyond. The image was crude and stylized, but the fire-fish's striped barbs and frills were easily discernible. Olenka glanced up and down the walkway and then pushed the door open.

The inside of the tavern wasn't much quieter. The meager wood walls kept out the storm's chill but none of its din. A rugged ugkoy couple sat behind the counter, eyes fixed on Olenka. The stench of pipe smoke and booze fumes was exceptionally heavy for such a drafty shack. A few siokoy crews were drinking at tables around the back, nothing but their tilted cups and tattooed shoulders visible in the yellow lamplight.

Olenka stepped up to the counter and leaned back on one forearm. Her fingers, webbed to the first knuckle, gently rapped against the wood as she scanned the crowd. There were at least three distinct crews here: one passing pebbles along a board game on a wooden crate, one laughing and throwing something sharp at the wall, and a third crew way on the other side that–

Olenka turned away to hide the thrill in her eyes.

The crew in the back was the one. It had to be. There were four of them in total: three gnarled siokoy and a single sirena in their midst. That was the first clue. The only real difference between sirena and siokoy was gender, but mixed-caste crews were *strictly* taboo. Only pirates would flaunt their blasphemies so boldly.

The second clue was the sirena's attire. Most sirena, Olenka included, wore a tight fish-skin vest and a girdle of straps for holding knives, fishing spears, and whatever else the sea might demand. It wasn't comfortable or attractive; it was practical. This sirena was not dressed for the sea, but for crawling the taverns. She wore a sweeping leather vest, open to a tight shirt of fine, pale cloth. Her neck and wrists were covered in tinkling ornaments, and she brandished a gaudy nose ring of traditional Bharatian stamped gold.

She wasn't a warrior. She was a captain. This *had* to be the crew Olenka was looking for.

"You orderin' something, miss?"

Olenka turned to see that the old ugkoy man had risen to her spot at the counter. He had the worn, wrinkled face of a Bantay Tubig that spent too much time in the smoke and not enough in the sea.

Olenka nodded. "Four shots of rice wine," she said, sliding a silver barya out onto the counter.

The old man chuckled, his gruff voice like crunching shells on wet sand. "We don't get much of that around here, miss. I can offer you four shots of lambanog, though. That alright?"

"Lambanog?" Olenka tilted her head and the old man dove under the counter, rummaging through the glass necks.

"We make it with coconut sap," he said with a smile. "Comes out strong and sweet. Perfect for a tough little thing like yourself."

Olenka rolled her eyes and peered over the counter. "Is it clear?"

"Clear?" The ugkoy glanced up with a puzzled look but pulled out a long, glass bottle and poured a shot into a bamboo glass. The alcohol flowed bright and transparent, and a sweet, spicy scent bit Olenka's nose, testifying to its potency.

"That clear enough for you, miss?"

Olenka nodded. "Should be fine. Get me one more glass of just water. Oh, and a tray."

"You know," he muttered as he poured, "for a couple more bai I could set you up with a *real* nice spiced bottle. Cinnamon and raisins is our house spec–"

"No." Olenka slipped her coin pouch back into her girdle and cleared her throat. "This'll be it."

The old man shrugged. "Suit yourself."

He slapped a metal tray up onto the counter and pulled a fifth glass through a basin of water.

"Thank you very much," Olenka sang, stacking the cups up onto the tray. "You know, now that I think about it, there is *one* more thing… I don't suppose you know anything about that crew in the corner. The mixed one?"

The old ugkoy's face dropped and he shook his head. "Listen, little sister, I never ask no questions about my customers that I don't need answers to. Spit and rain both fill the sea, ya hear me? If you pay your tab, then you're welcome here. That's all I gotta say about it."

Olenka smirked. "That's not really what I asked, but you answered my question anyway."

Olenka swiveled the tray so that the glass of water was directly in front of her and stood briskly. Before she could leave, the old ugkoy's hand shot out and grabbed her arm.

"Listen," he croaked, "I *do* know enough about them to not get mixed up in their business, alright?"

Olenka shook off the man's hand and glanced up into his worried eyes. Something seemed to click in his mind, and his gaze slipped up to Olenka's intricate, swirling forehead.

"You're not no sirena, are you?"

Olenka turned without a word, marching toward the table in the corner.

"Guess you'll just have to wait and see," she whispered.

* * *

THE MIXED CREW MEMBERS WERE ALL BENT OVER A sea chart when Olenka slid a seat over to their table. The siokoy to her right quickly rolled up the chart and all of them leaned back, staring storms at Olenka. She smiled and passed out the bamboo shot glasses in a very disarming way.

"With all that chatter, I figured you four might want something to wet your throats."

A siokoy to Olenka's left stood abruptly, nearly knocking over his chair as he grabbed her by the shoulder. His bare chest was a tangle of tattoos, leather straps, and jagged jewelry. Most were shark's teeth, but Olenka spied a few squid beaks strung along the cords. The left side of his face was streaked with scars that ran to a stump that had once been an ear and an unnatural divot in the man's trapezius.

"Leave us." His voice gurgled as he spoke, as if half the words got stuck in a flap of filleted flesh in his cheek. He pulled a thin, bone knife from a strap at his waist.

"Now, now, Hiroki. She's just trying to be friendly."

The siokoy turned back to his sirena captain then sat down. He released Olenka's shoulder but didn't sheath his knife. The captain leaned forward, resting her chin on her fist. Her nose ring caught the lamplight just right, throwing a brilliant gleam against the rows of ink in Hiroki's chest.

"What would a pretty minnow like you be doing out here in *such... deep...* water?" She drew out each word like Olenka was a little puddle pup who might not catch their true meaning.

Olenka smiled and lifted her glass. "I'm here to propose a toast."

The captain smirked in amusement that was quickly fading to annoyance. "And what exactly do you suppose we will be toasting, little sister?"

Olenka tilted her head toward the rolled-up sea chart being shifted off the table. "Well, for starters, how about a salvage contract?"

The three siokoy stiffened, turning to their captain. Unlike the others, the sirena stayed quite still. She smirked and shook her head.

"And what makes you think we have a contract for your ilk?" the siokoy holding the chart muttered.

Olenka set down her cup and leaned back. "Word on the docks is you four are looking for a crew that can pull off a salvage dive. A *deep* dive. If you're not too stingy about splitting the claim, then my crew will take the bid."

The three siokoy shifted toward their captain, uncertain of what to do. The sirena's skeptical smile never faltered, and her eyes never left Olenka's. She lifted her gifted glass and sniffed its contents.

"You should know that I don't take kindly to those who waste my time, little sister."

"We should get along just fine, then." Olenka motioned to the chart again. "So, are we going to go over the details or just spend the night glaring and flexing?"

The siokoy each twitched but suppressed their comments. The sirena captain laughed, glancing around at her flustered crew. "What's your name, little minnow?"

"Olenka. And you are?"

"Omi," the sirena whispered, her smile sharp as a knife. She slipped a stray strand of her matted locks back behind her ear as she leaned forward over the table. Her voice was low and tense. It was the voice of someone who was done being taken for granted.

"This is your last chance to leave," she whispered. "Walk away, and I'll let this all blow over. Stay, and your crew will finish the contract or die trying."

A ripple of adrenaline fluttered through Olenka's ribs. Not from anxiety or regret, but excitement. Olenka kept her eyes fixed on Omi's, studying the sirena's silver stare. Her eyes were like a crystal tide on an overcast morning. Omi waited, but Olenka's gaze matched her resolve. So, the captain smiled, leaned back, and raised a hand to the siokoy with the chart.

"Isko?" she prompted.

He grunted and unrolled the scrap of leather.

Olenka leaned forward on her forearms, taking it in. It was a map of all the currents and sea lanes down a one-hundred kilometer stretch along the northern coast. The ink scratched along the leather was harsh, but very precise. She quickly recognized the formation of islands depicted, but there were a few more marked here than she'd known existed. It was not a pleasing or elegant map, but, in the hands of one who could read the stars, it was priceless.

"We are here," the siokoy mumbled, pressing a webbed finger to a blotch near the bottom. Isko slid it along a current running north toward the shipping lanes. "There. Twenty kilometers from shore and about six cable lengths from these rocks."

Olenka nodded and looked up at Omi. "How deep?"

"About two hundred meters." She rubbed her eyes and sat back. "Two fifty at the most."

Olenka stared at the map as the adrenaline shot through her again. This time it *was* anxiety. She was used to great depths. Most of her childhood had been spent fifty to a hundred meters beneath the surface, but *two hundred and fifty?*

"You havin' some second thoughts there, short fins?"

Olenka glanced up at Hiroki. The scarred siokoy was glaring at her, humor and contempt splitting his mangled features.

"What equipment do you have?" Olenka turned away as she spoke, directing her comments to Omi. The captain was staring thoughtfully at Olenka, absently feeling the contours of her nose ring.

"A diving bell mounted to our barge, a few compression vests, and we can get ahold of a couple lanterns," she said, then she turned to the third member of her crew. "Weeping stones won't make it that deep, will they Aroon?"

The third siokoy scratched at his neck and shook his head. "Nah, that shrimp spit'll fade too quick. They'd be goin' dark before we got that bell halfway down there."

Omi nodded. "We'll need the shells, then. Or perhaps live fire-spitters?"

Aroon's scratching hand climbed to his chin. "Probably be needin' both, I's thinkin'. Them clusterwinkles'll be dim, but they's steady, too. And the shrimp'll help keep up the brights when they's needing it. The boys an' I'll be gettin' it all sorted, Cap'n. No worries."

Olenka nodded. "What's the timeframe?"

Omi shrugged. "We can have everything ready in an hour. Hit the mark in three. Your crew will ride out with us, and we'll take you to shore once the salvage is compl–"

"*No.*"

Olenka's voice seemed much louder than it was, and she glanced around the room to make sure she hadn't attracted any unwelcome attention. Omi's eyebrow rose sharply, and her three siokoy stiffened.

"Excuse me?"

"I said no." Olenka's response was flat and firm. "Tattered sails, sister. Do you think this is my first dive? We'll take our banca and meet you three just off the rocks. You can take us out from there if you like, but there's no buwisit way I'm running the risk of you stranding us twenty kilometers offshore, especially on a night job."

The table was silent for a moment, then Aroon chuckled.

"I ain't thinkin' this one's understandin' us, Cap'n," he croaked in his southern isles accent.

Olenka twisted her head toward him, not even attempting to hide the disgust in her eyes. "And what exactly do you think *this one ain't understandin'*? Hmm? That you're all kaizo? That you killed a lost crew running a load from the tall miners? That you were sloppy and sank their banca before you got to the loot? If we're going to do this, then you four need to stop playing games. This is business. You supply the gear and the location, I provide the divers. We split the claim fifty-fifty. Those are my terms. Accept them and we'll get the job done. If not, you can go make that uzai dive by yourselves. Two fifty should be nothing for a group of *bottom feeders* like yourselves."

"Alright." Hiroki stood again, his bone knife still drawn. "I've had *enough* of–"

"Sit down, you *buwisit*," Omi spat. Hiroki stopped, but he did not sit, and he did not take his gaze from Olenka.

Captain Omi snatched up a glass of lambanog and eyed Olenka suspiciously. "You have the spirit of a tempest, little sister. I will give you that. Very brave and very, very foolish…"

Olenka scoffed. "And you've got the heart of a shark, Omi."

The captain chuckled. "Well, flattery will get you nowhere, sister. Pretty minnow like you ought to know that by now."

Olenka raised her glass. "At the rock in three hours?"

The siokoy grabbed their glasses and raised them, eyeing their captain. Omi's face was calm and cold, like an eel peering from the corals. She nodded to Olenka. "Three hours it is."

They swallowed their shots, and Olenka hurried through the door.

CHAPTER 2

MORNING MISCHIEF

A PEBBLE FLITTED THROUGH CORIN'S WINDOW and slapped him against the cheek. He stirred and groaned and rolled over on his cot, but he did not wake. The second pebble was less subtle. Also, it wasn't really a pebble. The *rock* pelted him with decided precision, drilling Corin in the temple and wrenching him from the same dream he'd had every night for the past week.

Corin's body thrashed, and someone giggled. He raised himself up to his elbow, his long, pointed ears swiveling toward the window. Even groggy as he was, he knew there could only be one culprit of such a heinous act...

Adahy sat perched on the iron bar of the neighbor's laundry rack. The eight long toes of his hand-like feet were curled around the railing, his spindly telak-legs balancing his weight on his hind set of knees. He wore the typical clothes of a tribal outlander: long sleeves of vibrant colors and patchwork patterns, skin-tight red shorts decorated with white paint, and beads and feathers of all kinds woven into the braided locks of his cedar hair, all of it wound and bundled up in a crimson headscarf. He held a long spear wrapped in small carved charms loosely across his lap. He had all the grace and plumage of a songbird.

Corin sighed and threw his face into his pillow and groaned. "*Why?* What could you *possibly* want with me right now?"

Adahy laughed. "Wallie, wallie, my wallie…" he clucked, "this'll be the *highlight* of your morning, yeah? Guarantee it." His mahogany face stretched into an inviting grin. "Meet me out front!"

Corin's protest balled up behind his teeth as he watched Adahy bound away. He threw off the covers and swiveled his toes onto the warm stone floor as he rubbed his grubby, crusty face. He looked up through stretched, red eyelids and parted fingers at his barren room. A wooden shelf of clean clothes and a woven, reed basket of dirty clothes were his only decorations.

He stepped up from the bed, pulling at the unruly shag of his sandy hair. He reached for a shirt but hesitated. The crumpled texture of the dark, wrinkled cloth reminded him of his dream. It was the only dream Corin could remember having that didn't fade after he woke up. Instead it grew, drawing his thoughts out into something between fear and obsession, tainting his already weary mind with the most unsettling image. He saw it then: the long, black clouds of a fierce storm boiling across the horizon. There was something unnatural about them, like there was something terrible just beyond the edge of the closest cloud.

Something coiling.

Something writhing.

Something elegantly hidden.

Corin shook his head and dug through his pile of clothes. He thought briefly about bathing, but decided it wasn't worth Adahy's scorn. He sniffed a pair of grey shorts and pulled them on, first slipping them back, then forward over his set of opposing knees. He buttoned the fly in front, then fastened the strap over his tail set. He stepped out into the main room of the house, climbing into his linen shirt as he walked. Corin scoured the pantry for something to eat but found the bread and fruit bowls lacking. He settled for a handful of toasted wheat kernels in a clay jar by the wash basin.

He stared out the frameless, paneless window as he chewed, taking in the sights and scents of the shabby street. The morning air somehow balanced the last hint of night's chill with the dry scent of dust and cooking coals. The clamor of merchants and vendors pushing their carts to market was a constant roar against Corin's skull, one he had grown impossibly numb to. The southern district of Centile woke very early and very abruptly.

Corin didn't.

Contrary to his father's, and pretty much *everyone else's*, opinion, it wasn't because he was lazy. He just had a hard time finding the motivation to face the exact same day over and over again. Every morning felt indistinguishable: as far back as he could remember and as far forward as he could imagine. The same dirt under his nails, the same afternoons spent in the workshop, the same lectures about his future…

Maybe that's why he let Adahy get him into so much trouble all the time.

Corin brushed the chaff from his palms and stepped out into the alley. Three swollen barrels of rainwater were pressed against the side of the house. Corin dipped his hands in and took a long, cool draught. He used a second scoop to wash his hair and face and scrub the grit from the creases of his neck. He flicked his ears and wrists and tail and turned around to face his father's workshop. Across the alley he could hear his old man banging away inside. Corin stepped over the worn dirt and pushed open the door.

"Oh good, you're up," his father said. "Hand me that chisel there, would you son? The small one by the bellows."

Marcus' face was peering down at an unfinished cobblestone clutched in his thick, leather gloves. He seemed to be trying to smooth a stubborn divot off the edge. Corin sighed and turned to the unkempt stack of tools on the table to his right. His father's workshop was a tangled nest of perfectly structured chaos. Every meter dedicated to its own haphazard project, all of them in various states of incompletion. Corin picked the chisel from the pile with his toes and stepped over a casting frame. Marcus received the tool with a grunt and put it to use.

"Late start, don't you think?" Marcus blew some grit from the cobblestone and brushed at it with his gloved palm.

Corin sighed. "I suppose. Are we in a rush?"

"No more than usual." Marcus shrugged and looked up from his work. "We've got this order of four hundred cobbles due tomorrow to the plaza. Not to mention those six axes. Can you run the grindstone while I finish these up?"

"Actually," Corin cleared his throat, glancing around for a place to sit down, "I was hoping to spend the morning with Adahy. I guess he needs my help with something."

Marcus squinted as he wiped a bead of sweat from his brow. "This morning? But we have your brother's–"

"I know," Corin interrupted as he tried clearing a pile of nails from a stone block. They jangled and dangled a bit too precariously, so he gave up. "I won't be late. I'll run the grindstone when we get back."

Marcus' rugged features deepened as he regarded his son. All telaks had rich, tan complexions, but his father's russet face paled them all. Except maybe some of the outlanders. His skin was weathered and tough, blurring the lines between chin, neck, and leather apron. His clothes typically matched that haggard look, but today was special. His shirt was neat and pressed, with the suede strap of his collar carefully laced up in what could have resembled symmetry… at least from a distance.

Corin looked carefully up and down his father, but there were no grease spots or sparks holes to be found on anything he wore. *Merciful sun...* he might have even run a *brush* through his hair this morning.

There was something else, too: a subtle shine in the dark of his father's eye.

So subtle, in fact, that no one but Corin would have noticed it.

"Well, Cor, I suppose it's your choice," Marcus grumbled, "but I was hoping we might forgo the shop tonight to celebrate with your brother."

"There'll be time after. I'll get it done."

Marcus scowled but nodded. "Well, just don't be late, alright?"

"No worries," Corin called out as he slipped through the door. "I'll meet you outside the square!"

* * *

THE STREETS IN FRONT OF CORIN'S HOME WERE A smoky, sweaty river of wooden carts and hopeful merchants. The entire southern district seemed to be draining from their pressed, dirt roads, and sandy, clay hovels to line the streets along the way to Centile's central district. Carts loaded with baked goods, dyed cloth, and carved jewelry scraped and swerved as merchants fought their way to the prime peddling posts.

Corin turned, squinting in the morning sun, trying to spot his friend out somewhere in the bustling crowd. A telak dressed in all red should have been easy to spot amid–

In a heart-stopping smack, Adahy dropped onto the street in front of him.

He perked up, quickly biting into an apple.

"*Thunder and hail, man!*" Corin gripped at his forehead. "It's too early for that!"

Adahy glanced down. "For an apple?"

"No, of course I didn't…" Corin sighed. "Why would I… Whatever."

Adahy chuckled. "Hey, you want one, yeah? I been smuggling it around just for you!"

He held out the fruit, bright and crisp and perfect. Corin hesitated at first but then snatched it up.

"So, who'd you swipe these from?" he said, polishing the peel on his shirt.

Adahy's eyebrows shot right up to his headscarf. "*Swiped?* What a wicked, wallie word, yeah? A wallie like you is gonna be talking to me about *swiped?* These, my doubtin' Chiqalan, were picked out on *my plains*, grown from *my soil*, and made sweet by *my sun*, yeah? Wouldn't you say that makes them *my* fruit?"

Adahy sung his words with the subtle accent of the plains, each phrase arching a note too high at the end. It made his sentences sound correct and resolved, but also like there was an unspoken question drifting out the corner of his lips, as if every phrase held an impish caveat concealed in calming crescendo.

Usually that question seemed to be: You're a baca-brained buffoon, aren't you?

Corin rolled his eyes and bit into the apple. "Uh huh. And who *picked* all of *your* fruit?"

Adahy took another bite and shrugged. "Don't know. Some guy with a cart two blocks down."

Corin shook his head but kept eating. Reasoning with Adahy was like telling the wind to change directions.

"So, is this what you got me up for?" Corin asked. "Needed an accomplice in your morning mischief?"

Adahy smirked. "Well, yes and no. But we got *way* more important mischief to be mischiefing than some silly fruit, yeah? Come on!"

Adahy crunched into the last of his apple and tossed the core. He compressed his legs and used his spear to vault up onto a nearby roof.

"Seriously?" Corin groaned as the outlander flew away. "Can't we just stay on the ground today?"

Adahy twisted around and shot Corin a disgusted look. "Have you *seen* them streets? *Huh?* They'd run us down flat! Like ants, yeah? *Squish!* Come on! I'll pull your wallie tail up."

Corin bit the last mouthful off his apple and wiped his palms on his pants. He held a hand to Adahy. "You know this is illegal, right?"

"Don't be stupid!" Adahy grunted and jerked his friend up the porous wall. "Listen to me, Chiqalan, a rule's only a rule as long as it's enforced, yeah? The guards? *Pssh...* Them brillos got better things to do today than run us down."

"Better than run *me* down? Maybe. But you?" Corin chuckled as he got back up on his feet, pausing to glare at the outlander. "I think they'd make an exception. And my name's *Corin*, alright?"

Adahy feigned nausea. "Wallie through and through, huh? What would your poor mama say?"

Corin brushed some stray grit from his knees. "I think she would have said you're a bad influence on me."

"Wow..." Adahy smiled and clapped Corin's shoulder. "Thank you, yeah? My Chiqalan, that's the *nicest* thing anyone's said to me all day. Bad influence on a wallie, eh? Beautiful. Now, *come on!*"

And Adahy was suddenly two rooftops away.

"Where exactly are we going?" Corin yelled, but it was a gesture done out of principle. He knew Adahy wouldn't respond. The outlander bounded off across the sandy roofs, hopping breezily over crowds and alleys alike. Corin sighed but followed, hating himself for liking these shenanigans as much as he did.

* * *

THE TWO TELAKS SKIPPED THEIR WAY OVER THE DUSTY slums, passing piles of broken crates and clay bread ovens, baked brittle in the relentless desert sun. They wound around to the northwest, skirting the inner wall.

Dividing the outer districts from the city center was a shield of glistening, golden light. It rose from Vallin's Tower at the heart of

Centile and vaulted out in a great dome that enveloped the inner district. The buildings of Centile were squat and weathered outside the shield, but they surged up in stately grandeur beneath it. Sandy walls were replaced by molded brick, dirt streets with fitted cobblestone. And the wall of light ebbed and glistened in streams of sparks that bulged and stretched with the wind all around it.

Adahy suddenly jerked to a halt, crouching down behind a stubby, stone battlement. Corin slipped up behind him, trying to track his friend's gaze.

"There we are, yeah?" Adahy pointed and whispered, his tail flicking furiously. "You see that big building out yonder?"

Corin squinted and followed the gesture. Straight ahead was a collection of the city's grain silos and several massive, brick warehouses.

"Which one are you talking about?" he asked.

Adahy swiveled up behind Corin, gripping his ears like handlebars and aiming his head. "Right down there! The big one with all the glass. You see it, yeah?"

Corin pulled free of his friend's clutches. "Okay! Yes, I see it. What's your problem with it?"

Adahy crouched down, suddenly somber. "My problem is with *who's* in it, Chiqalan."

"Who?" Corin shook his head. "What are you talking about?"

Adahy bounced his fingertips against his lips, contemplating the warehouse. "Two days ago, a big group of guards came by our village. Spears, cyoves, the whole brillo show, right? Now, normally my father would have shown them the way off, but he was… well, he didn't, yeah? So, them nasty wallies went and rounded up half the baca herd! Just hauled straight them off the plains! Shoved 'em all up in that building."

Corin frowned. "Are you saying the city guard stole your tribe's herd of bacas?"

"*Our* herd?" Adahy smacked Corin's arm with his spear. "This is the problem with all of you wallies! Walls! Always *walls!* Yours, mine, ours, theirs, everything is *walls* with you! *Mi cola*, you all so boxed up in here you can't see the sky no more, yeah? No, they're not *our* herd, but we take care of them and they take care of us. And the guards? They skin them all for leather and chop up the rest for cyoves, yeah? No respect for nobody…"

Corin sat back and rubbed the sting out of his arm, trying to make sense of the situation. "So, what exactly are you suggesting? Wait… That's the wrong word. What are you *plotting?*"

Adahy smiled. "We gonna break 'em out, yeah? You and me."

"Absolutely not."

"Oh, come on! Chi–" He stopped himself and sweetened his pleading tone. "Corin, please. It won't be that bad, yeah? I figured it out already! Look, look, look, come check it out."

Corin sighed and shook his head but slipped back up next to the battlement.

"See?" Adahy pointed. "Count the guards. How many you see?"

Corin squinted, the shield's glare catching his eye off to the left. It looked like there were two fully armored soldiers at the door. Maybe a third through the warehouse doorway.

"I don't know," Corin muttered. "You tell me."

"There are only *four* of them brillos," Adahy sang. "Two outside and two inside, yeah? That's *nothing!*"

Corin laughed. "No, actually, that's *four.*"

"Yeah? Well it's usually it's a lot more, alright?" Adahy snapped. "But they all down at the plaza party waiting for all that shiny nonsense to come rolling in. This is our chance, yeah?"

Corin stood up to walk away. "Do you have *any* idea how stupid this is? What if they catch us? What if they catch *you?*"

Adahy stood too, placing both of his hands on Corin's shoulders. "Corin, *please*. I'm asking you not just as friends, but as family, yeah? The tribe *needs* this, and I can't do it all by myself."

Corin raised an eyebrow. "Yes, you could."

"Okay, maybe I could," Adahy admitted, "but it would be a *whole* lot harder, yeah? Come *o-o-on…*"

Corin shook his head, pressing his fingers into his eyes. "Why do I always let you talk me into this stuff?"

Adahy smiled and smacked Corin's shoulder. "Because deep down in that wallie, wallie heart of yours you know I'm right."

Corin slouched and shrugged off Adahy's hands. "I assume you have a plan?"

"No way!" Adahy cried. "Plans are too stiff, yeah? We got to be flexible. We gotta be the *wind*. Roll with whatever happens."

"I need a plan."

"I don't want one."

"Then I'm out."

Adahy rolled his eyes and threw up his hands. "Ay, *mi tonto!* Alright, alright, alright… How 'bout this? I go start something with the guards on the inside. Get them all riled up, yeah? Then, you slip in and let out all the bacas."

"No way!" Corin let out a nervous chuckle. "That's absurd. You want *me* to be the one to sneak in there?"

"Would you rather be the distraction?"

"Yeah!" Corin scoffed. "I would actually."

Adahy laughed. "Oh yeah? What are you going to do? Walk up to them and ask them how their day is going?"

"I mean… maybe."

Adahy squawked and whispered something to the sky that Corin couldn't quite make out, then he snapped back up into his friend's face. "No! You listen to me, my wallie. *I'll* get them all out of there, and *you* slip in and set the herd free, yeah? Sweet and simple as corn cake."

It was clear from his tone that further critique would no longer be tolerated. Adahy jumped up onto the battlement, crouched and ready to pounce…

…but Corin reached up and grabbed his tail just before the outlander leapt.

"Wait!" Corin hissed. "How am I supposed to *get in?* There'll still be guards at the door, won't there?"

Adahy flicked the barbed end of his tail at Corin, pricking his forearm. "*Then break a window!*" he snapped.

Corin recoiled and scowled. Adahy slipped off the edge, landing lightly on a crate below. Corin watched the outlander's scarlet head bob off into the distance. He sighed and sat back, feeling his heart starting to race.

"What am I doing…" Corin whispered to himself. "Am I really this bored?"

And he slumped down to wait.

* * *

THERE WAS A PIERCING CRASH FOLLOWED BY THE immense sound of stone tearing through glass. Corin jerked upright in time to see the two guards at the warehouse entrance rushing into the open doorway. His breath froze in his chest as he listened to the brawl echoing from within. Furious cries clapped out from the warehouse followed by the bright bang of metal.

Corin hopped off the roof, rushing for cover behind a nearby wall. He peered around the edge and was just in time to see Adahy burst shoulder-first through a window around the side of the building. He was wearing what could only have been a guard's helmet. He hit the ground and rolled up to his feet, his tail twirling in exhilaration as silver shards rained down around him.

Four guards rushed through the doorway behind him. Only three had helmets.

Two of the guards darted straight for Adahy, spitting obscenities and swinging spears with each step. The hatless one motioned for the last guard to stay by the door, and then joined in the pursuit.

Adahy was absolutely glowing.

He squealed with insane laughter as he threw himself into the race, dashing straight toward Corin's hiding spot.

"*Good luck, yeah!*" he sang.

The outlander banked up the wall of the far building and juked off into a tight side street. Corin slammed his back against the wall and listened to the swearing, scrambling scuffle of three very flustered guards scraping their ironclad way into a cramped alley.

The sound finally faded, and Corin slid down to a sitting position.

He was used to his friend's antics, but they had never involved the city guard before. Not so directly, at least. Sure, there had been that one time with the moldy corn husks... but that didn't count.

Corin took a deep breath and peered back around the wall. The last guard was still holding his post at the doorway. Understandably, he seemed on edge, but judging by the slant of his ears, he wasn't very focused on the warehouse behind him.

Corin wiped the sweat from his brow and crossed the street as casually as he could. The guard didn't even notice. Trying not to move too quickly, Corin ducked behind some crates and into the shadows. He slipped to the back end of the warehouse, giving the building a wide berth. Judging from the debris, Adahy had smashed three windows in total: an entrance, an exit, and... maybe a third for fun?

Corin scanned the empty street. The echoing thrum of distant crowds was strangely comforting against the silence of the area. Corin felt his nervous tail curl around his thigh. He stepped slowly and deliberately, letting the pad of each toe press in silence. Straight ahead was one of Adahy's broken windows, situated directly above a barrel. Corin leapt up and peeked his head up through the opening, trying his best to keep his ears down.

The warehouse was long but cramped with corrals. There was a narrow walkway down the middle lined with rows of stalls, each filled to capacity with squalling, baying bacas. On the far end was a small clearing by the doorway with chairs and a table. He could see the guard's elbow through the opening, but the room was otherwise clear.

Corin leaned back and examined the jagged edge of the window. He picked out a few shards and then hoisted himself up to the ledge. It was tall enough for him to crouch in. His feet crunched the broken glass under his weight as he clutched the edge with his toes, but the agitated bacas covered the sound. Corin swallowed and dropped down with a gentle pat. His eyes shot to the guard's elbow as soon as he landed.

Nothing.

With a nervous sigh, Corin inspected the baca corrals. There were four iron gates along the wooden fencing. Each was latched shut with a metal rod that fit into a hole drilled into the dirt, but none of them were locked. Corin reached for the first latch, but stopped, considering the outcomes.

Best case scenario? The bacas would stay where they were.

Worst? They would stampede.

What a plan…

Corin stepped back and glanced at the guard again. He had to get out of here. This was too risky. Maybe he could slip back out the window without him hearing–

"Hey Chiqalan!"

A yelp caught in Corin's throat as the sharp, whispered voice sent a chill of adrenaline through his sides. Adahy hopped down from the window frame with a beaming grin.

"What are you *doing?*" Corin hissed through his teeth. "Where are the guards?"

"Guards?" Adahy looked perplexed. "I lost them, of course. Silly wallie. Now, how come them gates are all still closed?"

Corin's eyes kept dancing between Adahy and the guard's elbow. "Because I don't want *him* to notice! What if they all start running at once?"

"Well, they better," Adahy chuckled, "or we ain't never gonna get them out of here, yeah? Come on!"

Adahy quickly wrenched up one of the gate's metal latches. There was a soft squeal of iron rubbing up on pressed dirt, but the sound was swallowed up by the growing grunts of the animals. Corin dug his fingers into the roots of his hair, shook his head, but jumped in to help. He pulled the gate open slowly, trying to stifle the metallic rasp of the hinges. Adahy bounced away to the next latch, totally unfazed by the noise he was making.

A baca stared Corin down through the newly opened gate. Its long horns curled off its massive head behind watery, brown eyes. It stamped a hoofed foot and shook off some drool from its wet, bulbous snout. Corin backed away, letting the burly thing amble up to the opening.

When he was certain he wasn't about to get gored, Corin rushed the opposite gate and pulled it open as well, then he glanced around for Adahy. The outlander was busy brushing the black head of an exceptionally ambivalent baca, cooing to it gently.

"*This is stupid!*" Corin whispered. "We're never getting all of these lazy things out of here…"

Adahy perked up, scanned the room, and nodded. "You right, yeah? These guys ain't going *nowhere* yet. They're too scared. Or maybe…"

A wicked smile curled across Adahy's lips and he jumped back up to the broken windowsill. Corin's face drained of blood as the outlander sucked air into his bulging chest.

"*Aaayyyee! Yip! Yip! Yip!*" Adahy belted the scream out, letting its shrill hits rebound through the warehouse. He then leaned forward and started smacking bacas with the blunt end of his spear. The guard at the entrance darted through the doorway, but nearly tripped over his tail as he was met by two hundred panicked quadrupeds rushing the narrow entrance.

Corin grabbed at his face. "*What have you done?*"

Adahy jumped down from the window onto the back of the baca he'd just been petting while Corin scrambled out of the way of the cascade of hooves bursting from the gates. One of the bigger horned animals thrashed its neck on the way out of the warehouse door, knocking the armored guard flat against the wall.

"Get on! Get on! Get on!" Adahy whooped.

Corin fumbled back against the corral's fence and felt the hot side of a baca press against it. He pulled back and saw the beams bending and splintering against the building pressure. With no options left, Corin hopped the divide and pulled himself up onto the flexing shoulders of the nearest hornless baca. The wood finally snapped, and, like water through a broken dam, the animals surged out into the open streets.

Adahy kept yipping and screaming, as the herd trampled through the warehouse and into the sunlight. Corin leaned forward, feeling the boiling blood pumping through the baca's brown hide while he slipped back and forth along the thin peak of its spine. The sound of the stampede was so immense that Corin couldn't even hear himself screaming.

The herd peeled off into the streets, crashing back and forth through cramped alleys, tearing up dirt and crushing carts. Corin's vision was a blur of horrified faces and whipped wind. His baca rammed into a clay oven, pelting his face with dust and gravel and crusty bits of burnt bread.

"Jump off! Chiqalan! Get up on the roof!"

Corin turned around. A few meters back, Adahy was pointing off to the right. Coming up, was a low roofed building with a patchy sunshade. Corin gulped, and rose to his feet, his long, thick toes gripping into the baca's loose hide.

He gauged the distance, compressed his knees, and he jumped.

Corin flipped over the lip at the building's edge and crashed onto his side, spinning and sprawling out onto the hot, sandy stone of the roof. Corin felt the air collapse from his lungs, tasting blood as he gasped. Adahy sprang up beside him with infinitely more grace.

The outlander crouched low beside Corin, pressing a finger to his smirking lips and a sweaty palm to Corin's gasping face. The stampede shook the building with outrageous cacophony that just kept *going*...

When the commotion settled, they heard the panicked howls of four unhappy guards, sprinting through the dusty air, and then, finally, blessed silence.

Adahy sat back, exhaled, and chuckled. He was about to say something, when the peal of distant bells perked up his long, pointed ears.

"Hey, you better get outta here, huh?" he said. "You gonna be late for the shiny nonsense!"

CHAPTER 3

DEEP WATER

OLENKA STEPPED OUT ONTO THE BOARDWALK and let the rain clear her waterlogged senses. Her heart was pounding, her fins were trembling, and she felt like she was seeing and hearing and thinking everything through a fog. There was no going back now, and the thrill of the hunt was starting to blur into doubt.

"Two-hundred and fifty meters…" she muttered to herself. A dive that deep was *probably* possible…

But was it possible for her crew?

Olenka exhaled and took stock of the moment, evaluating her senses to keep her grounded. It was a classic sirena trick to clear a troubled mind of distractions. She heard the tide thrash against the beams of the wharf, smelled the savory sting of pipe smoke in the air, felt the bloated, tropical drops pelt her shoulders…

…but she also noticed the two shadows in the corner.

Olenka's fingertips brushed at the knife sheathed to her thigh as she pretended to be adjusting her girdle. She dropped to one knee and peered across the darkness over her forearm. Two siokoy were leaning against a tavern wall across the plaza. Their shark tooth necklaces glowed clear and white and wicked in the yellow light, like monstrous, pearly grins across their bare chests. Olenka stretched her shoulders, stealing a second glance. There were only two of them, but they were clearly watching her. She sniffed and resumed a casual pace, dipping off to the right.

She didn't need to look to know that they were following her.

The pier was empty now, the haunting, smoking faces all retreated back indoors. Olenka quickened her steps. If she found the right spot, she could drop into the surf. She was a much better swimmer than fighter, and it would be easier to lose them in the water. She paused to scan the streaming edges of the planks, watching the water drain, and looking for a chum hole big enough to slip through. She didn't see any prospects, and the creak of fin-falls on wood was picking up behind her. She glanced back and saw the two siokoy pushing through the oily glow, abandoning all subtly as they marched directly toward her. Olenka exhaled and kept walking.

Then the siokoy started to sprint.

So did Olenka.

She darted frantically around corner after corner, quickly losing track of her way. The grid of shanties all looked the same and she wasn't sure which turn led back out to the open dock. Her webbed feet slipped to a stop in front of a fork in the boardwalk. She panicked and ducked left.

That was her first mistake.

Olenka sped out over the walkway only to find herself cornered at the end of an alley. She swore and desperately looked up at the surrounding rooftops. There was nothing to climb, and the beaten, tin roofs provided no grip or traction. She swallowed and leapt toward a nearby lintel, trying to hoist her torso up onto the beam.

But she wasn't quick enough.

A hand clenched around her ankle and wrenched her from the building, the edges of the rusty nails scratching across the skin of her arms as her slender frame was ripped off the wall. She smacked down against the boardwalk, all the air jolting from her chest. The two siokoy were chuckling, circling her as she crawled back against the wall. Olenka pulled her knife free and hopped to her webbed feet. The siokoy slowed for a moment of natural hesitation but resumed their sinister advance.

"Go *on*, then," one of them muttered. "Give it a try, short fins."

Olenka felt her jaw tremble as she exhaled. Her eyes darted back and forth between the two, unsure which one would come at her first. She took a step forward, swinging her knife at them to test her range.

That was her second mistake.

The two siokoy jerked back from the slash but quickly shot forward together. Olenka felt a shoulder sink into her chest as massive hands pinned her wrists to the wall. She struggled and screamed, but the men were too strong, and the rain was too loud. She felt their blood pounding through their flesh as they pressed their wretched bodies against her, and she heard her knife clatter to the boardwalk as the bones in her hand contorted together.

"Hey, hey, hey… *Shh...*" the siokoy whispered, his lips brushing her cheek. "We wouldn't want to wake up all these nice folks around here, would we?"

He leaned his forearm against the wall, using his right hand to grip Olenka's face. She felt her eyes trembling at the strain. She wanted to kick him, to bite him, to push her fingers into his uzai eyes, but the other siokoy had her pinned. She glanced between the two, searching for an opening. She flexed her thigh and slammed her knee into the gut of the siokoy to the left. He grunted but returned the blow with a solid fist to her abdomen. Olenka gasped as the icy shock branched up through the veins in her arms and chest.

"This could be easy, you know. If you just keep still for a moment, it will all be—"

A fishing spear ripped through the rain, sinking into the siokoy's flesh.

The spear pinned his hand against the wall, sending a spray of droplets from the swollen wood. The shocked fiend screamed, releasing his grip on Olenka to claw at his wound.

The other siokoy jumped back, the whites of his eyes as bright in the gloom as the sheen of his twirling knife. There was a distant crash down the alley. The confused brute bought the distraction, and as he turned toward the sound, a sirena dropped from the rooftop behind his skewered companion. The maimed siokoy howled as his good arm was wrenched up between his shoulder blades and a bone knife was pressed up against his throat.

Olenka coughed and clutched at her own throat as she crumpled to the pier. She stared up at the sirena. Her toned arms were tight and bare in her fish-skin vest. A long braid of matted locks divided the shaved sides of her head, accentuating the intricate tattoos that bloomed from her kudori and wove their way down her neck and shoulders and arms.

"Thanks, Di," Olenka managed as she stumbled against the wall.

Diwala smiled and tightened the knife against the man's throat, letting a thin line of blood run with the rain. "Did they hurt you?" Her voice was calm but strong, like a hidden riptide ready to sink a careless swimmer to the abyss.

Olenka shook her head, picking up her knife. "You made it just in time."

Diwala smiled and pressed up on the siokoy's elbow. The man bellowed as the pain in both arms tore through his spastic muscles.

"You have one chance," Di whispered into his trembling ear. "Leave us now."

The siokoy across the alley looked uncertainly between Diwala and his whimpering companion. Di pulled back on her captive's torso, and the pinned rogue screamed again as his wounded hand slid a centimeter down the spear's shaft.

"*Crushing depths!*" he cried, frothing spittle on his quivering lips. "*What are you waiting for? Gut her!*"

"Poor choice," Di whispered as the armed siokoy rushed her from across the alley. In a fluid motion, Diwala slit her hostage's throat and tossed his convulsing mass in front of her, ripping his hand free of her bloody spear. The attacking siokoy fumbled at the sight. His fins slipped on the slick wood, and he tumbled forward over his dying partner.

Di caught the siokoy's wrist as he desperately swung his knife at her belly.

She turned her own blade up into his chest, letting the force of his fall slip it into his heart. He bellowed a hot, gurgling cry as he slumped into his pooling gore. Diwala pulled free of the carnage and tossed aside the broken handle of her bone blade.

Olenka cracked her stiff neck and stepped up to the corpses. "I could have handled those bottom feeders on my own, you know. They just caught me off guard..."

Diwala scoffed as she pulled her spear free of the wall. "Could? What is *could*? If they caught you off guard, then you *did not* handle them. Is this not so?"

Olenka sheathed her knife and raised her hands to the warped walls. "Hey, it wasn't a fair fight, alright? I got turned around and they cornered me in this buwisit alley. I was trying to make it back when–"

"Do your excuses bring you comfort, dear sister?" Diwala was crouched down beside the bodies, searching through their tangle of straps. She pulled free a leather pouch and jingled it beside her ear.

Olenka sighed and pressed her fingers to her eyes. "Yeah! You know what? They kind of do."

"Well, they should not." Diwala tied a few coin pouches to her girdle as she spoke, then she began examining one of the siokoy's silver knives. She wiped it off on the dead man's pants and slipped it into her sheath as she stood. "Your excuses dishonor your mistakes, and dishonored mistakes never share their lessons."

Olenka opened her mouth to protest, but Di held up a hand to silence her.

"Come, we need to leave. Marikit is waiting for us, and sharks are always drawn to blood."

* * *

MARI SQUEAKED AND LEAPT TO HER FINS AS THE brittle door of the shanty creaked open.

"*Lightning upon you, Diwala!* You could have at least *knocked!*" Marikit clutched at her chest as she exhaled. "You two are *very* late, ya know…"

"My fault," Olenka mumbled as she crashed down on a wooden stool. She loosened the neck strap of her vest and motioned for the other two to join her at the table. Diwala and Marikit slid down beside her.

"So?" Mari offered. "How'd it go? Did you find them?"

"Oh, I found them…" Olenka rubbed her eyes. The adrenaline of the fight was gone, and she was left with nothing but doubt and exhaustion dulling her wits. "*And* they took our bid."

Di and Mari smiled to each other, but Olenka shook her head.

"Let's not celebrate just yet, sisters. We've got a problem. That uzai dive's a lot deeper than we thought… They estimated two fifty."

Diwala leaned back and Mari gasped.

"*Two fifty?*" Marikit pressed her face into her hands. "Is that even *possible?*"

Olenka shrugged. "Di? What do you think?"

Diwala didn't move. Her arms were folded tight across her chest, her tattoos thickening the creases of her rigid muscles.

"It is possible… but not for either of you."

Marikit nodded and stared down at the table, but Olenka glared at the stoic sirena. "What are you saying? You're going to do it *alone?*"

Diwala's eyes were distant. She rubbed absently at her forearm and shrugged. "I see no other option."

Olenka shook her head. "No way. Come on, Di. You can't pull a salvage job by yourself. Not a load this big, and *especially* not that deep. I'm coming with you."

Di sighed and leaned forward on the table. "Olenka, listen. This one is more than you are ready for. Two fifty… It is just too much. Too deep."

"Too deep?" Olenka spat. "Di, I *grew up* at half that depth! I'll be fine! I'm used to it. You're just being–"

"Being what?" Diwala sat up, staring straight through Olenka. "More careful with your life than you are? You are not ready for this, sister. I am telling you… something changes after two hundred meters. The water gets stronger. It starts to attack you from the inside. It gets inside your head. I have only ever done a dive this deep twice before, and the first time I almost did not make it back to the surface."

Olenka smacked her fist against the table and then slumped back in her chair. "So, what now? Do we just *abandon* the job? Run away and hope the kaizo don't come looking for us?"

"No, we do not run," Di said stiffly. "Not after what they did to Daisay. We go on with the plan, but you will stay topside with Mari."

"But Di," Mari whispered, "Kay Kay's right. Even if it wasn't that deep, hauling a full chest of jewelry on your own? You won't even be able to pull it out of the mud…"

Diwala stared at Marikit with a dangerous look that dissolved into a sigh, followed by a chuckle. "You too, traitor?"

"Oh, come off it, Di!" Olenka leaned forward and smacked her tattooed forearm. "Listen, you *know* we're right. You and I can do this. I'll follow your lead. Promise."

Diwala stared up at Olenka's garish grin. It was tawdry, but surprisingly effective. The tattooed sirena rolled her eyes and leaned back. "What equipment do the kaizo have?"

"Compression vests, shrimp lanterns, and a diving bell," Olenka counted off on her fingers. "I assume a salvage line as well."

Diwala bounced her fist against her lips as she considered the list. "The bell will only make it a hundred meters. Hundred fifty at most…"

"We can free dive from there, Di." Olenka had been feeling exhausted a second ago, but seeing Diwala so miserably pessimistic filled her with inexplicable optimism. "It will be fine, sister! You can show me everything I need to do."

Diwala considered her for a moment, then sighed. "This is not going to be pleasant, you know that?"

Olenka nodded. "Of course."

"Good," Diwala grumbled. "Now, let us *assume* for just a moment that you and I can make this dive. How are we going to fool the kaizo? They will be expecting our deceit, and we can certainly count on theirs."

Olenka smiled and turned to Mari. "Did you end up getting that spare banca?"

Marikit smiled, bright and charming. "A very nice shopkeeper told me I could take his banca out whenever I liked, just so long as I brought it back in one piece."

Diwala chuckled. "Knowing Olenka, that is not likely."

Olenka ignored the comment and turned to Di. "And the kaizo barge?"

Diwala smiled. "Simple. Our line is attached, and the rudder will be easy to break."

"And they had a lifeboat on board?"

"Just one." Diwala sat back, gazing up at an image in her mind. "Port side, opposite of their diving bell. Oars but no sail. It can probably hold two. No more than three."

Olenka leaned forward, brushing her fingers against the table as she spoke. "Alright, we can do this. The kaizo captain said for us to meet them at the rocks just west of the wreck. We'll take both bancas. Di and me together on the spare, and Mari on ours. We'll need to run another line from the spare banca before we go."

"Another?" Mari frowned. "But, what about the line we ran from the barge?"

"We'll need two," Olenka explained. "One for the haul and one to be a decoy."

"Decoy?" Diwala looked intrigued.

"You said it yourself, Di. They'll be expecting something." Olenka dumped a few coins onto the table and started sliding them around as markers. "Look, we make the dive from the kaizo barge here. You and I will break open the chest and load the jewelry into *our* line attached to their barge. Next, we fill the chest with rocks and swap out the lock. Then we load up the decoy line with rocks too. You follow?"

Marikit squinted at the coins and pressed her hand to her forehead. "Wait, so why would we need the second line if the jewels are already switched out of the chest?"

Olenka smiled. "Because they'll be *expecting* us to tamper with the chest! They're going to be looking for our second line, so let's give them a fake one."

"And the fake line…" Mari stared at the table as she spoke, "*isn't* the line we ran from the barge?"

Olenka grinned. "No, of course not. That's the beauty of it. They're expecting us to try to get the claim as far from them as possible. We'll hide it in plain sight right underneath them. The banca line is the obvious choice, so we'll use it as the bait."

Di nodded and stroked her chin. "So, how do we get them to bite the hook?"

Olenka motioned to Marikit. "Mari will disable the rudder while we're down. You and I will ditch the bell before they pull us up and swim to the spare banca. We'll light a lamp and start to hoist up the decoy line where they can see. The kaizo will try to follow us, but with the busted rudder they'll need to take the lifeboat."

Diwala grinned. "Meanwhile we ditch and meet Mari on their barge to haul the claim?"

"Exactly," Olenka said.

Marikit grimaced and pressed her fist to her chin. "I don't know… Won't they leave someone back to guard the barge?"

Olenka nodded. "I'm sure they will. We'll just have to take him out. There were only four of them in the crew when I met them at the tavern. Di, did you see any more on the barge?"

Diwala shook her head. "All clear there."

"Easy. The three of us can take one or two kaizo." Olenka smiled and sat back. "I mean, they're just buwisit pirates. No problem!"

"Oh?" Diwala's voice and folded arms were stiff and tight. "No problem, you say? Do you think it *will* be no problem, or it *could* be no problem? Perhaps we *could* take them as long as they do not catch us off guard, is that right, sister?"

Olenka sighed. "What do you want from me, Di?"

Marikit glanced back and forth between the two, a little concerned, but mostly confused.

Diwala spoke clearly and gently. "I just want you to be careful, Olenka. Overconfidence can be a selfish thing."

Olenka scoffed. "Selfish?"

Diwala nodded. "Very, very selfish. What happens to us if you push yourself too hard? What happens to our crew if our fearless leader does not come back up from the abyss? Hmm? Did you stop to think of that?"

Olenka tried to look away, but Diwala's eyes were unwavering. Mari's too.

"We just love you, Kay Kay," Marikit muttered.

Olenka felt the heat in her sinuses as her throat tightened. "What's gotten into you two…"

Diwala placed her hand on Olenka's arm. "Sister, you bear Heaven's blessings but reject the gift of temperance. You are strong and very smart, but you are not immortal. Will you promise us that you will be more careful?"

Mari reached over and gripped Olenka's hand. They smiled to each other as a tear tumbled to Olenka's lips. She sighed and pulled her hand free to rub her eyes.

"*Alright!* Tattered sails! I promise… Now, can we *please* go get to work?"

CHAPTER 4

SHINY NONSENSE

CORIN FRANTICALLY BUTTONED UP HIS KIND OF fresh, sort of clean, mostly baca-hair-free shirt as he ran. The city center was alive with color and commotion. Citizens of all districts had taken to the streets, lining the cobblestone ways, and filling the sidewalks. The sun was blistering, but it only served to feed the crowd of telaks with greater life and energy.

Carts and barrels of merchandise cluttered the alleys, and giant crimson flags clouded the sky. Each flag was decorated with the crest of Centile: a long, honey-yellow sword brightly engulfed in the light of a swirling six-point sun embroidered behind it. The scarlet banners were everywhere: draped over carts, hanging from windows, and frantically thrashed in the tiny clutches of children perched on their parents' shoulders.

"Corin! Over here, son!"

Corin almost tripped as he stopped hard against the curb, swiveling his ears to the sound of his name. Marcus' gruff voice boomed over the din, and his burly arms waved over the crowd. Walking on the tips of their long toes, all telaks were tall, but with his four knees extended, Marcus absolutely towered over the packed street. Corin pushed his way through the crowd, trying not to trip over the spiky tails of passersby. Carefully stepping over a toddler, Corin reached out and took his father by the hand. Marcus yanked his son next to him with the solid force of a working man's arm.

"Are they close?" Corin asked.

"Just up the street. You had me worried, son. I thought you were going to miss it." Marcus' *worried face* was calm and stern. It also happened to be his *proud* face, *happy* face, and *angry* face, but that didn't bother Corin anymore. His father had been that way for as long as he could remember.

Marcus grunted and then actually smiled. "You're shaking."

"Am I?" Corin swallowed. "Well, I guess I'm just so…" He paused. What should he be feeling right now? "Excited?" he offered. Was that the right emotion?

"*Ha!* So am I, Cor!" Marcus chuckled and beamed as he put a massive hand on Corin's shoulder. "So am I…"

A ripple of commotion moved through the crowd, and the applause came all at once, like a rush of wind against Corin's long, sensitive ears. Marcus jumped in with the others, roaring a deep cheer that might have split the stones in the street. Just ahead, beyond a sea of sun-bleached hair and tan, pointed ears, a massive procession was coming around a building.

At the lead were a series of six chariots pulled by enormous red-skinned lahartos. Each burly lizard was stout and intimidating, with thick, ridged skin the same color as wet clay loosely folded over a substantial knot of sinew. Each lizard stood over a meter high, and two lahartos pulled each chariot with bronze chains attached to a yoke mounted on their scaly shoulders. They were clad in golden, ornamental armor, as well as all manner of scarlet ribbons and flowery head dresses.

The chariots were likewise decorated with massive red banners baring the golden crest of Centile on their billowing surfaces. Standing before each banner was an old man dressed in a long, elegant robe with gaudy, ceremonial armor clad over the cloth.

They were the six Elders of Centile: the highest governing body in the city.

The elders stood upon their chariots in glittering extravagance, slowly moving two by two over the cobblestone street and through the twisting flurries of crimson leaflets being thrown down from the rooftops and skyline walkways. They were escorted by the elite guard marching with their broad shields, and ostentatious armor.

Mounted on the front of each of the elders' chariots was an inscription engraved into a brass plaque. They bore the title of the elder riding, naming the ancient position each held. The two elders in front wore, respectively, red and purple robes. The one wearing red was Elder Morten. His plaque read: *Defender of the Light and Captain of the Guard*. Beside him in lavender robes was Elder Sheig: *Ensign of Peace and Director of Commerce*.

Directly behind them were two more elders. In blue was Elder Duarten: *Vessel of Truth and Minister of Education*. To his right was Elder Aldren, dressed in green robes with a golden sash about his waist. His plaque bore: *Keeper of the Land and Director of Agriculture*. Two final Elders brought up the rear. In robes of white and silver was Elder Baltista: *Hearer of the Heart and Chief Judge*. Finally, one Elder remained. Dressed in yellow with an orange sash across his chest was Elder Lehonti. His title was: *He Who Remembers–Chief Historian and Advisor to the Five*.

Elder Lehonti was Corin's grandfather.

The high-ranking officers of the guard were next, all dressed in sparse decorative armor, with wreaths of wildflowers woven into sashes around their chests and torsos. They rode on mounts, but these were nothing like the docile brutes pulling the elders' chariots.

These were cyoves, the attack steeds of the guard.

Tall and sleek, standing several hands' breadths above the lahartos, the cyoves were covered in light grey-brown fur with a single dark stripe that ran from the tip of their muzzles to the ends of their curved, bushy tails. Their snouts were half a meter long, with sharp canine features and a grin of sharper fangs. They walked with grace and precision, long claws clacking against the cobblestones with each step, and their riders sat on hearty saddles of molded leather. Each saddle was situated on the cyove just behind their shoulder blades, on a long ridge formed from the massive mound of the creature's powerful shoulders.

As they passed, a swell of whoops and roars announced that the *true* stars of the parade had finally come into view.

Standing in rows of ten, came this year's graduating recruits. Clad in the finest armor the city had, they marched forward with unwavering resolve. The cheers from the onlookers hailed them on. Each face was hard and stoic, but Corin chuckled when he noticed their tails twitching in uncontrollable excitement.

At the lead of the new recruits were five telaks, their line spaced slightly ahead of the rest. These were the choice soldiers. The exceptional. The gifted. They had flown through the ranks and would now be appointed officers or trained to join the elite guard of the inner district. Farthest on the left of the five was a fair-faced telak with warm, brown skin and long blond hair that erupted like sunshine out from the bottom of his helmet.

He was Corin's elder brother, Lorenzo.

Corin pushed forward a step, crammed two fingers against his lips, and whistled as loud as he could. At first, Lorenzo didn't seem to notice. He and the other four marched on: an apathetic wall of toned arms and rigid spears. Corin's shoulders dropped, but he'd expected as much. Mister newly-appointed-captain must already be taking himself too seriously…

At the last second, Lorenzo's eyes darted to the right. Almost imperceptibly, he shot his younger brother a wink.

Corin smirked. "Typical."

* * *

BEHIND THE RECRUITS, THE CROWD HAD FLOODED OUT onto the streets, cheering and following the procession into the plaza. Marcus smacked Corin's back in sudden panic. "Hey! We've got to move or we won't see a thing!"

The two bolted through the crowd, joining a small stream of others who were already bounding away two steps ahead of the parade. Several streets down, the crowded sidewalks opened up into the expanse of the plaza. This was the city's center: the clean, nestled sprawl at the base of Vallin's Tower.

Like so many times before, Corin couldn't help but admire the colossal spire. Despite the great height of the other buildings encompassing the square, the central tower soared stories above the rest. It was different from the other structures: worn and outdated, almost akin to the sandstone hovels outside the shield wall. It bore no emblems of wealth or privilege. No banners or polished rocks adorned these walls. Its face was simple, smooth, and sandy, the whole expanse gently curving into a massive cylindrical edifice that gradually thinned to the top.

Despite its squalid style, this one central tower rose in unquestioned magnificence, like an ancient queen, calmly ruling over her subjects across the echoes of an antiquated age. It was stately in its simplicity, unapologetically baring its empty walls far above the gaudy streets and decorated buildings below in unparalleled, gargantuan excellence.

At the top, Vallin's Tower was crowned with a colossal iron lantern, just as worn and ancient as the rest of the structure. The lantern sloped out at the base to hold eight massive glass windows, all filled with a blinding, golden light. At the top of the windows the poles met at an iron canopy.

The lantern's pointed roof sloped into a thin spire. From this point, Centile's shield wall flowed. As the light left the pole, it erupted upward towards the sun in condensed streams of crisp sparks and golden gleams before curving down in a long, slow descent to the inner wall. It billowed around the tower, like a tent erected against a gale, circling the heart of Centile with the warm wings of a mother bird sheltering her young.

At the front doors of the tower, a large wooden stand and an enormous pulpit plated in beaten bronze had been erected for the ceremony. The crowd was divided into two halves, creating a path for the procession and space for the recruits to line up before the pulpit. The plaza was already brimming with telaks, and Corin's father rushed along the edge of the buildings, looking for a clear place to stand.

The cheers finally caught up with them from the street behind. Marcus turned. The six banners of the elders were just visible above the crowd. He panicked, and without a word, leapt onto a nearby stack of crates. The owner of the neighboring stand looked on with displeasure but stayed quiet.

Corin barked with laughter. This was most irregular behavior for his crusty old man. Corin leapt up next to him, promptly sitting down on the highest box. The view was great, but Marcus still craned his neck and stretched out his legs.

Corin kept quiet, taking it all in with a forced grin on his cheeks. He really was happy for Lorenzo, but it was hard not to notice the bitter taste the scene left on the back of his tongue. He glanced up at his father.

Marcus' shadow completely eclipsed Corin as he strained to see his eldest.

As they entered the plaza, the group of chariots split off into two rows, swinging wide in round, opposite paths before turning back and lining up on either side of the stand. The elders stepped down from their rides in practiced synchronization and walked onto the stage to stand before the central seats. One by one they met their wives lined up beside the stand and gently led them by the hand to their places on the stage. Next, the officers handed the reins of their cyoves to the escort battalion and claimed their seats just behind the elders.

Finally, the new recruits lined up before the stand. They split off and then condensed into long, even rows with military precision. The five officers-to-be remained in front, attentively watching the elders on the stand. With a quick glance among the six, the elders and their wives sat in unison. The officers followed suit behind them. An ear-splitting crack then echoed off the tower's rounded surface as each soldier in the plaza slammed the end of their spear to the ground.

The echo reverberated five or six times, and the crowd went silent.

And then a pebble hit the back of Corin's head.

He twitched and turned around reflexively, rubbing at the sting. Adahy winked from his perch on a second story balcony. Corin suppressed a scowl, mouthed something foul at the outlander, and then turned back toward the stage.

Elder Morten had just stepped up onto the podium, a haughty grin plump on his lips. He was a brusque, bombastic man with thick forearms and a square face. The crimson clad elder raised his hands to the crowd as he spoke, wide and inviting.

"Welcome one and all to Centile City's *annual accolade ceremony!*" The crowd exploded into cheers and a cloud of banners. Morten waited against the din and then continued.

"It is my great privilege to stand before you today and recognize Centile's *finest*. They have been trained, tested, and are forthwith sworn to defend our city from harm and uphold the sacred order of the light! Join with me, Centile, in welcoming *our 296th graduating platoon!*"

Once more, the crowd burst into applause.

Elder Morten cleared his throat and motioned to the young guards lined up before him. "I now turn my words to *you*, our newest soldiers. You stand in the place of our ancestors. For nearly three hundred years the new recruits of Centile's guard have stood at the foot of this ancient tower and sworn their allegiance to the city they love. You have taken upon yourselves both the great honor and the great responsibility of guiding our people on toward prosperity and safety. We have worked hard to shield our world from the cruel kiss of the plains. We have built our walls and paved our roads and lifted our people out of the barbaric life beyond. You now are the *only force* that keeps our way of life alive, the *only protection* from slipping back into the shadow of the past. From this day forth, each of you must act as though you alone keep our homes and our trade and our fields safe from the savagery of the plains beyond! Outside those walls, there is no honor. Outside those gates, telaks run wild without law. Beyond our haven, live the murderous packs of the wretched outlanders who *prey upon our prosperity*, who *scavenge from our stores*, and *who leech off our labor!*"

Corin flinched at the elder's words. He turned his head to offer a comforting glance to Adahy, but, unsurprisingly, he was already gone. Corin didn't blame him.

"Know this, my young friends…" Morten continued. "The training that has brought you to this point will guide you in all the days of your service. The fate of our city and the fate of our enemies are now in your hands. You here are all men and women of honor and valor. Else, you would not be standing before me. Your worth has been proven, and your courage been found pure. May the light of Centile burn within you! May it continue to fill your hearts with pride and keep your minds and spears *together sharp!*"

He lifted his arms and eyes to the thronging crowd on either side of the new recruits. "Centile, I give you our 296th *graduating platoon!*"

The crowd erupted once more. Corin smirked and clapped along for Lorenzo. As much as he hated to admit it, his brother had earned this day. Up on stage, Elder Morten bowed and returned to his seat. Elder Lehonti rose, briefly shaking hands with the red-robed captain before walking across the stand. He stood in silence at the lectern for a brief moment, calmly looking out across the soldiers. It took some time, wound up as they were by Morten's speech, but when the cheers finally died, Lehonti cleared his throat and gestured behind him.

"Thank you, Elder Morten, for your words of… encouragement and council." Elder Lehonti's voice was still and much quieter than the red-robed captain, demanding a new and poignant reverence from the audience. He turned once more to the crowd, his eyes quietly slipping over the stands.

"As chief historian of the city it is my duty to remember. I think that we, as elders, often forget the full magnitude of our callings. The first half of our title is seldom mentioned and seldom discussed. More than chief historian, I am *He Who Remembers*. It is my duty to impart what wisdom I may have beyond these grey locks, and to tell the stories that everyone else wishes to forget. Speaking now to you, noble youth, it is my hope that my words may find place in your hearts.

"As you hear the number of your title, our 296th platoon, I would ask that you also remember another number. It is three hundred and twelve. That is the number of years since our world was won back from the powers that sought to overtake it. It was on that great day, so many, many years ago, that our founder, Vallin, gave his life to reclaim what was lost. I invite you all to reflect again on the familiar lines of the ancient anthem:

> *"And when the darkness gathered in, and all that's*
>   *good was lost to sin,*
> *"Dear Vallin saw our need that it was dire."*
> *"He feared no horror of the night. He fought for us with*
>   *all his might,*
> *"And from his task his heart did never tire."*

Lehonti paused to give the words time to resonate among the silent listeners. He turned his head and coughed into his fist before continuing. "Vallin's sacrifice was one of purity and honor, not greed or conquest. I would that you might look to him as your model. For when he, on these very plains, fought the horrors that beset us, remember that he did it not out of pride or anger. He did it not for hate or vengeance. He did it out of love. He did it for peace. His goal was not to destroy life, but to save it. His sacrifice was one of healing. Let us not forget that, dear daughters and sweet sons of Centile. Let us remember his example amid the current... *excitement* of our lives. Vallin fought to preserve our world, and he died that we *all* may live.

"Yours, dear youth, is a truly noble calling. You follow in Vallin's footsteps, seeking to restore balance and justice to an imperfect world. No different really than his course those many years before. May your intentions ever be as noble, and may your hearts ever be as pure. As you fight to defend our world, do not forget that Vallin died to save every soul you may slay in battle."

These last worlds hung still and sour in the air.

The silence swelled around the restless crowd. It was several uncomfortable moments before the old man finally cleared his throat once more. "Now, on that note, it is my great privilege to present to you our five captains from the 296th platoon."

Applause followed with tentative renewal. The five telaks in front smashed their spears against the stone and stood at attention, and even from a distance, Corin could feel Lorenzo's grin bursting through his helmet.

"These five young men have proven themselves exceptional in all aspects of combat," Elder Lehonti continued, "but most importantly, they have proven themselves to be courageous leaders, and telaks of honor and integrity. We are proud to present their names to you. Would the five please join me on the stand?"

With another smash of their spears the young captains turned and marched onto the wooden stage, standing beside Elder Lehonti.

"Announcing Captain Paulo," the old man stated, "Son of Garian and Cynthia."

Cheers erupted through the crowd as one of the high-ranking officers tied a flowered sash around Paulo's chest.

Elder Lehonti continued. "Announcing Captain Sergio, son of Nathaniel and Yessenia." Again, the crowd's shrill approval sounded forth. The procedure was repeated for Captain Darrow, Captain Perry, and finally for Lorenzo. Before reading his name, the old man paused.

"And last, announcing Captain Lorenzo, son of Marcus and Elizabeth… my dear grandson."

The crowd roared especially loud for Lorenzo and continued on in honor of the other four. Corin smirked and coughed and took a single, cautious step toward the back of the crate, glancing up at his father. Marcus' voice boomed above the rest, his eyes fixed on the stand.

Corin took advantage of the commotion to quietly slip away.

CHAPTER 5

A KAIZO CONTRACT

THE TROPICAL RAIN DESCENDED IN TORRENTS around Diwala and Olenka, making the breezeless air heavy and humid against their skin. Olenka scanned the horizon. The sea and skyline were both as black as squid ink under the starless cloud cover.

The pontoons of the borrowed banca shifted gently on the sea's rolling surface beneath them. It was a stout vessel, not nearly as swift or streamlined as their own, and without the aid of any wind they had fought for over an hour just to keep it in the current's path. Despite the contrary weather they still managed to arrive early, giving Mari enough time to hide their own banca among the rocks. Every piece was in place, all their preparations double checked, but Olenka was still anxious. She could sense that the kaizo barge was close, and she was keen on not letting it sneak up on them.

"You need to relax, sister."

Olenka peeled her eyes from the sea to scowl at Diwala. Di was sitting back against the banca's mast, her shoulders pressed into its bound sail. In the darkness, Olenka could just discern the slits of her closed eyes and smirking lips.

"I *am* relaxed," Olenka grumbled.

Di chuckled. "Well, that is certainly up for debate, but you misunderstand me. You must relax when we *descend*. I know you too well, dear sister. You crave control. You will be tempted to tighten your muscles, to fight the pressure, but you cannot struggle against it. You must welcome it. Let the water slow you down."

Olenka frowned. "Slow me down? What do you mean?"

Diwala inhaled a long and gentle breath, letting the air fill the bottom of her ample lungs. "It is a strange world down in the abyss. One that is indifferent to time. And in that world, there are rules which you must respect."

"Like *relaxing?*" Olenka teased.

Diwala's head gently tilted up and down. "Yes," she stated. "It is one of the many rules you *cannot* neglect in the deep. You must move slowly and precisely. Glide more than you kick. Do not rise or dive too quickly. Do not jerk about or overexert yourself. And above all, do not breathe too deeply from our air in the bell. Not like you would on the surface. The air goes… *farther* down below. Too much of it can become a poison in your blood."

Olenka giggled and rolled her eyes. "Oh, come on, Di. A *poison?* You can't be serious."

Diwala sat forward, her eyes suddenly open and glaring at Olenka. "You promised that you would listen to me, sister. Did you not mean that? Because we will not survive this dive unless you keep your word to me."

Olenka sighed and leaned back. "Okay! I'm sorry. I'm listening. I promise. I just… don't really get it. How can it be a poison?"

Diwala kept her eyes fixed on Olenka's, studying her sincerity. Eventually she sighed and continued. "The air becomes more potent as it is compressed, and it will rob you of your senses. You must constantly exhale as we descend. Do not drink too deeply of our air in the bell. You must force yourself to sip it slowly. Do not fill your chest like you would on a normal dive. Too much of it and you will begin to lose your mind."

Olenka was puzzled. "I don't understand. Why would I need *less* air?"

"The weight of the water," Diwala explained, spreading her hands for emphasis. "It squeezes the air. You will see it happen as we descend." She brought her hands slowly together. "A single breath below is like ten breaths on the surface. If you drink too deeply of it, you will become sick and dizzy. Pass out, even."

Olenka nodded, contemplating the information. "I guess that makes sense… Tell me more. What else do I need to know?"

"How quick you are to repent," Di chuckled. "Well, the only other thing to consider is the return. It will likely be… painful. Much worse than the descent."

"Worse?" Olenka frowned. "Worse how? Why?"

"It just is." Diwala rolled her shoulders and closed her eyes, imagining the miserable sensation. "I cannot prepare you for it, but you must be ready to take it all the same. It is a throbbing pain that comes from everywhere inside of you at once. It is like all the blood in your body is ready to burst through your skin and skull." She shook her head and smiled. "But we will rise through it all the same."

"Okay…" Olenka swallowed and exhaled. It was too late to get freaked out now. "This pain… why does it only happen when you rise?"

Diwala shrugged. "We are not fish, sister. We are merely *visitors* to the deep sea, and it does wicked things to Bantay Tubig who do not respect its power. I wish I knew why. I only know that it does. We must rise ten meters at a time, no more, then we must rest. If you do not give your body time to adjust it could kill you."

"Wait, what? *Kill you?* Di!" Olenka leaned forward, pulling at the matted locks of her hair. "You didn't say anything about that earlier! It can *kill you?*"

Diwala smiled and nodded. "Yes. Or you could become paralyzed. I once knew a siokoy who lost all of the feeling in his arm. Up too quick," she snapped her fingers, "useless arm."

Olenka rocked back, clutching her knees. "Storms, Di! Why didn't you tell me this buwisit earlier? Oh, my goodness… I think I'm going to throw up…"

Diwala chuckled. "You said you could handle it, sister! I did not want to worry you before it was time. But do not panic. I will be there to guide you, and your body will tell you when it is time to stop. Just listen to it. You will feel it in your very blood."

Olenka sat back and rubbed her forehead. "Alright… No problem, right? We've got this! We'll be fine, right?"

Diwala shrugged. "I should hope so. The kaizo are here."

* * *

OLENKA WATCHED THE OILY LIGHT OF THE KAIZO barge slink across the waves. It was dim and gentle, but against the endless black it was a prominent beacon. Diwala and Olenka took hold of the oars, watching the barge float toward them.

"Should we light the lantern?" Diwala whispered.

"No, not yet." Olenka kept her eyes on the distant glow. "Not until we're ready to board. Let's see what they do first."

They followed the kaizo silently, giving their ship a wide berth. The barge pulled up to the far side of the rocks and drifted to a stop, and the sirena floated up beside it. They sat in silence, hoping to overhear something on board. Olenka could discern a few muffled voices drifting down from the deck, but the roar of the rain was too intense, and the kaizo were too clever to speak above a whisper. She soon gave up and motioned to Diwala.

Di opened the glass door of the lantern and scraped a few sparks into it off a flint block. The wick took, and she cradled the building flame, letting the greasy plume curl in her cupped hand until the light glowed blue through the translucent webbing between her fingers.

"No going back now." Di smiled and hung the lamp from a notch on the mast.

"No going back now…" Olenka echoed.

It didn't take the kaizo long to notice them. A fat coil of braided bamboo rope shot out of the darkness, slapping across the hull of the banca between them. Diwala wrapped it a few times around an iron cleat hammered into the bow, and their boat was quickly hauled up to the side of the barge. Four silhouettes peered over the edge, leaning against the gunwale.

"My, oh my…" Aroon croaked. "They's got some *real* pretty barnacles out this way, aye Captain?"

"Indeed." Omi's slender frame shifted weight from one leg to the other, her gaze drifting to Diwala as she spoke. "Though, this new one's got some sharp edges, wouldn't you say?"

Hiroki chuckled a throaty gurgle. "Might cut up your fins if ya ain't careful."

Diwala stood as the kaizo laughed amongst themselves. She pulled on the rope to bring the banca flush with the barge.

"The thing about barnacles," Di stated, "is that they always stay still. You only get cut if you swim too close."

"*Woo, hoo, hoo!*" Aroon clucked. "We's all gonna be havin' some *fun tonight*, that's what I's thinkin'."

Olenka exhaled, standing up beside Diwala as Hiroki extended a burly arm to hoist her up. Olenka ignored the gesture, instead pulling herself up by the rope. Hiroki grunted and stepped back as the two sirena hopped onto the deck.

"Welcome, sisters." Omi grinned. "What luck to have so many sirena on my ship! One to one with the boys, now. Are we not?"

"Good." Olenka straightened her vest as she scanned the ship. "Maybe we'll actually get something done tonight."

She crossed the deck to examine the diving bell. It was a bulbous structure with sloped sides, no windows, and several thick chains attached to bundles of rope. In the gloomy light it was hard to tell if it was made of copper or just really rusty. Olenka rapped her knuckles against it a few times, listening to the dull thud of metal too thick to ring. She stepped back, studying the surrounding machinery above it. There was a complex series of pulleys and levers, along with a set of sturdy metal arms branching out over the black sea.

"This is it, then…" Olenka mumbled. "Bit smaller than I was expecting."

Omi shrugged. "Any bigger and I'd need a new ship. But I think it will be more than enough space for the two of you."

Diwala stepped up, examining the bell's chains and attachments. "There are cargo hooks on the inside, I presume?"

Omi nodded. "And a handrail for ascent."

Di grunted her approval, circling the diving bell as she spoke. "And there is a sounding line?"

Omi pointed to a loose coil of twine snaking through a few metal loops and under the lip of the structure. Diwala studied the line and followed it to a tiny, *silver* bell mounted on the mast behind the big, *rusty* bell. Omi stepped up beside her, the back of her hand resting against her hip.

"Won't do much good on the way down," the captain lamented, "but there's more than enough line for you two to signal us when the cargo's loaded."

"And…" Olenka started, but hesitated, "you four will just pull us back up when we signal?"

There was a creak in the ship's boards behind her, and Olenka jumped as a thick hand fell on her shoulder. She spun back to see Hiroki's scarred face much too close to her own.

"Thinking maybe we'd just leave you two minnows down there?"

Olenka slid out from his grip, stepping to Diwala's side. "Actually, I was wondering whether you'll be able to lift that thing by yourselves."

Hiroki chuckled. "Don't you worry, short fins. We'll be getting your pretty face back up nice and easy."

He ended his words with a wink. Olenka almost punched him in the throat.

Instead she smiled. "Well, that's good to hear. It would be a shame if you pulled us up too quickly. You might knock the cargo free."

There was a long pause as the kaizo stared down at Olenka. She didn't move. The Great Sea taught many lessons to those who were observant, and those who weren't did not last long. Olenka had seen doomed ships foolishly try to outrun storms. She had watched schools of fish courageously ebb around a drifting shark's open mouth. She had noticed the way panicked crabs would sometimes take to their hidden fins when an octopus approached only to be snapped up all the quicker. In the ocean, you were either a hunter or you were prey. The first to flinch were usually the first to be eaten. Olenka was a hunter, through and through. This siokoy would learn that fact one way or another.

"Well," Omi broke the silence, staring at Olenka, "seems like we all… *understand each other* quite well, don't we? Shall we get you two suited up, then? Isko, show them their gear."

Olenka nodded, still glaring at Hiroki. Diwala brushed up beside her, and together they followed Isko to a table under a lantern. He was a tall, slender siokoy with no visible scars or tattoos. He had glazed, calloused eyes that harbored more intelligence than Olenka expected to see in a pirate.

"Alright, two vests and two lanterns. Here we are." The lanky siokoy hefted a pile of mahogany straps from the table and shoved it into Diwala's arms. The vests were thick and heavy, the leather woven around strips of metal designed to compress their chests. The sirena worked into the rigid things while Isko pulled two submerged iron lanterns from a bucket. As soon as he stirred the water, a cool, cerulean glow bloomed out from the glass, clashing with the murky glare of the fish oil.

"Mmm…" Isko hummed as he flicked the glass of the lanterns. "Beautiful, aren't they?"

Olenka leaned in, peering into the glowing aquarium. A small pile of shells was shifting at the bottom of the lantern as the water sloshed inside. Each was glowing a brilliant shade of electric blue. Thrashing above them was a swarm of shrimp. They dashed around inside the lantern, belching vibrant teal plumes whenever they hit the glass.

Isko cleared his throat, hoisting one of the lanterns up to eye level. "Now, the clusterwinkle shells will keep shining the whole time, but to get the shrimp to glow you need to flick the glass. Try and save them for when you need distance. Those fire-spitters only have so much juice in them, see?"

He handed one lantern to Olenka and then used his free hand to pull open a handle at the top of the other. A metal plate slid out, exposing several small holes in the lantern's top.

"Be sure to let in water as you dive," he explained, "or else the pressure will burst the glass. You understand?"

Olenka nodded as she messed with her lantern's lid. Diwala took the other and gave the glass a delicate tap. Three shrimp suddenly burst with light, flitting their way through their cage in luminescent jets.

"Beautiful," Diwala whispered, smiling into the glass. "Just like Pa Naing, is it not?"

"Ugh… Why'd you have to say that?" Olenka grumbled. She lowered her lantern and glanced around at the kaizo. "Well? What are you all looking at? Let's get down there."

* * *

THE METALLIC SCREECHING OF THE BELL SLIDING across the wet planks pierced through even the rain's relentless din. The three siokoy grunted in strain while the captain released a weight into the water that pulled at the bell's chains. With a tremendous impact, the diving bell crashed into the sea, slowly sinking below the tumultuous surface.

Olenka and Diwala were sitting against the gunwale with their eyes closed, trying to keep their hearts still and their minds clear. Their legs were crossed, and their backs were perfectly straight as they slowly breathed in and out, stretching their ample lungs. Omi stepped in front of the two sirena, her hands resting on her hips.

"Everything's in place, sisters," she said. "You two finished napping?"

Olenka opened her eyes. The bleak deck of the barge seemed strangely bright, and the pounding rain felt unnaturally comforting. Olenka cleared her throat, trying to focus on those calming, familiar, topside sensations while she still could. She clenched her fists as she exhaled to try to hide their trembling.

Omi smiled as she squatted down in front of them. "Don't you two go failing me down there. We sirena need to maintain our reputations, you know."

Olenka cracked her neck and rose to her webbed feet. "You keep your end of the deal and we'll keep ours, Captain."

"Fifty-fifty," Omi whispered, her eyes and jewelry twinkling as one.

Olenka and Diwala stepped up to the edge of the barge, pulling their fish-skin hoods over their matted locks and tightening the straps of their compression vests. The diving bell was fully submerged now, nothing but a few lines of bubbles betraying its location under the surface.

Olenka cupped her lantern against her ribs and stepped off into the water. She slid into the black brine, the shock of the cold instantly sharpening her senses. The familiar pressure of the water was deeply reassuring and deliciously silent. She drifted for a moment of peaceful suspension before bobbing back into the rain crashing against the ocean surface. Diwala splashed in beside her, and Omi crouched down at the edge of the ship, letting her forearms rest on her knees.

"Now, listen closely, sisters. The haul won't be easy. It's an iron chest with a big, rusty lock and latch." She spread out her hands shoulder's length in front of her. "It's about this long, and it'll be heavier than it looks. You'll need to work together to get the uzai thing up to the cargo hooks. Still think you two can manage?"

Diwala scoffed as she adjusted her hood. "We can handle your jewelry box, sister. Mind your tongue."

"Of course…" Omi paused, considering Diwala's stoic features. "How terribly disrespectful of me… Well, not that you two need any help finding it, but the chest should be somewhere under the hull, maybe a wooden trap door near the bow."

The two sirena nodded to Omi, and in a synchronized dive, slipped under the waves. The kaizo captain stayed crouched near the edge, staring into the black water. Finally, she inhaled too quickly, like she had briefly forgotten to breathe, and turned her ear toward the deck behind her.

"Hiroki, dear?"

The scarred siokoy stepped to the edge. "Captain?"

"Did you and the boys tell them that the chest was filled with jewelry?" Omi kept her eyes fixed on the water as she spoke, her finger absently scratching at the patterns of her nose ring.

Hiroki frowned and folded his arms. "You been with us the whole time, Captain. Ain't none of us slipped a word about the claim."

"How interesting…" Omi whispered. "Neither did I."

CHAPTER 6

BACK-ALLEY BALANCING ACTS

ORIN MOVED UNNOTICED ALONG THE cobblestone street, slinking quietly behind the crowd. Another cheer broke out with a flurry of red cloth to swirl it high into the still, hot air. Someone new was admonishing the masses, but Corin was too far from the podium to make out their words. He forced himself to walk slowly down the empty streets. Wooden crates and carts loaded with vegetables and tubers caked with red grit filled the walkways and corners. There was no one left on the streets but the occasional merchants guarding their wares with tired, drifting eyes, steadily shifting their weight and adjusting folded arms.

But Corin hardly noticed them.

He paid attention to his breathing as he walked, trying to time every third step he took with an inhale or an exhale. An inhale then an exhale… He was disturbed by what he'd just seen, and he couldn't fully explain why. It was the platoons of guards, the synchronized cracks of their spears, Morten's speech, the way he called for action. That was it. It was the way he stirred up the crowd until they were reduced to a screaming riot of flicking tails and pounding fists… Something about it all made his mind absolutely sick, like it was dredging up a nightmare he'd long since forgotten.

Corin couldn't control what his mind was doing, so he focused on his lungs instead. The smooth nails of his eight toes rhythmically clacked along the cobblestone, helping him keep the beat of the street and his breath pounding over his other thoughts: drowning them out, pushing them back down to his subconscious where they belonged.

He slipped down an alley to the edge of the shield. Its golden surface lighted upon a wall of enormous stone bricks and the massive archway to the southern district. Corin walked along the banner-shadowed path and through the southern gate. A guard nodded him through the arch with a vacant stare. He was leaning against his spear and swiveling his ears toward the sound of the distant celebration.

Outside, the lower-class districts carried on with their affairs, uninterested in the festivities. They were mending cloth, scraping dirt off potatoes, and maintaining an impressive level of apathy for the grandeur just beyond the wall.

Corin rounded a corner into a short, secluded alleyway. The end opened up into a small courtyard with spent crates, their dry, bristling planks piled high along the three walls. Corin leapt up and stretched out on one of the creaking things. It wasn't particularly comfortable, but the space was secluded and familiar. He came here often to think… Or, if he was being honest with himself, to *hide*. The alley was always warm and still. It seemed quieter than anywhere else in the city.

It also never changed, which was something great and terrible indeed.

Corin closed his eyes, hoping that he could nod off, but his mind was far too busy to allow for sleep. He breathed the fresh air, free from the shield's suppression, and tried to get the back of his head to sit comfortably against the panels of sun-bleached, brittle wood.

Corin's ear twitched at a creak in the box beside him. He opened one eye and tilted his head in the direction of the sound. With no more grace or secrecy than a rockslide, Adahy dropped down next to his face from off the rooftop.

Corin bolted upright, sighed, and then slapped his face into his palms. "Do you *have* to do that?"

Adahy looked legitimately surprised. "Do what?"

"Fall from the bloody sky!" Corin snapped. "You're going to drop down on an old lady someday and stop her heart cold."

Adahy laughed. "Well, you know, we murderous *plains barbarians* can't be too careful! Taking down one of your city-wenches would just be a lucky perk, yeah?"

"Come off it. No one takes Morten seriously," Corin muttered, more to himself than Adahy. He lay back down and closed his eyes. "Hey, thanks for coming today. I'm sure Lorenzo will appreciate knowing you were there."

"Oh? *Lorenzo* will appreciate my presence, yeah?" Adahy's eye twinkled in sarcastic pleasure. "Because, you know, that is of course who I came to visit."

Corin smirked. "Well, you know. A *captain* needs the support of... the *little* people every once in a while. Helps him know he's making a difference in this great and glorious struggle."

Corin couldn't see it, but he knew Adahy's features had tightened to hold back a snort.

"Now, you gotta refresh my memory, Chiqalan," Adahy sang. "It gets so muddle, puddle jumbled in all them wallie politics, yeah? You talking about the struggle *inside* or *outside* the wall?"

"Oh outside, of course! We city dwellers don't engage in such petty conflicts within. All is well in Centile..." Corin held onto his smile, but it was tough. All the life behind it faded as the bitter taste in his throat caught back up with his tongue.

Adahy tilted his head. He'd obviously noticed Corin's falling features, but he didn't acknowledge them. Not out loud, at least. Instead, he jumped down from his crate, the blunt end of his spear firmly fixed in the gap between two cobblestones. He pulled up on the shaft near the blade and wrapped his toes around the base. Gently pulling back as he stepped up, Adahy lifted off the ground, balancing his whole weight on the tilted end of his spear.

Corin chuckled despite himself. Adahy could never sit still, especially during a heavy conversation. Occasion, topic, tone, it was all completely irrelevant. The outlander had started practicing this absurd balancing act as a way to channel his fidgets when he felt confined.

Adahy tenderly crept higher up the spear, and then glanced at Corin. "You ready to be amazed, yeah?"

Corin raised an eyebrow and nodded. With empty-eyed concentration contorting his face, Adahy let go of the spear with his toes. Slowly he arched his back, lifting his feet up and outward and stretching them out at full length for balance. For an instant, the outlander was suspended over his tilted spear, his legs extended out like eagle's wings, his arms quivering with the strain…

…and then his grip failed.

Adahy slid down the shaft for a few centimeters before his weight shifted and the spear's end popped out from underneath him. He caught himself, but not before rubbing a hole in his crimson shorts. He kicked his spear aside and swore a string of unintelligible plains-curses, poking a finger up into the threadbare edges of the hole. Corin laughed deep and clean and true. The display had been for him, and he was grateful. Adahy grumbled bitterly as he sat back down on the crate beside him, but Corin could see the proud smile creeping up the corners of his lips.

* * *

THE TWO SAT CHUCKLING FOR A WHILE AFTER THAT, just taking in the sun. But once the laughter settled, and the heavy feeling started fogging up the alley again, Adahy cleared his throat and turned to Corin.

"Hey, I was hoping maybe I could go speak with Elder Lehonti and Lady Maria, yeah? Tonight, if he can. It'll be *real* squeaky quick. See, my papa… Well, he's sick, yeah? And I'm thinking that he might not pull through without some wallie medicine…"

"What? Really?" Corin turned to Adahy. "What's wrong with him?"

"We… don't know." Adahy twirled his spear as he spoke, his eyes distant. "He was attacked by something freaky, yeah? Happened last week. Cut him deep across the arm and chest. Right here, see? And the wound's not healing so good. Cold as winter wind, too, but he's acting like he's got a real achy, shaky fever." Adahy suddenly sighed, and the sound was filled with more trembling than Corin would have expected. "He won't come into town to ask you wallies for help, you know? Not that I can blame him, yeah? But… Well, you know how he is. My mama's worried too, but she's as stubborn as him…"

"What attacked him?" Corin asked.

"No clue." Adahy was staring off into the distance. "He didn't say much about it, and the others with him said that whatever it was came and went so squeaky quick that they couldn't get a good look at it, yeah? In and out. Like *lightning*."

"Lorenzo described something similar," Corin said. He sat up and jumped down off the crate. "Last week the guards lost a patrol of four men. The whole city's been talking about it. They were taking the eastern route from the old coast road to Dawn's Harbor. They were coming up to the southern gate when something attacked them. The group didn't check in that evening, so a squad was sent out to search for them. They only found two of the men. One was passed out from blood loss, and the other was bloodied up something terrible… Both arms broken, gashes all up and down his legs. There was one dead laharto about two hundred yards away, but the other men were just… *gone*. Three of their mounts too. They found a couple of blood trails in the grass, but they all came up empty…"

"And the two they found…" Adahy was very still as he spoke. "How they doin'?"

"They're both stable now, last I heard." Corin shrugged. "But neither of them had any idea what happened. They said the same thing you did. In and out. Didn't even see what attacked them. It was dusk at the time too, so–"

"Did they get sick?"

Corin turned and squinted toward Adahy. "Sick? Sick how?" Adahy shrugged. "Just sick. *Any* kind of sick."

"I don't think so…" Corin shook his head while he spoke but paused, looking at his friend. "But it's got the whole city tripping over their tails. You heard Morten's speech. People have been saying that the outlanders might be responsible."

Adahy's skin went rigid. "It's *always* them wicked outlanders, ain't it?"

"That's just what they think…" Corin mumbled, regretting he'd said anything.

"And what do *you* think? Eh, Chiqalan?"

"I think it's nonsense," Corin said. "I don't know much about the plains, but I'm sure it would take more than a raiding group to take down a guard patrol with four lahartos. Especially one that could slip in and out like that without notice…"

Adahy sat quietly, his ears twitching. "I don't know of *anything* that could do that… On or off the plains, yeah?"

Corin rubbed his eyes. "Just be careful, alright? Not that anyone really listens to them, but the elders have asked for all citizens to keep off the eastern and southern roads until they've figured out what happened. I know Lorenzo led a few squads doing search runs, but they haven't found anything."

"And," Adahy looked away at the sky, "those two brillos? You said they were all doing alright, yeah?"

Corin shrugged. "I've told you all I know. I haven't heard anything about them being sick."

Adahy nodded. "Just curious, you know? Anyway, what you doing out here, Chiqalan? I saw you sneaking away from your papa. Running away from all that shiny nonsense, yeah?"

Corin chuckled sourly. "I did not run. I just, you know... I just knew I'd be in the way."

Adahy tilted his head. "In the way?"

"Yeah, it's just... Well, today isn't about me. You see what I'm saying? Today is about *Lorenzo*, and if I'm there, then everyone will try to make it be about me too. They'd say things like *you're so lucky you have a brother that's a captain*, or *I'm sure we can expect great things from you, too*. You know what I'm getting at? Just the typical rubbish people say to prove they can still see you when they can't..."

Corin realized he had been pacing and forced himself to stand still.

"Uh huh," Adahy was squishing his thumb up into his chin in feigned perplexity. "Or they wouldn't."

"What do you mean?"

Adahy shrugged. "Well, I mean just what I said, Chiqalan. *Or they wouldn't.* Maybe that's what's really getting to you, eh? You're scared they wouldn't say none of that stuff, yeah?"

Corin chuckled again. It was less convincing this time. "Believe me, I would be *more* than happy with that, but that's just not the case. People are alwa–"

"Really?" Adahy interrupted. "Because I wouldn't have said none of that stuff to you."

Corin rolled his eyes. "Well, yeah, but that's because you only ever say what's on your mind. You guys don't really worry about trying to step around feelings and..."

"*You guys?*" Adahy smirked and raised an eyebrow, leaning into his spear across his lap.

"Oh, come on," Corin groaned, "you know that's not what I meant."

"Isn't it, though?"

"No." Corin was pacing again. He gave up trying to stop.

"So," Adahy said, "you *didn't* mean that outlanders, like me and mi familia, are more blunt and honest than wallies like yourself, yeah?"

"Well, yeah. I guess that was what I meant."

"So, why you so ashamed of it?"

Corin sighed. "I guess I thought you might take it poorly."

"And, if it was true, why would it matter if I took it poorly, huh?" He held out a hand to Corin's chest to stop his pacing. "Let the truth *sing*, Chiqalan! There should be enough of your mama in you to know that, yeah?"

Corin sat on the crate again. "Yeah, well… sometimes the truth really isn't what people need to hear."

The muffled roar of a cheer echoed its way to the alley. Adahy looked toward it briefly and then back at the sky.

"The only moments I know when the truth is best left unsaid are moments when *all* words are best left unsaid," Adahy explained. "You know why I wouldn'ta said any of that stuff to you today? Because none of it is true, yeah? You *not* lucky to have a brillo brother. It barely affects you, and from what I done seen, the little effect it has ain't no good. You're worried about his safety and you're too embarrassed to stand up straight beside him, eh? No one hopes you go following Lorenzo into the city guard, Chiqalan. And no one's worried whether you gonna *accomplish great things*, yeah? Nobody 'cept you, maybe. You not your brother, and you gotta stop weighing yourself against him, yeah? I don't let nobody else tell me what I'm worth."

Corin sort of chuckled and sort of sighed. "And how do you determine your worth, Adahy?"

The outlander twirled the gaudy display of charms on his spear. He pinched one between his thumb and the first knuckle of his index finger, gently rubbing the stone's polished surface. It was a tiny carving of the sun.

"I listen," he said gently.

Suddenly snapping from somber to anxious, Adahy shot up to his toes and bent his four knees into a tight crouch. "I need to leave now, yeah? And *you* should go find your brillo brother."

In a single spring, Adahy was back on the rooftops. He tapped Corin on the shoulder with his spear. "Hey, but not till you're ready for the truth, yeah?"

He smiled and bounded off before Corin could respond, his trailing giggles bouncing back down the roof at him. Corin halfheartedly threw up a hand to wave him goodbye. He sat there in the sun until he was sitting in a shadow. He was watching his hands for some reason, letting the creases fold and unfold.

Fold and unfold…

He was amazed at how dull and empty they looked.

Finally, Corin pushed off from the crate and walked back through the southern gate.

CHAPTER 7

A POISON IN YOUR BLOOD

THE DIVING BELL ECHOED THE SMALLEST SCRAPES and thumps and splashes into a tremendous, focused racket of reverberation. Olenka grabbed onto the railing inside and pulled herself up into its bleak dome. The darkness was oppressive, even with the glow of her lantern's shells. She loosened a strap on her waist and slid it through the lantern's handle. The blue light illuminated the water at the base of the bell far more than the air pocket above it.

Olenka stared up at the dim, twirls of light refracting through the water's ripples around her torso. They painted the meager, metal canopy with a chaotic beauty that only emphasized the bell's rigid ugliness. Somehow, it felt even smaller from the inside. Olenka had never been one to fear cramped spaces, she'd once stowed away inside a chest of scrolls, but something about this bell made her squirm. Perhaps it wasn't the *size* of the structure, but who *controlled* it that bothered her…

A line of bubbles snaked up from a blue bloom below, and Diwala rose up into the bell beside her.

"You got it?" Olenka asked.

Diwala nodded as she hoisted herself into place, gesturing to a hook clipped to a strap at her chest.

"The line looks secure." She pulled a net up out of the water as she spoke, draping it over the handrail beside her. "And we have about one hundred and fifty meters of rope to work with."

"Alright," Olenka whispered. She could feel her words speeding up as she said them. "Nothing to worry about, right? Everything's in place. The plan will work. It has to. This'll be easy, don't you think? Just another buwisit job, just like all the oth–"

"*Sister*," Diwala interrupted, pressing a sturdy palm against Olenka's chest. "You are doing a *terrible* job of relaxing."

Olenka tried to smile, but felt her cheeks awkwardly quiver instead. "You're right… I'm sorry. I guess I'm just–"

"Breathe with me." Diwala drew in a gentle breath, her hand still pressed against Olenka's chest. Olenka closed her eyes and followed the sounds of Di's air.

"Too much," Di whispered. "Be gentle with it. Sip. Do not chug. Keep your diaphragm relaxed."

"Okay," Olenka muttered as she exhaled. The bell trembled and something metallic screeched through the water above them. Diwala pulled her hand away and checked the lid of her lantern. Olenka did the same.

"Here we go." Di grinned as the bell quivered around them. "It is exciting, is it not?"

Olenka chuckled nervously. "You're insane, Di. You know that, don't you?"

"Oh, come on, sister!" Diwala was far too playful given their predicament. "Surely we have Heaven's blessing in this! Our cause is just. There is nothing to fear. Enjoy the thrill! But don't forget to exhale. Come on, let it out."

The bell shook again, harder this time. Olenka closed her eyes, focusing on her breathing. "I'm sure I'll enjoy it more as a memory…"

"Oh, Olenka…" Di clicked her tongue in pity. "What a terrible way to live! Your misery will do *nothing* to change our fates. Why, then, would you choose it over happiness?"

The bell's speed was clearly picking up. Olenka could sense the motion through the metal at her back. The temperature was dropping too, and the echoes from above were completely silenced now. She could feel the pressure building up behind her eyes and ears, and her shallow, ragged breaths were making her shoulders shake.

"You know, Di," Olenka grumbled, "you can't always choose how you feel."

"Ha!" Diwala spat. "Lightning on *that* thought. You are always in control of your mind. Here, I will prove it to you. Smile."

Olenka shook her head. "I'm more likely to vomit…"

"Hey! Come on. None of this stubbornness! Smile for me, sister."

Olenka sighed but forced her cheeks into a grin.

"Now hold it, there," Di said. "Give it some time to sink in."

Olenka rolled her eyes but kept on smiling. She felt ridiculous, but despite all her elegant skepticism, it was starting to work. A chuckle slipped through her teeth, and she was suddenly smiling in earnest.

"There we go, sister!" Diwala said. "Now don't forget to exhale. Keep your mind calm and keep your breath shallow."

Olenka let out her breath, a cool stream of air in the frigid ambience. She really was starting to feel better. She looked up at the light twirling across the canopy, then glanced down at the lantern at her waist. She briefly considered double checking to make sure the lid was open, but she cast the thought aside. It was probably fine. What did it matter, anyway? Di was right. What will happen will happen. Why worry about it? She looked back up at the ceiling. It was strange, but it almost looked like the ripples of light were getting *brighter…* swirling *faster…*

"It really is thrilling, isn't it, Di?" She smiled sleepily. "That light is something else… So much brighter now that we're this deep! How pretty…" she slurred.

Diwala's smile fell as she stared across the bell at Olenka. She pulled her hand up from the water and pressed it against Olenka's chest.

"Sister, exhale *now*," Di ordered. "You need to empty your lungs."

Olenka giggled. "Oh, calm down, Di! And you say *I'm* the one that needs to relax?"

Diwala switched sides, pulling up next to Olenka's freezing frame. She pushed two fingers up under Olenka's jaw, her eyes wide as scallops as she listened to her pulse.

"Olenka, *listen to me!* Breathe out, *now!*"

Olenka sighed and smiled, only vaguely aware of Diwala's pestering words. She let her head drift down, gazing into the blue light. The water was so much higher in the bell now. It seemed impossibly high. In fact, her head was almost pressed up against the bell's top! How funny! And the light just kept getting brighter, didn't it? White sparks and glares were dancing around the outside of her vision, like a tunnel of stars closing in on the azure glow beneath her.

She could feel Diwala screaming into her ear right beside her, but everything was numb and tingly and warm. Tiny fingers were tickling across her skin and pricking at her muscles. Her eyes were getting very heavy, so she let them close. The blue light faded, but she was delighted to find that the whirlpool of stars remained.

Was this the Silver River?

Had she stumbled upon Heaven's gate?

"It really *is* thrilling," she mumbled across her stiff, clumsy tongue as her words slurred to silence.

* * *

OLENKA FELT A STING ACROSS HER CHEEK, LIKE A NUMB wound thawing back to pain. She gasped and coughed and felt every centimeter of her body trembling.

"*Gently!* Breathe gently, Olenka. Come on, take it easy."

Olenka opened her eyes to see Diwala right in front of her. She blinked rapidly and tried to speak but was met by another round of coughing.

"I said easy, did I not?" Diwala scolded. "What part of that did you not understand, sister?"

"Di?" Olenka stammered. A shock of pain shot through her lungs, and she clutched at her chest. "Di, what happened?"

"*Shh...*" Diwala whispered. "Be still. You drank too deeply. I warned you, but you rarely listen..."

Olenka sighed, leaning back against the bell and grabbing her brow. "Oh, my uzai head..."

"The pain is normal." Diwala chuckled, and then pulled down on Olenka's eyelid, studying the red flesh inside. "I will not lie... You had me quite worried, sister. Are you feeling alright?"

Olenka exhaled very slowly, trying to gauge her level of discomfort. The pressure was obvious and much stronger than she had imagined, especially in her skull. She could still feel all her bodily functions pulsing and sloshing inside her, but they felt weaker. It was like her heartbeat was somehow distant, like the blood pumping through her neck had gotten thicker. Her lungs were still inflating, but it was a strained, shallow expansion. Di had been right. Everything had slowed down.

"I think I'm alright." Olenka stammered at a throb of pain in her chest. It almost felt like she had bruised her lungs.

Diwala gently pinched her friend's nose. "Equalize the pressure."

Olenka exhaled against Di's grip and felt the crackling in her ears and the relief in her skull. Diwala pulled away and Olenka sniffed and shook her head again.

"Okay... I think I'm good. You ready?"

Diwala nodded. "*I* am ready, but *you* will stay here."

"Di, seriously?" Olenka groaned. "This again? I didn't come all the way down here for nothing. I'm going down with you. I'm feeling better already!"

"Sister…" Diwala drifted forward, placing her hands on Olenka's shoulders. "We might still have another *hundred meters* to the bottom, yes? *Fifty* at the very least. This may only be halfway, and it gets worse after this. You must trust me in this… Stay here."

"Di, I am coming with you. You can't haul that chest on your own, and you need me to help comb the bottom. We have no idea how far we are from the wreck." Olenka closed her eyes, breathing out slowly. "If I wasn't feeling better, I would tell you, alright? I need you to trust me too."

Diwala felt Olenka's pulse again, and then pulled down on her other eyelid. Olenka rolled her eyes but surrendered herself to the prying. Diwala grunted and leaned back.

"Fine," Di muttered, "but you *need* to take it slow. The deep has little sympathy for those who do not respect its strength."

"I will." She clapped Di's tattooed bicep. "Promise."

Diwala nodded and checked her lantern. The shrimp didn't seem as agitated anymore, and the shells were all still glowing. She grunted and turned to Olenka. "What is the plan, then?"

Olenka smiled and gazed down at the abyss below. "I say we sink straight down and circle around from there."

Diwala nodded. "We will need to mark the bottom somehow or we will never find the bell again."

"True," Olenka mumbled. "We should also stay within sight of each other's lanterns. I imagine it's pretty easy to lose your bearings down there?"

"Easier than you could imagine." Diwala stated flatly. "Do not forget that we must rise slowly. We can come back to the bell for a quick breath if we need it, but then we must immediately dive down again before the change in pressure has time to poison our blood. Do you understand?"

"Of course."

Di nodded. "So, we are ready, then?"

"Yeah…" Olenka exhaled slowly. "Yeah, I think so."

"Then breathe with me, sister." Diwala extended her left hand to Olenka's right arm, her right hand still grasping the railing inside the bell. Olenka mirrored the gesture.

"Fill your lungs but be sure to fill them *slowly*. Gently."

They inhaled together, drawing in crisp, chilled streams from the compressed pocket in the bell. With a wink, Diwala released the handrail, and Olenka followed. They held onto each other's arms as they drifted down: still and cold as anchors. Olenka tried to guess how deep they were sinking, but in the empty, black void there was nothing to go by. She was completely blind in this lightless world. If it weren't for the lanterns, she wouldn't even have seen Diwala's face in front of her own. Di's eyes were closed, and her body was rigid. She seemed perfectly relaxed. Not the forced relaxation that comes with concentration, but genuine harmony with the crushing depths around them.

It was beautiful and terrifying.

Suddenly, Di opened her eyes and glanced down below them. Olenka looked too, just in time to see the abyssal plain lighting beneath their fins. They landed softly, a plume of silt rising from their gentle impact. Olenka scanned the area. The light of the lanterns was weaker than she had hoped, fizzling to gloom after just three meters of strained clarity. Diwala leaned down and felt the ground at her feet.

There was no vegetation anywhere, but the seafloor was surprisingly full of life. Crustaceans marched over rocks as pale as bone. Frills of scum waved from the backs of shells and broken branches. It was a grey and simple world, but far from empty. Diwala shifted a few rocks into a pile where they had landed, and Olenka joined with her. They formed a simple cross in the muck. Nothing complex, but it was large and bright. Most importantly, it was obviously unnatural.

Olenka turned to Di and slowly twirled a finger over her head. Diwala nodded, and together they started to circle out from their marker. They panned the plain gently, drifting more than swimming. The water felt thicker this far into the abyss, and Olenka found that she was easily suspended in the pressure. She loosened the lantern from her waist and held it in front of her as she crept along the muck. Crabs and lobsters cringed and scurried from the blue gleam, abandoning half-consumed fish with pallid flaps of tissue waving in Olenka's wake. She glanced back and could barely see the glow of Diwala's lantern in the distance. She realized then that, more than anything else, she was afraid of getting lost down here.

Olenka blinked the fear away and turned her attention back to the sea floor. She wasn't covering enough ground. She decided to slowly swing her lantern from one hand to the other, adding another meter to her sight in both directions. Back and forth she passed the light in front of her, a false thrill bursting through her chest every time she spied a large rock or a sunken log. It was hard to tell how long they had been looking, but Olenka was starting to feel the jitters in her arms. It felt like she still had at least another ten minutes of air, but she would need to save most of it for the ascent. She twisted around and spied Diwala's bloom in the distance, and with a simple kick started to drift back to their marker.

As she swam Olenka's heart trembled at the pale gleam of a branch off to her right. She swallowed the thrill, knowing it was just another false alarm. She didn't have time to explore it now…

…but the image stuck with her.

Something about it was wrong. The stick was too barren, and far too straight to be natural. Olenka leaned back into a gentle flip-turn, letting her body drift down to the sea floor again. She tapped the glass of the lantern, and three shrimp suddenly shot across the container in streaks of brilliant blue. The stick in the distance came into view, its barkless shaft protruding from the muck.

Olenka's heart began to race as she realized that its surface wasn't just smooth, it was *polished*. She sped over to the piece of wood, gripped its smooth handle, and pulled its wide, flat end from the slime.

It was an oar.

A line of bubbles burst from her mouth as Olenka let out a chuckle of excitement. She lifted the lantern higher, gazing around for anymore artifacts, but saw only scum swaying in the gloom. Olenka tucked the oar in the crook of her arm, letting its tip drag in the mud beneath her as she swam back to the marker.

Diwala was waiting for her when she arrived. The tattooed sirena raised her lantern and grinned at the sight. She motioned above, and together they rose back up to the bell. To Olenka's delight, Diwala did not make them stop to rest, but rose straight up into the air pocket.

"*Did you find it?*" Diwala exclaimed as she exhaled.

Olenka coughed and sucked in a fresh breath. "No, but it's probably close by! I left a trail back to where I found this."

Diwala reached over and took the oar from Olenka. "This was definitely from their banca, Heaven help them… You can tell by the carving at the base. Daisay always marked her oars with an octopus, you see it?"

Olenka leaned in and let her fingers slip along the simple carving, ten-thousand bittersweet memories assailing her. "Do you think there's any chance they're still alive?"

Diwala shook her head. "No. Those kaizo would not have let them go. My guess is Daisay probably sank their ship herself just so they could not get to the jewels."

"You're probably right…" Olenka paused, trying to suppress the anger building in her throat. It was tight and painful, almost like a sting. The pain shot down the side of her neck and into her arm, making her twitch.

Maybe it wasn't anger at all…

Diwala noticed Olenka's flinch and motioned back to the deep.

"Come," Diwala whispered. "We must descend again quickly, before we get sick."

Olenka nodded, and together they dropped back to the seafloor, Diwala trailing a net in her grip. They landed a few meters off from their marker, but quickly found Olenka's trail in the slime. They followed it back to its end, and once again panned out in a wide, sweeping spiral. Olenka moved quickly, eagerly pulling herself along the slick stones. She found a few more pieces of broken wood, and a length of twine suspended in the murk, but the rest of the wreck remained elusive.

Out of the corner of her eye, Olenka noticed the glare of Diwala's lantern waving quickly back and forth. Olenka turned and kicked off toward the light. First, Di came into sight, then another body, limp and pale against the sea floor. Olenka drifted down, gazing into the dead sirena's eyes. Olenka recognized her face as a member of Daisay's crew, but she had never learned her name. The sirena's throat had been slit, and the ashen wound was bulging out in grotesque rows of tattered, fish-nibbled tissue.

Olenka turned away from the grisly sight and noticed Diwala waving for her attention. She pointed out into the murk, tapping at the glass of her lantern. The light was catching something big in the distance, a reverse silhouette glowing against the eerie darkness beyond. They slipped through the water toward the glow, and the wreckage came into sight.

The banca had landed upside-down, half of the bow buried in the mud. Olenka set down her lantern and grabbed ahold of the exposed end while Diwala pressed up from underneath. The boat shifted easily, the tip of the pontoon casting a cloud of silt as it pulled up into the water.

Olenka drifted down next to Di as the boat settled, feeling surprisingly dizzy from the meager effort. The cloud of dust dissipated, and a line of bubbles slipped from the cavities of the sunken banca.

There, wedged under the ship's wooden beam, was Daisay's limp body.

Olenka stared. The sirena had been much older than her, but Daisay still should have had decades left on the sea. A spear was protruding through her gut just above her left hip, and it looked like she must have used the last of her strength to pry up a few boards at the base of the deck with her knife.

Olenka drifted over to Daisay's corpse and cradled her frigid face in her hands. Daisay had been one of the few people who trusted Olenka in the beginning, back when she was still just a lost guppy flopping free of her pampered puddle. She had offered them jobs they had no business taking because she believed in them. She had taught Olenka all she knew about trade on the Great Sea, but now…

Olenka tried to close the sirena's bloated eyes, but the stiff lids wouldn't stay shut. She needed to do *something*… She had to pay her respects *somehow*… Sure, Daisay had been a miserable old crab. She drank like a fish and could sniff out blood better than any shark, but she'd also been like a mother to her. A loud, salty, wonderful mother. Olenka felt the sea's immensity crushing in around her, and the silence of the deep roared through her frozen bones.

She felt Diwala's hand press on her shoulder, and she turned away.

Together they crept along the bottom of the banca. It was long and wide, but very simple in shape. The two quickly found the trapdoor that Omi had mentioned. There was a small cut-out in the wood with a rope handle. It pulled open easily, revealing the edge of the chest inside. Olenka tapped on Di's shoulder and pointed back toward their marker. She nodded, and together they hefted the box out into the muck and dragged it between them.

Bubbles kept escaping her lips as she hefted her end of the chest. It felt much heavier than Olenka had expected, but it might just have been the effects of the pressure straining her muscles. Diwala was either unaffected or very good at hiding her discomfort…

…but Di was also a buwisit force of nature, so she didn't count.

The marker came into sight, and the two dropped the box onto the muck. Olenka studied the latch in front and motioned for a rock. Diwala brought one, and Olenka smashed it against the big, rusty lock. After five hits, the busted mechanism slid free, and Olenka drifted back in fatigue. She gripped at her head, seeing the swirl of sparks close in on her vision again. Diwala slipped into her place and pried open the lid. She held her lantern over the contents, letting the blue light catch the facets of a hundred mountain rubies.

Olenka drifted back down to Di, gazing in over her friend's shoulder. It must have taken Daisay's crew *months* to get this many rubies from the tall miners. It was a dazzling fortune, enough to sail away on silk sheets, sipping coconut cream in a gilded captain's quarters, but the wealth didn't matter to Olenka. This was personal. As long as those uzai kaizo didn't get their claws on it, Olenka would be satisfied.

The two sirena offered each other one quick grin before piling the loot out into their net.

The pieces were gorgeous, much more elegantly crafted than typical Bantay Tubig jewelry. The scarlet rubies shone a deep violet in the blue light, their golden chains and brackets exploding into rows of stars. When the chest was emptied, Olenka filled it with rocks and clapped the lid shut. Diwala pulled a spare lock from inside her vest and briskly snapped it down on the latch. With one last nod, the two sirena gripped the chest and net between them, then kicked off back into the gloom above.

The exertion was tremendous.

The chest alone had been more than they could manage comfortably, but, with the added weight of the rocks, Olenka felt like her body would simply seize up. Her air was running very low, and the force needed to keep her fins going was sucking the last drops of oxygen from her chest.

A bolt of pain struck her neck and arm again, hitting the exact same place they had before.

Diwala noticed the burst of bubbles escape from Olenka's lips and pulled the lantern from her hip and placed it on the chest between them. She smiled and flicked the glass. The explosion of light filled Olenka's sight and, for a moment, she was able to forget the pain and just keep kicking.

Diwala's eyes and cheeks were pulled taut in discomfort, but her smile was a plume of warmth in the murk. Olenka gritted her teeth as she kicked and kicked and *kicked...* The weight of the chest was incredible, and no matter how hard she fought against the deep it felt like they were sinking instead of rising. She strained her eyes, pushing past the pain in her arms and neck and lungs to search for the elusive diving bell above. Burning panic was rushing up into her throat: the desire to gasp, to thrash, to drop the chest and claw madly at nothing until the void in her chest was filled with *something*.

Her eyes blurred, but through the fog she finally spied the rim of the bell, suddenly illuminated above her. Panic was replaced by desperation, and Olenka poured the last of her stamina into lifting the chest's handle over the bell's salvage hook.

The instant the cargo was secured, Olenka burst up into the pocket of air, letting the meager few centimeters of oxygen bloom to icy life inside her pounding chest. She gasped and leaned back and gasped again, color suddenly rushing back into her vision. She tightened her arm around the handrail while she massaged the twinge in her neck. Diwala shot up beside her.

"*Lightning*, sister!" Di cried. "You were right after all, eh? No way I could have hauled that without you." Diwala pressed her hand against her face, pulling down on her eyelids as she wiped the water from her chuckling features.

Olenka wanted to smile or roll her eyes or tease her sister, but instead she just sat there, panting in their oasis of air. It was all she *could* do.

Diwala smacked Olenka's arm. "Hey, I told you it would be exciting, did I not?"

Olenka shook her head and smiled as she panted, but a horrible thought struck her. "We need to go back down, don't we?"

Diwala rolled her shoulders and flexed her webbed fingers, staring down at the pulsing capillaries in the membrane.

"We will rest for now, perhaps it will be alright." She clenched her fist and glared up at Olenka. "But if you feel *anything* you must descend immediately."

Olenka nodded, contemplating the pain in her neck. Every beat of her heart brought a fresh sting that shot down her arm, but each new spasm was weaker than the last. She breathed slowly, letting the shocks numb to an annoying throb that grew softer and softer, but never quite went away...

Olenka shook the anxious thoughts from her aching head. It would be fine. She had run very low on air. Pain was to be expected. She just needed to hold still and breathe. Keep calm and breathe.

She pulled up on the handrail and closed her eyes. "Is the net secure?"

Diwala nodded, her exhausted voice like reeds in the breeze. "It is attached. As soon as we are ready, we can begin the ascent."

Olenka nodded and looked around at their sheltered, rusty bubble. "How much air do we have left?"

Diwala shrugged. "Hopefully enough."

"*Hopefully?*"

"Hopefully." Di smiled. "Stow your panic, sister! Give us a few more minutes to rest, then we will ring the bell, alright?"

Olenka leaned back. She wanted to relax. She wanted to give her lungs and muscles time to recover, but the water lapping at her throat was too unsettling, and the sea's chill had finally worked its way down into her bones. She waited in uncomfortable, trembling silence until their breathing steadied and Diwala finally motioned to the sounding line. Olenka reached for the rope, startled by how much her hand was shaking. She pulled up on the line, hauling two meters of slack into the bell before it finally went tight. She jerked on the taut end over and over, hoping the motions made it to the surface.

Finally, the bell started to lift.

Olenka leaned back and watched the blue light of the shrimp lanterns illuminate a thousand particles of marine snow drifting away beneath them. Diwala was also watching the water, studying the specks with warm curiosity that began to harden into unusual fascination. Her eyes started to dart around, suddenly concerned, then frantic. Olenka scrunched up her brow and bumped Di's arm.

"Hey," she said. "Everything alright, sister?"

Diwala jerked slightly at the touch but didn't respond. She gazed into the black depths as if she were straining to see phantom shadows that had just been there.

"Di? What's up?" Olenka pressed. "You're freaking me ou—"

Olenka clutched at her neck as a spasm split through her veins.

The pain sent an icy jolt through her arm and chest. Then another. Diwala looked up, her eyes wide and round and blindingly white.

"They are not stopping," Diwala stated. "We have to ditch."

Olenka cried out as the pain burst through her flesh again. She looked up at Diwala in panic.

"What do you mean, *ditch? Right now?*"

Diwala grabbed Olenka's arms, staring straight into her bleary eyes. "They are trying to *kill us*, sister! We are rising too quickly! Just look!"

Olenka's frantic eyes darted around the bell. The air pocket had swollen to more than double its size, and the illuminated particles were streaking below them at ever increasing speeds. Di was right. They were coming up too fast.

"*Olenka!*" Diwala shook her by the shoulders as she screamed. "*Ditch, now!*"

Diwala took a massive breath and then released her grip on the handrail, letting the bell slip away above her. Olenka looked down at the fading light of her friend's lantern. Her blood felt like it was bursting through her skin, violent throbs and pangs that shook her frame until she screamed and released her grip…

…and was swallowed up by the void.

CHAPTER 8

CAPTAIN BRILLO

THE CROWD AROUND THE TOWER HADN'T REALLY dispersed so much as widened. There was still an oppressive swarm of telaks clogging the square, but they had wound themselves up into tight, little chattering bunches. Many had rolled barrels of ale out onto the cobblestones and were toasting to decorated children and future glories on the plains. The benches and tables along the edge of the plaza were packed to capacity, with merchants wandering around the edges, pushing cheap jewelry and fresh bread on anyone foolish enough to make eye contact.

Corin wove his way through the masses and around the side of the central tower. The crowds were denser there, clustering around the front gate of an enormous square building. Two nearly symmetrical statues sat on either side of the gaping doorway. Each was a relief carved into ancient sandstone blocks at least four meters tall. The statue on the left depicted a kneeling soldier gripping a flaming sword in one hand and a massive gem in the other. To the right was another soldier in the same pose, but wielding a long, flowing banner mounted on a spear. The statues were well-worn and stained with clay smears of a slightly darker brown to patch the cracks in the failing stone. A steady gush of people moved in and out of the building, the dull roar of hundreds of voices reverberating through the cavernous walls and lofty ceiling of the training compound.

Corin squeezed into the closest trickle and shuffled his way into the building, stepping with the pulse of the crowd. The training compound of the guard had been re-imagined as a banquet hall for the after-party. It was currently obscured by the crowd and tables, but the floor was a grid of stone pathways, etching giant rectangles into a floor of bare sand. The training equipment had all been pushed against the walls into great piles of iron beams and mounted logs that Corin couldn't begin to fathom a purpose for.

The crowd opened up a little past the doorway, and Corin made his way past rows of wooden tables laden with clay dishes of food and great barrels of dark, bitter ale. Most of the trays were covered in fresh breads and pastries. At a glance, every crusty roll was identical to the last, but each was stuffed with a different culinary treasure. Corin noticed a tray of swirled pastries that were wrapped and baked around whole carrots, crisped green tops and all flowing from the end. Another tray held curiously knotted baskets of golden, flakey bread, each filled with a paste of tubers and lentils garnished with edible pink flower petals and deep, green sprigs of some dried herb too fancy for Corin to recognize. Likely something foreign shipped from across the Great Sea.

There was very little fruit present in any of the dishes, except a few baked apples here and there, and there was absolutely no meat. Fruit was just tough to come by out on the plains, but telaks weren't especially partial to eating flesh. At least not Centileans. There was no morality in it; it was simply a generally understood superstition that meat made you heat-sick, gave you a stomachache, and slowed you down.

The caramel walls of the cacophonous room stretched back for a great distance, periodically draped with Centilean banners. At the end of the hall was a crowded wooden stand.

There, near the left of the stage, was his family.

The first thing Corin noticed was his brother's sun-bleached, blond hair flipping around with the energy of one of his animated stories. His father was standing close to his eldest son, facing Corin's grandparents and a younger couple that Corin didn't recognize. He held back for a few minutes, pointlessly nibbling at a fluffy roll that turned out to be interspersed with flakes of smoked chilies and roasted garlic.

When the unfamiliar couple drifted down the stand, Corin meandered to the stairway. Lorenzo caught his eye first and flung himself over the railing at his brother.

"You, little *scoundrel!*" he cried.

Lorenzo crashed into Corin, knocking them both to the ground and spilling a woman's glass of something lavender and sticky. Impressively, it managed to get into Corin's eye, hair, and all over the sleeve of his previously white shirt.

"And what exactly do you think you're doing?" Lorenzo growled. "You think you can just charge into my party after bailing on me at the ceremony? You've got a lot of nerve." Lorenzo sat up, pinning his brother down with his first knees crushing into his chest. The surrounding crowd mumbled in distress, but that was nothing Lorenzo would ever choose to notice.

Corin pretended to hide his immense *physical* discomfort under the pretend *emotional* discomfort that his brother's display demanded. It was a familiar routine, and Corin knew the part: fake displays of anger resulting in an inappropriately public wrestling match and tied up at the end with hug-it-outs and slaps on the backs. All just a playful charade…

…for Lorenzo, anyway.

"Oh dear, was that *today?*" Corin choked out. "If only there had been a *parade* or something! You know, a big, loud, shiny show… Something really *full of itself* to help me remember…"

Lorenzo's eyes shone bright and bold as he shook his head down at him. For a moment, Corin thought he was going to pop him in the nose, but instead Lorenzo hopped off his chest and offered him a hand.

"It *was* a little modest for the occasion, wasn't it?" Lorenzo winked as he wrenched Corin up to his toes. The new captain's mood had obviously been loosened up by the ale, and he forgave his little brother his sass. They embraced with much back thumping and grunting, and Lorenzo pulled Corin up the stairs with a thick arm around the back of his neck.

The crowd parted easily for Lorenzo, probably for fear of further antics. The rest of their family stood in a half circle by a clothed table of drinks. Elder Lehonti grinned warmly at his grandsons while his wife, Maria, ran to embrace Corin.

"Oh, dear, where *were* you?" She reached up and grasped his face. "You should have been there for your brother!" She clucked her tongue and tilted her head in an exaggerated pout.

Marcus, too, reached out and placed a hand on Corin's arm. "She's right son. Where did you run off to?" As always, his face was stern but not angry.

"I'm sorry." Corin grabbed a cloth napkin from the table and wiped the purple smear from his brow. "I was talking with Adahy. We headed out of the noise for a minute and must have gotten carried away. Oh! That reminds me. Grandfather, Adahy really needs to speak with you. His fa–"

Lehonti raised a hand to cut him off. "He's told me all about it. An *hour* ago, actually." His grandfather arched a single, condemning eyebrow toward Corin. "Lorenzo and I plan to visit their village first thing tomorrow morning."

Lorenzo reached to the table and grabbed a mug. He was busy taking a gulp as he patted his brother's back again. "That's right, and you are more than welcome to come with us!"

His smile was starry-eyed and tipsy, but undeniably sincere.

"We'll see," Corin offered, tossing the soggy cloth aside. "I've got a lot to catch up on at the workshop, but I can probab–"

"Splendid!" Lorenzo barked. "You know, I could even round us up a couple of *cyoves* now! If you'd be interested, Cor. Wouldn't be a problem at all. You'd love it too, I tell you! What a way to travel. Nothing like those bulky red lizards. Perks of being an *officer*, eh?" He laughed and sipped and spilled a little.

Corin sighed. "I suppose congratulations *are* in order, aren't they?"

Lorenzo put down his mug and looked Corin in the eyes, suddenly serious. "Only if you mean it, Cor."

Corin put on a smile, swallowed his pride, and threw a hand up onto his brother's armored shoulder. "I do. I *really* do."

Lorenzo's serene, beaming smile trembled a bit at the corner. He slipped his arm onto Corin's neck and pulled him down into an awkward, drunken huddle.

"Corin, and I'm not," he hiccupped, "just saying this… that means *a lot*. What *you* think? Thunder and hail, I'm telling you… It means more than what *anyone else* in this whole bleeding building thinks!" He panned his hand out over the crowd and then smacked it against his brother's chest. "So, thank you, Cor. I'm serious, okay? *Thank. You.*"

"Oh, shut up." Corin laughed and threw off his brother's arm.

* * *

GROUP BY GROUP, THE CROWD OF TELAKS SLIPPED away into the failing heat and drawing shadows of the afternoon, the chaos of the banquet soothing to softer laughter and softer topics. Elder Morten rose to the stand and motioned for the guards lined against the walls to begin clearing the tables and shifting the stacked gear. Silently they went into motion, gently directing stragglers to the doorway, and hefting furniture back into place.

Elder Morten turned back to his wife, took her by the hand, and motioned to the remaining elders. They likewise each meandered off the stand, drifting to a small doorway to the left in a gentle, chipper cloud of brilliant cloth and half-empty cups. Corin's grandparents softly offered their departing formalities and kissed their grandchildren before locking arms and following the flow.

Marcus slapped Lorenzo's armored back and the three of them slid off the stand and past the clearing tables. Outside, the day was still warm but dimming with encroaching clouds. The buildings glowed amber with a light that seeped deep into the sandy brick and speckled cobblestones. The shield above looked more translucent than it had during the ceremony, the light more white than gold now. It was like the plumes of heat put off from a smoldering coal: a mere ripple in the air.

The Centileans laughed in great boisterous bursts that rumbled with their staggering, drunken steps. Their tails swept along streets littered with crimson paper and cracked, clay mugs. Dusk was still hours away, but to a people who rose and moved and lived by the sun, the overcast afternoon felt like the failing gleam of a sleepy twilight. It was a day that glowed, not glared, and so the crowds staggered pitifully through the warm haze like club-tailed children huddling from the coldest winter they'd ever endured.

Lorenzo stepped forward and took a long, deep breath. He turned back to his family, the stars of promise glittering at the corners of his obnoxious eyes.

"Father, you should head back home and rest. You must be *exhausted*." Lorenzo lovingly patted Marcus' brass shoulders.

His father grunted in grateful amusement. "It *has* been a long day for me, my son, but I do not yet wish to abandon you or this evening." He took Lorenzo by the shoulders. "Do you have any idea how proud we are of you?"

Lorenzo chuckled, but grew surprisingly serious. "Father, please. You can barely stand! Besides, I wanted to take Corin for a walk. I'm sure he's sick of all this formality."

"Oh, no." Corin shook his head. "Don't you dare drag me into this, *Captain*."

Marcus grunted as a smile cracked his lips, his eyes assessing his boys. "Perhaps you're right, son. It is late, and my day must begin well before the sun tomorrow." He embraced Lorenzo and then Corin.

"Stay with your brother tonight," he grunted, patting Corin's shoulder. "There will be more than enough time for chores tomorrow." He smiled and pressed down the street, a swelling pride lifting his knees and shoulders to new heights.

As soon as his father was out of earshot, Lorenzo spun to his brother.

"What's troubling you, Cor?" His eyes looked sincere, but Corin suspected it might have been the ale asking.

"Troubling me?" Corin tried to laugh off his brother's advance. "You're letting the party get to your head. I'm just tired. Been a long day, just like you said."

"A long day, huh?" Lorenzo repeated, leaning far too close to Corin's face. He studied him for a moment before shaking his head. "*Rubbish*. It's not just today, baby brother. For *months* I've noticed it. Whenever you're around me you get bloody quiet. You smile too much and talk too little. It's like you're wearing someone else's feelings. What's going on?"

Corin shrugged. "Maybe you just don't know me that well anymore. You've been training or running missions pretty much nonstop for the last year." Corin waited for a response, but the silence only grew. "So, were we going to walk somewhere, or was that just to encourage Father to go home?"

"*Of course*, we're going," Lorenzo scoffed. "Come on."

He motioned across the massive courtyard. They walked in silent, drifting steps, moving slowly through the staggering huddles and drained kegs. Corin knew that this was not the end of Lorenzo's interrogation, so he kept his head down and braced himself.

"Here we are!" Lorenzo announced, stopping in front of the massive wooden doors to Vallin's Tower. From this close it was clear that the tower's bare, sandy surface was actually etched with hundreds of designs. They were simple and repetitive, but beautiful in their minimalism. They looked out of place in the grander structure, like they had been scratched into the tower's walls years after it was built. None of them climbed more than a few meters up the stone siding. Corin had seen them countless times, but this time he noticed that some of the designs may actually have been words. Maybe even names. But they were too worn to decipher, rubbed smooth from hundreds of years of oily palms passing over their ridges and divots.

"Why here?" Corin asked with budding interest.

Lorenzo folded his arms and took a step back, his eyes dancing up and down the tower.

"When I was just a child, grandfather would take me here and tell me the stories of Vallin. Right here. To this spot. Do you remember?"

Corin nodded but kept his eyes down. "Of course. He took me too."

"Right…" Lorenzo swayed a little on his toes. "I never really understood why, but I think today I'm starting to get it. Do you remember how he ended his stories? He would *always* remind us that we were Vallin's direct descendants."

Corin nodded. This felt like it was turning into a lecture…

"Why do you think he did that?" Lorenzo asked.

Yep… *Definitely* a lecture.

Corin shrugged. "I assumed it was to make us proud of our lineage. You know, make sure we don't forget how important our ancestors were, or what they did, or something like that…"

Lorenzo took a few steps toward the tower. "But why would that matter, Cor? Why do we need to be so concerned about what happened in the past? Vallin did amazing things, but so what? It's all in the past. That's what I always used to think. Why not worry about *now?* Why not be concerned about what *we're* doing? It used to really bother me, you know?" He reached up and touched the wall. "But today's got me thinking… Maybe he told us those stories to help us see who we *could* be, not just who we are. It's almost like a call from the past, isn't it?"

Corin snickered. "You mean like destiny?"

Lorenzo turned to him. "Yes. Exactly like destiny. Something so much more than potential. Something that's in your blood. Something that's meant to be. Perhaps we too are destined for the same greatness as Vallin, if we're willing to work for it."

Lorenzo's preaching face was deeply serious…

…and Corin was deeply unable to take him seriously.

"Interesting," Corin muttered. He folded his arms, and stepped up next to his brother, pretending to study the wall before them. "You know what I think, Lorenzo? I think you've been drinking a little too much."

His brother laughed heartily and slapped Corin's back. "You know something, Cor? You're right. You are *absolutely* right. But why should that change anything? My lips are flapping a bit looser than I usually let them swing, but that doesn't mean I'm wrong! I've been thinking about this since I was a kid. Don't you ever just stare up at the stars and think about where you fit in it all?"

Corin took in a deep breath. Of course, he did. Corin spent every waking moment wondering who he was and what place in this world he could possibly hold as his own. This conversation was starting to make him feel more vulnerable than he was comfortable with.

"I try not to," he mumbled.

Lorenzo looked shocked. "Why?"

Corin shrugged again and shifted his weight. "Well, what if you don't fit in at all? What if you're such a small part of it that nothing you do or say could ever matter?" He glanced at his brother. Lorenzo's face was calm, but his eyes were filled with horror.

"Cor… How could you think that? Look at this." He reached up and scratched the sandstone of the tower. A few grains shifted and stuck to his skin. He rubbed them between his fingers, letting them roll and tumble to the street.

"Can you imagine if every grain of sand that made this tower didn't feel important? Or if they all felt too small to be a part of something this grand?"

"It's just sand," Corin said. "None of it feels anything."

"You know what I mean," Lorenzo grouched. "Just look at it! It takes each individual grain to make this one extraordinary whole."

"But it doesn't." Corin turned to him, pointing a hand to the street. "That's just my point. Vallin's Tower didn't *need* those grains. You scratched them off, and the tower is still here. It's fine. Nothing's changed. They're too little to matter."

Lorenzo twisted up his face and shook his head. "But you're missing the point, baby brother! Each one matters. Even if a few are lost, they still mattered. How can you decide which ones matter and which don't? Eventually, if you scratch long enough, it will make a difference, right? *Eventually* a significant dent will be made. You'll carve a hole straight through this wall. If a few grains would make a difference then, why don't those same grains make a difference now? What makes the sand within any more important than the sand without?"

"It's *just sand*, Lorenzo." Corin laughed. "It's not that any single grain is more or less important than the others. I don't care where it is, *none* of them alone have very much importance. But, add all of that minuscule importance together and you've achieved something spectacular through sheer numbers. But nothing matters all on its own."

"Well," Lorenzo paused, "for sand maybe… but I believe telaks are different."

"Why? Because you are one?" Corin folded his arms and stared at the stones.

Lorenzo watched Corin carefully, slightly confused by his bitter response. "I didn't mean to offend you, Cor. I was trying to help you feel better."

"I know," Corin mumbled, "and that's what was offensive."

Lorenzo nodded, went silent, and then smacked Corin's chest with the back of his hand. "You know, this wasn't the reason I brought you here. I was thinking you might like to go inside." He pointed up to the broad wooden doors off to the left.

Corin's ears twitched involuntarily. "Inside? How would we get inside?" Was his brother planning on breaking into the most securely guarded building in all of Centile? It wasn't as if Corin had any room to judge, but Lorenzo had only just been appointed to his new position. If he was caught, he would surely be stripped of his rank. Maybe even locked up for treason.

"Well," Lorenzo said, "when one is entering a building, one typically walks through the front door."

He took a few steps to his left. The four tower guards on duty straightened at Lorenzo's approach. He was smiling broad and clear, and Corin could see those stupid stars again, taunting him from the corners of his brother's eyes.

"Since when do you have *access to the tower?*" Corin followed him, too intrigued to be bitter.

"Since the ceremony today!" Lorenzo announced. "One of my newly appointed duties is to oversee the security of the major political and historical buildings within Centile's central district. I now have unrestricted access to the barracks, the training hall, the five departments of the elders, the archives, *and...*" he twirled and bowed, his arms outstretched to the great wooden doors, "Vallin's Tower!"

Lorenzo pressed two fingers to his lips and whistled a pair of shrill ascending notes. The four tower guards split, two lifting the massive wooden latch from the doors while the others pried open the brass handles. The sound echoed through the chamber beyond, and a soft line of golden light began to spread out onto the cobblestone street from within.

Lorenzo's hand clapped down on Corin's shoulder. "Well? What do you say, little brother?"

A small crowd of shocked, tipsy telaks was building behind them, straining to see into the tower's clandestine glow. Curiosity and pride grappled in Corin's mind, but eventually curiosity won. He couldn't resist the tower's pull. Lorenzo's grin broadened, and they stepped into the cavernous chamber together.

CHAPTER 9

AFOUL OF THE ROCKS

OMI SLID THE BLUNT END OF HER KNIFE UP THE side of Mari's throat, feeling the stunned sirena quiver as the steel traced the pulsing bulge of her artery.

"Such a pretty face, wouldn't you agree, Aroon?"

The siokoy wiped his mouth with the back of his hand as he grinned. "I can't be too sure, Captain. She be shakin' so bad I ain't seeing her straight!"

He brushed the backs of his fingernails against the small of Mari's back. She yelped and sat up straighter.

"Oh, shh, shh, *shh*..." Omi clucked as she leaned in. "Don't give us that look. You knew you were sailing into narrow straits, didn't you?"

Marikit stiffened as the point of Omi's knife pressed into the base of her throat. She twitched back but felt Aroon grip at her hair. The bones in her wrists crackled under the bamboo rope as she strained against it in vain.

Mari whimpered and closed her eyes. "I was just coming to help them with the haul..."

Omi pressed forward on her knife, gently piercing the tip into her chest. A bead of blood pooled to the blade but quickly streaked down Mari's vest with the coursing rain. Marikit trembled at the pain but bit her lip to keep herself from crying out.

"Don't lie to me, little minnow," Omi whispered. "Pretty little things like you should keep their lips *clean*." She reached up and gripped Mari's face, forcing her cheeks and mouth into a scrunched pucker. Mari tried to pull away but felt Aroon's hands tighten around her matted locks behind her.

"What do you want?" Mari managed through strained features.

"Me? Silly girl… You're asking about *me?*" Omi smiled and suddenly slapped Marikit with the ringed back of her hand. "But I'm not done talking about *you!*"

She leaned back in, her voice suddenly dripping with coconut syrup. "Just *look* at you… Delicate, little flowers should stay back on land where they belong. Yet, here you are! Slinking around my ship in the dark. It's like you're not a flower at all. More like an uzai crab picking at a sunken corpse. So, tell me, pretty minnow," Omi whispered as she crouched down to Mari's level, "what was your plan, hmm?"

The light in Omi's eyes was terrifying. It was a wicked gleam that didn't seem to notice the rain streaking before it, or the midnight pressing in against it. Mari didn't know what to say, so she held her tongue. Omi scoffed and pulled her knife away.

"You're a funny little contradiction," the kaizo captain said. "An ugly, ugkoy kudori mounted on a perfect, kataw face… and yet you're out here running dirty jobs for a sirena crew?" Omi wiped the blood from her knife off on Mari's vest and pressed the end of the handle up under her chin, forcing the frightened sirena's face up into the downpour. Omi stared down into Mari's eyes, chuckling as she flinched away from her gaze.

"Well, that's just it then, isn't it?" Omi grinned with open teeth, like she couldn't decide if she should laugh or sigh or bite. "Caught between worlds… You're playing dress-up, aren't you, little sister? Hiding your face in plain sight, trying to claw your way down to the holy city! My, my, my… Now I understand. You've gone and drunk yourself silly on those poison dreams, haven't you, little minnow?"

Mari didn't respond, but her eyes drifted away to the wet boards beneath them.

Omi stood and smirked. "Well, this may surprise you, but I know a thing or two about the dangers of silly dreams. I was young and stupid once, too, and I had my swollen heart broken by a harsh world and an unforgiving sea." She paused, cocking her head to the side as she regarded Mari. "Huh… You know what? I don't feel so bad about all this anymore. In fact, I do believe I'm doing you a favor, little sister. It would be absolute *cruelty* to let a dreamer taste reality, wouldn't you agree, Aroon? Much better to nip this pretty flower in the bud before she has time to wilt."

At that, Hiroki stepped up beside Aroon, pulling a knife from his vest and pressing it against Mari's quivering throat.

"Captain?" he growled.

Omi shook her head. "Oh, don't be stupid. You can't go fishing without bait."

* * *

OLENKA COULDN'T FEEL HER ARM. ACTUALLY, SHE couldn't feel her *anything* through the pain. It permeated every centimeter of her flesh, branching out under her skin like crushing, curling fingers that pulled her into a tight, miserable mass. Di had been right: it was a pain that was in her very blood, swelling and burning until her veins and muscles had tightened and burst, red splotches welling up all across her slate blue skin.

She tried to hold still, to calmly let Diwala suspend her in the water, but she couldn't keep her body from trembling, and she couldn't keep her limbs from jerking. She wanted to scream and plead with something, anything, to take the pain away…

…but they were still very deep under the water, and she had no more air left to scream.

Diwala held Olenka in place, clutching her tortured frame against her chest. She was kicking gently, trying to keep them from drifting into the depths, but with no light or objects in the void around them, it was impossible to tell if they were rising or falling. Olenka wanted to worry about that. She wanted to plan and analyze the problem and figure out a solution to their predicament, but her mind was somewhere far away.

Her flesh was at war with itself. Her blood was demanding that she descend, and her lungs were pleading for her to rise.

So, she did neither. She drifted and shook, praying that Di wouldn't let them drown.

The minutes crept by as Olenka shivered away her air. Each time the pain began to subside, Diwala would kick them higher, causing a fresh wave to bite into her neck and arm. She knew she needed to stay submerged. She knew that pressure was the only thing that could help the pain, but it didn't matter. She wanted to rise, to be free of the water and the cold and the crushing black, to feel the air and the rain against her skin. Nothing seemed to make sense anymore. She was fighting against her instincts. The depths had *caused* the pain, how could lingering help end it?

And for the first time in her life, Olenka felt like she was drowning.

When they finally reached the surface, the rain muffled Olenka's screams. The world around her suddenly matched the chaos within: everything flailing and pounding and bursting apart. They had come up a full twenty meters from the kaizo barge, but Diwala still wrapped her hand over Olenka's mouth to silence her. Olenka didn't resist. She couldn't resist. They bobbed across the heaving waters, the light of the pirate vessel fading to a dim bloom in the storm's haze. Di was pulling Olenka along the inky swell in utter darkness, and it occurred to her that Diwala must have had the good sense to abandon their lanterns before they reached the top.

Olenka wasn't sure how, but amid the rain and the pain Diwala managed to find their banca bound between two jagged rocks. She felt Di heft her into the ship followed by a burst of agony from the impact. Olenka scrunched up in the cramped space, clutching at her chest and throat.

Diwala was beside her in an instant. "Where is the pain, sister?"

Olenka tried to speak but couldn't force her teeth to unclench. It was a stupid question, anyway. Where *wasn't* the pain? Her fins and fingers were tingling like she'd held them too close to a fire, all her joints were aching with the cold, her neck and right arm each felt like they'd taken a spear, and her skin was being ripped open from the inside out. She managed to motion toward her neck and arm, and Diwala quickly swung her leg over Olenka's side and began to massage the burning muscles with her palm. Olenka screamed but submitted herself to the torture.

"Here?" Di asked. "From your jaw down?"

Olenka nodded, clenching her eyes against the storm. Diwala increased the pressure, dragging her hand from Olenka's neck down to the crook of her elbow. It stung, but it did seem like it might be helping.

"You feel nothing in your back, yes? Nothing down your spine?"

Olenka shook her head. Her breath trembled as she exhaled, and her whole body was shaking in distress.

"And your head?" Diwala asked. "Do you have any sharp pains in your skull?"

Olenka grunted. "Just from all your buwisit questions..."

Diwala laughed and smacked at Olenka's back. "You are lucky, you know! The poison blood seems to only be in your arm. There are much worse places it could be."

"Lucky..." Olenka mumbled into the swollen boards beneath her. She supposed she had been lucky. Diwala had warned her that she was not ready, but she had been stubborn and gone anyway. The kaizo had tried to kill them, and yet they were alive. They had all escaped. They were all...

"Di, where's Mari?"

Diwala paused massaging for an instant, but quickly continued.

"I have been wondering that as well," she muttered. "She was supposed to meet us here, yes?"

Olenka nodded. She tried to sit up, but a fresh burst of pain forced her down again. "Di, we *have* to go find her! *Before the kaizo do!*"

"Shh…" Diwala pressed down on Olenka's back. "Be still, sister. You cannot worry about her now. You are still not well. I will go find her. I am sure she just got lost in the dark. You know Mari."

"Di, this is serious!" Olenka pushed Diwala away, flipping up onto her side. She panted at the strain but was able to tentatively relax against the gunwale. "She could be in trouble! We need to go find her *right now!*"

A moment of blinding light flashed around them, followed almost immediately by a guttural swell of thunder. In that instant, Olenka could see Diwala's face clearly. Her cheeks were high and gaunt, strained with dread and guilt, a forced smile pulled too tightly across her features. She met Olenka's eyes, but quickly looked away.

And then Olenka understood.

It was a look she had seen before, the kind of look a worried parent gives to a frightened child. She was putting on a show for Olenka's sake.

"Di, what happened?" Olenka muttered. "Tell me what you know… *Please.*"

Diwala sighed and turned away, abandoning all attempts at reassurance as she began checking on the many knives strewn throughout the sheathes and pouches on her vest and girdle.

"The kaizo have taken her captive," Di stated. "When we came up, I could hear them speaking to her on the deck of the barge. They must have caught her disabling their rudder. I think that is why they tried to kill us."

Olenka leaned forward, gripping Diwala's vest. "You knew? You knew and you *left her there?*"

Diwala closed her eyes and wrapped a gentle hand around Olenka's wrist. "What would you have done, sister? You are in no state to fight. If we would have gone straight in like stupid, hungry sharks, then I would have lost *both* of you."

Her voice hung heavy, the quiet words somehow piercing the din of the storm. Another flash broke around them and Diwala stood.

"I will go get her," she announced. "And you will stay hidden and stay quiet."

Olenka screamed out her protests, but Di didn't wait. She flipped off the deck of the banca, launching herself into a smooth dive from the tip of the pontoon. Olenka thrashed up to her knees, reaching out after her, but Diwala was already gone, swallowed up in the black sea of her own resolve. Olenka swore and smacked her fist against the banca's planks.

She sat back and felt the rain streaming down her throbbing, burning skin. Her hands and feet were floating far away from her senses, and all her joints ached, but the pain streaking through her arm was different now. Like the fresh sting of an urchin quill finally pulled free. The pain was just as intense, but it was somehow… better? Maybe? She shook her head and slapped at her neck. She wasn't sure if it was just the adrenaline, but her mind felt quick and sharp. The haze was dissipating. She lifted her webbed hand up as a flash of lightning bloomed across the grey world around her.

Her skin was streaked with red, bulbous blotches, but her hand wasn't shaking anymore.

"Give me strength…" Olenka whispered to nothing in particular. She lit the banca's lamp and slipped into the water.

CHAPTER 10

JUST LIKE ME

CORIN WAS EXPECTING HIS EYES TO HAVE TO adjust to a dark, dusty room, but the inside of the tower was actually brighter than the streets. The immensity of the chamber was instantly apparent, and Corin felt himself tipping back as his eyes climbed ever higher and higher up the walls.

At first, he guessed that there were windows or torches casting the light in the tower, but the reality was so much more extraordinary. The inside of the tower was a massive cage of steel pillars and crossbeams, each streaked with swirling golden patterns that led to flameless lanterns lining an impossibly long staircase spiraling up the wall at a steady incline. Corin had always thought the tower was just built of stone. This was so much more than he had imagined.

Corin drifted to the nearest wall, vaguely aware of his brother's gloating gaze on his back. Corin leaned in, studying the glowing lines on the support beam. They didn't make any sense. It was as if the scratches in the metal were casting their own light: bolts of lightning illuminating the clouds of cold, grey steel around them. Corin raised his palm, hovering it over the light. He was half expecting the surface to be hot, like the cherry tips of his father's forging tools.

"Go ahead," Lorenzo offered, motioning to the wall.

Corin glanced back and then pressed his fingers to its surface. The glowing lines felt cool, exactly like the metal surrounding it. He slid his fingertips across its surface, feeling a faint seam in the steel. The golden designs must have been a different type of metal laid into etchings in the beams. But what metal would glow like this?

Corin stepped back, his eyes tracking the lines all the way up to the surface of the tower, hundreds of meters above them. "Does the sun gem do this?"

Lorenzo nodded, his dreamy, watery eyes drifting up the wall. "Sure does. Powers the whole thing. Day and night, just like the shield."

"It's… beautiful," Corin whispered despite himself.

Lorenzo chuckled. "I reacted the same way the first time I saw it. Shame it's not open to the public."

Corin nodded, the thought striking him a lot harder than he would have expected. "Why is that? Why would the elders cut us off from something… something so amazing?"

Lorenzo rubbed at his neck. "Well, little brother, *I* suspect it was for security of the sun gem, but grandfather seems to think it had something to do with *this*."

He stepped back and motioned to the chamber's tiled floor with a broad sweeping gesture.

Corin's eyes followed his brother's hand, and his mouth gaped. He had been so smitten with the light that he hadn't noticed he'd been walking across the most impressive piece of artwork he had ever seen. The entire floor of the chamber was one massive mural, composed entirely of hundreds of thousands of painted tiles.

The tiles spread out into the distance all around him, their hexagonal edges blurring and meshing to form fluid landscapes, faces, and vast battle scenes. The circular mural appeared to be divided into sections, with the great sun and sword crest of Centile sitting in its center. An intricate border of colorful patterns encompassed the whole piece, creating a natural path from which the mural could be admired one slice at a time.

Corin's mind and eyes were too busy for him to speak. He slipped along the tiles trying to understand its immense meaning. There were swords and spears, telaks moving through dark landscapes, horrifying monsters, and…

Corin froze, gazing down at the face of a telak at his feet. He stepped back, giving the tiles some distance so that they could properly blend into their intended image.

"Lorenzo…" he muttered, "who is this?"

His brother stepped up beside him. "Who do you think, baca brain? We're standing in *Vallin's Tower*."

Corin's eyes were frantically darting around the image. It was very bright, filled with hundreds of tiles of white and gold. The telak was kneeling on the floor of a cave, holding something in his hands, something that was illuminating all his features, clearly detailing every bend and crease and contour of his youthful face.

A face that was a mirror image of Corin's.

"Lorenzo, he looks… he looks *just like me*." Corin stuttered
His brother stepped back and squinted. "Maybe a little."
"A *little?*" Corin almost shouted the words as a stunned grunt escaped his throat. "Lorenzo, it's like I'm staring into my reflection!"
Lorenzo shook his head and pressed his fingers to his eyes. "Cor, I don't know what you want from me. Yes, he looks a bit like you. What do you expect? He's our *ancestor*."
"*A bit?*" Corin pressed his hands to his face, gripping at the roots of his hair. "How do you not see this! Lorenzo, he looks exactly like me!" Corin realized his heart was racing. He stepped back and felt his chest. What was happening to him? Everything was starting to drift and ebb around his feet, like he was losing control of reality. The image of Vallin's face filled his thoughts, digging into deep, uncomfortable places that made him nauseous and very, very nervous.

"Cor, don't you think you're overreacting just a little?" Lorenzo's voice was smooth and condescending, sobering up a tremendous amount from his previously slurred lines.

Corin shook his head, unable to respond. How could his brother be reacting so differently? Maybe Corin really *was* seeing too much in the tiles. There were hundreds of years between them, but Corin and Vallin were technically related. Distantly, but still related.

Maybe it was all just a coincidence…

"Perhaps we should come back when we're a little less… excited?" Lorenzo's arm patted down on Corin's back. "Sound good, baby brother?"

"Yeah," Corin muttered, barely managing to tear his eyes away from the floor. "Maybe you're right."

* * *

THE BROTHERS MADE THEIR WAY OUT OF THE TOWER and across the courtyard, kicking aside stray flags and paper. The crowds were gone and so were the merchants. Most of their food carts had already been wheeled back to their tents and sheds. Only faint, slatted lines of silt, ash, or crumbs testified of their previous locations of industry. Before dawn tomorrow, battalions of recruits from the barracks would be commissioned to sweep the streets clean, pushing everything into the nearby bread ovens. The chefs and bakers would silently accept the free fuel from the paper and flags, and loudly protest the extra dirt to shovel out into the weekly ash carts.

As they walked in silence, Corin racked his mind for something to talk about that wasn't the mural. Something safe and neutral, something that might distract him from the memory of his own face staring up from the three-hundred-year-old floor.

"So," Corin said, "Adahy told you about his father today, right? About what happened on the plains?" As he spoke, Corin noticed an older telak with piercing white hair perk up at his words.

He was busy brushing the red paper from his doorway and windowsill. He shifted a curious glance at the brothers, but quickly went back to his chore.

"Not really…" Lorenzo cleared his throat and clasped his hands behind his back, lowering his voice considerably. "He stopped grandfather and grandmother as they were walking into the banquet. I just happened to be near them at the time and volunteered to help."

Corin nodded. "How much did he say about his father's injuries?"

Lorenzo took a long breath in. "Well, he mentioned that something had caught his father and a few other outlanders off guard on the plains. He said that Mohe has a long gash across his chest and right bicep. Apparently the bleeding has stopped, but the wound won't close or come clean. Grandmother asked what they had done for it, and…"

Corin looked up. "And what?"

"Well…" Lorenzo chewed over his words, looking around to see who might be listening in. "Adahy said they washed out the wound, applied an herbal paste to it, and then stitched it up. But, he said the skin and muscle has gone grey along the cut's edge… The strength of the stitch ripped right through the sick flesh."

"What?" Corin asked. "The stitches did? How?"

Lorenzo winced and shook his head. "I'm not sure. He made it sound like the flesh had gone rotten. It just pulled apart at the stitches. Grandmother was very concerned that it might have been some type of poison."

"You mean like an insect sting?"

"I don't know for sure…" Lorenzo shrugged. "But yeah, like an insect. Or maybe a snake."

Corin shook his head. "But how could there be venom in a gash that size?"

Lorenzo glanced around the street again. "Well, that's the mystery, isn't it?" He smiled weakly at Corin. "Father actually had a theory about that. He said that when he was young there were stories of marauders who coated their blades in poison. They would hammer notches and scratches into their knives and then fill a sheath with something toxic. That way, every time they pulled out the blade it would have a fresh coat slathered along it." Lorenzo shrugged. "*I've never seen leather skins do anything that bold before, but scorched sands*, I wouldn't put it past those savages…"

Corin tried to convince himself that it was just the ale talking.

"Do you think this could be related to that lost patrol?" he asked.

Lorenzo nodded. "I do. I'm not sure why I do, but I do. There's not a lot of information about either attack, but I think that what *wasn't* said might mean more than what *was*."

He paused, but Corin kept silent.

"You see, none of the victims could identify their attacker," Lorenzo continued, "both incidents happened off the eastern road to the southern gate, and in both accounts, the witnesses said that everything happened too quickly to process. Like a well-planned ambush in the dark… I don't know. Something just tells me there's a connection. I think we might have a well-organized marauding party. One that specializes in night ambushes. It's like they're trying to send a message: attacking our guards, Mohe's hunting groups… They're testing out strength, Cor."

"What about the poison?" Corin asked. "Did any of your men show any signs…"

"No…" Lorenzo quietly shook his head. "One had two broken arms, but no open wounds. The other one was never stabbed or cut. It looked like he was thrown from his mount and bashed his head against a rock. No… No poison. Just a bloody lot of questions."

Corin nodded. "You seem scared."

"I am." Lorenzo's response was much quicker and more direct than Corin was anticipating. "We're *all* worried, Cor. It would be very unfortunate if this came to war."

Corin flinched. Were the guards *really* considering war with the outlanders?

"If it's just a group of marauders," Corin said, "then Morten's thugs will hunt them down pretty quick."

Lorenzo stopped walking.

"Morten's *thugs?*" he spat. "Are you referring to the *city guard?*"

"Yeah, but not *all* of the guards. Just…" Corin sighed. "Just those patrols you hear about that pester the farmers and outlanders, you know? Not any of *your* men, I'm sure."

Corin tried to keep walking, but Lorenzo didn't budge.

"Corin, how far, exactly, have you been out of the city?"

"*Ugh…* I don't know." Corin rubbed at his forehead, bracing for another lecture. "Adahy and I've run pretty far out into the plains together."

"How far?"

Corin shrugged. "Down the western fork of the southern road. To where it hits the foothills."

"So, not far at all," Lorenzo scoffed. "Just past Adahy's village."

"I guess. What's the big deal?"

Lorenzo began walking again. "The big deal is that you have *no idea* what is out there, Cor! You've never taken the merchant roads to the coast. You've never been over the southern mountains. You've never been attacked by marauders, alright? *I have*, and so have my men, and we need your *support* out there, not your cynicism."

Corin rolled his eyes and hurried behind his brother. "Can we at least agree that the patrols can be a little heavy-handed sometimes?"

"What do you mean?" Lorenzo spat.

Corin chuckled uncomfortably. "Well, do we really need to harass so many farmers? Seize unmarked crates of potatoes? Interrogate anyone wearing something too colorful? Doesn't it all seem a bit… *unnecessary* to you?"

"No, it doesn't." Lorenzo's words were quick and stern. "So long as we're losing men out there, I don't think it is unnecessary. In fact, I don't even think it's enough! Did you hear about what happened today?"

Corin felt his face flush. "Umm… no. What are you referring…"

"A gang of outlanders *raided our food stores!*" Lorenzo shouted. "Right here in the city! They assaulted four guards and made off with an entire herd of the city's bacas. Are you *really* telling me that things aren't getting worse?"

Corin swallowed. "I mean… I'm sure it wasn't *that* bad."

Lorenzo raised his eyes in skepticism. "Not that bad? Cor, that was just what a *few* of them did. Do you have any idea how many leather skins there are out there?"

Corin opened his mouth, but Lorenzo plowed right over the top of him. "Did you know that less than a quarter of all telaks live in the boundaries of Centile? *One. Bloody. Quarter.* That's it, Cor. Another quarter live in small settlements like Adahy's village. That means that half of the telaks on the plains are undocumented and uncivilized. And there's probably more than we know because we have no way of tracking them!"

"*Uncivilized?*" Corin snorted. "So was *mom* uncivilized too?"

"Don't you *dare* bring mom into this, Cor," Lorenzo shouted. "She *chose* to leave them. She *knew* how barbaric the outlanders were. They roam the plains hunting whatever they can. Sometimes that means animals, but often it means *men*, Corin. Men like Mandel, who may never be able to use his hands again, and Eduardo, who still hasn't regained consciousness since the attack. Or how about Sy and Manuel? Did you know the *names* of the two men who went missing? Did you *care* to know them?"

"Lorenzo, I wasn't…" Corin stuttered. "I'm sorry…"

Chapter 11

Blood on the Waves

"There she is, Captain!" Isko bellowed across the deck. The crew scurried to the gunwale, Aroon and Hiroki abandoning their posts at the bell crane's crank. A column of bubbles was erupting up from the black water, and the rope was giving way to the bell's iron chains.

"Aroon, Hiroki," Omi spat, "get down there and check it out!"

Without a word, the two siokoy dove off the barge, steel knives clenched between their teeth. Mari watched and listened anxiously from the deck, waiting for any sign of her sisters. Omi leaned back from the water and turned around, thoughtfully regarding their prisoner.

"Isko," she called up to the bell crane, "mind the port bow! A beached fire-fish can still sting."

Isko nodded and descended the crane's rigging, taking a spot behind Mari. Omi glared at the bound sirena once more and then turned back to the emerging bell. Aroon and Hiroki slipped up to the surface.

"Did you find them?" Omi called over the torrents.

"Them minnows musta split, but the chest is still here," Hiroki called. "Toss us a line."

Omi pulled at a coil of rope with a rusty hook clamped to the end and threw it over the side. In a moment, Aroon and Hiroki were back on board, hoisting the chest onto the deck. As soon as the box crashed down over the gunwale, Omi was at its side.

"You three, get that bell back up on deck!" She pulled a small, brass key from her vest. "Isko, you work the crane!"

The three siokoy scrambled to their places: pulling levers, releasing weights, and turning cranks. The diving bell screeched horribly as it slid up the barge's hull and onto the sodden deck. The siokoy hurriedly secured the lines, leaving the bell mostly extended over the water. Omi knelt down in front of the chest and situated the box before her, running her hands along the polished top. She paused for a moment, the smile suddenly drifting from her lips as she lifted the latch and studied the untarnished lock. Her brows furrowed and she brought the key to the lock's hole. She tried several times to turn it, but each time the device held firm.

"Clever eels…" Omi stood as her crew gathered around her. "They switched the buwisit lock."

Omi suddenly threw the useless key across the deck, the handle pelting Marikit sharply in the ribs. She yelped and contorted from the blow, her wrists and ankles bound behind her.

"Where's *the key*, little sister?" Omi hissed as she strolled across the deck.

"I don't have any key…" Mari mumbled to the floorboards. Omi grabbed a fistful of Marikit's matted braids and jerked her face up into the greasy lamp light.

"That's not really what I asked you, was it?" Omi drew her blade and pressed it against Mari's throat. "*Where is the key?*"

Mari's skin twitched and trembled as the knife's force bit a thin line of blood into her throat.

"M-maybe…" she stuttered at the blade's sting, "maybe it's just rusty? Did you try wiggling–"

Omi's ringed fist sank into Mari's temple, sending her toppling to the floor.

"Hiroki! Crack that thing open!" the captain screamed. *"You two, search her!"*

Omi stormed across the deck to the diving bell. She felt her way up and down its surface, double-checking the sounding and cargo lines, but there was nothing to find. No chests, no nets, and definitely no jewelry. She turned back and watched as Isko and Aroon pulled away cords and money pouches off Mari, even a knife they had somehow missed in their previous search, but still no key.

Omi drifted to Hiroki's side, her arms folded tight across her chest. The scarred siokoy was using a blade to try to pry the latch off the chest.

"Not like that, you waterlogged fool! *Hit it!*" Omi screeched. "Go grab an anchor!"

Hiroki grunted, but stood obediently, motioning for Aroon. The two siokoy fetched a massive iron anchor from across the deck and bashed it against the lock. On the second hit, the metal gave in, and the whole latch was ripped free of the chest.

Omi forced the two siokoy aside and tore open the lid, revealing the muddy rocks and filthy water within. She swore and kicked the chest over, letting its contents drain out onto the deck. She twirled around, slamming her palms against the ship's railing.

"*Very*, very clever…" she whispered, gazing out across the ebony waves. She paused, her sight adjusting to the dark. The sirena crew's banca was still bound to the hull of her barge, empty and drifting with the swell, but there was a glow off in the distance. It was soft and subtle, barely illuminating the wet sides of the rocks around it. Omi's breath caught in her cheeks as she felt every muscle in her body tighten.

"Hiroki, dear?" she cooed, and the burly siokoy stepped silently beside her. "What do you see over there, my friend? Out across the waves?"

Hiroki leaned over the gunwale and then shook his head. "Nothing that will last the night, Captain."

He pulled his knife free from its sheath and stepped up to dive over the railing, but Omi's hand shot out and grabbed his arm.

"Wait," she said, "take Aroon with you. And leave the boat here. Do this quick and quiet, you understand?"

Hiroki nodded as he whistled for Aroon, and the two siokoy dove over the edge together. Omi ran her hands down her face, stopping to brush against her nose ring, gently tapping at the delicate metal, over and over... Finally, she turned around, staring at Marikit.

"Isko," she called, marching to Mari's side, "come drag that anchor over here."

* * *

THE WATER'S PRESSURE FELT WONDERFUL AND terrible on Olenka's battered flesh. On the outside, it pressed painfully against her tender, blistering skin, but on the inside? That was different. A weight was lifting from her organs. Her lungs felt clear and lithe. Even though she was deep under the swell, it felt like she could finally breathe again. She drifted slowly through the muted void, reclining back in the water and savoring the healing sensations.

Olenka's heart skipped as she noticed two blue gleams of shrimp lamps streaming through the darkness above her. She stiffened, letting herself silently sink as the two siokoy passed. Once they were gone, Olenka smiled. The kaizo had taken the bait. Their plan was working.

She kicked off toward the barge, slipping through the brine and almost colliding with the ship's hull as it suddenly came into sight. The only light filtering down from the lamps on deck quickly dissipated under the barge's shadow, and Olenka crept blindly down the keel until her hands clasped around their hidden salvage line. She pulled on the rope, feeling its weight in the gloom, then she checked the metal stake, still securely screwed into the wood.

Olenka walked her hands back up the barnacled hull, carefully approaching the light above. She stared up through the turmoil of the water's surface, straining to see if anyone was visible along the gunwale. She slipped her face up from the waves, the roar of the rain suddenly pounding all around her. She could hear Omi on board, talking quickly over the sound of something heavy scraping across the deck. Olenka scanned the hull, looking for anything she could use to climb. Near the bow, she spied an iron ring mounted halfway up the side of the barge. She swam over and strained to reach it, but the ring was higher than it had seemed. Again, she stretched her arm up to grab ahold of it, her fingertips just barely brushing–

The pain shot through Olenka's arm and neck once more.

It was so sharp and sudden that she couldn't control the scream splitting her lips.

The deck above went silent, and Olenka sank down under the bow, clutching her throbbing arm. Her chest was littered with tingling, stinging warmth, her skin going numb around her neck and shoulder…

…and the water exploded into a stream of bubbles as a siokoy dove into the sea beside her.

Olenka reached for her knife, but the pain had made her weak, and her trembling fingers fumbled around the handle. It didn't take Isko long to find her. He slipped through the black water, slamming his shoulder into her chest, his blade drawn. The knife grazed her arm, a sudden bloom of warmth against her frigid skin.

Surprisingly, the pain seemed to help, the shock to her nerves bringing fresh strength and adrenaline to her limbs. Olenka grabbed the siokoy's throat and kicked her fins into his gut.

Isko coughed, letting out a curtain of bubbles between them. His free hand rushed to pry her grip from his throat, but his right hand stayed at his side. It was then that Olenka realized her error. She saw the siokoy's jaw clench, the muscles in his chest and shoulder flex as he swung the knife forward. Olenka closed her eyes, bracing for the pain of the blade as it sank into her neck…

…but the pain never came.

Isko's throat was jerked from her hand. Olenka opened her eyes to see Diwala's furious face, glaring at her over Isko's shoulder. She had slipped her arm under the siokoy's wiry bicep and curled it back behind his neck. Her right hand was tight around Isko's wrist, the knife quivering in his grip as he struggled against her. Di barely seemed to notice his efforts. She was staring expectantly at Olenka.

Olenka didn't hesitate. She drew her knife and slit the stunned siokoy's throat, blood and bubbles emptying from his gullet. He dropped his blade and clutched at his wound, but there was nothing he could do. Diwala released her grip, and he sank into the deep beneath them.

Diwala met Olenka's eyes as she gripped her vest in anger. At first Olenka thought she was going to hit her, but instead Diwala embraced her. Apparently Olenka had misjudged the look in her eyes.

To be fair, Olenka wasn't sure she'd ever seen Diwala look *afraid* before.

Olenka motioned to the surface, and they rose together. The rain's explosion of sound had felt oppressive before, but now it didn't seem like enough cover. The two sirena pressed themselves flush with the hull, listening to anything on the deck, but the barge was silent. Di tapped on Olenka's shoulder and motioned up to the ring. Olenka nodded, and Di helped lift her to the handhold. Apprehension gently thrummed through her, but the pain stayed subdued. Nothing but a meager ache taunting her nerves. Diwala motioned around the bow, and then slipped back into the surf.

The message was clear: they would take the deck by surprise, attacking from both sides at once.

Olenka pulled a knife free and passed it to her teeth. Getting onto the barge would be easy. There was a cleat up to her right, and there was a cross beam below it that she could kick off from. Even in her weakened state, climbing up wouldn't be a problem, but fighting… That worried her. She would need Di's support. In fact, she expected she wouldn't be any more useful than a convenient distraction.

Olenka held still. Listening. Feeling. She decided to give Diwala until the count of ten, then she would hoist herself up onto the deck.

One... Two... Three...

She heard steps on the deck above her: quiet, gentle pacing up and down the length of the bow.

Four... Five... Six...

The gentle steps became hurried, and Olenka heard a bright, sharp whistle break across the deck.

Seven... Eight... Nine...

A rope ladder whistled through the air, splashing down into the water just down ship from her. Olenka's blood went cold as she saw two blue gleams drifting toward the barge.

Ten.

Olenka pulled herself up by the ring, catching the cleat with her free hand and kicking up against the beam. She dove over the gunwale, pulling her knife free as she rolled forward onto the wet deck. Omi was standing on the far side of the ship, a few meters down from the bell teetering over the water. Marikit was bound on the floor beside her, a snare of rope leading to an anchor tied to her ankles. Her fins were dangling over the edge of the barge's docking plank, no railing between her and the open water below. The instant she saw Olenka, Omi swiveled behind her hostage, pressing a blade to Mari's neck.

She opened her mouth to speak but was cut off by the sound of Diwala flipping up onto the barge.

Everyone froze, and everyone tensed.

Olenka's eyes darted from Di, to Omi, to Mari, and finally to the rope ladder draped over the edge of the far gunwale. So many variables… and the other kaizo had almost returned. Her mind was frantically searching for a solution, but there simply wasn't one. Omi's calculating eyes were likewise passing back and forth between the two sirena, unsure who would spring forward first.

"I wonder…" Omi whispered. "How long do you think your friend can hold her breath? What do you two guess? Any wagers?"

Mari whimpered and thrashed against her bonds, a gag cord pulled tight between her trembling teeth. Olenka and Di each stepped forward, trying to close the gap while Omi was still speaking.

"No guesses?" Omi muttered. "What a pity…"

She pulled the knife free of Mari's throat, and slammed the handle into her gut. Mari flailed as all the air burst from her lungs, and then Omi kicked her off the deck. Her body surged down to the water, pulled into the depths by the immense weight of the anchor.

Diwala was over the edge in an instant, diving after Mari.

Olenka rushed forward, closing the gap to the kaizo captain and her twinkling blade. Omi smiled, her face and stance unflinching. Olenka knew it was a trap. She knew that Omi had the advantage. She knew that Omi was luring her in, taunting her into a fight she probably couldn't win. She knew that she had purposely distracted Diwala so that she could take them on one at a time. She knew that, really, Omi was just stalling for time: waiting for Hiroki and Aroon to return.

Olenka knew all of that buwisit, but she didn't care.

Enough was enough.

Omi slashed out with her blade, and Olenka dropped to the side of her thigh. The boards were streaming with rain, and she slid smoothly across the last meter of the deck. Omi flailed to recover as

Olenka crashed into her shins, but her balance was thrown off by the attack. She fell forward, barely catching her fall, but dropping her knife. Omi's blade clattered across the deck and dropped down to the sea.

What a pity... Olenka thought with a grin, her own knife still tight in her grip.

Olenka slammed the blade into the captain's calf, feeling her muscles convulse and tighten around the steel. The kaizo screamed and thrashed, and they tumbled out onto the docking plank together. They slid to a halt as Omi caught the edge of the gunwale, Olenka's legs and hips dangling over the water. Omi bellowed in pain and fury as Olenka's weight tugged on the blade in her flesh. She clawed at the railing but kept losing her grip on the sopping wood. Olenka hefted her knee back onto the plank, pulling the knife free of Omi's calf and burying it again in her thigh.

The kaizo shrieked and swore, but Olenka couldn't hear anything. The pain had returned in her arm, burning through her mind and body. She trembled and released her weapon, slipping off the plank in tortured spasms, tumbling back toward the sea.

But a hand wrapped around her throat just before she fell.

The pressure on her already tortured neck was simply too much for her broken mind, and she felt her senses blurring and failing all around her. She was lifted up from the bloody board, a cascade of sparks and stars and darkness crashing in and circling around her sight. She was staring through a pinhole, but she could still discern Hiroki's scarred face moving toward hers. She watched him bring a second hand to her vest, his fingers never loosening from her throat. She was going limp, the world losing the little light and warmth it had.

There was a sudden impact, a massive crack that rang through the back of her skull and filled her dark vision with a fresh explosion of blinding light. Olenka's eyes drifted open, and she found that she was lying on the deck now, her torso slouched against the edge of the diving bell that was swinging weakly behind her. Hiroki reached forward, pulling Olenka back up onto her feet. He slammed his fist against her face.

Once.

Twice.

She felt her cheek swelling and the skin splitting at the corner of her lip, but she barely noticed the pain. Even the force of the impact seemed weak and distant, muffled like sound through water. She was suspended in the void once more, adrift in the cold and the dark and the empty, far away from anything happening to her fragile body.

Was this dying? How odd…

She'd always imagined it feeling more… *substantial*, a great flourish of strength and tragedy to garnish her life's parting song. She thought it would have been loud and terrifying, but this felt so weak… so *anticlimactic*. Her mind rejected the idea. She couldn't be dying; this was too gentle to be death.

She just needed to *open her eyes* again, but for some reason she couldn't. Why was it so hard? It was such a simple task.

She just needed to *breathe* again, but her lungs weren't responding. Her chest was stiff and still, and the harder she pulled at her diaphragm, the more unresponsive it became.

She just needed to *not let go*, to *not drift away* from consciousness. But she felt so tired. She scolded herself, demanding her body to quicken, but the weight of fatigue pulled her deeper into the vacuum. Why was this so difficult… Why couldn't she just fight through it…

Child, be still. You are not alone. This is not your end.

A breath of fresh, crystal air filled Olenka's lungs as they jolted back to animation. Warmth flooded through her extremities as the gentle voice echoed through her blood. It soothed her tortured mind, reviving her broken senses. Only, it hadn't been a voice. Not exactly. It was more of a feeling, a knowing, a glorious, comforting hope that came from deep within her own mind.

She opened her eyes to the nightmare around her.

Omi was screaming over the deafening rain, her blood seeping out across the deck. Hiroki was standing over Olenka's crumpled frame, his knife drawn and ready. Aroon was beside him, his greasy eyes slipping up and down Olenka's helpless limbs, his lips moving, muttering.

"Not be needin' her now, is we Captain?" the siokoy croaked.

"*Kill them!*" Omi stumbled toward the two siokoy, ripping strips from her vest to bind her wounds. "Just kill them all! We'll find those buwisit jewels on our own."

Aroon smirked and licked his lips, tapping his blade to his fingertip to test its edge. Olenka felt like she should recoil, like she should be afraid of this man falling upon her to slit her throat, but she simply couldn't. She had been promised she would live, and for some stupid reason, she trusted that promise. Even with the pain bursting through her anew, she felt entirely at peace. The warmth of the voice was fading, but she could still feel it. Her eyes drifted from Aroon's bloodthirsty sneer, to Omi's screaming face, and then…

…to Diwala and Mari, gently creeping up the rope ladder behind them.

Olenka smiled. All three of the kaizo were gazing intently at Olenka. Aroon passed his fingertips down her cheek and neck, raising his blade as he tenderly caressed her face.

"Oh, short fins…" he clucked. "A pretty smile ain't be doin' *nothing* to save you now."

Olenka closed her eyes and turned away just as his blood sprayed across her skin. Aroon coughed and groaned and stepped back, examining the tip of Diwala's spear poking through his bare, tattooed chest. He collapsed in front of her, his eyes unfocusing as the color drained from his dying face.

All at once, the deck exploded into chaos.

Hiroki twirled behind Olenka, bringing his knife to her throat. Omi stumbled on her lame leg, falling to the deck as Marikit rushed her. The captain screamed as she fell back onto her wounds. Mari wrenched Omi's arm up between her quivering shoulder blades, crushing the kaizo's face against the deck. Olenka felt Hiroki's arms tense, his whole being urging him toward his captain. She could almost feel his reflexes rippling through his fingers, the instinct to slash Olenka's throat and bolt across the deck. One simple motion, cocked and ready, was all that stood between her and death.

"*Stop!*" Diwala screamed, and, miraculously, the deck obeyed.

"Drop the knife, little shark," Hiroki muttered to Di.

"First, drop *my sister*." She stepped forward as she spoke, her blade tight against her palm.

Hiroki shook his head. "You ain't playing fair. Caught us all with our backs turned, you did."

"And you caught us two hundred meters under the Great Sea," she moved closer as she spoke. "I would say we are on pretty even footing, kaizo."

"Step again and she's dead." Hiroki tightened his grip, and Olenka felt a trickle of blood tumble from the corner of her jaw.

"Kill her and we kill your captain."

"Better her than me."

"Better none at all," Diwala offered.

"*None?*" Hiroki laughed. "You tell that to Isko and Aroon, why don't ya!"

"They chose their fate," Di stated. "You haven't yet. Let her go and we will give you back your captain."

"And be outnumbered two to three? Not likely."

Diwala pointed to Olenka. "She can hardly stand."

Hiroki motioned to Omi. "Neither can she."

"Then perhaps we should trade," Di said. "A life for a life would be a fine deal, I think."

"What then?" Hiroki scoffed. "You three sail off with our jewels?"

"The jewels… are *here*," Olenka whispered. She was shocked at just how weak her voice sounded.

Hiroki and Diwala both froze. Di's face was grim and shallow, staring at Olenka with a blend of sorrow and confusion.

"What did you say, little minnow?" Hiroki's knife tightened up against her jaw as he spoke.

Olenka tried to swallow but only managed to drool some of the building blood and saliva in her mouth. Her face was swollen tight, and she kept accidentally biting the inside of her cheek as she spoke.

"The tall miner rubies…" she slurred. "They're on the barge… Well, *under* it, actually."

"Olenka…" Di whispered, a pleading look in her eyes.

"It's alright, Di… They're not worth it. The kaizo won." Olenka winked to Diwala. Or, at least she *hoped* she winked. Her face was so swollen it was hard to tell. Fortunately, she saw a flicker of understanding pass through Di's features, imperceptible to anyone but Olenka.

"You best not be playing games." Hiroki's voice was hot and hushed in Olenka's ear. "I've had enough of your sirena chum, you hear me?"

"I'm done with games," Olenka mumbled in feigned defeat. "I just want to go home…"

Hiroki chuckled. "Well, bring me up my jewels and we can see about that real quick."

"Let me go, first. I'll bring them right up…" Olenka let her head roll to the side for effect.

"Don't listen to her, Hiroki!" Omi called across the sodden deck, her own blood streaming off to the sea. "It's on their *buwisit banca!* They're trying to trick you!"

Olenka sighed and gently shook her head, a single drop of blood dripping free of her chin. "You saw our banca yourself. We ran a fake line. It was a distraction. Please… I'm done with the games. I just want to see my family again…"

Olenka felt Hiroki's indecisive voice rumbling in his chest, not quite forming words as it bubbled up to his throat. Finally, he shook his head, pointing his knife out toward Omi. "Let her free first."

Marikit glanced to Olenka who nodded. She stood up, hopping back a pace toward Di. Omi staggered to her fins. Her face was bloody and contorted, and it looked like Mari might have broken her nose. Good for her.

Hiroki smiled as she limped across the deck to him. "Alright, now tell me where you hid my jewels."

"Under… under the bell," Olenka mumbled, letting her body grow increasingly limp and heavy against Hiroki's grip. She really needed to sell it…

"That's a load of chum," Omi spat. "I checked that bell top to bottom!"

Olenka sighed. "Not *in* it… *under* it. We ran anoth–"

"Olenka, no!" Diwala stepped forward, and then pulled herself back as she saw the blade tighten against Olenka's throat. Olenka choked a little as she strained to keep her giggles contained. She'd always known Di was quick, but she had no idea she could *act* too.

"Easy there, fire-fish," Hiroki threatened. "Don't ya be slippin' too close, ya hear? Not now that we're making some progress, eh? Come to think of it, why don't you two be kicking them knives over to us. Just to be good and sure."

Diwala tensed, but she and Mari dropped their blades and sent them clattering across the streaming boards.

"Very good," Hiroki breathed through his beaming, mangled features. "Now, you two listen *real* close. There's a couple pairs of iron cuffs in that crate behind you. You two clap them on and it'd make us feel a whole lot better about all this chum."

Olenka gave Diwala a subtle nod of confirmation. The sirena glanced back at the crate. "How foolish do you think we are?"

"Foolish enough to nip at our fins, little minnow. *Put on the irons*," Hiroki spat, turning his attention back to Olenka. "Now you. What were you saying about my jewels?"

Olenka let her eyes drift and roll in her head as the siokoy shook her. "We... we ran an extra line... attached to the hull. It's right under the bell..."

"A third line, huh?" Hiroki sniffed. "Sounds like more games to me. What do you think, Captain?"

Omi limped up in front of Olenka, grabbing her swollen face and contorting it up into the light. She glared into her eyes, studying them with cool calculation. Olenka relaxed, letting her face and body go limp in her grip.

"If you're lying to us," she whispered under the pounding rain, "I won't just stop at your friends. I'll find your family too. I'll make them pay me back for every drop of blood I've wasted on you uzai eels, you understand me?"

Olenka bristled, feeling her wounded façade slipping off with her rage. She clenched her fists for a moment and then dropped her head.

"The jewels are there. I promise." She lifted her sunken eyes to meet Omi's. "I just want to go home."

A smooth grin crested the captain's lips as she turned around and glanced at Diwala and Marikit, iron cuffs clapped over their wrists.

"Well, if the jewels really are under the ship, then it shouldn't be any trouble for one of you three to go down and grab them for us. How about you, sister?" She motioned over to Diwala. "A razor shell like you ought to be able to swim in cuffs just fine! Unless, of course, there's something you want to tell us–"

"Fine." Di kept her face stiff as she spoke. "But my sisters stay safely on board until we make the trade."

Omi smiled. "Very good. Hiroki, get us all down to their banca."

"The banca, Captain?"

Omi hobbled toward the docking plank, her bleeding leg dragging with each step. "Does it *look* like I can swim? And check their cuffs, too!"

Hiroki's fist slammed into Olenka's gut, dropping her to the deck. She let her face slap against the wood for effect, forcing herself to not catch her fall. The kaizo needed to be *certain* she wasn't a threat. She heard the jangling of Hiroki checking her crew's cuffs, and then Omi wincing as she lowered herself into the boat below. Olenka swiveled her head just in time to see Diwala wink at her before hopping off the deck and into the banca.

Olenka cautiously lifted her head, scanning the barge's deck. Mari was in the corner, eagerly staring at her. Olenka sat up and strained her ears. When she was certain they were all in the banca below, Olenka motioned Mari to her side. She scrambled over, holding her chains to her chest to suppress their jangling.

"*Look at your face!*" Mari whimpered under her breath. "Are you alright, Kay Kay?"

"*Shh!*" Olenka hushed. "Never mind me. Hurry! Go get us some knives."

Mari nodded and scurried off across the deck. Olenka slipped along the wood, retrieving Diwala's dropped blade. She rose to a crouch, wobbling at the sudden exertion. She shook her head and blinked away the fresh swirl of stars.

Maybe she hadn't been acting as much as she'd thought…

Olenka crept up to the side of the bell crane as Mari stepped to her side. She examined the many cogs and levers, trying to find a weak point in the contraption. Finally, she found what she was looking for: all of the bell's chains were clamped to the ends of several massive ropes, their salt-bleached fibers brittle and frayed around the coils.

"Mari, we need to cut these three ropes, but we have to time it just right."

"Cut them?" Marikit asked, her eyes wide as scallops. "You're not planning to…"

"Of course, I am!"

"But what about *Di?*" Mari hissed. "What if you hit her too!"

"She knows," Olenka whispered. "At least, I *think* she knows…"

"You *think?* Kay Kay!"

"*Shh!*" Olenka glanced back nervously. "Look, we don't have a lot of other options, alright? We have to trust her. On my mark, start cutting through these two ropes."

"Okay…" Mari half whispered, half whimpered.

Olenka slid across the deck, pressing her cheek flush with the boards. She crept to the base of the gunwale and peered under the railing and over the edge of the barge. Di and the two kaizo were sitting in the banca below, drifting toward the bell's gently swinging shadow.

Good, she thought. *Just a little more…*

Olenka couldn't hear what the pirates were saying, but she could see Omi's mouth barking orders. Diwala was kneeling in front of her in the boat, the point of Omi's knife pressed into the base of her neck. Hiroki's blade was ready too, hovering just behind her kidneys. Despite the danger, Di was the picture of poise. With her jagged, warrior's tattoos running down her shadow-creased muscles, it was hard to see the two kaizo as the real threat. The knives withdrew, and Di stood. She stepped to the edge of the boat and dropped into the water, just as the banca drifted under the teetering bell's shadow.

"Go!" Olenka mouthed to Mari as she dashed across the deck. She started sawing frantically at the ropes, her manacled arms barely reaching both at once. Olenka dove to her own rope and began carving into the fibers. They broke away in strips, but it was slow. Much slower than they needed. Olenka glanced up at Mari's progress. She wasn't doing much better.

"*Hurry, Mari…*" she mumbled.

They sawed into the fibers, feeling them peel away bit by bit. Olenka grew desperate, stabbing into the rope, feeling its sopping girth absorb the blows. It was like they had stopped making progress, like the rope had somehow grown thicker.

A creak sounded from the crane above, and the rope suddenly tightened under Olenka's grip. She felt the adrenaline rip through her as she sped up her cutting. All at once, the three ropes burst, peeling apart in a sudden flurry of fibers and droplets that hissed like serpents as they sped through the pulleys. Olenka turned and saw the bell slip and then drop, scraping the side of the deck before punching into the black depths. There was a horrible shriek, followed by the snapping of crushed wood, and then everything was silent.

Olenka and Mari froze, waiting for the silence to end.

What had they done?

Time snapped back to them, and the two sirena rushed to the edge of the barge. Trails of bubbles were boiling up through the flotsam, the banca's shattered bow and pontoons drifting away in the storm. Olenka's blood was cold and slow, her heart breaking against her static lungs.

"Di…" Olenka whispered.

There was a burst of motion in the water, and the sound of someone gasping for breath. Olenka leaned forward in time to see Diwala bobbing out of the shadows.

"*Lightning upon you, sister!*" Di roared. "*What in the Great Sea was that?*"

Olenka gasped in relief and fell back onto the deck. Marikit squealed and rushed to get the rope ladder.

"Di… don't scare us like that!" Olenka yelled.

"Oh, *you* were scared?" Di shouted. "What was that chum, huh? You dropped *the bell* on us?"

"I thought you knew!" Olenka wanted to argue with her, but she couldn't stop laughing.

"I thought you two were going to drop down and *ambush* them! Cut their throats while they were distracted!" Diwala explained. "Something *reasonable*. Not drop the whole buwisit *bell* on us!"

Mari tossed the ladder over and helped pull Di up onto the deck. She stomped up over the railing, glaring down at Olenka.

"Merciful Heaven, sister," Di said. "I'd slap you if your face did not already look like a chewed clam…"

Olenka smiled and jumped up to her feet. She and Mari rushed Diwala, knocking the sirena against the gunwale as they embraced her.

"Alright, that's enough," Di grunted, holding up her wrists. "Get these things off me. It is time we got our jewels."

Part Two

The Light From the Darkness

CHAPTER 12

WALLS

THE BROTHERS WALKED IN GROUCHY, FUMING silence. As they moved down the street and passed from underneath the buildings, a pale light gently grew around them. The buildings opened up into a modest square filled with closed vendor stands, stables, storehouses, and a steady trickle of telaks. Just ahead was the southern gate. Two guards sleepily leaned against either side of the stone arch. Another pair rested on the southern face just beyond the shield.

A thick stone wall extended from either side of the arch as far as eyes could follow. The wall completely circled inner Centile, dividing the fortunes of the citizens. The arch and wall were elegantly adorned with carved bricks of varying shades of sandy tan and rich brown. The arch itself was taller than three telaks, and wide enough for five grown men to comfortably walk through shoulder to shoulder. Two broad iron doors were folded open and latched down to the wall on either side of the arch. Resting on top of the wall, and rippling across the archway, was Centile's golden shield. It shimmered and billowed in the failing light, casting beautiful waves of white and gold on every surface in the square.

As the brothers approached, a high, clear whistle split the still air.

The four guards at the arch shifted from their rest and stepped into the opening, spears and shields lifted into position. The pedestrians all stopped and slowly backed up into small crowds on either side of the wall. Lorenzo's ears twitched as he jogged toward the closest archway guard.

The four soldiers slammed the ends of their spears against the cobblestone at Lorenzo's approach.

"Excuse me, gentlemen. What's going on here?" Lorenzo sauntered up to them with great presumption, but just as much charm.

"My apologies, sir," a guard grumbled, "but the southern gate will be closed for some time. I recommend taking a detour around to either the eastern or western gates. It may be faster."

"What's happened? Why have you closed the gate?" Lorenzo folded his arms low and loose across his chest.

"Sir, we have received reports of a storm coming in from the northeast," the guard explained. "A large caravan of outlanders has been spotted on the southern road carting agricultural items under the shield wall tonight. We've been ordered to restrict all travel through the southern gate until the caravan has passed, sir."

The soldier never made eye contact with Lorenzo as he spoke. He stared straight ahead at the guard standing opposite of him.

Lorenzo nodded. "I understand, soldier, but I am an *officer*, and I would like to escort my younger brother to our home outside the wall before the storm reaches us." Lorenzo motioned for Corin to join him. "There should be plenty of ti–"

"Please, sir," the guard said. "I *cannot* let you pass. If I allow one, then I must allow all. I recommend that you and your brother detour to either the eastern or western gates, *sir*." He spat the last word.

That was it. End of discussion.

The guard's tone made it quite clear that he was not about to be undermined by a new recruit, captain or otherwise. Lorenzo stepped back and nodded. His face was placid, but his tail was twitching. Corin quietly smirked at the blessed, bureaucratic justice that had been rained down on his brother's self-righteousness.

Lorenzo could feel his brother's pleasure, so he smacked him once on the back, a bit harder than playfully.

"Not a word out of you, Cor. Let's go find somewhere to sit."

* * *

AS THEY LIFTED THEMSELVES ONTO A ROW OF CRATES by the stables, the brothers could finally make out the line of carts and wagons approaching the gate. A throng of farmers trudged into sight. Some were sitting on wooden carriages, leading dusty lahartos, but many were simply pulling handcarts piled high with tubers, gourds, and leafy greens, all filled to tedious, tenuous capacity. Many were overflowing with brown sacks and open-topped barrels. Others with massive haystacks haphazardly tied down with meager scraps of twisting, bristling twine.

As the crowd entered, they split in two lines, following the stone wall on either side of the arch, and searching for an empty hollow to hold down in for the night. Time came and went, smudging the shadows in the cherry light, and still the caravan drifted into the city.

Corin studied the eclectic group shuffling in. Some were dressed in plain, rugged shirts and pants, with worn, dusty hats pulled low over richly tinted brows. Others sported the gaudy beads and bright colors of the outlander tribes. Many had deep smoke-stained wrinkles carved into their tired features, and all of them had their heads down.

"There are so many," Corin said.

Lorenzo shrugged. "They come from everywhere, Cor. Centileans, outlanders, villagers… Once *one* farmer hears about a storm, the rest panic. They pack up everything they're afraid to lose and head in for the night. Before long, it turns into *this* scorching mess…" Lorenzo shook his head in frustration.

"What's wrong?" Corin teased. "Still mad he wouldn't let you through?"

"No." Lorenzo looked up, raising his hand to the crowd. "Look around you, Cor. Use your head. These guards haven't examined *any* of these people! Anyone could be filing into the city with this group. No inspections. No paperwork. No accountability… I'm just glad this security breach isn't mine to clean up."

Corin actually laughed at that.

"Oh, *come on*, Lorenzo! This is exactly what I was talking about before. They're just *farmers*. Look at them. They're harmless! Tired, dirty, and looking for a place to weather the storm. What exactly are they going to do?"

"I get that you want to save these people more discomfort, but isn't peace of mind worth a little discomfort?" Lorenzo leaned back, shifting his weight to his hands. "You don't understand what it can be like out there, Cor. There's a reason for all of these extra security measures, believe me. You should learn to appreciate them."

Corin suppressed a sigh which turned into a yawn. "Adahy's right. All these walls… Don't you think all this nonsense is causing more problems than it solves?"

Lorenzo snorted. "And what *problems* do you think our security measures have caused?"

"Well," Corin hesitated, "I'm not really sure how to put it into words."

"Oh, no, no, no…" Lorenzo shook his head. "If it was important enough to mention, then it needs to be important enough to explain. So, go on! *Enlighten me*, baby brother."

"Alright, fine!" Corin grunted. "Look at the outlanders. Their way of life can't be easy, but there must be a reason why they chose it. Any one of them could decide to take their trade and set up a shop in the city. Most rely on us to sell their wares, anyway, but still they choose to travel the trails for dozens of kilometers to get here when they could just… well… stay put. Haven't you ever wondered why? Why would they choose a life on the plains?"

Lorenzo nodded. "I have, but I want to hear *your* take on it."

Corin sniffed and looked at the falling sun in the distance, burning across the short, clay rooftops. "Adahy says we've lost touch with the land. They call us *wallies*, you know. They're always talking about our walls… At first, I thought it was just because of the shield, but I think there might be more to it than that. Something about *how* we live, not just *where*. He says that our lives are too chaotic for us to hear anymore."

"To hear?" Lorenzo snorted. "To hear *what*, exactly?"

Corin shrugged. "I don't know. Adahy won't explain it to me… He says that if you can't already hear it, then you'll never understand it. But that's why they live on the plains, I guess. To keep their minds and ears sharp enough to…" Corin paused, realizing just how ridiculous he sounded. "To hear whatever it is they're listening to."

Corin became aware of Lorenzo's stare.

He turned just in time to see his brother's smirk crack into a chortle. "Corin, do you even *hear yourself?* You sound like one of those leather-faced shamans selling sun charms by the outer gates! When did you start buying into all this outlander nonsense?"

Lorenzo laughed again, but he saw the hurt on his brother's face and backed off a little. "Listen, Cor. I'm sure there's *something* to what your friend's been telling you. Some mornings when I'm out on the plains, and I get to watch the horizon change from night to dawn… Well, it's a powerful feeling, Cor. The whole sky starts off real dim, and then this deep blue light fills in the space between the mountains. The light sort of bursts over their tops and into a little strip of pink. It stretches out across the sky, bouncing off the night's clouds. It picks up its pace after that, faster than you think it should, and then, before you know it…" he sighed and closed his eyes, "everything has gone from pink to orange to clear golden shine. It looks just like the shield. Those mornings can wake up something inside of you, *for sure*," Lorenzo chuckled and bumped Corin's shoulder, "but I'm *not sure* I'd go so far as to make a whole bloody *religion* out of a pretty feeling."

Corin shrugged. "I guess I just like to keep an open mind to these things. I'd hate to wake up one day thinking I could explain away all the magic in the world…"

"Magic?" Lorenzo scoffed. "What *magic* do you feel is out there that needs explaining?"

"Everything!" Corin cried. "Look around you! The stars, the storms, the seasons. Look up! Just *look* at the shield, Lorenzo! Do you have any idea how it works?"

Lorenzo nodded. "Of course, I do. The tower mounts and channels the sun gem's power to the spire, and the spire casts the shield to the inner wall. Easy. Where's the bleeding magic in that?"

"No, that's *what* it does." Corin sighed. "I want to know *how* it does it. Did you even look around while you were in there with me? Did you see the light running down the walls?"

"Yes, I saw the bleeding light, Cor." Lorenzo shrugged. "Thunder and hail, why does it matter? It works! Our ancestors built the system hundreds of years ago, and it's still there to guard us. We need to protect it, and care for it, but why on the scorched sands would we need to know how they did it?"

"*Why?*" Corin honestly didn't know how to respond to that. "Doesn't it bother you? How can it *not* bother you that we use its power and have no clue how it works?"

"Corin, *relax*," Lorenzo laughed. "Farmers don't worry about how seeds grow, do they? Who knows what makes the grain sprout? Thunder and hail, who *cares?*"

"That's different!" Corin protested. "You can't compare *grass* to the shield! Telaks didn't *build* the grass! What if the gem's dangerous? What if its energy fades? What if it breaks and we can't fix it?"

Lorenzo laughed. "Cor, if it was dangerous, we would know by now. And if it fades or breaks or whatever, *so what?* If the leather skins can survive out there without it, then so can we. We still have our walls and the city guard. It's convenient, and it's safe, but the shield's not a necessity."

Corin shook his head. "I just can't see it that way. Grandfather says that no one alive really knows anything about it. He told me that the city was first built around the sun gem, and that the tower was made to mount it years later. He says that the shield suddenly appeared the first time the gem was placed at the top! How could that be? How could it just *appear?* Doesn't that bother you?"

"Cor, those stories are almost three hundred years old. I don't think that our city's history is particularly reliable." Lorenzo shrugged. "Grandfather takes the stories literally because it's his *job* to remember them. It's hard to say what's fact and what's myth. I think what *is* important are the lessons those stories teach us. It's like I was saying before! Vallin and his legacy are there to inspire us, Cor. To help us see our own potential. Think about it. Do you *really* believe Vallin could move with the wind? Run the whole world round, or whatever rubbish the song says?"

"I don't know..." Corin said. "It might have been a little exaggerated."

"A *little* exaggerated?" Lorenzo rolled his eyes. "What about shooting lightning from his fingers? Speak in any language? Do you honestly believe he could wield a sword wreathed in flame? Those are just *myths*, little brother! Myths!"

"Well," Corin said, "myths come from somewhere, don't they?"

"Sky above..." Lorenzo slapped his forehead. "You're just not getting it... They're *metaphors*, Cor. Silly stories meant to frighten club-tailed runts, not grown men! They're meant to be pondered, not taken at face value. I'm sure there are powerful lessons to be found in the stories surrounding the sun gem as well. You just have to not take them too literally. Or too seriously, for that matter."

Corin tilted his head as he considered these words. The line of carts seemed to be approaching an end now, the sound of creaking wood dimming slightly against the muffled echoes waving out into the shield's canopy. He sat back and scratched his chin.

"I don't know, Lorenzo. I don't take Grandfather for a fool."

"Neither do I, Cor," Lorenzo quickly added. "I just think his role is a little different from ours. Like I said, it's *his* job to remember. Not ours. We need to act, to think. We need to *move*, baby brother. Defend the present. Not lock ourselves away in the archives. Which... actually, reminds me of something."

Lorenzo leaned forward and pulled out a folded piece of paper he had tucked away in his waistband. "I've been meaning to talk to you, Cor. You'll be nineteen next month, and Father and I think it's time you started taking your future more seriously."

Corin sighed and leaned back. "What, the *dating lecture* again? Listen, I'm just not–"

"No, not dating," Lorenzo cut in, "though, that's certainly something you *should* get a move on..."

"Then what is it?" Corin groaned.

Lorenzo cleared his throat. "Well, as a captain, I now have certain... influence. Here, I want you to have this." He held out the folded paper.

Corin's brow scrunched involuntarily, but he reached out and took the parchment. The paper was thick and tan, folded in thirds and held together with a tight crimson ribbon and a blotch of pressed wax.

Pressed with the official seal of...

"Lorenzo," Corin mumbled, "what is this?"

Lorenzo smiled. "Open it."

Corin lifted the ribbon and gingerly snapped the seal. The ribbon fell forward, and the paper unfolded into his lap. Corin scanned its content. Centile's emblem was stamped onto the top corner, and the sharp printed ink was addressed to him.

"Lorenzo, what *is* this?"

His brother smacked the back of his head. "Will you just *read it?* Thunder and hail, Cor!"

"I did. Lorenzo," he looked up. "I've been accepted into training for the city guard?"

Lorenzo smiled. "You have."

"But I didn't *apply* for the guard," Corin said. "I haven't even taken their preliminary fitness test! I haven't even spoken to a recruiting officer!"

"I vouched for you, little brother." Lorenzo patted Corin's shoulder and gave him a wink. "We'll think of a way for you to pay me back later."

Corin realized that the flush running up his ears was anger, not embarrassment. "Lorenzo, I…"

"Cor, listen. I knew you were worried about applying, but Father and I agree. This really is for the best. You and I both know you're more than capable of this position. Or, at least you *could be* if you cared to try. What you lack is confidence, not skill."

There were those stupid stars again in his stupid eyes, ready to spill out over his lids and glisten across everyone else's dreams…

"Lorenzo, stop," Corin said. "*Listen* to me. I didn't ask for this! I–"

"You didn't need to." Lorenzo couldn't stop smiling as he spoke. "I know you, Cor. I've known that this is what you've wanted for years! I *also* know that you get nervous at the worst moments possible. This is your chance, little brother! You're in. You've made it! All you need to do now is show them who you are."

"Lorenzo…" Corin wanted to hit him. He wanted to run. He wanted there to be some way for him to explain to his baca-brained brother that this was the absolute last thing he would ever want to do with his life. He had nightmares about this: miserable, disturbing, bloody nightmares of being clad in bright, shining armor, of riding out on the back of a cyove, of meeting a clash of swords and spears only to be smitten down by terrible, bloody hands. The thought alone sent his heart streaking away into his stomach, made his sight go weak and distant…

Lorenzo had taken Corin's worst fear and packaged it up like a box of honeyed corn cake.

Corin looked down at the paper again, trying to find balance in his words. "I get that this is an incredibly kind offer. I'm sure you really had to pull some strings to make this happen, but this *isn't* what I want. I need you to understand that. This has *never* been what I've wanted!"

Lorenzo chuckled. "Cor, stop. There's no use trying to talk me or yourself out of it. This is the right thing for you. For our family. Just because you didn't apply doesn't mean you didn't earn it. I know you can do thi…"

Corin blinked and cocked his head. Lorenzo's voice had drifted off, his eyes slipping away to something in the distance. Corin spun around to the archway. The caravan was finally coming to an end, and Lorenzo's gaze was fixed on a single cart approaching the gate.

One very average, very full cart of hay.

Without warning, Lorenzo hopped off the crate and stretched out his knees to stare over the crowd by the arch. The cart was drawn by two brown lahartos, one with deep red streaks along its shoulders, the other with a creamy underbelly. The man at the reins sat slouched against the cart's wooden back, his head dropped against his chest and his forearms resting in his lap. His load was bulging over the lips of the wagon, but it was just a stack of hay.

What was the emergency?

Why was his brother acting like a spooked prairie cat?

Corin tilted his head, trying to figure out what he was missing. Everything seemed fine, nothing worthy of such an unusual reaction. If it was Adahy going all bottle brushed, that would have been one thing. But Lorenzo wasn't one to jump at shadows. Corin turned to his brother. Lorenzo was standing incredibly tall and still, his hands drawn into tight fists at his sides.

"Lorenzo? Hey, what's your problem?"

His brother didn't move, his eyes unblinking on the approaching cart. Then, in a burst of motion, Lorenzo suddenly started for the arch. His pace was a fast trot, almost a run. Corin sighed and jumped down to follow his brother.

"*Soldier*," Lorenzo called out to the closest arch guard. The armored telak turned on the spot and slammed his spear end to the road.

"Sir?" The guard glared at Lorenzo with disapproval sunken into his dim eyes. His stance shifted, but his feet never moved from his post.

"Soldier, you need to inspect that cart!" Lorenzo motioned to the wagon. It was less than twenty meters from the arch.

The guard did not move. "Sir, I need you to stand down and step away from my gate."

Lorenzo quickly wiped his upper lip on the back of his wrist and stepped firmly to the guard. "Soldier, you need to *listen* to what I am telling you," he spat. "Stop what you're doing and *inspect that cart*."

The other three guards had brought their spears down and were watching the scene unfold. Lorenzo glanced to them and then back to his victim.

"Sir, my orders are to allow this caravan to pass quickly into the city uninterrupted! I will *not* have you interfere with this directive, regardless of your bloated rank or temperament. Now, I need you to stand down, sir."

Lorenzo smiled and loosened his knuckles as he took half a step back, and the guard dropped his shield.

That was foolish.

In one burst of motion, Lorenzo stepped right against the guard, grabbed him by the cloth at the neck of his breastplate, and cracked his back against the arch's stone wall.

"What is your job, soldier? Hmm? *What is your job?*" Lorenzo's voice was harsh but quiet. The crowd instantly tensed: two hundred sets of eyes wide on his grip. The other guards were rushing to Lorenzo's side when he threw the man to the ground.

"Your job, *soldiers*," he turned to face the approaching guards, "is to *protect this city!* Not to blindly follow a low-priority traffic errand!"

The three guards were on him in an instant, forcing him against the wall. Lorenzo struggled at first, but then went still and tense, his gaze fixed upon the approaching cart. The hay wagon passed through the arch unimpeded and uninspected. Lorenzo's eyes followed the man sitting at the head of the wagon, his face growing paler the longer he watched.

When the cart was through the gate, the guards released Lorenzo, and stepped back into a loose circle around him. Lorenzo didn't even look at them. He pointed at the passing cart.

"That man," he cried, "has not twitched or blinked *once* this *whole time!*"

The guards looked around at each other in nervous confusion. One glanced at the cart over his shoulder, but the others seemed too afraid to take their eyes off Lorenzo and his unpredictable fists.

Lorenzo pushed a guard aside and jogged up next to the cart.

"Excuse me, *outlander!*" He called out to the man sitting at the reins.

He didn't respond.

Lorenzo ran up beside him, tugging at his pant leg. "Sir, stop this cart immediately for an inspection!" Still the man sat motionless, empty eyes staring into his lap.

Lorenzo grabbed the slack of the reins around the lahartos and pulled them to a halt. The beasts grunted roughly but slowed to a standstill. Lorenzo patted the back of the closest brute and swiveled back to the driver. The features on Lorenzo's face melted from frustration to confusion in less than a heartbeat.

The hay on the back of the cart shifted.

CHAPTER 13

THE BEAST

IT WAS SUCH A DELICATE MOVEMENT THAT WERE IT not for the scene at hand, none of the guards would have caught it. Keeping his eyes on the man in the cart, Lorenzo raised a fist to the guards at the arch. With a flick of two fingers, and a quick, sharp whistle, the four men approached the cart with lowered spears and raised shields.

Lorenzo stepped forward gently. The whole square had gone rigid and silent. He passed a hand before the cart driver's face, pulling back his hood. Then he felt for his wrist dangling between his knees. Lorenzo's features hardened at what he didn't feel. He pushed up on the man's forehead. The sickly flesh was drained of any hue, and his eyes rolled limply with Lorenzo's touch, one drifting unnaturally to the side. Lorenzo sat the man back against the cart and inspected his torso.

At the center of his chest, barely visible under the folds of his shirt, was the rusted end of a tarp stake.

Lorenzo tilted his head as he examined the body, then he jerked slightly on the dead man's shoulder. His back peeled away from the wood. Short strings of dirt and coagulated blood stretched thin and then broke against the stained back of his shirt. The man had been nailed upright to the wood. His hunched position had almost perfectly hidden the blood and the stake.

Almost.

The load of hay shifted again, a few individual straws fluttering to the cobblestone. Lorenzo's eyes snapped up as he straightened his spine. The four guards stepped back, knees bent like pressed springs. Lorenzo stepped gently to the wagon's side, his hands raised to chest-level. He approached cautiously and gently pulled down on the closest loop of twine, releasing the rope from its hook…

…and in a shatter of light and sound, the stack of hay burst around them.

The crowd screamed as the guards fell back on their tails. A flurry of straw coursed through the sudden pandemonium. From his place in the crowd, Corin watched a massive brown figure burst over the cart, splintering the far side of its wooden frame. The brown thing kicked out through the street with incredible speed. The guards scrambled up to their toes as citizens were thrown from theirs. Through it all, Corin noticed Lorenzo standing very still while the world burst into panic around him.

The bounding monster dug into the street on the far side of the cart, the force of its impact sending cobblestones flying like gravel kicked up from a runner's toes. Its body tensed and then blurred with motion as the massive thing surged out of the crowd and onto the side of the nearest building.

There, from its perch, Corin could finally see it clearly.

The beast was easily four meters long and covered in fur that bristled like shards of rust. Its black skin shimmered beneath the hair like coal oil, sending off glimmers of green and violet and blue across the sandy wall behind it. It held onto the building with six muscular limbs, four in front and two behind. They ended in a cross of blunt toes, each crowned with thick, chipped claws that splintered the building's plaster like it was eggshell. Its limbs and knuckles were grotesquely wrinkled, covered in ridges that slipped and bulged over its bones with each flex of sinew beneath.

Long slats of ribs pushed against the taut skin of its barrel chest leading to an abdomen so thin it seemed insect-like. Boney hips held quivering haunches ready to pounce, and despite its immense size, the beast's movements were quick and spastic. So much quicker than it should have been.

But the face… Corin was most disturbed by the creature's horrible *face*.

It was as round and bulbous as the back of a skull, with ribbed horns protruding from its rusty mane. Tight wrinkles ran from the crown of its forehead to the folds of its neck, splitting around either side of its maw. Its mouth opened from side to side instead of up and down, exposing row after row of jagged teeth. The creature's pointed eyes covered most of the rest of its face. They were sunken, watery things, with cloudy pupils that seemed rotten.

Corin felt a rush of cold, putrid air escape the monster's lips as it suddenly bellowed. Rough, vibrating tones clashed and echoed from its throat in metallic dissonance, momentarily paralyzing the crowd. The telaks scrambled to cover their long, sensitive ears, screaming in pain and terror.

Then the sound stopped. The plaza stood still for a single heartbeat.

And then everyone ran.

Corin was knocked back against the wall of crates by the frantic clawing of a hundred hands pushing past him all at once. Through the blur of clothing and tanned skin, Corin saw the creature launch off the wall and crash onto a ledge on the opposite side of the road. Again, it thrust itself into the air and came down hard on the cobblestone street, splintering a peddler's abandoned stand, and tearing off into the distance.

Corin felt someone hoist him up to his toes.

"*Come on!*" Lorenzo's words were fast and tense, and his ears were high and sharp.

But Corin just couldn't make himself move.

Lorenzo might as well have been coaxing a tree to take up its roots and follow him. Corin could hear his brother roaring in his ear, and he could feel the crowd bursting around him, but he wasn't really there. His mind was drifting away, totally disconnected from the moment and horror and the need to run away.

A quick slap brightened his eyes with a flash of pain, and Corin gasped as his brother shook him.

"*What are you doing?*" Lorenzo screamed, and Corin swallowed against the raw, dry feeling building in his throat. "Move! *Now!*"

So, without thinking or feeling or choosing, Corin raced after his brother. In the coursing madness of the crowd, they seemed to be the only ones heading *into* the city center. Crimson smears and broken bodies adorned Centile's stone walls, and great gouges of shattered stone adorned her floors. Ahead lay two guards propped unconscious in the shattered remains of a cloth stand. Lorenzo grabbed their spears and threw one to his younger brother. Corin fumbled with it but caught the end of the weapon's shaft.

The beast was out of sight now, but the screams guided them on.

Lorenzo swore under his breath and stretched out his legs to look around. Decision flashed across his brow, and he ran up the cloth stand's broken table, kicking off its sunshade and landing on the ledge of the building beyond. In another massive spring, Lorenzo was on the rooftops racing with all his might.

Corin followed his brother's acrobatic path, scrambling to keep up. His mind was frozen, but his body pressed on independent of his fears. He couldn't stop, and he couldn't think. He was only running. His breathing was harsh and bloody, but he couldn't wait to catch it. Something was happening inside him, and he rode the reaction in salty waves of adrenaline that broke across his mind and seized his legs. He leapt again and again, clearing the rooftops and spinning past cracked tiles. Lorenzo was close ahead now. Something had slowed him to a trot. Corin cleared one last roof and matched his brother's gait.

"Did you see where it went?"

His brother's eyes shot along the buildings ahead, leaning and peering to see down into the web of streets. The rooftops had risen substantially, and the beast was completely obscured somewhere on the cobblestones below.

Lorenzo didn't have time to respond to his brother's question.

A massive crash split the atmosphere as the side of a nearby building webbed and cracked. The monster threw itself to an opposing wall, bounding its way up to the rooftops. Lorenzo's eyes unfocused as he slowed to a standstill, watching the beast scrape along the tiled roofs.

"By the sun…" he whispered. "It's heading for the tower."

* * *

LORENZO PUSHED OFF INTO A SPRINT, QUICKLY leaving his brother behind. Corin tried to follow, but his energy was sapped. More than that, he couldn't stop trembling. Three rooftops later he skidded to a halt, his numb, clumsy toes crunching against the shrill of the grinding clay.

Lorenzo was gone.

The creature was gone.

Everywhere he looked, he could only see the sweat stinging his eyes in blurred clouds and hear the pulsing ache in his skull tearing across his temples and cutting into his stomach.

But then he saw it.

There was a distant smear of brown as the creature leapt onto Vallin's Tower. Corin could only gape at the destruction as the beast scaled the building's immensity in only a few leaps, leaving crisp gouges in its sandy walls. With a final bound, the monster leapt straight to the tower's top chamber, bursting through its glass wall in a spray of diamonds and silver powder. A blinding flash seared from the iron building, and the shield wall began to recede. The dull, bubbling roar of the frightened city suddenly spiked into the cascading peal of ten thousand voices crying out in unified panic.

Corin wiped his face obsessively, trying to process what was happening. His adrenaline was wearing off, and his senses were dimming. Through squinted lids, he could see the beast's torso emerge through the hole in the tower's upper chamber. Clasped in its distant maw was a speck of golden light. The sun gem was dazzling and impossibly bright. There was nothing Corin could compare it to…

…except, perhaps, the sun itself.

The creature pressed against the jagged glass for a moment before shifting its hind legs out onto the tower wall. Scraping its way down the sandy surface, the beast slid along the stone with claws sunk firmly into the wall. When it was halfway down the tower it leapt to the nearest building, crashing down hard on the rooftops.

Corin watched the beast stumble as it ran, all of its grace and ferocity strangely gone. Something was wrong with it. The woolly creature was staggering on the roof as if it were wounded or dazed. Perhaps it had underestimated the fall to the rooftop. Perhaps the broken glass had injured it. Whatever the reason, the monster staggered like it was drunk on corn whiskey. The beast shook its head and a spray of golden particles swirled around its face.

But then it ran.

It ran with renewed effort: blinding, focused speed. Scores of chipped tiles erupted out from each of the monster's bounds as brick walls popped and buckled beneath its weight. It was headed back for the southern gate, back the way it had come.

Corin gripped his hair in panic, but, across the street, he spied Lorenzo. His brother was running low, crouched with his salvaged spear held tightly in both hands. He stopped at the edge of the roof, squatting close to the tiles. Corin looked around in confusion, but suddenly understood. The beast's tracks were gouged deep into the street below.

This was its path, and Lorenzo was waiting to ambush it.

Corin looked out into the distance and saw his brother's plan unfolding. The monster had returned to the street. The crash of bursting stones and screams was approaching, reverberating off every centimeter of wood and rock. Corin looked at his brother. His eyes met Corin's, and he offered him a quick nod.

Before Corin could respond, the street below exploded into motion.

Around the farthest corner, the beast emerged, blindly scrambling across the broken stands and shattered stones. It banked hard against a brick wall, its right three legs clawing high up the sandy surface before kicking off back into the street, gouging devastation into the tan bricks. The beast rushed ahead, gaining speed once more as it surged into the center of the cobblestone road. It was then that Corin noticed that its eyes were closed: squinted shut in thick, bulging wrinkles.

Its features were contorted in what could only have been pain.

Clutched tightly within its putrid mouth, the sun gem's light filled the street with a searing white. It was so bright that it dulled all colors into brilliant prismatic shades and shimmering sparks that twirled across every surface. Around the beast's face the gem splintered and twirled in shards and drops of golden light. They twisted off the gem with each of the creature's mighty bounds, like dew shaken from a blade of grass. They swirled and fragmented and splashed together, tumbling back into the gem: a golden swarm furiously circling its hive.

As the beast approached, Lorenzo crept to the edge. His tail was twirling in restless spasms. Lorenzo lowered his spear, placing his right hand at the weapon's blunt end. His legs flexed and twitched, sizing his target, timing his strike.

Through the flare of light, Corin watched his brother lunge.

As the beast pushed through the street, Lorenzo brought his spear down in front of him, falling five meters from the rooftop, and landing a crushing blow into the creature's right flank, just higher than its double socket shoulder. The blade sank deep into the monster's flesh with the plunging force of Lorenzo's fall, releasing a spray of wretched black blood that misted the ground and sandy walls.

The beast tripped from the blow, skidding into the cobblestones that popped out and flew with a blast of gravel. Its right, front limbs folded under its barrel chest and a series of cracks echoed through the street as its ribs broke. The creature crashed into a vegetable stand, crushing the frame into a cloud of splinters. It exhaled, and Corin saw the shower of sparks from the gem swirl back into the main gem, splashing like liquid, but instantly calcifying back to crystal.

Lorenzo pulled back on the spear, trying to cause as much damage as possible.

The monster didn't even seem to notice him.

In a shroud of twisting black fluid, the beast leapt back to its feet. Its middle right limb dragged limply below it, but the brute acted as if nothing had happened, as if it wasn't mortally maimed. Corin couldn't see his face, but Lorenzo's body tensed as he hunkered down into the matted fur on the creature's back. With that, they were gone. A smear of black on the broken stone was the only evidence of the grisly episode.

CHAPTER 14

TAKEN

IT TOOK A MOMENT FOR CORIN TO FIND HIS NERVE. The shock of the scene was still splitting across his throbbing brow. Once he could feel his feet he jogged to the edge of the building and peered over onto the street. Whipping his tail around for balance, Corin dropped to a porch railing below. He staggered briefly but caught himself. The road was still another three meters down and crowded by the shattered remains of a cart. Trying not to overthink it, Corin made himself jump, aiming to clear the splintered wood below.

His leap was short, and a shard of the ruined stand pierced his foot.

Corin yelled and crumpled to his side as he landed, the momentum of the fall flipping him into a puddle of the creature's blood.

It was a frigid fluid: the heat of life absolutely absent.

Corin twisted up his head, momentarily panicked that the beast might somehow return, but the streets were barren. He felt for the wood in his foot, and as quickly as he could, he wrenched it out. The sensation of the alien material slipping through his flesh was more painful than the actual puncture.

Biting hard on the inside of his cheek, Corin threw the bloody stake aside, and got up to a knee. He wasn't sure if he could walk, but he didn't really have a choice. He reached for the spear he'd dropped and used its shaft to push himself to his toes. His foot flinched and clenched as the muscles flexed within the raw wound, and a hot flush of blood wet his toes. He tried to put weight on it, gauged the pain, and then stepped forward.

He could manage.

He didn't know if it was the adrenaline or the strange numbness still caging his mind, but the wound felt more uncomfortable than painful.

So, fearing he'd lose his nerve, Corin started to run, trying his best to ignore the jolts shooting up his calf. He left a single row of crimson footprints beside the beast's black trail. The monster's blood seemed to be everywhere, making the stones slick and rancid. The creature was out of sight now, but Corin knew they couldn't be too far ahead. He could still hear the screams.

Corin tried to close the distance to those screams, but they were growing fainter.

He was growing fainter.

He stopped, bracing himself against his spear. In the stables to the left, Corin noticed three lahartos struggling against their restraints. Corin ran for the closest beast and slit its harness with the tip of his spear. He made no attempt to calm the brute. He needed speed, not temperament. The laharto flailed and stumbled out of the stall, and Corin threw a leg over its back. The beast charged forward, but Corin wrenched on the reins, steering the mount down the ebony smear ahead. The laharto obeyed, and together they pursued.

Everywhere the monster had run, the crates and stands had not survived.

Often, their proprietors had not either.

Corin slapped the end of his spear against the laharto's rump, and its weight shifted forward into a sprint. As they came to the southern gate, Corin could see deep gouges in the wall with thick, black stains adorning the street. It looked as if the creature had lost control, careening into the stones before shifting back onto its course through the arch.

The laharto instinctively veered away from the gore, but Corin jerked on the reins, steering the brute through the gate and into the southern district. The tall brick structures quickly faded to squat, sandy shacks and chipped clay ovens. Entire buildings had been leveled: brought to rubble and sprayed sickly black. Just ahead, past the last row of buildings, Corin could see the decrepit outer wall. To the left of its meager opening was a massive hole, burst through by the beast.

As they shot out into the open plains, Corin squinted at the evening sun. He wiped his forehead as the wind chilled the tips of his ears. His mind felt nauseous and drifty, the sting in his foot pulsing and building through his knees. At least it *had* just been a sting. Now it was an *immense* pain. What had happened? Was his adrenaline wearing off? Whatever the reason, the wound was quickly becoming more than he could ignore.

Corin tilted the crown of his head toward the sun, trying to regain his vision and his heading. The sky was a rich, disorienting froth of charcoal ahead, the smear of rain accenting the encroaching storm.

But off to the left, Corin saw a light.

He squinted against the gleam, feeling the spots forming on his eyes in bright splotches of white and blue and green. The light pulsed from the distant gem in radiant waves crowned with glints of rainbow spectrums that all melted back to white. Against the glare, Corin could just make out the creature's outline, and what must have been Lorenzo's figure protruding from its back.

Corin pulled tight on the reins, shifting the laharto's gaze and stride toward the sun gem's light. The brute frothed and grunted, but it was remarkably well-trained. It obediently coursed on through the sea of brittle grass. This was faster than Corin had ever gone, and he could feel his balance shifting poorly with the animal's might and his inexperience. The pain in his foot wasn't helping either. He leaned forward, resting his chest against his forearm against the laharto's back. He desperately wished he had another free hand as he tucked the spear tight against his thigh. The wind pulled on the shaft, tugging against the waning strength in his knuckles, threatening to rip him off the mount.

As the laharto approached, Corin could see his brother's mad thrashings. He wrenched back on his spear, carving out as much damage as he could into his enemy. The trail of blood came into view as Corin's mount lined up behind the beast.

There was a tremendous *pop* as something burst in the creature. It tripped and crashed into the dirt, sending a wave of soil over its black, sticky frame. Corin closed the distance then. As he came up beside it, the mangled beast lifted itself back onto its five working legs and began to trot forward.

"*Hit it, Cor!*" Lorenzo screamed from the monster's back, pulling desperately on his spear's shaft. Even though the blade was slipping and sawing through the creature's grey flesh, it didn't seem to be causing any pain.

Corin raised his spear and sank it into the beast's left, rear leg as he passed. It didn't go in very deep, and the creature began running again. Before it could pick up speed, Lorenzo threw himself from the creature's shoulder and clasped onto Corin's spear. He pulled and twisted the shaft, sinking it deeper into grey, rancid meat. A fresh burst of black bubbled up and coursed through the monster's fur.

But still, the creature ran.

Its pace was blinding now: just as clumsy, but faster and more determined than before. It was as if panic had suddenly taken it. Corin smacked the reins against the laharto's shoulders, but the beast pulled away, steadily leaving the red-skinned brute behind.

Ahead, something caught Corin's eye. Beyond the bursting light of the sun gem, he could see a violet gleam on the plains. It wasn't much, but it stood out against the endless gold and brown of the surrounding grass. Corin screamed out to his brother, flailing an arm toward the purple shimmer beyond.

"Lorenzo! Ahead!"

In a flash of movement, Lorenzo glanced back to Corin and then to the approaching gleam. If he was going to act, it had to be now. Lorenzo adjusted his grip and then swung off the beast. He held the spear firm and used the twist of his fall to sink the blade down the creature's leg, ripping through tendons and hide and cords of flesh. A fresh wave of black blood streamed across Lorenzo's arms as he slid down the shaft, crumbling into the golden grass.

The beast's leg went limp, and just meters from the violet gleam, the monster's shoulder sank into the dirt, flipping it onto its side. With titanic force, the beast's limp body cut through the soil, one of its gnarled horns snapping on impact. Corin pulled back on the reins hard, bringing his laharto to a skid. He sat upright, carefully watching the still, woolly mass.

This time, it didn't get back up.

* * *

LORENZO WAS ON HIS HANDS AND KNEES, TRYING TO regain his footing in the smear of black. He finally managed to stand and staggered toward the beast with a heavy limp. Corin leapt from his mount. The beast was utterly motionless. At first, Corin was hit with a blessed wave of relief.

Then he was hit by the smell.

The sweet and sour sting of rotting flesh wafted up heavily from the furred creature, carried in the storm's building breeze. The brothers gawked and grimaced across the ebony puddles, waiting to see if the hairy thing would amble back onto its broken limbs.

But it never moved. It didn't even look like it was breathing. Corin carefully stepped to his brother's side, trying his best not to gag. The two were silent, catching their breath in the dying light.

Lorenzo turned to Corin. His blond hair was thick with the creature's black blood. He smiled and together they laughed.

Corin shook his head. "I *cannot* believe you did that."

Lorenzo rolled his stiff shoulders, grabbing at a sting in his neck. "You know… I can't either."

Corin swallowed and wiped his damp hands off on his pants. "Do you think it's dead?"

Lorenzo blinked and took a few heavy steps closer to the creature. He leaned back a little, stretching his back. He sniffed before speaking. "I'm not entirely sure it was alive to begin with. Do you smell that?"

Corin nodded. "Yeah, I do. Spoiled meat."

"Just about…" Lorenzo wiped his hands, realized how drenched his clothes were, and gave up. "Its whole body is ice cold too. I've never felt anything like it." He shook his head and cocked his jaw in thought.

"Maybe it bled out." Corin stared at the long streaking puddles of black on the plains. "Nothing can bleed like that and stay warm."

Lorenzo nodded. "That must be it… but," he shook his head and grimaced, "*thunder and hail*, Cor, it didn't feel *a thing!* I swear, by the end I was sawing that spear against bone and it never even *flinched*."

"Something was getting to it, though. Did you see how it was running near the end?"

"See?" Lorenzo barked a short laugh. "I was *on it*. It's like it couldn't open its eyes. It ran into everything it could. Did you see the wall back there?"

"Rubble," Corin agreed.

Lorenzo shook his head and swore. "Totally blind. At first I thought the bloody brute was just trying to knock me off its back, but now… I don't know what happened."

Corin nodded in agreement. "I think it was the gem."

"I think you might be right."

The two walked closer, stepping gently around the beast's rancid mass. Corin winced at the excruciating pain in his foot, but his curiosity drove him on. From up close, they could clearly see how dead the beast really was. Its chest sat rigid and silent, its still eyes wrinkled shut. Corin pressed his hand against its gut and shivered. Lorenzo was right. The creature felt chilled and soft, like a rotten corpse. The flesh peeled open around its shoulder was grey and sticky, with frothy white beads budding between the strings of muscle. The whole area had gone black with the beast's chilled, fetid blood.

"Do you think this is what attacked that patrol?" Corin asked.

Lorenzo nodded as he stepped up to the beast. "Had to be. It certainly could have taken down a cyove."

"It was fast, too," Corin added, trying to suppress a gasp as he stepped on his wounded foot. "I can see how those men could have missed it. What do you think it is?"

Lorenzo folded his arms. "Now *that* seems to be the right question, doesn't it? It's definitely nothing local."

"It could have migrated down from the north. That might explain the fur." Corin stepped back. The smell was overwhelming his senses. And that *pain*… What was happening to his leg? He rubbed at his thigh, trying to push the burn back down his veins.

"Maybe…" Lorenzo muttered, "but I just don't understand how something like this could go unnoticed for so long. You think we would have heard about a sun scorched monster like this. And why would it suddenly attack the…"

Lorenzo shifted his gaze to the sun gem lying off in the distance.

The beast's impact had sent it flying several meters ahead. Lorenzo rushed toward it. Corin limped behind, cautiously eyeing the beast's corpse as he passed, and bracing his hand against his thigh as he walked.

The gem sat nested in the grass. Its light was so intense that everything around it was shades of brilliant white. Lorenzo walked up to it and crouched down, his four knees folding snugly together.

"What would an animal want with…" He reached a gentle hand toward the light and gasped.

Corin rushed to his side. "What is it?"

"Cor… *look*." Lorenzo showed him his hand. His fingers were clean. The creature's blood was still damp and sticky around his wrist, but by his fingers it had gone dry and charred, like the flaking edge of a burning piece of paper. He leaned farther into the light, and the dry edges of the blood peeled and lifted gently from Lorenzo's skin, silently shriveling to ash in the breeze. With a delighted laugh, Lorenzo reached forward and touched the gem.

In a flash of movement, its surface shifted.

Lorenzo jerked back, his hand and forearm were completely clean. The gem seemed to have rearranged itself. A spout of light shot out along its far edge, immediately hardening back into a perfect crystal shaft. A spray of particles had flared off of its surface, but they all splashed back into the whole. It was like it had been liquid for a moment. But, more than that, it was like it had been alive… like it had recoiled in fear.

Lorenzo leaned back and stared at the gem. "I think I owe you an apology…" He gave Corin a quick glance. "Maybe there *is* some magic in the world."

Corin couldn't respond. He couldn't even think. With the pain in his leg, with the confusion in his mind, he was lucky to even be standing.

"We have to get this back to the tower," Lorenzo stated.

And that finally loosed Corin's tongue.

"Lorenzo, *what was that…*"

Lorenzo stood up and turned to his brother. "Cor, please. I'm just as lost as you, but we need to bring the gem back to Centile. We'll come back later with a platoon and–"

"*But it moved!*" Corin shook his head. "Come on, we *at least* have to talk about this for a moment! What just happened? It moved! You saw it!"

"Corin, stop. Listen to me," Lorenzo insisted. "I don't think that creature did this on its own. I have no idea what it is or where it was going, but this isn't something an animal would do by itself! *Think!* It's like it was *trained* to do this. Like it was *sent*. We need to get the gem back to the city."

Corin nodded. Lorenzo was right. This would all have to wait. He swallowed hard and clutched at the searing pain in his thigh. The light stings of the storm's first rain were hitting his brow, helping to distract him from the ache as he turned to hobble back to the laharto...

...but something caught his eye.

He squinted through the gem's light. Just beyond its glow was that same violet sheen he had spied before. Lorenzo followed his gaze. He stood for a minute, puzzled by what he saw, then he knelt down and gingerly lifted the sun gem into his arms. It shuddered but did not shift this time. A few drops twisted off and back into its golden surface as Lorenzo lifted it. He pressed it to his chest, and the beast's blood peeled away in crisp flakes and particles all throughout his body.

But Corin's eyes were fixed on something else.

Something was sprawled out across the ground, like a web of tangled, violet vines. Corin squinted against the glare, studying the anomaly. It was a mostly round patch of ground that seemed to be covered in knotted roots, like the base of an ancient tree. The roots were mostly black, but in the gem's light their rounded edges shone with an inky, purple light. It was the same dark spectrum of color one might see rippling across a puddle of coal oil.

The roots were very dense and, though they were static, they looked like they were clawing across the grass with a thousand boney fingers. They were bulbous, unpleasant things, and seemed to bubble and protrude in unnatural ways, like poorly blown glass pulled and bent at odd angles as it cooled. The whole knot was perfectly still, but the grotesque ripples and ridges and bulges along each twisting stem gave the scene the surreal optical illusion of hot, writhing movement.

Lorenzo knelt down again and stared across the black and purple mass, and then he pointed up to the air above it. *"Look…"*

Corin bent his neck and stared across the violet mass. There was a shimmer in the air, like the twisting waves of heat rising from a flame. In fact, it behaved *exactly* like a flame, but there was no heat. No flashing streaks of gas, or lifting trails of sparks, or hazy bursts of smoke. It was only the distorting, transparent ripples of a heat that wasn't there. Corin couldn't believe it, so he raised a hand toward the invisible flame.

"Do you feel anything?" Lorenzo asked.

"No…"

Lorenzo stood back up. "Neither do I." He tucked the sun gem under his arm and reached for the roots.

"Don't!" Corin spat out. *"Look!"*

He pointed to a root off to the left. One of its bubbling edges was pulsing, steadily inflating and deflating like a bubble of tar. Lorenzo stepped back from it, and as he did, the bubble burst. A slick black tendril shot out into the soil. Quicker than a flash of lightning, it split into two branches, one of them splitting again. The branches shot through the grass, bubbling and bending as they sank into the dirt, and suddenly becoming just as still and crystalline as the others. It was all over in less than a blink of an eye, faster than the two brothers could even process what they had seen. They jumped and scrambled back with delayed reflexes.

"We need to leave…" Lorenzo muttered. *"Now."*

"Yeah," Corin whispered. "Yeah, I think you're right."

✳ ✳ ✳

THE SCENE HAD BEEN TOO ABSORBING, AND NEITHER OF the brothers had stayed aware of their surroundings.

The wind and rain had started to pick up, so neither of them had heard it. Their senses were tired and worn from the chase, and they had not noticed the beast slowly rising to its feet at the edge of their peripheral vision. They did not feel it step across the soil and creep up behind them. They did not hear it gently press the brittle grass, moving into position. But as they turned, the brothers saw it there: ghastly and wretched, with two grey eyes silently watering down on them.

As they turned, the beast leapt. As they turned, its putrid maw sank into Lorenzo's belly. He screamed as a red mist painted his teeth and lips. With a second bound, the creature dove for the violet mass, Lorenzo tightly gripped and screaming. He only had enough time to toss the sun gem aside, a spray of light twirling around it as it spasmodically shifted and shifted and re-shifted in the air. The transparent tongues flailing above the roots suddenly flared up like a cyclone, swallowing the beast and swallowing his brother. In a single, silent shimmer, they were gone, and the mirage twisted out of existence.

Corin stared at the empty network of roots and fell helplessly to his knees.

CHAPTER 15

A BRUSH WITH THE ETERNAL

THE STORM WAS COMING. THE SHARP STING OF THE icy rain hit hard against Corin's ears. Soon the rain would give way to wind, and the wind would bring blinding, coughing clouds of dust. But Corin could not move. He stared out over the convoluted mass of crystal tendrils. The meager light faded with the rolling clouds, and the pockets of violet shimmer had dulled to dusty graphite. Still Corin could not move. His mind was quiet and cold.

And then, like a blade, the pain pierced his thoughts. Sudden and unwelcome, he screamed as tears stung his skin and blurred his sight. He held tightly against his stomach. His intestines felt chilled and tense. His mind was rejecting what it had seen: flushing the poison of reality down through his torso, killing his flesh from the inside out. He couldn't accept what he had witnessed. Lorenzo couldn't be gone. It didn't make sense. It was a thought so cold and so impossible…

The pain in his gut spiked and Corin vomited onto the grass. He felt the bile burn his throat and palate, somehow helping to clear his mind. His voice was yelping and tumbling from him as he wept, and he realized that he was not in control. He was not in control of his body or his mind. He was shaking violently and couldn't unclench his grip against the stabbing pain inside him. Could this just be sorrow? Was this truly the power of anguish?

He had to move. He had to get help, anything to dull the burning in his mind and body. Corin tried to stand, but only managed to scream into the storm. A bolt of pain shot through his leg and he fell to his side.

He could hardly feel the blow of the fall.

Corin thrashed and wept as the stiff grass scraped his skin. He realized then that something was happening to his body, something much greater than grief. There was something wrong with him; there was something wrong *inside* of him. He thrashed forward and managed to pull his wounded foot into view. The puncture was grey and pale with black veins throbbing and streaking under his fragile skin. Convulsing in the brittle grass, Corin grew very cold and very afraid.

But he also noticed the light.

Through the dancing shadows of the plain, Corin saw the sun gem. It was pulsing gently, blooming coronas of gold out from its shifting surface. With each flare, the rest of the world looked darker, greyer, less interesting, less inviting. It was calling to him, somehow dimming the distractions. But there was something more to it, something Corin could feel in his stricken mind.

It was something soothing and warm.

It was a feeling Corin could only describe as love.

Tenderly, Corin crawled through the grass on his forearms, trying to keep his breathing smooth, and dragging his useless legs limply behind. The pain returned in violent shots, like thorns splitting his flesh. The horror of his broken body should have been growing to panic, and yet, as he crept closer to the light, his thoughts actually began to settle. What had once been a gale of anguish was calmly aligning into a plan:

Lorenzo is gone, child. Accept that. There was nothing you could have done to save him then, and there is nothing that can be done to save him now.

Amazing, Corin thought. He hadn't even realized there was guilt floating through his mind, and yet the answer swept his psyche clean before he even had time to confront it. It had come to him quickly, with a certain flavor of necessary pain: like the sting that comes from dipping freezing fingers into warm water. It hurt, but it was over in a flash, leaving nothing but the comforting ache of healing.

Again, the strange, warm thoughts came:

Return the gem to the tower. The city is vulnerable, and you are dying.

Dying? Really? How could that be? It had only just occurred to him that what he was feeling was something more temporal than mere sorrow, but *death?* Seemed excessive.

Also, why wasn't he more upset about all this? It was an odd sensation. Corin had just received a clear, unmistakable impression that his life was in mortal peril, and yet he felt no panic. That ache was still present in his mind, but none of the terror that a thought like that should have brought to him. Was it because he did not believe it? That must be it. He hadn't processed the thought. It had not yet sunk in.

But, no… that wasn't it either. His mind was moving faster than it should have been. He had processed the thought. It came and went and moved through his mind and into his heart almost before he was aware that it was even there. He felt like a baby suddenly thrust into the mind of its parent. More than that: an ant given the mind of a god.

All his senses had been heightened, but he was not accustomed to operating at such an extreme speed. In a single flash of mental pain that he had barely noticed, Corin had felt panic, horror, denial, sorrow, regret, and a bitter, jaded acceptance that now urged him to crawl closer to the rippling gem before him. It hit him again that he truly was dying there on the plains, but apparently that would be an easy fix… so long as he continued to crawl toward the light.

Things have finally been set in motion, and what is done cannot be undone. The sum of ten thousand past ages has been placed upon your shoulders. But first, you must not die out here in the grass.

There was a clear objective, now. His panic had been burnt away by the drive to meet a precious goal. But, how? How had these thoughts come? A second ago, Corin had felt that he was not in control, but now… Now it felt as if he had been *given* control. Not that he had found it or overcome what was keeping him from it. He felt as though he had been given the clarity to process and proceed. The influence was so obviously foreign, and yet it felt so familiar.

Familiar… That wasn't the right word. It wasn't a memory he had lost, or an old habit kicking in. It was deeper than that. It was something instinctual. He had been reconnected to what he had always belonged to: something sweet and natural, and vaguely terrifying.

As Corin crawled to the crystal he noticed the black smears on his fingers burn and crack and flake away to ash. He paused and watched. The light was singeing the creature's black blood. It seemed to boil in a flash and then shrivel to nothing before gently lifting from his skin, a harmless scrap of paper pressed against a coal. Despite the blood's volatile reaction, Corin felt no pain on his flesh. The black blood peeled off, leaving him clean and dry.

Heal your leg. Hold the gem.

My leg… Corin thought back on the pursuit. He had been wounded. His foot had been wounded and then he had run through puddles of the creature's black blood. Corin shifted to his side and then lifted himself up onto his knees. The pain flared with each burst of his pulse, shooting the icy feeling through his veins. In a spasm of pain, he reached forward and clasped the golden thing before him.

Corin's world went white: startlingly, strikingly white.

An exquisite heat burst through him, perfectly permeating every centimeter of his body. His flesh was on fire, being consumed by the light.

But no… that wasn't it at all. His flesh *was* the fire. It was as if he had died and been born anew. He was desperately ill and healthier than he had ever imagined possible, broken and rebuilt. His life was suddenly a blinding, brilliant paradox of surreal, cosmic sensations. He flew from the ground, passing through the sky, drifting higher and higher until blue became black and black became laced with diamonds. His vision burst into vast scenes of stars and clouds of incomprehensible colors, and great constellations clustered in patterns so empyreal and immense that Corin screamed in terror and threw the sun gem.

Corin leapt to his feet and scrambled away from the crystal.

It rolled once in the grass, a cloud of splintered pieces swarming its surface before splashing back into the whole. The gem coursed and pulsed with delicate ripples of cubic patterns waving silently through it. Corin looked down at his hands, certain that they were raw and burnt. He flexed his fingers and turned them over several times.

They were fine, and they were clean.

Corin shifted his weight on his feet and then noticed that there was no pain. He twisted up his foot and looked at its bottom. His wound was gone. The icy feeling, the pain in his blood, and even the hole in his flesh… They were all healed. A simple white scar was all that remained.

For a moment Corin just stood and stared at the gem, letting the fading rain prick his neck. He felt strange now that he had released the gem, like he was no longer whole. His mind especially felt small and broken. He could feel the chill in his temples.

Something warm was slipping away beneath his skull, pulling back and recoiling from his inadequacies.

Corin held his forehead trying to remember what had happened. It had happened in an instant, but it had seemed so much longer than that. It was like his mind had moved quicker than it should have: noticing more in less time. It had frightened him, but now that it was over, he could not stop thinking about it. What was it that had frightened him, exactly? It was something he saw. Something great and terrible. It was like the night sky but far more vast… infinite even. It was like seeing the sky from a different angle. The difference between seeing from the view of an insect and the view of a bird.

Corin shook his head and looked out across the plain. The rain had stopped, and he could see the dust rising. A massive cloud of sand and grit was billowing toward him, turning the grey sky tan. Corin considered the sun gem for a moment and then ran to the laharto. The brute was still standing patiently by the black puddle where the beast had fallen, but the storm was making it twitchy and skittish.

"Shh… Hey, come on, now. Stay with me." Corin gently tugged on its reins, and the laharto obediently trotted along behind him. As they stepped up to the sun gem, Corin turned to the mount's saddle. Tied to the side was a thick, rolled cloth, probably used to cover its back at night. Corin pulled the knots loose and unrolled the blanket, holding it up by its tasseled edges. He walked to the gem and threw the cloth over it, bunching it tight and scooping it into his arms. He tied the gem to the side of the saddle and mounted the red beast.

As he climbed up, the agitated creature was instantly, perfectly calm: soothed by the crystal's presence.

Corin rolled his eyes. "Oh, you like that? Why don't you try *touching* it… you might feel different."

* * *

THE RIDE BACK WAS MISERABLE. THE SANDSTORM HAD descended, stinging Corin's eyes and skin with each thrash in the atmosphere, but that wasn't what was truly bothering him. He kept hearing the thoughts in his head repeated over and over. He couldn't pin down the words, exactly, because there had been none. They were just ideas, unfettered by the bonds of language. They were pure knowledge and emotion and instruction, and they disturbed Corin more than anything he had ever known.

What had they said? Lorenzo was lost, the city was vulnerable, and something had been set upon his shoulders, something that could not be undone. It was as if the universe itself had stooped down to send him a message. But that wasn't quite right either. It was not a message coming *to* him from somewhere else. The ideas and emotions had come from *within* him, some part of him that Corin did not understand. Something he didn't even know existed.

That was what was most unsettling. The ideas had been harsh and terrifying, but he knew with a perfect surety that they were true. They had come from within his own mind, but he trusted them far more than he had ever trusted himself. It was distressing. It made him sick and dizzy, like there was a place in his thoughts where he was not permitted to go. There was a wall in his mind, and each time he thrust his thoughts against it he was washed over with a wave of nausea and bitter frustration.

In the end, that frustration was too severe.

He shook his hands wildly at the wrists and breathed in the cold air of the storm. He couldn't let himself dwell on it. Somehow, he knew it would destroy him. Somehow, he knew that time was short.

When he reached the outer wall, the city was still deep in its panic.

Great bells of distress were ringing in the distance, and people were scrambling to get indoors. Corin followed the main road, moving quickly through the clearing streets. When he reached the central wall, he could hardly comprehend the sight. The perfect plants and banners of the inner city were being torn and twisted in the wind: exposed to the elements for the first time… ever? What a thought.

There were no screams, but a swell of anguished voices wailed in the dying light. The southern gate had been abandoned by the guards, but the creature's cart of hay was still sitting peacefully in the square. The city, which had been so vibrant and alive only moments ago, felt cold and grey. The shield's light had always been Centile's greatest comfort, and now it was exposed. The inner district throbbed like a wound laid bare for all the world to pick and prod.

Corin smacked the reins against his mount and raced through the broken streets. The storm wasn't so fierce within the buildings, but the dust still choked, and the sunlight had been all but extinguished. Through it, an obstruction came into Corin's view. Several wooden stands had been crashed together, blocking the street as they met the enormous wreckage of a collapsed building. Corin prodded the laharto forward, but the brute wouldn't take another step.

Corin swung off the beast and searched for a path through the rubble. It turned out to be an easy fix. Part of a broken cart could be moved to clear a path. He ran over to it and hefted a protruding board.

No sooner had he applied force to the wood than a shrill voice cried out in pain.

There were no words. Just a desperate, short-breathed agony. Corin jumped back. Beneath the cart was a guard and a young girl wrapped in his arms. The girl was unconscious but still breathing. It had been the guard who had screamed. A broken beam from the cart was lodged into his shoulder. He was lying on his side, using his mass to shield the girl from the crushing weight of the cart. He was trapped beneath the wood, unable to lift himself free and unable to collapse from exhaustion without crushing the unconscious girl. The guard was a thick, muscular man, with a hard jaw and cropped brown hair, but he looked weak and spent. He shot a devastated plea to Corin, unable to even find the strength to speak.

Corin ducked down to the man's level, examining his wound. The wood had pierced straight through his shoulder blade. A small crimson tip was protruding from his chest. It was a miracle he had been able to hold the wood at all.

Clearing the debris away, Corin caught hold of the little girl's arm. He pulled her gently from under the cart, trying to keep her skin away from the splintered edges. The guard under the cart quivered as blood and sweat dripped down his brow. Once the girl was free, Corin went back for him.

"I'm not going to leave you," he whispered, and Corin knelt down by the broken cart. The angle was the problem. If Corin lifted straight up on the wood, it would pick the man up with it. If Corin pulled back on the wood, it might shift the cart and crush the guard. As quickly as he could, Corin cleared all the excess lumber from the cart, lowering the weight and searching desperately for an alternative. Once the cart was bare, Corin could see the street underneath.

His heart jumped.

The ground was black and slick with the beast's wretched blood, and the poor guard was soaked in the stuff.

There wasn't any more time. Corin got behind the cart, facing the man's pierced back. He found a suitable bit of timber and wrapped his fingers around it. He stretched out his knees, lifting the cart as high as he could. The man screamed and thrashed once more, frantically clawing at his chest. As soon as he was lifted free of the stone, Corin raised his foot and pushed against the man's back.

Blood, pain, and shrill screams, but the guard slid off the jagged edge: the metal of his breastplate scraping splinters against the beam. The man landed roughly on the stained stone below. As soon as he was free, the guard began bellowing and twisting and clawing at his chest and belly as he folded in on himself.

It took very little imagination for Corin to see himself in the man.

His mind raced back to the ice in his intestines, that burning cold that seemed to creep up his veins and nip at the tethers of his feeble mind. With all the strength he had, Corin pushed against the beam, tipping the cart up onto its side. It creaked and swayed but stayed balanced. Corin rushed to the guard. He tucked his hands under his arms and dragged him out into the clear street.

There was a brief, stupid moment where Corin wasn't sure what to do for the man. He removed his dinged helmet and peeled off his sticky breastplate. Shards of metal had been folded into his wound, but the guard was somehow past feeling them, and they pulled out of his chest unnoticed. Instead, he held his abdomen and wailed into the storm.

As soon as Corin saw the man's grey, soft flesh, he knew what had to be done.

Beneath his chainmail shirt, thick, black veins bulged across the guard's skin, exploding into thin webs that pulsed and coursed through his dying body. The smell was overpowering. It was pure putrescence: the sweet, sticky decay of spoiled meat.

Corin pulled the man up to the laharto, and the beast stayed surprisingly calm and subdued. With a quick glance around the street, Corin loosed the crystal's cloth and placed it in the guard's lap. The man relaxed and opened his eyes, staring blankly into the storm above, apparently not feeling the sand and grit biting at his corneas. Corin knelt down beside him. He wasn't sure what he was doing, but it seemed as if he had no other choice. He lifted the man's now limp arm, pulled back the gem's covering, and placed his hand on the crystal's surface.

The flash of light was instant and overwhelming.

Corin turned away and noticed the little girl beside him. In the blinding light it was clear that her legs had been scraped and cut by the wood. He lifted her into his arms and placed her hand on the gem as well. The light flared through her, and for a moment her skin turned an impossible, celestial color that was almost clear.

Corin pulled their hands from the gem and sat back, the little girl silently pressed against his chest. The guard blinked as fresh tears tumbled down his cheeks. With a free hand, Corin pulled the cloth back over the sun gem and pulled it onto the street next to him.

"What did you do to me?" the guard whispered.

"I was… trying to help you."

The guard smiled and felt at his chest. The wound was gone. The black blood was gone. He laughed. "Was it all a dream?"

Corin sighed in relief and looked at the covered crystal at his thigh. His mind ran back to his vision on the plains. He had seen so much in so little time. Perhaps…

"Did you… see anything?" Corin asked, cautiously.

The guard blinked and then looked at Corin. "You're Lorenzo's brother, aren't you?"

He forced himself to nod. "My name's Corin."

"Corin… Well, I… thought I was dead. Not even *dying*, but all out *dead*." The guard chuckled and cracked his neck. "Sky above… I thought my heart had stopped. Everything hurt so bad…"

"I know," Corin urged, "but what did you see?"

"See?" The guard seemed a little confused at the question. "I, um… I saw that creature. It came at me down the street, just there, smashing every cart in its way. There was a little girl standing in the road screaming. I'm not sure if I did the right thing, but I dropped my spear and dove over the girl, trying to protect her. That's when the wood came down over us. I didn't see what happened, but I felt my shoulder rip open…" He shuddered. "Bloody nasty, that was… The little girl must have gotten knocked out by the fall. After that, I… Well, I don't really know. That pain… it was too much. I must have passed out, huh? Did you get me out?"

Corin nodded softly. "But, *after* that? Did you see anything else? Anything in your mind?"

The guard shook his head gently. "I don't… wait. There was… a light? Does that make sense? I saw a light. And I felt it too…

I felt peace, like… like everything was going to be alright. *Thunder and hail*, did I die? I could be dead right now, huh? Or was it…" His eyes wandered to the wrapped object at Corin's side. "It was the sun gem, wasn't it?"

The guard looked back up at Corin, a kind of eager concern in his sunken, weathered eyes.

Corin grunted and turned away, ignoring the man's naked desire for information. "I need to get it back to the tower. Can you take the girl?" Corin lifted the child into the guard's solid arms.

"Of course, but how…"

Corin grabbed the crystal by the cloth and lashed it back onto the laharto's saddle. He leapt on and kicked mildly at the brute's sides.

"Corin, wait up a moment!" the guard called, climbing to his feet. "My name is Darrow, by the way. I was in your brother's platoon in the guard. Where is he? I would have bet my life that I saw him *riding* on the back of that thing!"

Corin turned away without answering, and he smacked the laharto's reins.

CHAPTER 16

HE WHO REMEMBERS

THE CENTRAL PLAZA WAS BARE AND COLD. THE remnants of the celebration still cluttered the streets. Here in the open space the storm was dense, with swirling, brown clouds of dust blinding the way. When Corin reached the tower, he found its massive doors limply hanging open, leaving a half meter crack to the gale.

Corin dismounted and loosed the gem. He braced to heft it but realized how incredibly light the thing was for its size. He thought about tying the laharto to the nearby stalls, but realized he had no idea who the lizard even belonged to. He left it there in the storm and pushed his way into the tower. Inside, the walls were dark and bleak without the gem's light, and his eyes were useless for a moment against the sudden black. As they adjusted, a hunched, cloaked figure faded into his sight.

"Grandfather?"

Lehonti quickly glanced up. He had been sitting on an enormous chunk of stone that must have been knocked loose from somewhere high in the tower. The impact had left a huge gash in the tiled floor.

"Corin?" The old man rushed to his feet. "*Corin!* Where have you been? Do you know what's happened?"

When Corin saw his grandfather, it was as if all his strength and courage were suddenly spent.

His mind had been closed until now. Sealed tight with the desperate tide of adrenaline carrying him on. He had been riding a high of sorts: fueled by all he had seen, fueled by what the gem had shown him. He felt in that moment that he had not been entirely himself, that some greater force had buoyed him up and kept him from collapsing into despair. But as the old man rushed toward him, Corin finally collapsed, overcome by grief. Lehonti moved swiftly to his grandson and held his shoulders.

"Corin? *Corin!* Speak to me, son! What's happened to you?" There was palpable panic in the old man's eyes. Corin tried to speak. He tried to scream. He tried to tell him everything that had happened, but amid the bursts of tears only his trembling gasps echoed through the tower's dark chamber. He hunched forward, clutching the wrapped gem against his gut.

"He's *gone...*" Corin whimpered. "It took Lorenzo."

Lehonti's face grew dim and pale. "What took him? Corin, what are you saying?"

Corin trembled as he wept, leaning lower as his strength seemed to fail him. His voice rose and shook, and the words suddenly burst from him.

"*That thing!* That terrible *thing* that stole the gem! We tried to kill it, but it took Lorenzo!" He stopped and sobbed some more. The old man was perfectly still and perfectly silent, absorbing all Corin had to say.

"Grandfather, they just *vanished!* We were out on the plains and… we thought we had killed it, but then it took Lorenzo and they were just gone!" Again, Corin shrank and collapsed within himself. He glanced up at the old man. Lehonti's face was streaming silent tears, the whites of his eyes blurring to red.

He held his grandson, and together there, in the dark of the empty tower, they wept.

* * *

IT MIGHT HAVE BEEN MINUTES. IT MIGHT HAVE BEEN AN hour. The two telaks mourned in silence as the shrill storm wailed against the hollow chamber. Dusk fell, and for the first time in three hundred years, inner Centile felt a storm's bitter sting. Lehonti leaned back and stared out through the open door.

"All is truly lost, now," the old man whispered. "Without the sun gem, we will all share Lorenzo's fate."

Corin sat up with the gem cradled in his lap and gently pulled back a portion of the crystal's cloth, letting the golden light fill the chamber. Lehonti stopped short, the pain in his features melting under the gem's shimmering light.

The elder was suddenly on his toes.

"Come with me, son. *Now*." Lehonti motioned toward the curling stairway that wrapped around the edge of the tower. With surprising speed, the old man rushed up the steps. Corin staggered at the abrupt shift, but followed his grandfather, leaving the gem partially unwrapped to light the way. They ran as fast as they could, but the tower was immense. The stairway was much steeper than it looked, and it felt as if they were making little progress in the climb.

Corin had a thousand questions bursting into his thoughts, but he was too winded to speak them. As they ran, he gazed out into the center of the tower, straining his red eyes to understand the optical illusions created by the immense cross work of iron beams and metal ribs hiding in the shadows of the tower's inner surface.

When they finally reached the narrow top of the tower, the stairway abruptly turned left onto a thin walkway. There was an iron ladder at the center of the path leading up into a broad, metal ceiling. The old man hurried up the rungs, unfazed by the dizzy heights of the meager path. Corin felt a thrill of fear run over him but walked forward. He was accustomed to running across rooftops, but this was much worse. He grasped the cold iron bars and realized that he didn't know if he could climb with one hand. Trying his best to not look down, Corin passed the bunched-up cloth to his nimble toes and pulled himself up the ladder, awkwardly hopping along the way. He tried to not imagine what would happen if he slipped or dropped the gem. He guessed that it would probably just shatter and regroup like it had on the plains, but that was a precarious assumption to rely on.

When he reached the top, his grandfather pulled him up the rest of the way. Corin lifted the gem to his hands and stepped into the room. They were standing in the iron lantern at the top of Vallin's Tower. It was much larger than Corin had imagined, and the whole metal surface of the structure was etched with beautiful swirling designs. The room had eight tall, glass windows, divided by iron beams that supported a conical roof. A window off to Corin's right had been blown inward by the beast, casting diamond slivers across every centimeter of the floor. Some of the creature's loose fur was still caught in the meager shards around its shattered frame. The wind was catching the window at such an angle that the whole room whistled and screamed. It felt like staring out over hungry, crooked teeth.

"Corin, quickly now!"

Corin flinched out of his stupor. His grandfather was standing in the center of the room, beckoning him toward something Corin hadn't noticed. Directly underneath the sloped point of the roof, was an iron stand about waist high, with a cupped top to cradle the sun gem. Careful to not touch its surface again, Corin rolled the crystal out of the cloth and onto its altar.

The room filled with light, and the gem convulsed in excited, cubic spasms. Its surface rippled and shuddered and flooded out over the ridges and poles of its altar. The sun gem crusted the metal like salt crystals climbing the shore. The gem itself seemed to bloom, crowning out into a vast display of spikes. Spikes, Corin realized, that looked strikingly similar to the end of a telak's tail.

Sparks of white light travelled quickly down the etchings in the metal stand, illuminating them as they went. They continued with blinding speed, lighting the designs on the floor, the beams of the walls, and finally the roof. The little trails of light swirled and tightened and eventually converged at the center of the roof. In another flash of light, the shield began to melt out over the city, thinly spreading like golden wax over a polished stone.

As the shield descended, the wind ceased. Fragments of dust and sand fell from the air, and the world went suddenly still and silent. It could be felt across the entire city. As the dome was restored, all of Centile collectively exhaled and relaxed.

* * *

CORIN'S GRANDFATHER STARED FOR A MOMENT AT THE sun gem, as if he wasn't certain it would stay put. He was still dressed in his yellow ceremonial robes and orange sash. He looked perfectly at place here, overlooking the city by the light of the gem. He turned to Corin, swift tears slipping across his wrinkled skin.

"We have so very much to talk about," he whispered.

Corin swallowed and tried to find words, but none came. He was tired in a way he had never known. His mind felt full, but his heart was sunken and empty.

"Corin, tell me what you saw. How did you retrieve the sun gem?"

Corin shook his head. "I didn't."

He stepped to the wall and pushed aside the shards of glass. He slumped down hard on the floor, leaning against a glowing, iron beam. He tried to speak calmly, but he felt his eyes puff and flare and his sinuses warm and fill. Through ragged breaths he explained that Lorenzo was dead, taken by the black beast they thought they had slain. He told his grandfather of the tangle of crystal roots and the cold, clear flame that had swallowed them both. He described the ice in his blood and the surreal pain in his mind. He spoke of the crystal's terrifying vision, rescuing Darrow and the girl, and the rotting smell in the guard's flesh that had reminded him of the beast's putrid wound. He described how they too had been healed by the crystal, but mostly he just cried. He cried out of shame and weakness, and he cried for Lorenzo.

The old man listened. He never spoke, and he never interrupted. He knelt down by Corin and let his grandson weep. When the words stopped, and his wails cooled into silent puffs and trembles, the old man wrapped his arms around his grandson and held him close. For the first time, Corin realized just how cold he had been.

He gently pulled back from his grandfather and leaned his shoulders against the beam. He closed his eyes and breathed through his nose, his nerves finally settling.

"Corin," Lehonti offered, "I know this is more than you can take right now, but I need to speak with you. If what you have told me is true, then we have to act immediately."

Corin opened his eyes and stared at the sun gem, its light pulsing and growing. It felt so alive, so busy: like it was engaged in some incomprehensible task.

"We thought this day might never come, Corin," Lehonti muttered. "We hoped that we would be safe forever. Over three hundred years we grew negligent and lost our caution. We stopped telling the old stories, and our history became superstition. But that is why I am here. There must always be one who remembers. When the world grows forgetful, it is my job to tear open the scar and reveal the splinter still buried within."

"Grandfather," Corin muttered, "what *is* that gem?"

The old man smiled and shook his head. "I don't have the faintest idea… but I *do* know where it came from." The old man stood and offered his hand to Corin. "Come with me, son."

CHAPTER 17

THE MURAL

TOGETHER, THE TWO DESCENDED THE LADDER and the stairway. Inside, the tower's beams had all been lit up once more, the swirling designs perfectly illuminating their path. Corin gazed around in wonder.

"No one ever sees this…" Corin gently lamented.

Lehonti shook his head. "It's a travesty… It truly is. The tower used to be open to the public. Now only the elders and highest guards are permitted within these lonely walls. The last council declared that allowing citizens access might become a *security hazard*. In reality, though, they believed it entertained *flagrant fantasies that might prove dangerous to progress*, to use their words from the official report. What baca chips. Your great-grandfather fought their decision, but in the end the majority ruled against him. For more than fifty years, this chamber has remained silent and forgotten, and with it, we have lost our capacity to learn from the past."

The familiar lecture was taking on new strength and purpose in Corin's mind. He could not explain what he had seen, but neither could he comprehend what his grandfather was explaining. Not yet, at least. Perhaps the two mysteries would meet in the middle.

"What is this tower, Grandfather? I don't think I understand its purpose."

"Of course, you don't, my boy! No one does!" Lehonti laughed bitterly and threw his hands about the enormous, cylindrical chamber. "It is a relic of the past. It is something ancient and sacred, something designed to encourage us to never forget! So, naturally, we have all forgotten. It has become a part of our lives as common as the rising and setting of the sun. We never question what we have always known. We lose our curiosity with our clubbed tails. We become frustrated searching for answers on our own, and we are scolded for asking too much when we are young. Thus, the truth is pushed ever further from our reach..."

"Yes, but Grandfather, *what is it?*" Corin suppressed a groan. He needed answers, not philosophy. "Why was it built? What is it actually for?"

The old man stopped and whipped around. "Have you heard nothing I have said? This tower was built to help us remember, and it was built to save us when we forget!"

The elder pressed on.

Corin frowned deep in his brow, trying to understand his grandfather's cryptic words. "Alright... Then what is it we were meant to remember?"

"Now *that*," Lehonti laughed, "is a question I have waited a lifetime for someone to ask me. Look out there, Corin. Look out over our people's forgotten memories." Lehonti pointed down to the vast floor of the tower. They were still a hundreds of meters from the bottom of the stairway, but the whole room was now clearly lit by the curious etchings in the tower's metal skeleton. Corin could see the massive mural in its entirety, the thousands of colored tiles seamlessly weaving together a vivid, horrifying picture. They were arranged in a perfect circle, with Centile's sun and sword crest framed in the center, the tip of its blade pointing to the double door entrance, and the six points of the crest's sun dividing the mural into six pointed slices.

"What is this, Grandfather?"

The old man smiled. "The history of our people. Our records say that it took ten artists seven years to finish the whole masterpiece. It was meant to preserve the story of Vallin and the great war."

They continued down the steps to the face of the mural. Corin's eyes darted wildly along the work. The color was dimmer than it must have once been, but the images were still vibrant and sharp. The sheer enormity of the project was what impressed him the most. It's size really couldn't be appreciated from the ground. Each tile was smaller than the tip of a thumb, and yet they laid out full telaks and sweeping vistas in intricate detail.

"It's incredible," he whispered.

The old man smiled and nodded. "It is truly breathtaking. Unfortunately, the story it tells is not one of beauty. Come, stand there first. Tell me what you see."

Following the old man's summons, Corin descended the last few steps and stood before a portion of the giant mural. Depicted in the tiles was a woman. She was young, maybe in her twenties, but her skin looked worn and frail. Her features were far older than her physique. Her short years had no doubt been ones of great grief. Two children were clinging to her, their pointed ears and unbloomed tails pulled low and tight in practiced caution. A young girl rested on her hip while the boy leaned against her thigh. Their backs were pressed against the bare frame of a ragged, dead tree.

With a shock, Corin realized that this little family was not alone in the scene.

All along the sides were creatures. Most of them portrayed as black shadows lurking in the distance, barely distinguishable from the broken foliage that surrounded them. They were everywhere: mounted on rocks, flying through the sky, there was even one sitting atop the family's tree. Its frame looked almost like a telak, but its legs were shorter with less joints. Its face was flat, with slit nostrils and wide, watery eyes. Its body was naked, and its skin seemed to be pulled too tightly over its protruding bones. By all means, this creature looked dead… All but the eyes. Those watery, swollen eyes held a dim light in them. They were grey and chaotic, like a storm cloud.

The memory crashed back into him. Those were the eyes of the beast, the eyes that had killed Lorenzo. Corin turned to his grandfather, but the words choked up in his throat. The old man took a quivering breath and then stepped out onto the far side of the scene.

"I know…" he whispered, patting Corin's shoulder as he walked the length of the image. "See here, son. Recently, I have become quite intrigued by one, particular character in this rendition."

Corin stepped to his side and the rest of the world seemed to fall away at the surreal sight.

At Lehonti's feet, skulking in the background of the image, was a long, six-limbed, woolly creature with twisting horns and massive, sunken eyes. Corin could feel his features go limp as he stared into an almost perfect likeness of his nightmare. That was it. It had to be it. There was nothing else that looked even remotely like that beast.

"You knew?" Corin shook his head and looked up at the glowing frame of the tower. "The elders knew for all these years… How could it be sitting right here at our feet? How could that thing be *right here* in the middle of the city, and yet *no one had ever seen it before?*"

Corin felt his anger rising with his voice. He realized that what he was feeling was a chance to redirect his guilt. Something else could have saved his brother. This knowledge might have spared him.

Lehonti stared at the tiles with hands clasped thoughtfully behind him. "I have tried, my boy. For all the years of my appointment as elder, I have tried to convince this city to remember the past. There is an ancient adage written in the archives. It states that those who forget the past are doomed to repeat it. I have truly failed, Corin. I am *He Who Remembers*, he who is meant to keep these stories alive, but I was always dismissed as a nuisance to progress. And now this day has come. The great day of my failure. I ha–"

"Tell me everything, Grandfather," Corin spat. "I'm ready to listen. What are we up against?"

Lehonti glanced up with high brows. "Corin, I–"

"Tell me *everything* you know," Corin pressed. "Please."

The old man's shock melted away with a nod, and he smiled bitterly at his grandson. "No one knew what they were, or where they came from. All the records in the archives say they sprang up overnight and swept down any resistance placed before them. In a matter of weeks, the world was overrun. They were called by many names in many lands. In our own records they are sometimes called *creatures of the void* or the *dark ones*, but most commonly history labels them as *demons*."

As his grandfather spoke, Corin's eyes drifted up the image. The tiled sky was dark, almost black, but the artists had managed to sculpt motion and tumult into its static surface. As he stared, the memories of his repeated dream rushed back to his mind. He saw the clouds: horrible, black clouds racing across the plains. The storm was coming, almost upon them. He could feel it, see it in his mind. They had to act before–

"Are you alright, son?"

Corin jerked alert and nodded. He stepped back, trying to better examine the whole mural. "Do we know now?"

"Know now?" Lehonti looked puzzled. "Know what?"

"You said no one knew what they were or where they came from. Do we now?"

"Ah... well." The old man sighed. "I'm afraid we still know very little about them. Come with me."

Lehonti walked to the left, moving around the edge of the mural to the next scene. It was a cross-section of a large underground cavern. Telaks were moving along every surface, tending to a herd of bacas, carrying baskets of corn, and drawing water from a well at the floor of the cavern. A small village of animal skin huts had been built at the cavern's base, and at its center, mounted on an altar of wood, sat the sun gem. In the artist's interpretation, the crystal floated above the wood, a perfectly cut jewel.

It was a bright, gold color and cast a pure, white light throughout the cave. At the entrance, the cavern was guarded by a group of telaks wielding spears. Just beyond the edge of the gem's light, several black creatures sat and waited.

"Apparently our ancestors found shelter in some sort of cavern… I'd give my tail to know where, but…" He sighed and rubbed at his tired eyes. "Regardless, somewhere deep inside they discovered the sun gem and built a new life for themselves. Not much has been written about this, but it seems clear that the gem's light repulsed the demons and allowed our people to survive while the world rotted around them."

Corin stared at the image, darkly fascinated by the creatures prowling the entrance. "What are they doing?"

Lehonti shrugged. "I'm not sure. You have to understand, Corin, I have spent a *lifetime* trying to interpret this mural, and what I'm telling you is just what I have pieced together from the few shabby records our people have retained. You would be *astonished* at how little anyone wrote back then…" He glanced back down at the sprawling chaos depicted under his toes. "Anyway, there is one, brief entry that describes rules and cautions for hunters. I assume it must have been necessary for small parties to leave the cave once in a while, possibly in search of food and supplies. According to this record, these groups were to stick together and follow three rules. First, never be seen. Second, never be smelt. Third, never bleed. Apparently, these creatures hunted mostly by smell, particularly the smell of blood. If one caught the scent of your blood you were instructed to lead it as far from your group as possible, never back to the cavern."

"That's awful," Corin whispered as he studied the picture. He mulled over his grandfather's words, considering the bleak rules. The guards at the front were staring down a vicious pack of demons, and yet they didn't look anxious or alert. They just looked tired. They stared weakly at the pacing monsters beyond.

"Is that what happened here?" Corin asked. "In the picture? Did someone lead these things back home?"

The old man shrugged. "Your guess is as good as mine, son."

"How long did they live like this? Just… hiding in this cave?"

"It could have been years. It could have been centuries. Nothing exists from before the demons, you see. Any records of the old world have since been… *erased from history*." Lehonti muttered the words like they were a string of curses. "But we do know that eventually something extraordinary happened. Look here."

Lehonti pointed out past the scene to another slice of the mural. The whole image seemed like it might have been built of nothing but white and yellow tiles. Corin moved in front of it and his mind fell to reverent stillness.

This was the portion of the mural he had seen before.

This was the image of Vallin.

"You see it don't you?" whispered the old man. "You see his face, yes?"

Corin couldn't answer. Even knowing that it was there, seeing his own features perfectly depicted in the mural was still overwhelming. It was the most striking likeness of himself he had ever encountered. It was like an ancient, tiled reflection. He might have been standing at the edge of a pool. Corin forced himself to look past Vallin's face, to examine the surrounding image as well. The ancient hero was knelt down beside the sun gem. In his hands he was holding a sword that shone as bright and golden as the crystal before it. The whole village was gathered around the scene, stunned looks on every face.

Lehonti chuckled. "What you are looking at, my son, is one of the few visual depictions we have of our famous ancestor."

Corin hesitated at first, thinking back on Lorenzo's mocking dismissal, but the need to know grew and grew within him. This couldn't be coincidence.

"I'm not crazy, right?" Corin asked. "He really looks just like me, doesn't he grandfather?"

"Yes, Corin. He certainly does."

Corin nodded and exhaled. "But how? This is hundreds of years old, but… I mean, it's like they were looking at *me* when they made this…"

"Yes, I know." The old man smiled. "I have wanted to bring you here for some time, but your father thought it best to not fill your head with any of my *wild fantasies*."

"He's seen the mural?"

"Of course, he has!" Lehonti snapped. "He's *my* lump of a son, after all! Corin, I showed him all of this years ago when I still hoped he might take my place as elder one day."

Corin shook his head. "But… how could he not tell me about this? How could he know and keep it to himself?"

Lehonti laid a gentle hand on Corin's shoulder. "Your father has always been remarkably stubborn. He believes that we see what we want to see. Some things are merely chance to him. Some things have a reasonable explanation. Perhaps he's right. Maybe it is reasonable to accept that after ten generations the line of Vallin might happen to recreate his face in yours."

"But what do you believe, Grandfather?"

The old man stepped away to the next scene. "I believe that what you told me upstairs has confirmed something I have held in my mind for years. I believe that history is repeating itself, and I believe that you are fated to save us."

Corin froze. "What? *Save?* What are you saying, Grandfather?"

Lehonti offered a loving yet firm smile to his grandson. "Corin, please. *Think* about what has happened! Think about what you have told me! You heard a voice, did you not? You saw a vision! What is done cannot be undone. Is that not what you said? You have been chosen, child."

Corin shook his head. "No, that's ridiculous. Do you even hear yourself? Chosen? Chosen by what?"

"Heaven. The universe. The sun gem. I don't know, Corin. But you must see what I am telling you, yes?" The old man's eyes were frantic. "More than three hundred years ago, when our world was in danger, Vallin was chosen to defend it. The same signs have been revealed. History has truly repeated its course, and here we now stand, at the very evidence of its repetition." Lehonti threw his finger down at the mural, letting the image do his accusing for him.

"So, what are we going to do about it, boy?" The old man paused to glare and flare his nostrils. "Because unless you're lying to me, Corin, something reached out to you on the plains! Something gave you a mission. Something saw your courage and placed our fate upon your shoulders. Those are not my words! That is how *you* described it. So, I ask you again. What are *you* going to do about it?"

Corin could not speak. That same piercing surety that had hit him on the plains was hitting him now. Something in his mind would not let the old man's words fall to the floor. With a strange knowledge that came more from within than without, Corin knew that all of this was true. And that was more terrifying than anything Corin had seen or felt on the plains. His heart pumped wildly, and adrenaline shot through his flesh as the stress of it all folded onto him.

"Corin?" the old man pressed.

"I don't know, yet."

Lehonti sighed, the blush of shame rising in his pointed ears. He swallowed and shook his head. "I'm sorry, Corin… I didn't mean to… This is more than anyone should ha–"

"I need to know more."

The elder glanced up. "More?"

Corin nodded. "Tell me more. Tell me everything. About Vallin. About the demons. What happened? How did he win?"

Corin blinked and realized that fresh tears were trailing his face. When had that happened? He wiped them away and clenched his teeth. He had been asked what he would do, and he had decided. He would keep going. He would keep learning. He felt like he was running down a hill, going much faster than he was able to maintain. If he stopped now, he would crash. If he paused to consider his chances, he would fall. There was nothing left to decide. Run or fall. That was it…

And he would keep running.

When Corin looked up at his grandfather, he saw that the old man's eyes were filled with tears as well.

"Don't ever feel alone in this, my boy. You never will be."

Corin nearly rolled his eyes, but instead he nodded. "I know."

The old man sniffed hard and blinked. "Well then, what happened next? The songs and stories are very clear on *what*, but they fail to mention *how*. You know the words, my boy:

"And when the darkness gathered in, and all that's
   good was lost to sin,
"Dear Vallin saw our need that it was dire."
"He feared no horror of the night. He fought for us with
   all his might,
"And from his task his heart did never tire."
"But all the world was filled with blight, and clouds of
   death obscured his sight,
"So, Heaven blessed him with a sword all filled with fire,
"Yes, Heaven blessed him with a sword of fire."

Corin studied the tiles as the familiar lyrics came to life before him.

They were not nearly as metaphorical as he had supposed.

Like the last scene, Vallin held a golden sword in this image. He and a group of telak warriors were walking through a swamp of some sort. They were entirely encompassed by demons, but the creatures seemed to be cringing in pain and keeping their distance beyond the circle of light. Vallin was standing in the lead, the filthy water up to his hips, and the burning sword held high over his head.

When the old man's dusty voice finished reciting the words, Corin gestured to the mural.

"A sword of fire?" he repeated as he gestured to the image. "But what *is* it, Grandfather?"

"It is the sword of Vallin." Lehonti shrugged. "There's not much more to it than that. I already told you, son. We know what but not how. Vallin was able to transfer the light of the sun gem into his blade, or at least that's what seems to be happening. With the power of the sword, he was able to light a path in the demons' darkness, searching for help. It is said that Vallin's golden blade was the only instrument capable of actually causing the demons pain."

"That's it… *That's* what happened," Corin whispered to himself. Realizing how odd that sounded, Corin turned to his grandfather.

"That beast, the one that took the sun gem! It started acting… strange once it had the crystal. It was shaking its head and crashing into things. It was like it couldn't see where it was going, but there was nothing we could do to hurt it. Lorenzo nearly sliced the thing's leg off, but it just kept running."

The old man shook his head, as if to shed the horror of the thought. "Well, that is consistent with the stories. The records say the demons were a type of living death. Rotting bodies that did not sleep or eat. They felt neither pain nor cold. They lived only to hunt, and they feared only the gem's light. Didn't you say that you two thought you had killed it out on the plains?"

Corin nodded. "Yeah, we did. It passed out just before it got to that dark, twisted patch. We thought it must have been from blood loss."

The old man considered this for a moment. "I'm not sure what to make of that. It's clear from the stories that warriors other than Vallin were capable of killing demons, but there's no mention of how."

"Other warriors," Corin whispered. "You had said before that Vallin went searching for help?"

Lehonti nodded and smiled. "I did. And he found it."

The old man motioned to the next scene of the mural. It depicted a top-down view of a horrific battle. At the far, pointed end of the scene was that mass of twisted, violet crystal. The artist had included wispy, white lines flowing up from it. Clawed torsos and horned heads protruded from gaps in the lines, like hands and faces parting an invisible curtain.

Down further, the demons were in a massive throng, almost like a pulsing stream of insects tumbling over each other. Near the edge of the tiles, Vallin and his army fought. His golden sword was bursting through a fallen horned beast that was screaming at his feet, its body engulfed in white flames. Hundreds of others were fighting beside him. At first, Corin saw only the telak warriors, but as he studied the mural, he noticed others. Some of the fighters had pale, cream-colored skin with slate blue streaks down their backs and arms. They were tailless creatures with only a single set of knees.

With a start, he realized that what he had initially mistaken for boulders on the battlefield were actually warriors as well. They were massive, grey creatures, wielding steel axes and wooden staffs.

"Are those the other races?" Corin asked. "The ones across the sea?"

The old man smiled. "Indeed. The people of the mountains and the people of the sea. You might know them as the golems and the sprites, yes? Though I have heard they are not fond of our nicknames for them. Proud and mysterious peoples. Both of them."

Corin was fascinated by what he saw, and also disgusted at his own ignorance. He had heard that there were other intelligent races far across the Great Sea, but he had never *seen* one before. Not many telaks had. The lands beyond the plains were not a topic commonly addressed in Centile.

"I had always imagined them being more," Corin fumbled with his words, "you know. Like *us*... Ordinary people, just... from a different climate, you know?"

Lehonti laughed. "Just because they look different doesn't mean they're not like us, son. We owe the golems, especially, more than I can say. Most of our raw ore comes from our trade with them across the sea. Our records tell us that they were the ones who built this tower for us, as a gift to honor Vallin."

"And the sprites?"

His grandfather shrugged. "No one really knows. We were able to maintain some frail trade relations with the golems, but I don't think a telak has seen a water sprite for more than two hundred years. Barriers of language and distance, you see. Both races live on the far side of the ocean. Only a handful of merchants are brave enough to make the voyage each season. They occasionally bring back stories, but things have been quiet for some time. I'm afraid that after Vallin's victory, our peoples became rather insular. The telaks stayed on the plains, and the other races returned to their homes to the east."

"But what brought them together in the first place? How did Vallin find them?"

Lehonti laughed again. "Corin, you sound so much like me. You are asking all the questions I have spent a *lifetime* trying to answer. I am afraid that what you see here is all we know. There is tragically little written about Vallin and his journeys. He never kept a memoir, and truth has been lost to lyrics. All we know is that he left with a handful of warriors and returned years later with an army that changed the future. One that could break the demon ranks and snuff them at their source."

The old man motioned to the twisting, purple rock at the tip of the scene. "You've seen that, haven't you, Corin? The demon source?"

Corin nodded, and the sight made him squirm. The artist's interpretation was crude and simple, but that made it all the more horrible. It felt like an idea more than a place, like a symbol of something too terrible to be captured in realism.

"That's where the beast took Lorenzo," Corin muttered. "It jumped into the air and just... *vanished.*"

Lehonti was silent for a moment, quietly watching Corin study the tiles.

"That is where it all began." Lehonti explained. "I imagine it must have been in the exact spot you saw it today. That was where the demons came through. That is how they entered our world. I can't imagine what it must have taken for Vallin to discover that fact, but somehow he learned that the only way to stop the demons was to destroy them at their source."

Stepping tenderly to the next scene, Lehonti folded his arms and stared down into Vallin's face. The great warrior had stabbed his sword into the twisted, purple mass. There was an explosion of light from the blade, and a look of pain on Vallin's face. All around him, the demons were writhing and convulsing and dissolving to dust.

"He was fatally wounded in the process," the old man muttered, "but Vallin finally pushed his way through the demon horde and plunged his sword into their source. The records say that there was a burst of lightning. When the flash faded, the demons were all dead, and the twisted patch on the ground was gone. Vallin's sword remained, though. Sticking out of the soil… its master lifeless beside it."

"Wait," Corin thought for a moment, "if he died that day… then how…"

"How can we be his descendants?" His grandfather finished. The old man smiled bitterly. "Vallin left a family that day he ventured off into the dark. I imagine it must have been the love of those he left behind that drove him to continue. Many times I have considered what it would be like to abandon my wife and son. I have wondered whether or not I would be able to do it."

Corin considered this for a moment. "It was an easy decision," he stated.

Lehonti turned to his grandson with a look of gentle skepticism at his youthful naivety.

"Think about it," Corin began. "If he stayed, he knew that they were all going to die eventually. If he left them… then there was at least a chance he could save them. How could he stay behind and lose that chance? He had nothing left to lose but that hope."

"I believe you may be right, my boy." The old man smiled. "Come. There is one last image."

They walked to the next scene. Having come full circle around the slices of the mural, they now stood just to the side of the double doors. It was a depiction of Centile, though it was much smaller than it stood today. A few, squat buildings were huddled around the central tower, but there was no outer wall and no outer districts. The tower's metal frame was complete, but the top half of the structure had not yet been clothed in stone.

"This city was built in the decades following Vallin's death," Lehonti said, "to honor the fallen hero and to set a watch over these plains. I suspect this tower was intended to be a military fortress for when the demons returned. Can you see the symbolism?" Lehonti mused. "A massive watchtower on the plains, set to guard the future, but built upon this mural of the past." The old man chuckled to himself. "Our ancestors must have been rather poetic, don't you think?"

"I guess," Corin said, gazing up into the tower's glittering heights. "How did they build it?"

Lehonti smiled and stared up into the glowing bones too. "The three races worked together, using lost techniques from across the sea to channel the crystal's light into a shield around the city."

"Just like Vallin did with his sword," Corin whispered.

The old man looked down and nodded to his grandson. "And now, here we are. Three hundred years later, and the long-expected war has returned, but we have forgotten that it even existed in the first place. We were so busy squabbling among ourselves and glutting our bloody pride that we didn't even see the signs."

"Signs?" Corin glanced at the old man.

"Yes. There have been *many* signs," the elder stated. "The weather is changing. Storms have been growing stronger and more frequent. It's like the world is afraid, wailing at us through the wind. Think about Adahy's father Mohe. The outlanders have spotted strange creatures moving out on the plains. Creatures that have attacked them in the night, and the injured have been getting sick… Their flesh has been rotting away at the wound."

"Like that beast…" Corin said, remembering the stench of decay in its black blood.

Lehonti nodded. "Precisely. There have been plenty of signs, and yet we have done nothing. *Thunder and hail!* How could it come to this?" Lehonti spat. "The other elders take me for a superstitious, old fool, but now… *Now* things will be different. They *have* to be. What has been happening in the shadows has finally been brought into the sun. There is no denying it now. A demon has attacked our city and managed to steal the sun gem. We have you as a witness that their source has been restored. The rest of the elders will have *no choice* but to act now that–"

A cold feeling that wasn't quite a shudder whipped across Corin's shoulder. The double doors of the tower were thrown open with a metallic shriek.

A dozen guards rushed into the room, surrounding Corin and Lehonti.

"Indeed, you *have* forced us to act."

It was a deep, pleasant voice calling from the doorway. The guards parted, and Elder Morten stepped into the tower. His features were rigid, and his eyes were fixed on Corin.

"Detain the traitor," he ordered.

The room exploded into pandemonium as three guards rushed Corin at once.

He gasped in pain as a spear shaft cracked against his skull. His body lurched forward, and his arms were wrenched behind his back.

Corin heard his grandfather shouting protests to the guards, but his ears were ringing too much for him to make out the words. There was a brief flash of uncertainty in the guards' eyes as several realized they were receiving contradictory commands from two different elders. It passed quickly. Corin felt his own voice grunt and gasp in his throat as his wrists were bound behind him. He could see his grandfather screaming into Morten's face, the veins in his neck popping as he roared at the captain of the guard.

Corin could *see* it all, but his ears felt stuffy.

He felt, more than heard, the crackling sound in his shoulder, the pop of the bone shifting too far in its socket. The motion was met with a jolt of pain as the guards jerked too hard on his restraints. Corin thrashed involuntarily, kicking a guard square in the chest.

He paid dearly for it.

Corin felt his body seize up as a fist sank into his abdomen. His mouth was gagged as he tried to scream. A blindfold was cinched across his temples as his blurry eyes searched the room for his grandfather. He struggled, trying to break free of the burly arms gripping him, but the guard behind him slipped Corin's neck into the crook of his elbow.

He gasped and tried to scream, but his eyes went dark.

PART THREE

PRECIOUS IN THY SIGHT

CHAPTER 18

SOMETHING MUCH BIGGER

THE SUN WAS WARM AND WELCOME ON OLENKA'S skin, but despite the heat she was still shivering away the deep's frigid touch. It was like her bones hadn't quite thawed. She stretched out along the powdery sand, feeling the sea ebb and whisper all around her aching body.

It was a solitary island, if it could even be *called* an island. It was more like a sandbar that managed to crest the swell. Nothing more than an old atoll mounted on the remains of an ancient reef. But who cared? The sun was warm, the tide was just right, and most importantly, she had found a place to be alone.

Olenka held up her left arm, stretching her hand out to the sun and casting a meager shadow across her face. She studied the blue shine of the light dancing through the webbing between her fingers. Her skin was still streaked and blotchy from the diving sickness, but she would heal quickly. She always did.

She was just grateful that she could still use all her limbs.

Olenka laid her forearm across her eyes, shading them from the glare. It was a good day to rest, and after all that had happened, Olenka deserved the break. Marikit and Diwala were back at the wharf working their charm with the tall miner jewelry. Olenka had stayed long enough to help them unload and set up, but that was all she was willing to do today.

And if Di and Mari didn't like it? Well, then they could fight her.

It was for the best, really. Even on a good day Olenka's distaste for crowds scared away most of the customers drawn to Marikit's allure. Haggling and advertising simply were not her roles in the crew. Mari was charming, Di was tough, and Olenka was smart. It was a powerful balance, and sirena crews needed to play to their strengths.

Making a living on the Great Sea was not especially difficult, the tide alone could provide for any ugkoy with half a brain and a net, but making a name for yourself? And as a sirena? That was the real challenge.

And it was one that Olenka simply could not resist.

She had no idea why she was so obsessed with success. It was a stupid, reckless thirst to prove herself, one that often got the *whole crew* into trouble. Trouble like taking on an entire barge of murdering kaizo by themselves. She absolutely had to take responsibility for that shipwreck of a job. It was Olenka who'd demanded they avenge Daisay's murder, Olenka who'd refused to lose their jewels to the sea, and Olenka who'd insisted they take a salvage dive they had no business attempting. Whatever the odds, she just couldn't convince herself to back down.

Maybe it was just for the thrill of it.

Maybe she was trying to prove something to herself.

Or maybe she was sailing through storms just to say she could.

Whatever the reason, it was foolish. She didn't have any excuse for all the risks she took. But Marikit and Diwala, on the other hand, had dreams worth fighting for, and they wore those dreams like tattoos.

Mari was young and beautiful, but she had been born to a poor ugkoy family on the southern coast. Life on the shore had never suited her. She kept the crew up late rambling about her plans to make it to Lunsod sa Dagat. There, in the underwater city, she would find a place of comfort and ease with the kataw. She could start a family, live in wealth, and be forgotten with the rest of those boring, beautiful, city fish faces.

It made Olenka sick.

Diwala couldn't have been more different. She was a warrior, through and through. Her sirena kudori was sharp and jagged: a dozen spears perfectly mounted on her brow. The life of a merchant was too mild for her. She too longed for the holy city, but not for its comforts. She was in it for the challenge. Her dream was to one day join the sacred bushi of Pa Naing. To explore the unknown with kataw divers, to fight for Heaven's glory, to seek the hidden riches that lurked in the crushing black depths, to defend Pa Naing with her dying breath.

But passion and piety could only get her so far. The bushi's recruitment process was tight, and no siokoy or sirena who had not first proven themselves to the monks were ever invited to compete. Di was only a merchant for the experience. She sought wealth and challenge not as a means to retirement, but as a chance to grow stronger, to earn a reputation. Chasing sharks and gutting kaizo was all just a means to a glorious end.

So, what did Olenka work for?

She had asked herself that question more times than she could remember. She hadn't come from poverty like Mari. Quite the opposite, actually. She had no warrior's aspirations like Di. And yet, job after job, she worked harder than the others. She pushed them when they were ready to collapse. She sought out the most dangerous, lucrative jobs. She had made their crew what it was today.

But why? What was she looking for?

Maybe she wasn't looking for anything…

Maybe she was just running…

Olenka growled and flipped over onto her front, resting her face along her forearm. Her white underbelly was too fair for that much direct sunlight, but her back was designed for it. The sand was hot when she first rolled over, and what little water had remained on her skin and clothes sizzled away. She pondered the series of reckless, uzai choices she called her life, and the temperatures in and around her gently equalized. She found herself terribly, dangerously comfortable.

The sea rocked the air with a resonating ambiance and a gentle breeze. The gulls cried their lullaby. The comforting smells of the ocean filled her drifty head, and Olenka was soon asleep.

* * *

THE FAMILIAR PRESSURE OF THE CURRENTS AGAINST HER skin and eyes and ears beckoned her to look and Olenka looked.

She gazed into the shimmers of light that broke around her sight like gossamer in the endless blue. Horror, cold and vivid, pierced her senses as she saw that the water was filled with swirls of something black and viscous and somehow vicious. The black fluid twisted and spread but did not dissipate into the water. It stretched and swayed but would not dissolve or fade. She suddenly realized, or perhaps remembered, that there was a knife in her hand: a serrated blade of polished bone. Olenka lifted the weapon and found that she loathed its sight. It was drenched in the same wretched ink that would not be lost in the water and would not be forgotten from the horror that once more flashed through her chest as Olenka saw the black ooze creeping its way down her knife, slipping closer and closer to her hand. It was almost like it was crawling, scratching, searching, hunting, feeling.

It was almost like it was alive.

She dropped the knife and screamed in the water with a flurry of bubbles that blurred her face and hid her eyes...

...and when her scream became very bright and resounding, deafening in the chilled wind around her, Olenka looked up to see that she was now standing on the wooden floor of a raft. The ship was thrashing wildly: the pontoons on either side crashing hard into the chaotic crests. All around her, the sea was somehow on fire. The

waves of light flicked and jerked with the waves of water beneath them. Great crimson tongues flared around the boat, casting oily plumes of smoke that choked out the sweet, ocean air and obscured the night sky. The greasy black belched and smacked and tasted the clean marine sky that was no longer clean.

Mari and Di were frantically maneuvering around the boat, cutting cords off barrels and dumping their cargo into the inferno. The barrels fell right through the flames, dipping oblivion one brief, bobbing bow before drifting to obscurity below. Olenka felt smoke sting and blur her vision, twisting the light of the fire into distorted shimmers and dim sparks that smeared and stretched the colors around her that were suddenly much brighter than they should have been...

...but, it wasn't the light of the fire anymore.

With striking clarity of both sight and mind, Olenka stared through the azure light of Lunsod sa Dagat. The great city's shield filled in the subterranean tunnels with an impenetrable cerulean barrier, sheltering the massive upside-down castle under the covering of the island above. All around her, sirena and siokoy were diving into the exit pools, all of them heavily armed for battle, all of them streaming great aisles of bubbles through the dark. Olenka was also armed: covered with a thick shirt and hood of pleated scales, with a serrated spear in her grasp.

Through the shield's glare Olenka watched the warriors converge on a convulsing, crashing, coursing spot in the distance. Her heart sank as she saw daiow ika rise from the depths. The massive squid was flailing wildly, like it wasn't fully in control of its body or its mind or its sinister intention that brought it so very, very far up out of the frigid void and into the sacred, blue light of Pa Naing. The sirena and siokoy threw themselves relentlessly toward the monster, one by one being swept away or crushed by the creature's grotesque appendages.

Olenka stared out into the water, trying to see past the distortion of the shield's rippling surface. The squid looked wrong, like it was sick. Its flesh looked grey, with great, black, bulbous veins pushing out to the surface. They were almost like...

...then, in a strange corridor of metal, Olenka stared at a row of beady, black eyes. Flailing corpses shook with rage against their restraints. They were all shackled to the walls, iron cuffs around both their hands and feet. Their mouths chewed at the air in front of them, but they were silent. Olenka gazed at the wretched creatures. They had the same pulsing black veins as daiow ika. The same madness. The same sinister intent. Their muscles were tight against their gaunt limbs and faces. The blue and cream of their skin was grey and streaked like the bleeding patterns of ink leeched through dried drops of water.

But their eyes were the most disturbing detail.

Their pupils were so dilated they seemed to consume everything else. They were dead, hungry eyes, only the faintest glimmer proved them to be more than sunken sockets in a row of empty skulls.

But then the silence became chaos. The iron hall was filled with thunder and lightning and horrible, burning, screaming...

...and Olenka was startled, but she no longer felt afraid. As each image passed through her mind, she became more and more aware of something growing inside her: a purpose of some sort. It was a feeling unlike anything she had ever known, building off her selfish intentions and changing her thirst to prove herself into something clean and pure and noble.

That feeling of purpose grew stronger now as she looked up from the depths at a strange ship crashing in the waves. Cargo was leaping from the wreckage as the swells snapped the ship's wooden beams and ripped the mast from its place on the deck. In a crash of bubbles, Olenka saw a very unusual young man fall from the wreck. He was not Bantay Tubig, but one of the foreign runners of the western plains. His body looked deformed, and Olenka marveled at the impracticality of his awkward legs and water-dragging tail sinking into the sea like a drowned rat.

The boy did not thrash or fight or tread in the water. His body was limp and heavy. Olenka swam up to meet him and took him in her arms. As she held him, she looked into his unconscious face, and a wave of memories, none of them particularly pleasant, overtook her.

It was the face of the ancient hero...

...and that shock and horror and disgust lingered and grew and festered inside her until Olenka was standing at the edge of a dark pool with vegetation of all kinds growing all around her on every surface all around her and there was no sun or ocean or breeze anywhere around her, but there was a sound. A sound that was also all around her, but somehow inside her. It was the sound of frantic, desperate, perfect, balanced life. As she stepped into the dark pool of water, her body began to tingle and burn. She lifted her hand and watched with terrifying awe as the webbing between her fingers began to recede: the very color of her skin changing before her eyes. Changing from the creamy sheen of dry sand to the rich brown of damp soil...

...she gasped and looked up to see a sight truly beyond her sight. It was like the swirling light of the night sky, but it was closer, somehow. Closer and much more colorful. Like the smear of sun-dried salt stained onto black fabric, and like the life and energy of the reef, and like the deepest, coldest depths of the crushing sea below the currents. But there was something within that darkness, something beyond it, something trying to punch its way through the very fabric of existence.

Something coiling.

Something writhing.

Something elegantly hidden.

But there was also glory there in the dark. Standing in that empty void before her were two beings of pure light and radiance.

They were filled with it, quickened by it. They were impossibly beautiful, and their whole frames trembled with courage and compassion and competence. These two benevolent gods smiled, and Olenka shook, her whole body filled with indescribable joy and yearning and something more. Much, much more…

She was filled with the undeniable feeling of purpose.

* * *

OLENKA GASPED AND JERKED IN THE SAND, frantically flipping herself into a seated position. The beach was warm and calm all around her, quite oblivious to her brush with the metaphysical. To her amazement, she was still sitting on the beach. The sun was still bright. The breeze was still gentle. Everything was still exceptionally, painfully peaceful everywhere she looked.

But none of it brought her comfort.

Olenka stood too quickly, her legs and heart quivering, and she placed her hands on her hips to steady herself. She faced the sun and closed her eyes, trying to relax her breathing. She focused on her bodily senses: the warmth of the light, the sound of the sea, the smell of the salt, the absolute fatigue in her joints.

"Take stock of the moment," she whispered. "Clear your mind of all distractions…"

As soon as she had calmed herself Olenka looked around at the beach where she had lain, evaluating the memory with a calm, fresh perspective. What had happened? Had she been asleep?

She looked down at her torso and wiped the sand from her skin and clothing. She must have been dreaming. She must have had a nightmare, right? Of course. Just a silly dream.

But it had been so much more than a dream.

Who was she trying to fool? The images she had seen were things her mind *never* could have crafted on its own, and the emotions she felt… It was like the knowledge of a lifetime compressed into a series of sights and sounds and poignant flares of feeling. They felt like memories. Memories of things that had not yet happened.

The sun was still in its same place in the heavens, but Olenka felt as if she had experienced hours of exhaustion and fatigue. With an abrupt tremor in her knees, Olenka fell to the sand again, quite unable to find the strength to move. She stared at the perfect, cloudless sky, trying to remember what she had seen. It had all been so clear and vivid at the time, but now that she tried to recall it, the images all slipped from her mind, the vision fading faster and faster the harder she grasped for it.

She lifted her hand and watched it shake. She rested it against her chest and felt her heart banging away like a flap of loose sail. Why was she so frightened? What had she seen? She couldn't even remember any of it now… She tried to sit up again but fell back in a dizzy, helpless slump.

Eventually, Olenka came to the very reasonable conclusion that she must be working too hard. These crazy delusions were nothing more than her overworked brain processing the stress of almost being murdered by pirates. Since it seemed to be the responsible thing to do, and since she was too exhausted to do otherwise, she closed her eyes and tried to remedy her malady by getting some sleep.

Sleep, however, would not find her.

It was hours before Olenka found the strength and mental capacity to move. When she did, the sun had dropped considerably, ushering in the hottest part of the day. She walked to the water's edge, testing her strength, and sat down in the rising tide. The sea was cool and refreshing and helped to wake her rattled mind. She cupped her hands and splashed the water against her face and neck, running her fingers down the long, matted locks of her hair. It was time to get back to Sotay Wharf.

Olenka stood and stretched out her legs and shoulders. She breathed in and out once, twice, and then held it. An experienced sirena like Olenka could hold her breath for a full fifteen minutes if she took the time to prepare. She reached her arms over her head, stretching out her rib cage, letting the air fill the very bottom of her lungs, feeling the blood pumping from her face to her fins.

And then she dove.

The edge of the atoll was shallow, but in the space of a single kick it pulled away into a black drop. Olenka skimmed the surface for a moment, but then she went straight for the depths, letting the cold and the pressure clear her mind and sharpen her senses.

Her loose clothes and long, unbound hair pulled against her strokes, but that was what she wanted. When her crew was on a job, she always wore her fish-skin vest and hood. The gear cut her water resistance down extensively, but it was also miserably uncomfortable. On her days off she wore a simple shirt and skirt of fitted cloth, and she *always* let her hair flow free. As she swam, her matted locks spun and twirled nearly a meter behind her in the tropical water. The added resistance was an excellent workout. If she could swim well like this today, then she would race the wind tomorrow.

Before her, Olenka could see the edges of the Karafuru Reef. The ancient coral was piled high with vibrant fronds and anemones. Vast schools of fish swarmed its surface, shooting along its contours with synchronized precision. Everywhere around her, there was life and there was color. The grasses below were filled with crustaceans, the water above her twisted with the shimmer of a million scales in the sun, and the reef ahead blossomed with folded patterns of violet, pink, and gold.

Olenka smiled. This was her world. This was where she truly felt at home. The ugkoy seemed content with their fins in the sand, and the kataw hid themselves away in their bubble of light, but the siokoy and sirena had found a life filled with far greater riches. Here in the water there was no cruelty. There was no filth or toil. There was only freedom. Everything about the reef was a beautiful and unforgiving balance. In one moment, a sirena could be bewitched by the beauty and serenity of the reef, and in another she could find herself with the spines of a fire-fish through her fin. It was not a place for the weak or foolish, and it filled Olenka with a deep and abiding *sense of meaning*...

In a flash, the memory of her dream split across her mind.

Olenka didn't see or hear anything, but she *felt* something powerful. She remembered what she'd *felt* in the dream. She had found purpose in it. *True purpose*. Not this shallow communion with nature, or her reckless thirst for danger. This was deep and profound, but it was also perfectly distracting... Painfully unsettling...

Suddenly, her underwater paradise felt empty, and that unpleasant thought scratched over and over at her mind until she coughed up her breath of air and had to chase the bubbles to the surface.

Her face broke through the water and she gasped. She floated for a moment, panting. It was such a strong, profound sensation, and yet she had immense difficulty wrapping her mind around it. It was like she had stumbled upon the answer to her heart's deepest desire. A trained, ethereal eye had searched out her greatest weakness and brutally exploited it.

Olenka ran her hands over her face, wiping the salty water away from her eyes. In the distance she could see dozens of green islands painting the horizon. She focused on them, trying to find her feelings.

"Okay, time to talk this chum out..." she whispered. With no one but the gulls to hear her, Olenka often spoke to herself.

"I saw the reef... and it made me, what? Happy? No, the reef *always* makes me happy... I wasn't thinking about the reef at all. I was thinking about how the reef made me *feel*... Feel like I belong..."

Olenka stopped. The thought had gone too far. There were very few topics in this world that made Olenka uncomfortable, but she was getting dangerously close to one of them.

Fate.

She shook her head and teased out her hair. Time to refocus. She thought about the warmth of the sun and the contrast of the breeze on her wet cheeks. She thought about the drag of her hair and her webbed feet pushing against the water. She pictured it, feeling the way her toes curled around the water, imagining it being shoved down to the seabed in twisting balls. She pictured the reef and its balance. She was a part of that balance. She was at one with the world around her. This was *where she belonged...*

With that thought, the feeling struck her again. It was almost palpable, like her consciousness had brushed up against a great void she had been neglecting in her mind. There was something there, something her mind was trying to show her. Her reality became hollow and empty again. Everything she loved felt trivial and small...

And then a voice came to her from within.

There is so much more than this reef. Things have finally been set in motion, and what is done cannot be undone. The sum of all future ages has been placed upon your shoulders. But first, you must not forget what you have seen.

Olenka was unable to move.

Her subconscious kept her fins gently flicking, but her body buoyed steadily and helplessly in the water. The voice had been so clear in her mind, much more than a passing thought. It was the same voice she had felt on the kaizo barge, the one that told her she wouldn't die on that buwisit deck.

The message struck her to the core, seeming to weave itself deep into the very fibers and sinews of her restless soul. As a child she had always been desperate for more. A voracious appetite for adventure had compelled her to leave her pampered life and seek out something more robust, something surprising and new. She had spent her life seeking out a niche, or perhaps purposefully crafting one.

But no matter where she lived or what she did, Olenka had never truly felt complete. She had spent years of her life searching for that one, perfect, Olenka-shaped hole in the world that it was her undeniable destiny to fill, and she had long ago dismissed the search as futile fancy and entombed the dream deep within her heart. She was older and wiser now. She knew that it was no more than a silly, little girl's dream. It was just the tug of her bored spirit against her pride, trying to validate her inborn certainty that she was exceptional.

And yet, here were those same, tired, childhood feelings. The voice had exhumed them.

But the feelings felt fresh and new and, most dangerous of all, they were *hopeful*. They somehow felt possible, undimmed by their years in the crypt. Despite herself, Olenka cradled those feelings. Despite her better judgment, she delicately cupped that dream in the palms of her mind. It seemed purer now, clearer and more refined, but it was still obviously that same youthful dream: the desire to belong somewhere. It was still the same urge to feel needed, to be a part of something much bigger than the reef or the crew or even the Bantay Tubig.

But it was a dream that had grown up.

"*Fine,*" Olenka growled, "but only for one last job. I'll go searching this one, last, uzai time…"

CHAPTER 19

THE MARK OF HEAVEN

THE WATER AROUND THE WHARF ALWAYS FELT warmer somehow. It was no different from any other part of the reef, but Olenka swore she could feel the temperature rise around her the closer she got to Sotay. As she swam the length of Karafuru Reef, Olenka began to see the familiar markers. The local siokoy had driven brightly painted stakes into the coral to guide travelers back to civilization.

For Olenka, they marked the end of privacy.

As if on cue, there was motion off to her left and Olenka noticed two fishermen ugkoy hauling a tied net bursting with the day's catch. Ahead she could see the bobbing shadows of bancas being steered toward the docks, and in only a few meters the sea went from quiet and secluded to the rippling, echoing marketplace din of Sotay Wharf.

Olenka kicked hard and tucked in her arms, letting the force of the thrust slip her away from the reef. The water shallowed, and the colors of the reef melted into shimmers of sunlight dancing across the barren sand and isolated patches of porous rock. There were boats all around her now, dotting the seafloor with their silhouettes. Through the blue haze Olenka spotted the maze of wooden poles that was the pier.

The sounds from above penetrated the watery world below, vibrating through Olenka's ears in dull, muted echoes. She slipped between the poles of the docks, avoiding the jagged barnacles, and listening carefully. Several docks down, Olenka heard what she was listening for. Marikit's singsong voice was clear and penetrating even through the water.

Olenka gently slipped against a pole, hiding in the shadow of the walkway. She lifted her head carefully from the water, peering up onto the dock. Mari and Diwala were there, each standing before a table of their rare mountain jewelry. Mari's whistling voice was actively overselling their product to a pack of older ugkoy women.

It was a strange thought, but Olenka realized that if she and Mari hadn't been such good friends, then she probably would have hated her. She was thin, sweet, and ferociously flirty. Her voice was high and honeyed, and her clothes were always sheer and sparse. She wore her hair in the traditional matted locks, same as Diwala and Olenka, but they were much thinner than theirs. Dressed for market, she had them braided and twisted back into ornate rows that curled and swirled around her head and neck, sitting elegantly along her collarbone in a neat, spiral tail that never ceased to annoy Olenka.

And Olenka simply couldn't resist the opportunity.

* * *

"I DON'T KNOW," AN OLD WOMAN MUTTERED. "I USED TO have a necklace just like this, many years ago, and it didn't cost *half* as much…"

Mari smiled and shifted the strand of metal into the sunlight. "I'm sure it didn't, and here's why. Come closer. Do you see that? Look at the light here. That is the light of mountain rubies. It's not something you can fake with glass. My crew just brought these south from the giant stone miners themselves! You have to go deep into their caves to find these gems. Here, feel it. Can't you feel the power of the mountains in this necklace?"

The old woman's face was skeptical, but Mari was clearly getting to her. She felt the gem for just a moment longer than would have been a casual brush.

"Nothing, and I mean *nothing*, stands out in a crowd like these rubies," Marikit declared. "Would you like to try them on?"

The old woman was cautious, but she took the necklace. Mari quickly skittered around behind her and fastened up the brass clasp.

"There. Oh! It suits you… Sister, it suits you *wonderfully*."

The old woman glanced down, feeling the weight of the rubies on her chest. She sighed and tried to subtly assess the meager bulge of her pouch at her waist.

"I don't think I can go the full thirty barya, child. Would you take twenty and five?" The old woman looked defeated. The necklace had her hooked.

Mari pouted and pressed a fist to her chin. "Well, twenty and five barely covers the shipping and marketing expenses for a piece this rare. Getting it out of the deep mountains alone takes… Well, I do have some other, albeit slightly *less impressive*, pieces that I could let go for that low. Perhaps you would care to–"

"Twenty scales and seven bhai, then. But that is as high as I can go."

Mari smiled. "Alright, but only because it would be a shame to pass this piece off to someone who appreciated it any less than you."

Coins were exchanged, and Mari bowed to her victim. Olenka smirked. She kicked off the shallow seafloor and grabbed the straps of Marikit's skirt. She shrieked and tumbled and the two of them splashed back into the water.

Mari bubbled out of the water, gasping and screaming.

"*Olenka! Lightning upon you, traitor!*" Mari thrashed away, reaching for her dropped money pouch.

Olenka laughed and wiped the water from her face. "Mari, you are the only sirena I have ever met who hates getting wet."

Marikit turned to Olenka with enough heat to roast a fish. "I do *not* hate getting wet. I hate getting dragged into the uzai water by a mad woman when I am trying *to finalize a buwisit sale!* And look! *Look at my hair!* Do you have *any* idea how long it takes to look presentable for market day? Pull me up, Di."

Diwala somehow managed to look both sympathetic and amused. It was a practiced skill: trying to appease both halves of her crew at once. She reached down, and Mari grabbed one wrist while Olenka grabbed the other. With seemingly effortless force, Diwala pulled the two up high enough for them to get a fin up on the walkway of the wharf.

Olenka chuckled and embraced Diwala. "Thanks, sister. So, how'd you two sharks do today?"

Mari huffed and took a seat on a nearby crate. "Well, assuming you don't scare the rest away, we'll probably get through the last of the jewelry before sunset." Mari twisted her hair, cinching the water out of it. She flicked the drips from her hands and tried to wipe the water from under her eyelashes.

Olenka glanced at the jewelry crate and frowned. "Speaking of which, I thought we agreed to sell the necklaces for twenty silvers each."

Mari stood and smirked, wiping a piece of seaweed from her leg, "No, *you* decided on twenty. I decided that we should actually *get paid* for our effort."

Olenka shook her head and glanced up to Diwala. "And what do you think, Di?"

Diwala rolled back her shoulders and folded her arms, glancing down at the jewelry crate. For those who didn't know her, Diwala was a truly intimidating sight. While the other two had since changed into something more comfortable, Di still wore her fitted fish-skin vest. She had it tightly strung all the way up to her neck, emphasizing her bare, toned, tattooed arms. If it weren't for her feminine figure, she would have looked exactly like a typical siokoy thug from a distance. But Olenka knew her better than that. Her eyes held glittering kindness and curiosity. She was a hard fist but a soft heart.

"I have always been under the impression that if someone is silly enough to buy jewelry, then they are silly enough to pay too much for it. Why should I care how some ugkoy women waste their money? Mari is good at what she does, so I let her do it."

Olenka chuckled and shook her head. "Spoken like a true hunter."

Mari smirked in discomfort. She glanced down at her gaudy, decorated wrists, unsure which side of the fight Diwala had taken.

"So, what are you doing back so early anyway?" Mari turned away as she spoke, going back to messing with her hair. "You should be enjoying your day off! Healing! Not bothering me!"

"Yeah, well… relaxing can be exhausting." Olenka smiled and glanced up at Diwala. She nodded and smiled back. Clearly, she understood.

"Well, why don't you go *not relax* somewhere else? Some of us are busy. Di, can't you go entertain her for a little bit?" Mari flipped her hair back around and started straightening out her wares, loading her table back up with fresh pieces from the crate.

Olenka scoffed and stood up. "Alright, you grumpy crab. I'll make myself scarce."

She turned to leave and Diwala gently caught her arm. "I will come too. I have had just about enough of jewelry for today."

Olenka smiled her approval, and the two walked off down the wharf. It was a beautiful maze of walkways, docked boats, and huts of warped wood. The thinner docks ran out into the sea for the merchants to tie up their boats and unload their stands. Farther toward shore, the docks widened into grand platforms piled high with baskets of rice, vegetables, and spices. Most of the fish were kept alive in net corrals built off the sides of the dock. Crowds lined up to point out their future meal from the tiny school. The fish were gutted, filleted, and thrown straight onto the coals right then and there: always served on a massive, waxy leaf with a heaping mound of white rice and a splash of vinegar.

"So, Olenka, why did you come back so early? Have you found us a new job?"

Olenka glanced over at Diwala's overly inquisitive face. "Now, why would you say that? I thought we were going to skim the gossip tomorrow as a crew?"

Diwala nodded. "Yes, but few hooks besides a new job could drag you back to the wharf before it was time."

Olenka shook her head. "Well, if you *have to know*, I have heard a few rumors, but nothing that I'm excited about."

"Go on." Diwala's mood was strange: excited and friendly, but also vaguely aggressive.

Olenka stopped to examine a set of spears for sale. The ugkoy merchant glanced over excitedly as Olenka thumbed over the most expensive weapons.

"Di, look at the binding on these! And, there's enough in the set to get ones for the whole crew. Do you think it's time we refined our tools a bit?"

Diwala pulled Olenka away. "No, I do not, *and* I think we need to stop spending money as fast as we earn it."

"What are you saying, Di?" Olenka stopped and looked up at Diwala's somber, disgruntled features.

"What I am saying is that Mari and I have been feeling *trapped*, sister."

Olenka was shocked and also a little nervous. A crew leader never liked to hear that her companions were unsatisfied. "What do you mean?"

Diwala shrugged her shoulders and folded her arms. "Stagnant. Stuck on the doldrums. Lost upriver with no clear view of the sun. What I mean is that things have not been very *lucrative* lately, Olenka. Ripping off kaizo is fun, but we have been running this crew for over a year now, and we still have not gotten a single kataw contract. We are all getting older, Olenka, and our goals are slipping away with the tide."

"Is that all?" Olenka chuckled and started walking away. "This is what's been worrying you? Mari too?"

Diwala nodded gravely, impervious to Olenka's dismissive optimism. "Yes, sister. It feels as if your heart is no longer with ours. It feels as if you are comfortable with what we have achieved. *Do not* walk away when I am speaking with you."

Olenka stopped and turned around, exhaling her frustration. "Okay, you have my attention."

"Good." Di smiled and stepped closer. "Perhaps it is insensitive to say, but now that Daisay is gone, we have an opportunity, yes? An opportunity to *grow*. We are not a guppy crew running guppy jobs for our big sister anymore. You need to find us a kataw contract, something big and impressive. It must be something that will make us lots of money and stand us out from other crews."

Olenka shook her head and rubbed her eyes. "Di, that just isn't how it works..."

"And you are one to tell me how it works?" Diwala retorted. "When we first met, you were the most clueless puddle pup I had ever seen tripping over her own fins. You remember, do you not? You did not know which end of the spear went *in* until I taught you to fight. You could not have guessed which side of the banca went *up* until I taught you to sail."

Olenka sighed. "Di, you know how grateful I am for everything you've done for me, but don't you think you're being a little... unrealistic? Most crews don't make the higher bids until their fifth year. We've come so far in just a few seasons! How can you not be happy with that?"

Di shook her head. "You misunderstand me. I *am* happy. I am just not *satisfied*."

"Well, then perhaps you need to learn some patience," Olenka snapped. "This is how things go! Sirena life builds slowly, you know that. We just need more time. I mean, glance around at the other new crews, will you? They're still hauling *rice* down the river from Siyel Baryo, for Heaven's sake!"

"No." Diwala's voice was overly firm. "Those crews do not matter. They are not us. We are stronger than that. Stronger than them. You know this, and yet you pretend we are average, like we are just the same as every other crew. We have done so much because we are exceptional. We have come this far because you are clever, and you always manage to get us the best jobs. On top of all that, you are in a unique position to negotiate with the holy city. There is no reason we should not regularly be winning their contracts, but for some reason you have stopped trying. It is like you have grown lazy with our success."

Olenka stiffened. "Lazy? You honestly think I'm *lazy*?"

Di sighed and looked down. "No, I misspoke. I am sorry. I do not believe you are lazy, but I believe you are afraid of success."

Olenka laughed out loud at that remark. "Afraid? And what exactly am I afraid of, Di?"

Diwala stepped close to Olenka, and with no more respect for personal boundaries than a bandikan suckerfish, she placed her fingertips against Olenka's forehead.

"You are afraid of *this*."

Olenka stepped back and swatted away Diwala's hand. "Hey, claws off, you buwisit."

Di shook her head. "You know I am right, sister!"

"No, I don't, Diwala, and I don't appreciate you telling me what I feel either. If you want me to find us a tougher job, that's one thing, but don't go telling other people what they're afraid of."

"Olenka, please… you should have your kudori read. You will not be at peace with yourself until you know what it says. The line readers… they are never wrong." Di's voice was soft and sweet, but her words couldn't have been more bitter to Olenka.

"Never wrong, huh?" Olenka stepped back towards Di, trying to keep their conversation from all the unwelcome ears perking up around them. "And why do you think that is? Perhaps the only people who have their foreheads read are the people who *want* to believe what they say. Hmm? Have you ever thought of that? Di, you're better than all this superstitious nonsense!"

Diwala was calm but growing irritated. "Olenka, reading the kudori is not superstition. It is a glorious tradition of our people, and it is *true*. I have seen it for myself. As soon as the reader told me my fate it was like a hole inside me suddenly filled up! I knew then that I was a hunter and made for the spear. Please, sister. You can have that same peace! Just let me—"

"*Well go on then!*" Olenka shouted, stepping right up to Diwala's face. Several ugkoy in the crowd jumped and glared as they hurried away down the pier. "Go on, Diwala! Why don't you tell me exactly what *my fate* is? Don't act like you don't know. Don't act like you haven't studied the caste charts enough to instantly identify what my forehead says about my future."

Di's eyes dimmed with hurt and alarm, but she didn't look away. "Your kudori says that you will be a great spiritual leader. It is the clearest and most perfect pattern I have ever seen in someone's flesh."

"Di…" Olenka exhaled, stepped back, and looked down at her fins, "do you really think I didn't already know that? The *instant* I was born, my parents read my pattern and sealed my fate. And not just them, Di. *Everyone* who has ever taken one look at me. Can you imagine that? Never getting to choose your own path, never feeling like you had a say in your own future… This mark has never brought me peace or guidance, Di. It's just gotten in my way."

Diwala's wilting face suddenly perked back up, and she stepped closer to Olenka, taking her by the arm. "Is *that* why you are afraid of progress?"

"Progress? What are you…?" Then she rolled her eyes. "*This* again? Di, can we please just forget about all this kataw buwisit?"

"No, no! I am finally beginning to understand you." Diwala smiled, looking very pleased with herself. "You are not afraid of success. You are afraid of the holy city! You will not take a kataw contract because it will bring us too close to Lunsod sa Dagat! You are running from your fate!"

"Di, seriously?" Olenka's glare somehow melted into a smirk. Diwala's enthusiasm was obnoxious and dogmatic and everything Olenka had learned to hate from her youth, but it was still charming and sincere. Olenka didn't buy into any of Diwala's faith, but it was the sirena's way of saying she cared.

Olenka could respect that.

"Fine! Maybe you're right." Olenka threw up her arms and tilted her head, "Maybe I don't want to go back to the kataw. Maybe I am running from those city fish. I like where we are, okay? I like being free to take any job I want. I like being able to swim alone in the reef. I like not having the clergy constantly sizing me up for a sacred shawl every time I walk down the wharf. Is that really so bad?"

Diwala smiled and placed her hands on Olenka's shoulders. Her eyes were bright and watery. Olenka glanced across her face, studying her tattoos. They were meant to expand her sirena kudori, protracting the martial pattern along the shaved sides of her head and down into her spear-wielding arms. They were an act of faith, not fashion.

"No, it is not so bad, Olenka. But your fate will find you someday, sister. You are a gull flying against the storm. Perhaps your very efforts to avoid your fate are what will make you find it in the end." Diwala smiled in condescension, now openly, obviously, *insufferably* pleased with herself. Olenka tried not to be too annoyed.

"You are free to run, my leader." Di winked. "Just see that you run us into a kataw contract, yes?"

Both Olenka and Diwala laughed, but for very different reasons. Olenka checked her senses and grounded herself in the moment. The sun was hot, and her clothes were already dry. The salty wood was brittle and creaked below her fins. The crowd was loud and fluid, and the smell of charring fish was lofting through the breeze. In that moment of clarity, Olenka reflected on the deal she had made with herself.

One more job... I will go searching for my place again, but just for one more job. Perhaps Di is right. We're more than ready for a kataw contract...

And Olenka knew just where to find one.

CHAPTER 20

THE SAMAY LAWAS

SOTAY WHARF WAS NOTHING FANCY, BUT IT WAS situated in a very special location. The Padmaputra River emptied into the Great Sea right at the edge of the Karafuru Reef, and Sotay was directly built over its delta. Not only did this make it an integral trade hub between the sea and the jungle, but it meant that the reef blocked most of the damage caused by incoming storms. The area flooded periodically, but it was a relatively stable location for a town built on top of the water. Because of its ideal locale, Sotay Wharf was the place to buy and sell anything.

And that included new contracts.

Diwala and Olenka followed the wharf north. The eastern docks were for merchants, the central walkways were for established local business, but the north end was something else entirely. There, the siokoy and sirena crews went to drink, show off, and pick up new jobs. It usually wasn't dangerous, but it wasn't friendly either.

Siokoy and sirena culture was stringent, and young crews were generally unwelcome under the northern tent. There was a strict hierarchy to be followed. Younger crews ran ugkoy contracts along the coast and upriver: mostly shipping rice and other types of produce. More experienced sirena crews could take on some larger shipping, fishing, or salvage contracts to the far islands and ports, but it was only the most experienced siokoy that were entrusted with the big contracts. Among these, kataw contracts were the most highly prized and sought after.

The kataw were a wealthy caste, and their contracts paid handsomely. However, the contracts they gave were typically difficult, often dangerous. The siokoy used this fact to assert their unspoken jurisdiction over them, bullying sirena crews away from the most rewarding jobs. This gender division had always irked Olenka. It was a false barrier, a wall of bloated pseudo-authority, and she gained great pleasure by blatantly disregarding etiquette.

Little had changed from her youth.

The northern docks were much more cramped and isolated than other sections of the wharf. The walkway was raised up higher than the rest, creating a divisive set of stairs about fifty meters wide. The whole area was covered by a massive canopy of stretched cloth, mounted on tall stakes. It built a smoky, shadowy haunt with a bit more privacy for transactions of a sensitive nature. There were no guards or gatekeepers to turn people away, but it was painfully clear who was welcome under the canopy and who was not.

Diwala and Olenka were not.

So, they stepped inside.

* * *

THE TWO YOUNG SIRENA KNEW THE PROCEDURE. THEY jogged up the stairs and immediately went for the bar. It was important to look like you were here to drink. Di and Olenka each ordered a strong cup of tea and a plate of coconut-rice krok cakes, casually taking a place at one of the many tables along the edge of the canopy. The tables were set up in a semi-circle that cupped the entrance of the tent, ostensibly for easy access to those only interested in grabbing a quick drink. However, the perimeter created a perfect vantage point to spy out into the crowd beyond.

"Anyone catching your eye?" Olenka sipped her tea as she spoke, keeping her head down.

Diwala sat up very straight in her chair, glancing around the crowd. "The samay lawas seem… *crowded* today."

"So, you noticed, too…" Olenka smiled and nibbled a krok cake. Not only were they delicious, but Olenka always felt like they served as a rich metaphor for her method of picking up contracts. The krok cake was both a sweet and savory dish. It was filled with robust strips of green onions, and the occasional fried shrimp or minnow, but the outside was a syrupy paste of rice and coconut milk. The whole cake was then quickly crisped in scalding hot oil and dumped onto plates before drunk, unsuspecting customers. You see, the sweet aroma of hot coconut milk drew them in, but what really hooked them was that green onion's kick in the teeth. It was potent and surprising, and somehow exactly what you didn't know you were looking for in a snack.

Olenka leaned back and glanced over her shoulder. The samay lawas were a horrifying but popular obsession among the siokoy: one that sirena were generally too sensible to frequent. Fresh sharks were captured once a week and thrown into pools cut right into the docks. The edges of the pools were enclosed by a perimeter of crisscrossing wooden beams so that the animal was stuck listlessly swimming in a hungry circle, getting more and more desperate as its week-long incarceration progressed. Drunken siokoy would jump into the pool, showing their combat prowess by outmaneuvering the frantic animals.

Fatalities were rare, but it was not uncommon for some empty shell to lose a fin or a finger in the pools.

Eventually, someone with something to prove always volunteered to take out the old shark so that it could be skinned, butchered, sold, and replaced. The proprietors of the tent allowed the practice because it brought customers, and they generally got to keep the meat from the animal. The teeth, however, went to whoever picked them out first. Shark tooth necklaces were a popular way of advertising your skill on the Great Sea, and scavenging the remains of a poor, bullied animal was a cheap way to beguile your clientele.

Di stretched out her neck to see over the crowd. "Do you think they killed one?"

Olenka shook her head. "No, look again. There's no huddle, no one crouching down. If they killed it, they would be skinning it. And listen. There's no one in the water, either. I'm not sure what's happening. It looks like they're afraid of something."

Diwala shrugged. "As they should be. Karma always comes to those who upset the balance of the sea."

Olenka chuckled. "Now *there's* one of your superstitions I can get behind."

And then something caught Olenka's well-trained eye.

It was a man wandering around in the crowd, and that was just what caught her attention. He was not a *part* of the crowd; he was simply *in* the crowd. Like most of the other siokoy he was shirtless with shark skin trousers cinched around his waist. His torso was a collage of belts and shark teeth, but he didn't wear them well. They seemed out of place, like he was hiding behind them…

With a thrill of excitement, it all clicked in Olenka's head. He was not a siokoy at all. This man was kataw! It was all so obvious now. He had no tattoos, no scars, and no bulging physique. He wore the traditional siokoy garb, but it was ostentatious and impractical, obviously an outsider's ignorant parody of utility. He didn't even have *a knife* strapped to his uzai hip.

Olenka swiveled around to study him better. Was he really kataw, or was she just seeing what she wanted to see? The man moved through the crowd very gently, trying his best to politely shift past the swarming siokoy. While everyone else was staring into the pool or talking with a friend, this man appeared to be studying the crowd itself. When he turned, Olenka noticed his hair. His head was not shaved, even on the sides, and more importantly, his hair was not matted. He had it combed back into a tight bun at the top of his neck.

That did it. That was the detail she needed to be certain. No one but a pampered city fish would ever go through the trouble to keep their hair un-matted. Even Marikit with all her vanity accepted the practicality of the matted locks. There was simply no reasonable way to spend that much time in the saltwater and still have untangled hair.

Olenka stood quickly, completely abandoning her cup and unfinished plate of cakes. Di looked surprised but remained still in practiced silence. She could recognize a hunter at work. She calmly drained her tea, tossed a few bhai onto the table, and stood to follow.

As Olenka got closer, she slowed down to match the tipsy stroll of the crowd. It gave her an excuse to take in her surroundings. It was very loud around the samay lawas, but not as loud as usual. No swearing, no cheering, no thrashing in the water. The crowd was congregated around one particular pool. Olenka held back and listened.

"No way, man. Is you seeing dat t'ing?"

A younger siokoy was chatting with a group of his friends off to Olenka's left. She held her distance and stared straight ahead. The siokoy's southern isles accent was so thick that he was easy to pick out from the clamor of the crowd.

"Ah, come on! Our crew's needing the money, and you's our best chance wit' it!"

The young siokoy shook his head and stepped to the side, peering over shoulders to look at the pool.

"Nah, is sick or somet'ing, man. You go jumpin' yourself in dere an' maybe I's followin' to fish out your corpse."

"Interesting," Olenka whispered to herself. She needed some more information. She pulled out of the crowd to a nearby table of sirena. She bowed her head respectfully and then took a seat with them.

An older sirena with a vast array of shells woven into her hair smiled warmly, pleased with Olenka's manners.

"Welcome, little minnow. What can I do for you?"

Olenka smiled back, trying to soften her up a bit. "I am so sorry to bother you, big sister, but I was hoping one of you ladies could maybe explain to me what is happening over there?"

Olenka glanced around at their experienced faces. Most were skeptical, but the one who had spoken looked sincerely flattered.

"First time at the samay lawas, huh?"

Olenka smiled and nodded, trying her best to whip up a blush. "Is it that obvious? I'm sorry. I must be embarrassing you all with my presence." Olenka bowed again and motioned to leave.

"No, no! Not at all, little minnow. We were all there once, weren't we sisters?" The old sirena smiled in maternal compassion. "Have a krok cake and I'll tell you everything you need to know."

Olenka smiled and gratefully popped a cake into her mouth, her eyes disgustingly enthusiastic.

"Now, the pools over there are for the men to test their courage, see? Each week, the hunters bring in the sharks, one per pool, and the siokoy jump in to *dance* with them."

"*Dance?*" Olenka feigned astonishment and leaned forward. "But, isn't that *dangerous?*"

One of the other sirena scoffed and turned aside. "Just you stay on the river, little one. The open sea is no place for fear of danger."

Olenka looked back to her false mentor. "I'm sorry. It's all just so new to me. So, what happens when the shark needs to feed?"

The salty old sirena grinned maliciously. "Well, after a few days with no meat, you can imagine how a shark might start to act. After its week is up, when its hunger is at its peak, it's time for the *truly* courageous to show their strength."

Olenka widened her eyes and faked a silent gasp. "You mean, someone gets in there and fights it?"

The old sirena laughed and leaned back, tipping her cup of rice wine toward the pool.

"Well, normally, child. But that one there? It's been in that pool for *nine days* now, and no one seems to be able to take it on. Can't even get close! The savage thing bites at shadows!" She chuckled and drained her cup. "Pretty exciting though! No one's giving up because they're offering a pretty high prize to whoever takes it out. I'm not leaving until I see one of these cocky bruisers lose an arm."

The other sirena chuckled in agreement and turned back to their drinking. Olenka nodded to herself quietly, deeply intrigued. There was so much opportunity here…

Olenka bowed to her hostess and pushed back from the table. She slipped back into the crowd, trying to get closer to the disguised kataw. There was a huge splash and suddenly the crowd shifted. Olenka stretched out her legs and could barely see the action. A muscular siokoy with swirling chest tattoos was leaning over the pool, holding tightly to a pole behind him. It looked as if he had sliced open his hand and was dripping some of his own blood into the water.

There was another mighty crash and Olenka watched the shark slam itself into the side of the dock, breaching a full meter and almost snapping up the man's arm. The siokoy jumped back excitedly, the adrenaline high fluttering through the crowd. He turned back and collected a few coins from a nearby siokoy who brushed off his smug, drunken display with a toss of his hands.

Olenka turned away, rolling her eyes in disgust. She peered through the crowd and saw the kataw man standing a few meters ahead of her, watching the crass siokoy pour rice wine over his bloody palm. Olenka felt like this was her chance.

She slipped up next to the kataw and bumped his shoulder. "Hey, you alright?"

The man jumped and turned. "What? Yes, of course, I'm alright. What do you want?"

Olenka nodded to herself and slipped up next to him. "First time at the samay lawas, huh? It's a bit stressful, but you get used to it."

The kataw man turned to Olenka, both annoyed and charmed by her presence. "Listen, I don't have any money on me, if that's what you're here for. You'll have to seduce a drink off someone else."

Olenka laughed and folded her arms. "Please, don't flatter yourself. So, why are you here, anyway?"

"Why are *any* of us here?" The kataw spat. He glared at her and then turned his attention back to the huddle of siokoy. "Those men shouldn't be doing that…"

Olenka chuckled and followed his gaze. "Doing what? Wasting wine?"

The kataw rolled his eyes. "No, taunting the shark."

"Well, that's just how things *are* around here. Do you pity the creature?"

The kataw shook his head and turned away. "No, of course not. It's just… there's something wrong with it. Did you see how it jumped? It's like it didn't feel the blow of the dock… It's far too dangerous for all this."

"True," Olenka nodded her agreement. There was something familiar about this kataw… Tattered sails, did she *know* him? That would be a disaster… She had let her matted hair grow long enough to partially cover her kudori to prevent such awkward encounters, but you could never be too careful.

"Why *are* you here?" Olenka asked again.

The man turned to her, quickly glancing up and down her figure. Olenka pretended she didn't notice, but the tactless gesture added substantial fuel to the determination already welling up inside her. She *really* wanted to take this man's money.

"If you *must* know, I need a strong crew for a particularly dangerous job. I thought these pools might be the best place to look. Now, if you don't mind, I think I've found some reasonable prospects." He bowed with hollow, compulsive formality, and skulked away.

"Oh, no you don't," Olenka whispered. She glanced up to see Diwala watching her from the edge of the crowd. She let out a quick, shrill whistle, and with a flick of her head followed the kataw man's wake in the tumult. Diwala nodded, and circled the edge of the crowd, converging on the unsuspecting throng of siokoy.

The kataw reached them first. Olenka kept her meager distance, listening in on the details of his proposition.

"Excuse me, fine siokoy." The kataw stepped into their circle, and the thugs glanced up in annoyance.

The one with the split hand scoffed and tilted his head back as he spoke. "And who's we talkin' wit', eh?"

The kataw's composure stumbled for a barely perceptible moment, but he quickly translated the accent's broken grammar and cleared his throat. "My name is Krit, and I am seeking the assistance of warriors of your... your *stature*."

The band of thugs laughed loud and hearty, leaning into the circle and making exaggerated faces at each other, but their leader smiled and shook his head. He stepped forward, casually wrapping a strip of cloth around his wounded hand.

"You's listenin' to me, short fins. You's gonna hafta find another crew's what can handle yo' job. Me boys here, they not been takin' anyt'ing less than the best, these days, alright?"

The siokoy went to close their circle around him, but Krit stepped up again. "Gentlemen, please. I am not a man to be taken lightly. The contract I represent comes from the monks themselves. We need a crew that can handle immense danger and help us solve a rather egregious shipping blunder."

The five siokoy perked up.

So did Di and Olenka. The two glanced at each other, and began to move in.

"Da monks, you's sayin'?" The siokoy tilted his head in interest and offered Krit his un-bloodied hand, "Da name's Takashi. What you say to you's buyin' the boys here another round and we's listenin' up really close to dat monk job o' yours, eh?"

Krit nodded in compliance and moved to walk away with his mercenaries. Diwala and Olenka intercepted them.

"If your contract really is as important as you say," Olenka interjected, "then why not allow some... *friendly competition?*"

Olenka stepped into the newly emptied space behind the moving band of siokoy. They stopped and barked out a fresh chorus of haughty amusement. Krit looked shocked and nervous. Takashi looked hungry and annoyed.

But, maybe just a *little* curious, too…

One of the other siokoy spoke up first. "Little sister, don't you know what happens to minnows who swim with the sharks?"

Diwala stepped up next to Olenka. Olenka smiled and tossed a gesture toward the siokoy. "What an excellent proposition. Care to follow up on your boasting?"

Takashi motioned for his thugs to stay back as he stepped up to Olenka.

"What's you got in dat head, little sirena?" The sour scent of rice wine fogged the air around Olenka's eyes.

She blinked away the burn and smiled in spite of herself. "It's simple really. The one to kill the shark gets the contract."

The siokoy thugs were clearly startled, several of them laughing uncomfortably. Takashi tilted his head, trying to size up the profound oddity before him that was Olenka and her pride.

"You's wantin' to jump in dere with dat t'ing?"

Olenka nodded. "It seems reasonable, doesn't it? This fine man came to the samay lawas looking for warriors who could handle some danger. What a shame to not at least show him what *true* courage looks like. I mean, anyone can act tough when their fins are high and dry on the docks."

Takashi smirked at the insult, but Krit quickly stepped forward between the two. "Young lady, that is quite enough. I cannot in good conscience leave this wretched place with your blood on my hands."

"Now, be holdin' up dere for a moment, short fins." Takashi placed a hand on Krit's shoulder, holding him off to the side. "The little sister, there… she's makin' us a fine point, no? You be deservin' some o' dat action dere. And, o' course, only the best should we be trustin' wit' the work o' the monks, is you hearin' what I'm sayin' to you?"

Takashi smiled down at Krit who brushed the drunk siokoy off his shoulder. He shook his head and looked up at Olenka. "What exactly did you have in mind?"

Olenka folded her arms and looked up at Diwala. "How about it, Di? Want to set the terms?"

Diwala smiled and turned to Takashi. "We will keep it simple. The first one to kill the mad shark gets the monk's contract and the barya for the kill."

Takashi nodded in amusement. "The firs' one what kills the shark, or the last crew what's livin' to tell 'bouts it?"

Diwala smiled. "Whichever comes first, I suppose."

Takashi rubbed his thumb against his lip and glanced back at his chuckling crew. "What's you sayin' to raisin' up them stakes a bit, eh? Ochay up dere's been offerin' two golds to the crew what cleans out his pool. Match his wager an' we's in. Unless, o' course you don't got dat kinda barya jus'a lying 'round…"

Olenka grinned. "Perfect."

Takashi smiled back and held out his hand. "Alright then, little sister. We be shakin' on it den?"

Olenka clasped hands and the two crew leaders each gave their two gold barya to Krit who had turned a truly impressive shade of green.

He bounced the coin pouches in his hand and shook his head in disgust. "This is blood money."

Takashi laughed and slapped the kataw's frail back. "Ah, yes! Blood an' coin! The two truest faces o' life on the seas, little brother. If you wasn't in the business o' death you wouldn't be here wit' us now, am I right?"

He laughed loudly with his crew and turned to face Olenka. "And since we all be havin' the real *sportin' mood* today, we's gon' let your crew try first, eh?"

Olenka smiled and laughed to herself. How could it really be this easy? She glanced up trying to look professional, but she couldn't suppress one last chuckle.

"Takashi? You just made my day."

CHAPTER 21

DANCING WITH SHARKS

NEWS OF THE BET SPREAD THROUGH THE CROWD like blood in water. Without even needing to be summoned, Ochay came over from his place at the bar, ruthlessly shoving aside anyone in his path. He was a gruff man in his mid-forties, with a stained white shirt and a shaved head that could really use another shaving.

"What's all this then? I haven't got much patience for liars and braggarts."

Diwala and Olenka bowed to the proprietor and stepped forward. This was not a man it would be wise to infuriate, so Olenka let Di do the talking.

"We are here to remedy your shark problem," she said. "Takashi has told us that you are offering two hundred silver scales to the crew who can kill it for you. We will take you up on your offer."

Ochay's face was cold and sour. He was the kind of man who always looked like he was squinting into the sunlight no matter how dark the room. He shook his head and turned back to his bar.

"Forget it. I'm not about to let a couple of pretty minnows bleed out in my pool. Looks bad for business."

"Sir," Diwala stepped forward and took the man's arm, "you do us a great dishonor. We are sirena of the Great Sea, and you will keep your end of your bargain if we meet ours. Now, clear a perimeter around this samay lawa unless you would like your customers to be too close when the dance begins."

Ochay glanced at Diwala's hand at his arm and she released her grasp. He glared at the two of them and grunted loudly.

"Listen you two, I ain't responsible for what happens in the pool, you understand me? There's something wrong with that uzai shark in there, I won't tell you no different. You go in there with it and I can't guarantee anyone'll be able to pull you out in time if things get prickly."

Di nodded. "We understand the risks. Please clear the perimeter for us. If you do not mind."

The old man grunted his disapproval but turned his booming voice to the crowd.

"Alright, you barnacles, clear out! Let's nobody be chum today, eh? I want everyone a full three paces away from the pool. Let's go!"

He threw his arms up repeatedly, walking his way around the samay lawa. The shark inside seemed to notice the movement and began thrashing wildly. It rushed the edge a few times before drifting away from the stimulus. It rolled listlessly from its belly to its back and over again.

Takashi and his thugs had bullied some younger siokoy crew from their table and were busy setting up their front row seats and ordering a fresh round of rice wine. Krit stood nearby. His bloodless face looked like a shucked clam as he fidgeted with the bet money.

Olenka exhaled and crouched down, sliding her fish-skin hood out from the pouch at her belt. She pulled it over her head and tucked in her matted locks with practiced fingers. She stripped off her bulky cloth shirt and skirt, leaving only her watertight vest and girdle underneath. She focused on her breathing, calming her mind and taking stock of the moment. She felt the crowd thrumming around her, the smell of sweat and alcohol filling the still air. She sensed Diwala's energy next to her: calm and reassuring. She heard the mutterings of the many speculative spectators…

And she watched that strange, ill fish writhing in the water.

The shark coiled and twitched in unnatural, disturbing ways that showed no rhyme or reason. Its movements were fast and jagged and completely unpredictable. Sometimes it was as limp as a blade of kelp, others it crashed against the boardwalk like a tsunami. Olenka swallowed as she studied it, the full weight of her rash decision finally resting on her mind.

"So, my leader," Diwala whispered, "what is your plan?"

Olenka looked up to see Di kneeling on her knees and the balls of her feet, her fins splayed out on the dock before her. Her hands rested on her thighs, and her face was calm and eager. It was almost comical. For a hunter like Diwala, this was business as usual. Just another necessary risk on the path to glory. Olenka forced a smile and went back to watching the grey smear in the water. Even without its strange behavior, this would still have been a formidable shark.

"No clue... What do you make of its behavior?"

Di shook her head, as if she was saddened by what she saw. "This animal is sick. All else aside, we need to put it out of its pain. I am happy to be here to help bring balance back to this animal's life."

Olenka swallowed again and glanced around the cramped pool. Maneuvering would be a serious complication. The water was little more than a meter deep, basically eliminating the third dimension of combat that Olenka relied on so heavily. She was not the kind of fighter to charge straight into a brawl. She liked room to slip up and down and away from her opponent's line of sight. In the pool, the shark would have a brutal advantage. It was much quicker and *much* more powerful. Diwala and Olenka would have to coordinate their efforts to confuse and distract it while one of them sank a fatal blow.

"We'll need to work close together on this one, Di..."

Diwala nodded. "I agree. We must stay very near to its flank. Do not give it room to charge you. Look there, you see? It favors its left side. Always drifting this way around the pool. Keep to its right when you can."

Olenka nodded. "I think you should take a spear. I'm quicker, so I'll try and bait it to the middle. I'll have my knife, just in case, but it will be on you to bring it down. Nothing fancy, alright? Go for the gills. Stick it and bleed it."

Diwala nodded. "Agreed. No need taking chances on this one, yes? It is not worth our pride to stay in the water for a fight we cannot win. Will you ditch the pool if the necessity arises?"

Olenka faked a cocky laugh and threw back her hood. "Ha! Please, Di. You think I would just surrender four hundred scales to a pack of bottom feeders like them?"

"I expected as much, sister. You always were a typhoon." Diwala smiled and stood. "I believe I will need to find a spear before we–"

"Here you go little sister."

The two turned around to see the older sirena that Olenka had hustled earlier. She smiled warmly, the shells in her hair jangling as she held a spear out to Diwala. Di bowed, gratefully receiving the gift.

The old sirena winked at Olenka. "Quite a bold move for your *first time* at the pools, wouldn't you say, little sister?"

Olenka smiled and blushed. "I guess I've always been a bit… *ambitious*."

The sirena laughed a deep, smokey chuckle and leaned in close to Olenka's ear as she passed. "Put them in their place, sister. It's about time someone clipped their buwisit fins."

The old sirena sauntered away to the gentle chime of her shells rattling with each step. Olenka exhaled, feeling both the pressure and comfort of the old woman's support. She turned to Diwala who was busy twirling the spear and testing its weight. With a mutual nod between them, they stepped to the illuminated surface of the clear pool.

The shark's reaction was instant, rushing the dock and cracking its head against the wood. Olenka jerked back in shock as a piece of board splintered beneath her. Despite the blow, the shark acted as if it felt nothing. It twisted back, banking out for a brief flare of momentum, and then it struck the walkway again. The crowd gasped and shifted, and Olenka unsheathed her polished, bone knife.

She glanced around and heard the laughter of Takashi's crew behind her. A thought crossed her mind, and she trotted back a few paces.

Takashi grinned at her approach. "Wha's the matter, little minnow? Bit bigger den you two was all t'inkin'?"

Olenka grabbed a cup of wine from their table and dumped it out onto the dock.

"Hey, how deep did you cut your hand earlier? Let me see it."

Takashi looked around to his crew in hesitation, but he held up his bloody palm. "What you askin' 'bout, eh?"

In a quick motion, Olenka slipped her knife behind the back of his bandage and slit it in half. Takashi pulled back in shock, but Olenka ripped the bloody thing away in time. She rammed the ratty bandage into the glass and whistled for Diwala. Di was crouched and ready, waiting just outside the shark's line of sight. With a quick toss, Olenka threw the glass across the pool. It splashed and began to sink.

In a blinding moment, the shark flipped on its back and crashed toward the wine cup, drawn to the sound but hooked by the scent. Olenka and Di wasted no time. They sprinted along opposite edges of the samay lawa and dove smoothly into the water with practiced synchronization.

* * *

THE TEMPERATURE WAS ALWAYS THE FIRST noticeable change in sensation, but it was followed instantly by the crushing swell of the water dulling all sound to a dark, thumping reflection of its bright, former quality. The chaos of the blaring crowd was lost to the sea, and Olenka's world was filled with the coursing hum of the shark rippling through the swell. The two sirena swirled off behind the brute, kicking vigorously. They knew that they didn't have much time to get into position.

Ahead of them, the massive creature dove at the cup, swallowing it effortlessly. It thrashed in confusion for a moment, and then wrenched its body around, heading straight for Olenka. No hesitation in its bleak glare, just hunger.

Olenka twisted off toward Diwala, hoping to bring the shark within range of her spear before she ditched off to the side. The filthy fish burst forward, its own split flesh flapping and dangling from its ragged jaws. Its eyes were empty and cold, but its body was so full of life: unnatural and unimaginable vitality with which Olenka simply could not compete.

She swerved away, trying her best to judge the shark's speed, but it wasn't enough.

The monster was too fast and slammed its blunt nose into Olenka's stomach. She kicked wildly, trying to keep the lower half of her body clear of its teeth. She coughed bubbles and tasted blood in her mouth, and the shark's abrasive skin sawed into the bare flesh of her belly and thighs.

The shark jolted to the right, and Olenka was able to slip over the top of its head, brushing past its fin. As she passed, she saw that Diwala's spear was already rammed into the beast's gill. The shark was flailing against the pressure of the blow, but it did not retreat from the pain. It snapped savagely to its right, trying to get its jaws around Diwala's leg. Luckily, the force of its efforts spun Diwala as well, and the two splashed around in white-water chaos.

With a sickening *snap*, Olenka heard Diwala's spear break off near the tip. The shark sank its snout into Di's side as the brute burst free of the water. The force of the monster's flailing was so immense that Di was flipped clean out of the pool, crashing hard against the walkway above.

The shark wasted no time.

It charged for Olenka, mindlessly following the scent of the blood drifting from her lips. Olenka knew she had no time to move into a more advantageous position. It was going to be her or the shark; there was nothing more to it than that. She kicked off of the dock pole behind her and raced to meet her fate. Despite her burning fear, or perhaps *because* of it, a single thought drifted through Olenka's mind.

I bet Di will be proud of me...

Olenka raised her arm in front of her as she swam, the knife tucked tight against her thigh. She waited until the last possible moment. Her fear had made her move too quickly before, and her timing needed to be perfect now.

And it was.

Just as the two made contact, Olenka pushed off the creature's face, flipping around beside it. It was so close that she felt its jaw scratch her knees and the tops of her fins as they passed.

With the full force of their combined momentum, Olenka pressed the knife into the shark's surprisingly tender belly, dragging the blade along the full length of the beast's gut.

Olenka pulled up from her attack, amazed to be alive. She gazed into the shimmers of light that broke around her sight like gossamer in the blue pool.

Horror, cold and vivid, pierced her senses as she saw that the water was filled with swirls of black. The shark was off in the distance, flailing around in confusion, and the black fluid was twisting and coiling from its ample wound. It spread out into the water, but it did not dissipate. It stretched and swayed in front of her but would not dissolve or fade into the pool. It did not act like blood at all.

She remembered the knife in her hand and glanced down at it. The blade was somehow drenched in the same wretched ink that would not be lost in the water. Terror flashed through her chest again as Olenka saw the black ooze creeping its way down her knife, slipping closer and closer to her hand. It was almost like it was crawling, scratching, searching, hunting, feeling…

It was almost like it was alive.

And then the memory flooded back into her heart.

Time and thought all slowed as Olenka recalled the vision. That dream… her dream on the beach. Somehow it had shown her this moment. She had seen the swirls in the water; she had seen the knife coated in black. It was all there in her memory. Even this frigid feeling was familiar, this moment of perfect horror as she felt completely alone with a monster far beyond her ability to slay.

Somehow it was not new.

She dropped the knife and screamed into the water with a flurry of bubbles that blurred her face and hid her eyes and blinded her to whatever inevitable attack was coming.

A shock of pressure shook through the water, and Olenka felt something else tumble into the pool in front of her. She blinked hard, control of her body gradually coming back to her frazzled nerves. She twisted off to the side, trying desperately to avoid the sinister coils of black. From somewhere to the left, she felt Diwala rush against her. The sirena wrapped a tattooed arm around Olenka's torso, knocking out what little air remained in her lungs. With the coursing speed of her dive, the two arched through the water, and cleared the angled distance back to the dock.

They punched out of the pool, slamming onto the wood and sliding into the ankles of the screaming crowd in a shimmering kinetic spray.

Diwala rolled over panting, and Olenka gasped for air and grabbed at her throat. Her mind was so full, and every sight and sound and feeling and breath overwhelmed her until she thought she would vomit onto the dock.

"Look out!"

Someone in the crowd screamed the warning, and Diwala smashed the full force of her weight into Olenka's side. The two tumbled along the dry dock as the putrid beast burst out of the water behind them. The shark thrashed madly out of the pool, completely beaching itself. As it writhed forward, its inky insides spilled out onto the dock's foaming surge.

But somehow that didn't stop it.

The stained, bleeding thing leapt and flailed and fought its way across the dock, slithering toward them like a slug lubricated by its own murky gore.

Olenka screamed as loud as she could, but it was not in fear.

She pushed off of her knees, pulling Di's knife from the sheath at her friend's hip. She clambered over her exhausted companion, arms stretched high over her head, and plunged the blade into the shark's skull. The monster convulsed with titanic power and crashed back against the splitting wood below its girth. Its grey, cloudy eyes seemed to lose their meager light, and in an improbable instant of deep cessation, the beast's corpse rested limply on the dock.

The whole tent was silent then.

Olenka was draped across both Diwala and the remains of the mad shark. Both of her hands were still fiercely clutching the hilt of the sunken blade. Her heart was beating so quickly that it hurt, and her ragged, desperate breathing was shaking her vision. She realized with disgust that it wasn't just her breathing, but that *she* was shaking. Quivering like a scared little puddle pup on the carcass of this fallen brute…

Quivering in the middle of a crowd filled with fellow sirena and siokoy…

Quivering before a kataw who was assessing her courage for a prized contract…

Diwala sprang up to her knees and pulled Olenka back from the shark, wrenching her shaking body from its toxic mass.

"Sister!" Di roared. "Are you hurt? Show me your arms? Did it get you?"

Olenka froze, kneeling with her dear friend, too overwhelmed to speak. She closed her eyes and tried to calm her breathing but couldn't keep from trembling. Diwala grabbed her with oppressive force and hugged the very breath from her frame.

"I was certain that you... I am so sorry, Olenka! I left my dear sister alone in there. I did not mean to... It was just so strong, and... and..."

And then Di started laughing.

And then the crowd could contain it no longer.

Cheers burst around the two trembling women as swarms of Bantay Tubig rushed to their sides. Sturdy arms hoisted them to their fins, and Olenka realized just how limp and helpless her body had become.

She swung an arm around Diwala's shoulder, grasping for anything to keep her vertical. The crowd either didn't notice or didn't care. It sounded like they were being bombarded by questions and compliments, but the praise all felt like an unintelligible, reeling din to her frazzled mind.

She lifted her head weakly to Di. "Where... where's our money?"

Olenka glanced around the crowd, trying to spot Ochay or Krit. To her surprise, both men were standing right in front of her, beaming and shouting their approbation.

"Oh, there they are... How odd," she whispered, and a wave of dizzy nausea began to crest her senses.

Ochay shook his head and tossed a sack of coins to Krit. "Here, you better hold onto their winnings. They don't look so good."

Ochay slapped a hand against Olenka's shoulder and smiled. "Crushing depths, especially *this* one! You had me worried there near the middle, little minnow! But, lightning upon us all if you didn't take it out in the end. What a fine finish. You razor clams have certainly earned this."

Ochay laughed to himself and walked off toward the sick shark's corpse, which had already become the crowd's new point of focus.

Krit stepped forward and offered his shoulder to Olenka's other free arm, lifting her posture straight and level with the crowd.

"It appears I have underestimated your crew," he stated with a grin. "You have my sincerest apologies, as well as my complete loyalty to our agreement. If you would like, I can gather your things and meet you at your place of operation?"

Olenka nodded happily, not fully understanding any of what was happening. She drifted and dragged and smiled and slipped. Diwala appeared to be more coherent, and Olenka trusted her to guide them back to Mari.

"Hey, you eels! I got a word to be givin' you hustlers!"

Takashi pushed his way through the crowd, slamming his fist onto a nearby table.

"Dat you did out dere? That wasn't no *clean* fightin'. You was pullin' some tricky business on us. When we was shakin' on it, ain't you sayin' not'ing about pullin' no shark outta the pool so you can be finishin' it off on the dock! We wantin' our two golds back or—"

Olenka couldn't have held it back even if she tried. Which, of course, she didn't. A sour spew of rice and tea tumbled forth hot and abundant: a cascading column that coursed right into Takashi's tattooed chest.

Olenka smiled in her sickly stupor and then blacked out completely.

CHAPTER 22

ONE LAST JOB

A CALM BREEZE FLUTTERED ACROSS OLENKA'S face, causing a stray strand of hair to tickle her cheek. She opened her eyes to find herself lying comfortably in her crew's banca, a knitted blanket tucked around her torso. The air was cool, and the sky was dark. She blinked several times, trying to gauge her level of fatigue. She inhaled deeply, breathing in the sweet smell of the sea mixed with the powerful aroma of roasting fish.

Olenka pushed down the blanket and sat up in the boat. It rocked a little, but the pontoon stabilized it on the sand. She glanced around. The banca was tied up to the three stakes her crew used for shore anchors. The sun wasn't visible on the horizon, but its cherry glow was still dusting the sky a rosy pink. She recognized the stretch of beach instantly. It was a little alcove just south of Sotay Wharf: a familiar camping spot for her crew. It was sheltered by a pile of boulders to one side and thick mangrove jungle everywhere else. The view from the beach panned out to the west, always providing immaculate sunsets that helped them stretch the already long summer days.

Olenka heard voices and glanced over to the beach. Diwala and Marikit were sitting around a campfire roasting rockfish. Krit was there with them, picking at the last, meager morsels that still clung to his fish bones.

"Oh! She's up!" Mari's voice sang out as she splashed over to the banca.

Olenka swung her legs over the side of the boat and rubbed her aching temples.

"How long was I out?" Olenka was surprised to hear her voice sound so dry and harsh. It reminded her of that salty old sirena with the shells in her hair…

…and it reminded her of Daisay.

Mari hopped up onto the side of the banca with her, popping the cap off her bamboo canteen.

"Not too long. It's still *today*, if that's what you're asking." She handed Olenka the water. She received it eagerly and scarfed too much, coughing a little before handing it back.

"Thanks Mari… So, what happened exactly?"

Marikit smiled and took a sip of the water. "Well, you two *thugs* picked a fight way out of your league, almost got eaten by a mad shark, made enemies with the strongest siokoy crew on the wharf, and made us an obscene amount of money all in one night. Oh, and then you blacked out once things started getting awkward. Sound about right?"

Olenka chuckled and rubbed her head. "Yeah that pretty much sums it up. Hey, you forgot to mention *got us a kataw contract.* That's got to be worth a little redemption, right?"

Mari's face tensed, and she smacked Olenka's arm with the back of her hand. "Speaking of which, why didn't you tell me you were bringing *a kataw* back to camp with us! Ugh, I look like I've been scrubbing off barnacles all day!" She reached up and scrunched her hair.

Olenka shook her head. "Don't worry, Mari. I doubt he'll notice anything below your forehead anyway. Speaking of… you seen my clothes anywhere?"

Mari scowled and nodded toward the floor of the banca.

Olenka pushed the blanket off her lap and pulled on her shirt. Diwala and Krit were discussing something in the distance, but the surf was too loud to make it out.

Olenka tossed a quick glance in Krit's direction as she straightened her sleeves. "Hey, has he said anything about the job?"

Marikit shook her head and groaned. "No, and it's the *worst*. He said he wanted to wait until you were up. I guess he must have figured you were the *crew leader* or some chum like that." She winked and offered a hand to help Olenka to her fins.

Olenka smiled and took it. She never would have admitted it to anyone, but she was actually pretty worried about falling over while trying to get out of the boat. Her legs were solid as sea-foam at the moment, and the back of her skull was radiating a persistent ache that shot through her teeth and threw off her already diminished balance.

"Di mentioned something about it being dangerous, but I know *nothing else* about the buwisit contract!" Mari steadied Olenka as she spoke, sensing her friend's wobbles.

Olenka stepped into the water, feeling the refreshing chill launch up her ankles.

"He represents the monks," Olenka explained.

Mari's interest soared.

"*The monks?*" she hissed. "You mean *the* monks? *Why didn't either of you say anything?* Tattered sails, sister! I smell like something the gulls hacked up! Is he going to take us down to Lunsod sa Dagat?"

"I hope not," Olenka groaned. "He was out scouting for fighters at the samay lawas. I don't know what the job is, but it definitely sounds big."

"Big?" Mari grimaced. "Like, killing-mad-diseased-sharks big?"

Olenka smiled and nodded. "I mean, one can only hope."

* * *

KRIT SHOT TO HIS FINS AS SOON AS OLENKA AND MARI were within the glow of the fire.

"Welcome back," he said with a bow. "I was a little worried you might not awaken before I needed to leave."

Olenka gently folded her legs and carefully slid down to the sand. "Leave? Where do you need to go?"

Krit sat back down and stared into the fire. "I'm afraid I must return to the holy city. The monks will want an update on the contract before the night is through. Tell me, are you feeling better?"

Olenka reached for the fire's spit and ripped off a sizzling fish, placing it on a nearby rock to cool.

"Of course. I think I must have hit my head on the dock. Nothing I can't sleep off." Olenka chuckled, but Krit looked at her very seriously. Once again, she was struck with the distinct impression that she knew this kataw.

"You're sure you are feeling fine? No... pain in your stomach? Sort of like a burning?"

Olenka glanced around at the others who seemed to be just as confused as her.

"Um, no," she muttered. "I don't think so. Why?"

Krit sat back and shook his head, looking relieved. "Well, I suppose it's nothing. Just a hunch really... Regardless, I'm glad to see you feeling better." He smiled and bowed a little to apologize for his direct questioning.

"Um... okay. So, let's talk business?"

Krit sat up straighter. "Yes indeed. Time is short." He cleared his throat and glanced around at the crew. "I think you two might have overheard me earlier, but I represent the monks. There has been a rather tragic shipping error. The situation has become complicated, and we need a strong crew to help us recover what was lost."

Diwala shifted forward, resting on her knees. "So, it is a salvage job, then?"

"Well, in part, yes." Krit seemed a little nervous as he spoke, like he was worried he'd scare the sirena off if he said too much. "Perhaps it would be best if I explained what happened before I give you the details of the job. As I am sure you all know, the summer solstice is next week. As per Heaven's decree, we have been preparing for the Sacrament of Light to honor *the ancient hero*."

The phrase struck Olenka harder than the mad shark's nose to her gut.

It brought back memories of her dream. The ancient hero had been there, sinking into the water. She had seen him… She had saved him… How could that be?

"My dear, are you quite alright? You look like you've gone ill again…"

Krit was sporting his impressive pale green complexion, clearly worried that she had been lying about the quality of her health. Whatever disease he thought she had must have been serious. Mari leaned in and touched Olenka's arm.

"What is it Kay Kay?" she whispered. "Are you sure you're alright?"

Olenka nodded. "Don't worry about me. I'll tell you everything later." She turned back to Krit. "I really am fine. I just didn't realize how hungry I was." She reached for a piece of her cooling fish to sell her story.

Krit nodded, markedly unconvinced. "Yes, of course. Well, as I was saying, the summer solstice is almost upon us, and with it, the Sacrament of Light. Each year, to prepare, we send a crew to deliver the hero's armor to a certain, secret location for it to be polished and refurbished before the ceremony."

"You mean Ka Jiya Island?" Olenka blurted the words on impulse, her mouth bulging with half-masticated fish.

Krit sighed and shook his head, staring into the snapping coals of the fire. "I see our secrets are not what they once were. So, you know of the island?"

Olenka shrugged. "Not really. Rumors, mostly. It was just a guess," she lied.

Krit looked annoyed, but he swallowed it. "And what *rumors* have you heard?"

Diwala spoke up from her shadow to the left. "Those who live south of the tall miners say that a reclusive caste of kataw blacksmiths makes their home on the island, crafting special treasures to decorate the sacred city."

Krit nodded and offered a sour smile. "Well, they have told you the truth. The blacksmiths there are descendants of the very kataw that worked with the stone giants to arm and clothe the ancient hero and his army. Every year we send a convoy to deliver the sacred armor to them for upkeep before the solstice."

"But something went wrong." Olenka's voice was quiet and terse. She was beginning to understand just how lucrative this job was going to be. The sacred armor had supposedly been worn by the ancient hero into battle against the yokai hoards. It was the most prized object of the church, and they would do just about anything to retrieve it if it were lost.

Krit nodded again, his gaze becoming more and more distant.

"Something went *very* wrong." He sighed and removed his fake siokoy necklaces, rubbing a sore spot on his chest. "By Heaven, I don't know how those thugs wear these trinkets all the time… Teeth should remain *inside* the shark, if you ask me."

He chuckled at his own joke, but the crew remained silent, eager for Krit to continue. He looked down at his hands and exhaled loudly before he spoke.

"It seems that the crew I chose this year was attacked on their way home. Only one of them made it back, and he hasn't been especially… *coherent*. As far as the monks could tell, some animals were aggressive towards them and capsized their banca. The crew was killed, and the cargo was lost to the depths. Only one of the siokoy managed to swim to safety on a nearby reef, but he was gravely injured. When he arrived back at Lunsod sa Dagat, his wounds were infected. The monks didn't know what to make of his injuries. His whole body stank of rotting meat, and his skin had gone grey and cold in places. I never saw anything else like it," he paused to rub his tired eyes, "until today…"

Suddenly it all clicked together in Olenka's mind. "The mad shark…"

"Yes," Krit sighed. "That animal seemed to share the same illness as my siokoy. When he first came to us, he was delirious. Muttering gibberish and screaming in pain. It was an outright blessing of Heaven that we learned as much from him as we did. The night after he arrived, his behavior became very violent and erratic. He had to be dealt with before he harmed or infected anyone else."

Mari's jaw dropped. "You *killed* him?"

Krit chuckled. "No, no, not killed. But he was placed in quarantine until the source of his illness could be identified. But I fear that I may have found evidence that the infection is spreading."

Olenka shook her head. "That doesn't make sense… What kind of sickness could affect both sharks and people? We don't catch any of the other fish diseases."

Krit shrugged. "I am only telling you what I have seen. It is my suspicion that creatures like the one you two fought today attacked my convoy and killed my men. And… I fear that these creatures may be able to infect those they wound. That was the cause of my concern for you when you did not wake up after your fight."

The crew was silent, but the night was full of life.

The setting sun had dimmed to an auburn line that gave no true luminescence. The fire roared and crackled, and the jungle chirped and swayed. Olenka tried to clear her mind and stay focused on what the kataw was saying, but it was no use. The more the man spoke, the more Olenka remembered her dream. It seemed like every phrase he uttered was directly referencing her vision. Every ounce of sense in her system wished to expel the memory, to cast it out like the toxic hallucination that it clearly was.

But hard as she tried, she simply could not bring herself to doubt it.

The impressions were too real, and she had already witnessed the first scene prophetically pan out for herself. Something deep within her was certain that the rest of her vision would inevitably follow. It was a dreadful prospect, especially since she couldn't recall anything else from the buwisit dream. It was like she could no longer feel safe in her own mind. Nightmares were meant to be dismissed and forgotten, not foretold.

And certainly not fulfilled.

Marikit leaned forward, slapping her knees to lighten the mood. "So, you need us to go look for this lost armor? Is that it?"

Krit laughed and looked up from the fire. "No. *Heavens* no, child. I need you and your crew to hunt down and slay whatever killed my men, and I need you to recover the sacred armor and return it to the holy city in time for the Sacrament of Light."

Olenka laughed and tossed aside the sand she had been playing with. "Oh, is that all?"

"Merciful Heaven…" Diwala whispered. She pressed her fingertips to her lips and scrunched her brow.

"Before?" Mari stammered. "But isn't that…"

"The summer solstice is in less than a week," Diwala answered, turning her hard eyes up to Krit. "Where exactly did your crew lose their cargo? The voyage to Ka Jiya is long. Is it even close enough to collect by then?"

Krit rubbed his forehead as he spoke. "Unfortunately, they were attacked just south of the island, at the edge of a reef that runs west into the Great Sea."

Marikit shook her head. "Whoa, wait… Isn't Ka Jiya off the Bharatian Peninsula?"

"*Yep*," Olenka chuckled in vicious pessimism. "Sure is."

Mari held her palms to her hairline, her eyes begging for an explanation. "There's no way we can sail that in less than a week! That's nearly to the border of the far mountains."

Krit nodded in agreement. "You are not wrong…"

"So, what then?" Mari exclaimed in exasperation. "You've just been leading us on about an impossible job?"

Krit laughed. "And waste my time as well? No, child. We would be willing to part with a pod of our fastest plalomas to carry you. You would have to travel light, and it would not be pleasant, but it would be possible."

Diwala perked up. "Plalomas? Is there any chance that we could keep them after we finish the job?"

Krit frowned. "I suppose your salary for this venture is *negotiable...* I will talk with my superiors if that is truly your concern."

Diwala nodded, in perfect sincerity. "Please do."

Olenka scoffed and held up her hands. "Hold on. What are you saying? You expect us to cross the Great Sea, kill a pack of diseased sharks, and haul a crate of armor back to Lunsod sa Dagat on the backs of three, *already burdened*, plalomas? And all this in *less than a week?*"

Krit exhaled and tilted his head slightly. "The return journey does present a technical problem to be sure, but I am confident that your crew is more than capable of figuring it out. Perhaps you can salvage the previous convoy's banca, or maybe you could barter passage home. Regardless, I need your answer now. Your crew has won first rights to this contract, but I must begin searching immediately for a different crew if you refuse the terms."

Krit stood and glanced around at the sirena. "So, what do you say, sisters?"

Diwala and Marikit both turned expectantly toward Olenka, but she was too busy staring into the coals. The fire was warm and comforting in the chilled, breezy night, but for some reason it was also terrifying. There was something scratching at Olenka's mind. Something important... Something about fire... But the harder she focused, the less she could remember. It was like a childhood memory distorted and duplicated so many times that it barely resembled the original.

"Kay Kay? What do you think?" Mari's voice was soft and a little scared, but still perfectly kind and sweet.

Olenka stood as well, feeling her limbs take on new strength and resolve.

One last job…

"Ladies, get a good night's rest," Olenka said. "We ride at dawn."

The group let out a collective sigh, and Krit triumphantly placed his fists against his hips. "Well then! I shall leave you all to your rest and see about the necessary preparations. Meet me tomorrow at the seabird carving off the western edge of the wharf. Do you know it?"

Olenka nodded and glanced out across the sea. The lights of the wharf were just visible flickering in the distance.

Diwala stood up and approached Krit. "Do you need a lift back to Sotay?"

Krit smiled and shook his head. "No, I believe a brisk swim by moonlight might do me some good. But I thank you for your hospitality."

Diwala nodded and walked off to retrieve her bedroll from the banca.

Krit motioned to leave, but then took a cautious step toward Olenka. "It was *Olenka*, was it not?"

Olenka nodded, too emotionally exhausted to force any more substantial of a response.

Krit turned away and locked his hands behind his back. "I apologize. This is truly none of my business, but I couldn't help but notice your kudori. It is a rather remarkable pattern. I'm sure you are quite aware of its significance?"

Olenka rolled her eyes and looked the kataw in the eyes. "What do you want from me?"

Krit stepped back a pace and cleared his throat. "It's just that I believe I have once seen its equal. You wouldn't happen to be the child of Chatri and Kamala, would you?"

Olenka sighed and stepped into the surf. "They're my parents."

Krit smiled with excitement for a brief moment before coughing away his expression. He sniffed the sea breeze and closed his eyes.

"The child of promise..." Krit reverently muttered. "That knowledge brings me great comfort, little sister. I believe you were *meant* for this task. Perhaps it will even be what reunites you with your family below?"

Olenka glared into the water, folding her arms progressively tighter across her chest. "Perhaps it will."

Krit beamed another tactless grin and then clapped his hands in front of him, rubbing them together as he stepped into the water. "Well, I have overstayed my welcome and the sea bids me return. Farewell, child."

"Krit?" she called.

"Hmm?" The Kataw paused mid-dive.

"Don't tell them. Don't tell *any* of them, alright?"

Krit chuckled and turned back to the sea. "I wouldn't dream of it, sister. That is your message, not mine."

With a quick splash, the kataw was gone. Olenka stared out into the ocean for a considerable while. It was as if her mind was being torn apart by what she felt and what she believed. She *felt* that something great and terrible was happening to her, and that forces beyond her limited sphere of comprehension were tugging her into the proper place. She *believed* that she was the captain of her own fate, and that nothing but her own stubborn will could steer her path.

And then there was what she had *seen*...

Prophecy fulfilled was not an easy thing to discredit, especially when the vision came to you personally. She sighed and pulled a fistful of her long hair over her shoulder, absently stroking the soft, matted locks. The worst part of all of this was that Olenka didn't even feel like she had come to a crossroads. The decision had already been made; whether *by* her or *for* her, it didn't really matter. How could she have chosen against everything that she had seen?

"Olenka? You coming?" Mari called out over the clamor of the tide, beckoning her to the fire.

Olenka took a deep breath, retrieved her bedroll from the boat, and confronted the inevitable conversation she was so deeply dreading.

* * *

DIWALA AND MARIKIT WERE ALREADY BUNDLED UP next to the fire, huddling up close to the subsiding light of the coals. Neither Di nor Olenka seemed particularly eager to talk, but Mari was like a bubble ready to burst. The other two weren't really willing to vent what was on their minds, and the silence grew more and more strained.

Finally, Mari flipped over to her belly, gazing at Olenka.

"Okay, you said we'd talk later, and it's officially later. Time to tell me what's going on."

Olenka shifted her weight forward, leaning against her knees. "I don't really know how to begin…"

Diwala grunted and rolled over onto her back, draping her forearm over her eyes. "How about you start by explaining how you feel. You appear to be both confused and distressed, am I wrong?"

Olenka rolled her eyes. "No, you're right… That pretty much says it all." She groaned and flopped back onto her bedroll, feeling her tired muscles throb and tingle.

Mari giggled. "Well, that's a start. Now why don't you tell us what's *confusing* you?"

Olenka lifted her arm and stared at the webbing of her hand, subconsciously recreating the ghastly scene that had triggered the dream.

"Okay, but you two have to *promise* not to laugh, alright? And you can't tell anyone what I'm about to tell you. They'll think I'm crazy... *You're* probably going to think I'm crazy."

Mari groaned and threw her face down into her palms. "Kay Kay! We already know you're crazy! Will you just *tell us already?*"

Olenka forced a smile and continued to study her hand as she spoke. "When I went out this morning, I fell asleep on this quiet little island, and I had... I don't know. I guess you could call it a dream."

"Ooh, here it comes Di!" Mari's smile broadened as she snickered. "Was he cute? At least tell me he was cute."

"Seriously, Marikit?" Olenka snapped. "Do you want to hear what happened or not?"

Mari giggled again and hid the bottom half of her face behind her bedroll. "I'm sorry. I'll behave. Promise, promise."

Olenka shook her head, trying desperately to find the right words. "It's all so hard to describe, you know? There were emotions involved, especially fear. It felt more like a memory than a dream."

"What was it that you saw?" Di asked.

Olenka looked up to see that Diwala was now staring intently at her...

...or maybe just at her kudori.

"I don't really remember, Di. That's the buwisit problem... It keeps coming back to me when something else triggers the memory. But the thoughts never stay. It's like the harder I try to remember them, the farther they drift out of reach. All except..."

Olenka thought about the samay lawa. She remembered the coils of black shark blood pulsating through the water.

"Except what?" Diwala whispered.

"Except I remember seeing our fight with the shark. At least part of it anyway. Do you remember when I froze up in the water after cutting open its belly? Right before you saved me?"

Diwala nodded to the stars above. "I do."

"Well," Olenka paused, searching for the words. "I had already seen that moment in my dream. I remembered it perfectly in the water. I remembered seeing the shark's black blood swirling around me, and I remembered feeling terrified that it would touch me. In my dream I even saw it crawling up my knife… It looked like it was alive or something. It was… *crawling* down the blade to my hand. See, I saw all that *twice*. Once in my dream, and then again in the pool. It was exactly the same."

Mari shook her head. It looked like she was ready to explode. "Wait, wait, wait. Spill the wind, Kay Kay. Are you trying to tell us that you had a dream about the future? A dream that actually came true?"

Olenka groaned and pushed her palms against her eyes. "*Ugh…* I don't know what it was, but yeah… I guess so."

Diwala's breathing was slow and deliberate as she spoke. "And you are sure about this? What you saw in your dream truly was what happened in the samay lawa today?"

Olenka sighed, not wanting to confirm her words but being unable to resist.

"Yes, I'm sure," she admitted. "It was exactly the same, down to the tiniest detail. That's why I froze up. It overwhelmed me to see it all again… I was frightened."

Diwala grunted her acknowledgment. "And, in this dream… did you see anything else? Anything after the shark pool?"

Olenka nodded. "Yeah… yeah I did. I can't remember all of it, but I saw *a lot*. I just remember that it all felt perfectly real… It was so strange. It was like having a memory in reverse, one that you recall when you recognize it coming true."

"Try, Olenka." Diwala's voice was clear and firm. She rolled over onto her side, studying Olenka with penetrating eyes. "You must try again to remember these things that you have seen. They were shown to you for a reason."

Olenka groaned and clawed at her hair. "Di! Are you even listening to me? The harder I try to remember, the farther they slip!"

Di shook her head. "That is not good enough. Talk it out with us. Tell me everything you remember and see if the rest tumbles out with it."

Olenka frowned but took a deep breath. What had she seen? She started where she remembered, thinking about the shark's blood in the water… It was everywhere, and it was terrifying, and she had screamed.

"Okay, I remember screaming. First in the water, and then… somewhere else. Out on the sea, maybe. Something was wrong, but I just don't…"

Olenka glanced at the dying campfire and it all suddenly rushed back.

"There was fire everywhere. It was all around us, but we were standing on a boat." She frowned and shook her head, realizing how ridiculous that sounded. "It was like the very face of the sea was on fire. I know that doesn't make sense, but that's what I saw. Everywhere I looked, the waves carried orange flames that boxed us in… and I screamed."

Olenka clutched at her sinuses, feeling suddenly nauseous again.

"Listen, I know you two want more details than that," she said, "but that's really all I can remember right now. Thinking about this is making me sick…"

She glanced up apologetically to Mari and Di and was shocked by their expressions. She expected humor and skepticism, but Mari's face had gone absolutely ashen, and Diwala looked even more austere than usual. Mari exhaled and briefly widened her eyes as she rolled onto her side. Di stayed very quiet, considering Olenka's words.

"Perhaps you are right," the tattooed sirena said. "We must rest now. Tomorrow will not be easy. But you must tell us if you remember more."

Olenka nodded quietly, rubbing away at her tender mind.

Di turned in her bedroll, silently isolating herself from the fire's light. Mari was quiet as well, too spooked to speak. Olenka, however, was not tired. She sat in the darkness, watching the fire fade, and trying her best to forget what she had seen.

CHAPTER 23

PRIDE, PLANS, AND PLALOMAS

SOTAY WHARF WAS ITS ROUTINE HAZE OF HUSTLE. The sun had not yet fully crested the eastern horizon, but the merchants and fishermen were already well about their day's labor. Olenka and her crew paddled their banca to the edge of the western dock where Krit had promised to meet them. It was a strangely solemn event. The crew had never taken on a job even remotely similar to this one. They knew that they would be stretched, and they knew that they would be tested.

As the appropriate dock came into view, Olenka pulled her oar up onto her lap, carefully studying the crowd. Krit was nowhere to be seen. She glanced at the horizon and then shook her head.

"What is it, Kay Kay?" Mari reached forward and placed a hand on her shoulder.

"I just didn't sleep very well last night," she muttered. "I'll be fine."

Diwala was standing near the bow. She looked down at Olenka with solemn curiosity. "You are worried that he will not honor our agreement?"

"No, of course not. I'm just trying to work out some of the details."

Diwala nodded and sat down next to her. Olenka shifted her position, allowing Marikit into the conversation.

"I'm starting to get a bad feeling about all of this." Olenka confessed.

Mari nodded. "Like your dream?"

Olenka scowled. "No, not like that *uzai dream*. Will you squawking gulls lay off that already?"

Mari rolled her eyes but let the sass slide. "Alright, well what kind of a *bad feeling* are you getting?"

Diwala chimed in before Olenka could respond. "Do you suspect Krit has not been honest with us?"

Olenka sighed and rubbed the chill from her arms. "Maybe not *dishonest*, but… blind, perhaps."

Diwala frowned but nodded. "Blind in what way?"

"Well, just look at the full situation," Olenka said. "What do we really know? The church's most prized possession was lost by a group of siokoy thugs up on the northern trade routes, only one member of the crew made it back, he is apparently too sick to be allowed in public, but not too sick to explain that his group was attacked by aggressive animals, and a mad shark just *happens* to show up at the wharf a few days later." Olenka paused, distractedly still rubbing her arm. "It just seems suspicious."

Diwala shook her head. "I do not think so. I think his story is consistent."

Olenka nodded. "You're right. His story is *consistent*, but it almost seems *convenient*, too. Don't you think?"

"Wait up," Mari's voice clipped in. "What are you saying? That Krit is setting us up?"

Olenka sighed and looked down at her lap. "I don't know. Krit seems sincere enough, just naïve… I'm more suspicious of the other crew. Do you know how much a crew could make selling cargo like that?"

Marikit nodded thoughtfully. "Yeah, but the monks choose crews for their faith, don't they? Not just their skill. That's why they don't usually go public with their contracts, isn't it?"

Diwala grunted her approval. "She is right, Olenka. More likely they were an incompetent crew who could not handle an attack.

You and I were barely able to handle just one sick shark. Imagine many."

"See? This is just my point!" Olenka sat up, stretching out her hands to nothing in particular. "We're making just as many assumptions as Krit. Who's to say that shark had anything to do with this job? What evidence is there?"

Mari's voice was strangely timid. "There was your dream."

Olenka glared. "Are we *really* talking about this again?"

"You dreamed about that shark specifically!" Mari said. "It *must* have been important."

Olenka laughed in disgust. "By Heaven... I never should have told you two about that buwisit!"

"It was *by Heaven* that you received that dream," Diwala stated, "and it was *by Heaven* that you shared it with us." Diwala's voice was strangely agitated.

Olenka turned to Di, and her tattooed brows softened slightly. She reached out and placed a reassuring hand on Olenka's knee. "Sister, please. You must swallow your pride and learn to see. There are no coincidences, just silly minnows who fail to see the tides that shape their shore. I have faith in your vision, even if you do not."

Olenka shook her head. "Is that how you see me, Di? A silly, faithless minnow?"

"Only a little." Diwala smiled. "Mostly I see my sister. I *also* see that my sister is too afraid to *tell us* that she is afraid."

Olenka smiled and felt her sinuses getting all warm and fuzzy. "Aren't you two scared?"

"Oh, *for sure*." Mari's response was almost too quick. Di and Olenka chuckled and glanced over to her. She smiled and laid her hands on Di and Olenka's forearms. "But I also know that you two are way too stubborn to let anything bad happen to us."

Olenka laughed loud and clear and clapped her hand down on Mari's. "To our stubborn, frightened family, then?"

Mari smiled. "To our family."

"To us," Di whispered.

* * *

A SPLASH OFF TO THE RIGHT DREW THE CREW'S attention. Olenka glanced over in time to see the spray of several exhaling plalomas breaching the swell. Diwala and Marikit were instantly moonstruck.

"*Oh...*" Mari squealed. "I've never seen them *this close* before! And on the surface! Look at them!"

Olenka tried to smile, but plalomas carried little of their typical guileless fancy to her. They were a status symbol: possibly the Great Sea's most magnificent treasure, and yet they were chiefly used to entertain the city fish. She had seen many of them in her youth. They were gentle and smart and beautiful, but Olenka resented everything they were affiliated with. However, seeing them now…

…maybe she could separate the associations.

The crowd on the docks was peppered with gasps and squeals as ugkoy of all ages rushed to see the pod. They were truly gorgeous creatures. They looked like giant fish, but they breathed air like the Bantay Tubig. Their skin was thick and smooth, and colored much like their riders', a deep blue that ran their length, with a soft white underbelly. Plalomas even had a natural kudori of their own adorning the underside of their tails.

The pod gracefully swirled its way to the dock. The two mounts in front bore riders, while three more in back did not. Olenka's crew stepped from their banca, casually pushing aside the gaping crowd. At the lead, Krit pulled off a fish-skin hood and shook his hair free.

"Ah, good morning, ladies! Glad you all made it on time." He slipped off the side of his plaloma and swam to the edge of the dock. The kataw behind him slid off his as well and followed Krit up onto the walkway.

Diwala and Mari bowed to the two kataw, anxiously awaiting their chance to ride. Olenka folded her arms and silently judged them from behind. She didn't think she had ever seen Di acting so youthful. The five plalomas skittered away under the docks. The crowds followed, fanning out to chase their various trails of silt and bubbles.

Krit stepped forward and motioned to the kataw next to him. "Sirena, I would like you to meet Father Decha. He is the monk appointed to oversee the training of the holy city's plaloma pods, and he has been kind enough to agree to give you three a last-moment course on plaloma riding."

Olenka tried to be a good sport about all of this, but she knew she couldn't fully hide her sour stare. Father Decha didn't bother to remove his hood. He held his back straight and his arms tight behind him, staring at the three sirena.

"First, let me be clear with you all. I did not, and *do not*, approve of any of this chum," he growled. "That being said, you three have been given an abnormal privilege by the church. All of this is most unorthodox, and I expect you three to treat these creatures with absolute respect. Do you understand me?"

The crew nodded, and Father Decha attempted to suppress a grimace.

"Now," the monk continued, "the first thing any rider must know is that you do not ride *on* a plaloma, you ride *with* a plaloma. These are incredibly intelligent creatures. If you try too hard to control them, they will resist and humiliate you. If, however, you accept their superior skill in the water, you will find they are more than willing to lend you their talents. There are even stories of plalomas defending their unconscious riders from sharks."

Father Decha flipped around a bulging sash tied taut against his chest. From inside he pulled out several dead squid.

"Each of you, take a squid. Hurry up!"

The crew members each took one and watched as Father Decha turned to the water, crouched down at the dock, and blew a small, shell whistle from around his neck. In an instant, the pod was circling the dock below him, clicking and squealing. Father Decha smiled at the pod and then glared at the girls.

"Watch what I do carefully. Each of you will follow suit. And by the *powers of Heaven*, strap on your hoods and gear! *Let's go!*"

Mari and Di scrambled to get their hair put back and their pouches cinched down. Olenka followed with *slightly* less passion. This kataw was driving her crazy, and she had seen all this buwisit before. She just wanted to get out onto the water, and he was wasting what little time they had.

Father Decha lifted a squid over the water, waiting for a ploma to choose him. A long snout emerged and sang from the rippling surface. Father Decha chuckled and tossed the squid into his mount's ready jaws. The ploma snatched up the morsel and drifted closer to the kataw who gently stroked the length of its muzzle.

"Ah... there we are, good boy." He glanced back at the crew, his voice suddenly stern. "It is imperative that you allow a ploma to choose you. Never force a ride from a mount that finds you undesirable. Is that clear?"

Father Decha jumped into the water, not even waiting for a response from the crew.

"Once a mount has chosen you, you must immediately get on while your bond is still strong. Wait too long and they will not tolerate you. It is not an *indefinite* invitation."

He slid along the creature's side and grabbed ahold of its straps. "The harness slips around the neck just before their pectorals and connects down under the belly. Reach around their dorsal and grab the straps from both sides, like so."

Father Decha gently straddled the ploma, which clicked and chirped at his touch. He then leaned forward against its back, assuming the most streamlined position possible.

"Keep your face tight against one side of its dorsal, and let your legs move with its tail. You can kick with the ploma if it is making an especially tight turn, but mostly you just want to hold on for the ride. I'm sure you all have plenty of questions, but experience is always the best teacher, and we don't have the time to pretend otherwise. Krit has some whistles for you, so get going."

Diwala and Mari scrambled into a line. Krit passed them their whistles, and they quickly went to crouch at the edge. Olenka took a whistle but stayed back to watch the situation unfold. Mari was the most excited and blew her whistle first. Almost instantly, a spray of mist and bubbles erupted to meet her. She squealed in delight and tossed her squid to her new comrade.

"Very good," Father Decha said. "Now hop in and take your place at the harness."

Mari was a little timid, but her excitement overwhelmed her apprehension. She splashed into the water and stroked her ploma's smooth, blue head. The creature chirped and buzzed and slipped along Mari. She climbed onto the harness, and the ploma playfully flipped off into the sea.

"Alright, hurry it along. You next then, tattoos?" He pointed toward Diwala who nodded her approval. She blew her whistle and waited. Eventually, another shy creature bubbled its way to her. She followed the demonstrated routine and slipped effortlessly into her harness.

"Alright, last one," Decha growled.

Olenka coughed, grimaced, and then knelt down at the water. For some reason, this whole buwisit business made her very uncomfortable. She leaned over the edge and blew the quick, shrill blast.

Nothing happened.

She blew again, and again no ploma came to greet her. Olenka sighed and rubbed her face.

"Of course," she whispered.

Krit stepped forward. "Perhaps try moving the squid about in the water for them? You know, to advertise it a little bit."

Olenka did as was suggested and swirled the dead squid around for the remaining two plomas to see. Eventually, one did approach her. She smiled and tossed the squid which was quickly snatched up. The ploma, however, did not even come close enough for her to pet it, and it repeatedly dodged her stretched out efforts to do so.

Olenka's patience snapped. "Okay, Decha. What am I doing wrong?"

The monk had slid off his ploma and was floating beside it, softly stroking its back. "You didn't do anything wrong. They just don't like you."

Olenka rolled her eyes. "Alright, well *why* do you think they don't like me?"

Father Decha shook his head and looked down at his ploma. "I told you before. They are very intelligent animals. They can sense what you're feeling. You don't like them. You think that you're better than them. So, they will not approach you."

Olenka exhaled and pressed her eyes against her palms. "Lightning upon all this chum! We don't have time for this madness. We have to leave *now* if we hope to make it to Ka Jiya in time!"

Father Decha snorted in amusement. "I couldn't agree more, little minnow. So, clear your heart of all your hate, and only then will the ploma come to you."

Olenka scoffed and sat back on the dock. "The only thing I hate is your barbed tongue and this fish's uzai attitude…"

Father Decha let go of his mount and pulled himself up onto the dock. He stood over her dripping and simmering.

"Do you think I do not know who you are, *child of promise?*" Decha spat. "Three years is not so very long, child. Do you think I take pleasure in tormenting the daughter of my dear brother? Well, I don't, even if she has grown to be an entitled little urchin. Your hate is as plain on your face as the kudori you so inexplicably ignore. If you cannot overcome the blackness in your heart, then you will *never* ride this ploma, and you will *never* retrieve the sacred armor." His face was fierce, but there was something else there, an emotion he was trying to hide.

He was desperate.

In that moment, Olenka realized just how much this man was depending on her, and she also realized just how much she didn't care. He was absolutely right about everything he had said, and it was infuriating. If he had just been blowing hot air, she could have swam it off. But no. He had looked deep into her past and dredged up the rotting chum at the end of her slacking line.

She glanced around at Diwala and Marikit, both of whom were staring up at her from the backs of their obedient mounts. Olenka sighed and leaned into the water, gently placing her hand on the surface. She closed her eyes and took stock of the moment.

She felt the cold water lapping at the back of her hand.

She smelled the oily juice of the squid still clinging to her skin.

She felt the warmth of the sun just beginning to peek over the eastern islands.

And she felt the hate within her: the burning, gnawing desire to not be told what to do.

It was a poisonous pride that had fueled her success over the past three years, but now it was eating away at her from the inside. Olenka felt it souring her stomach and sending chills up the veins in her arms and chest. It was a toxin, as wretched and black as that filth she saw swirling in the shark pool. But why was it there? Why was it flaring up now? These animals worked for the monks, but they *weren't* the monks. They weren't the ones who had stripped her of her childhood. They weren't the ones who had locked her away to study the ancient texts. And they were certainly not the ones from whom she had run away three years ago. They were just animals. They had a pulse like her, breathed air like her, and loved the reef like her. They were just…

She felt a sleek, wet surface pass along the back of her hand.

Olenka opened her eyes to see her ploama stroking and nuzzling her wrist. She smiled, and gently turned her hand, resting it against the charming creature's snout. It was beautiful in a way that transcended physical appearance. It was an animal of calm compassion: free of the vices that so often plagued her own mind.

"There she goes…" Decha smiled at the coy creature. "Now you just keep on thinking whatever it is you've gotten ahold of in your head, you hear me?"

Olenka sighed and swallowed and nodded. "Sure thing."

"Alright, it looks like she's as warmed up to you as she'll ever get. This is your shot." Decha jerked his head to the water and Olenka nodded. Keeping her palm on the plaloma's snout, she slipped into the shallows. The plaloma backed away from the dock and clicked its invitation. Olenka smiled, her heart softening.

"It really is smart, isn't it?" Olenka giggled as the plaloma sweetly spun around her.

"*It* is a *she*," Father Decha corrected, "and her name is Akia."

Olenka nodded. "Akia, huh? Well, Miss Akia, if I apologize, will you let me ride with you?"

The plaloma chirped as it twisted, and Olenka reached for the straps. Akia let her slide into position, and Diwala began to clap.

Olenka rolled her eyes and smiled. "Yes, *thank you*, Di."

Krit nodded from the docks and plopped into the water beside them. "Well done you three! Father, are we ready to proceed?"

Father Decha didn't respond. He glared at Olenka, studying her interactions with Akia. Finally, he grunted and hopped back onto his mount.

"Well, no time to waste, I suppose. You there. Tattoos. Your plaloma's name is Yashiro. He's the pod leader now, so let him take his place in front when I'm gone. Giggles, yours is named Hoshay. She's a good girl, and won't cause you any trouble as long as you keep her well-fed. They will respond to their names, so do not forget them. Now, follow my lead."

Father Decha pulled himself tight against his plaloma. He tapped the top of its head and stretched his pointed hand and finger forward: first straight in front of the creature's brow, and then veering off to the left. The plaloma understood the message and began swimming in the direction he pointed.

Olenka felt Akia twitch and drift after Decha, but she waited for the appropriate signal. Olenka tapped her head, and the plaloma swam after the leader, quickly diving half a meter under the surface, barely giving Olenka time to suck in a breath. Olenka glanced around the water to see the rest of the pod trailing along. It was not an orderly procession, but a pack of free spirits playfully bumping and teasing one another as they swam farther out to sea. Akia swirled and rippled through the water, purposefully kicking up little storms of silt. As they swam, Olenka felt the power beneath her. Akia's whole body was densely muscled, and each kick sent a tremendous force into the tide behind them. It was impressive, and Olenka began to feel ashamed of her own comparably tenuous skill in the water. Even at her top performance, she knew there was no way she could match this creature for speed or stamina.

Ahead, Father Decha pulled to the surface, and the pod obediently followed. He exhaled through his nose and wiped his face before speaking.

"Okay, now that you've moved with them, tell me what you've noticed. What did you see and feel? You there, tattoos. You go first."

Diwala wiped her mouth and leaned forward to lovingly pat her ploma. "They move together. As a single pod."

"Very good," Decha nodded. "Plalomas are naturally social and will want to stick together. If you ever ask them to go separate ways they will likely resist you. What else? Giggles, what did you notice?"

Mari scrunched up her face and looked down at her mount. "Well, they certainly make you hold your breath."

Decha nodded. "True indeed. The plalomas do not come up to breathe very often, and when they do it is quite quick. New riders often find themselves getting lightheaded. Don't be fooled though. Their lung capacity is comparable to ours. They just *breathe in* much quicker than we're used to. If you're going to ride plalomas for any distance you must learn to breathe with them. Recognize when they are heading to the surface and begin to exhale. They will breach the water for only a brief moment, so you must spend all of it filling your lungs. Focus on your diaphragm. Pull in with your gut, not your lungs."

Father Decha sat back and met eyes with Olenka. Neither of them blinked or looked away.

"And what about you, *child of promise*? What did your holy eyes notice?"

Olenka kept her gaze steady. This man was sizing her up, and it was testing her patience.

"I noticed how much stronger they are than us. Faster too."

Father Decha nodded. "Right you are, and you would do well not to forget it. Plalomas only ride with those who respect their talents." He looked away, glancing at the now rising sun. "Tap them twice on the head to stop or to go. Guide them with your hand, but never jerk on the harness or force them. If you want them to speed up, click your tongue in the water. It doesn't need to be very loud. Their hearing is far keener than our own."

Father Decha turned to Krit. "I believe that's as much as they need to know to get started, but I still think this is a fool's errand, Krit. I don't care how the conclave voted…"

Krit nodded and waved a dismissing hand. "Yes, yes, Father. Your concerns have been *well* documented."

He turned his attention to the crew and tried to smile. Olenka marked the gesture. He was sincere and hopeful, but that hope was fading fast. Was there something important Krit wasn't telling them? Perhaps he was just questioning his own judgment for sending sirena.

Strangely, Olenka found herself hoping it was both.

"Olenka," Decha called out, "a word before you go?"

Olenka sat rigid as the kataw drifted closer. Uncomfortably closer. His words were stiff and quiet as he leaned in, whispering so that the others couldn't hear. "I know you couldn't care less what I think of you, but your pride will be the fall of this crew. I don't think any of you minnows have what it takes, but I'm not so petty as to wish misfortune upon you or this mission. So why don't you prove me wrong, huh? Prove you're worthy to bear *Heaven's Hand* upon your brow. Shove it right back into my pompous teeth when you bring my pod home bearing the sacred armor."

Olenka scowled. "You can count on it."

Decha grunted and nodded. "One more thing. Akia there is the fastest ploma I've ever trained, and she knows it. Don't cross her. You can bump heads with me, and you can bump heads with the monks, but you do as she tells you. You understand?"

Olenka sighed and stared up at the sky. "Will you two just *let us go* already?"

Father Decha smiled and bowed as his ploma drifted away. He tapped his mount's head, and the two slipped down into the sea.

"Oh," Krit squeaked. "Well, I guess that's it then. I'll take care of your banca for you while you are gone! *Good luck, you three!*"

And then he was gone too. Without any further advice or instruction, the two kataw retreated under the surface, abandoning the sirena to their impossible task.

"Well," Olenka said, "looks like this is it. How should we proceed, ladies?"

Mari flared her eyebrows and rubbed her ploma's back. "How fast can the pod go, you think?"

"Fast," Diwala said. "Krit was convinced that we could make the journey in time."

"Only one way to find out," Olenka muttered. "Di, you think we can make Ka Jiya by morning if we ride straight through the night?"

She shrugged. "I have heard boastings that would suggest we could, but your guess is as good as mine."

Olenka nodded. She clapped her hands and gripped her harness. "Alright, enough drifting the doldrums. Di, if you would?"

Diwala nodded and gazed out into the horizon. She tracked the sun and followed its glow out to the north. She slid herself down tight against her ploma and imitated the way Father Decha had tapped the creature's head. She stretched out her hand and pointed the gentle beast down its path.

Her plaloma obediently eyed her course and crashed into the water. He was followed by the simultaneous taps and splashes of Mari and Olenka. The plalomas moved with exhilarating speed. Together their pod rushed past the docks, barreling along the edge of Karafuru Reef, and bursting out into the cruel expanse of the open ocean.

Part Four

Instruments of Cruelty

CHAPTER 24

TRAITORS

COLD. THERE WAS A SUDDEN SENSATION OF COLD followed by burning discomfort in his nostrils. Corin opened his eyes, feeling them peel apart from the crust of sleep. The next thing he felt was a sensitive pulsing in the back of his head. His breath was ragged as he looked around. He was in a very dark room, or maybe it just *felt* dark. He was sitting on something hard which he realized must have been a wooden chair. It was uncomfortable, but that didn't matter. He was so very tired…

He slumped a little, and let his eyelids press back together.

There was a jarring impact against his cheek and temple that was almost a sound. Corin sprang back in pain, now fully alert. Two guards were standing in front of him. Corin felt water trickling down his chin and neck and noticed the empty bowl in the guard's hand.

"Go tell Morten he's awake."

One of the guards left the room. It was a sandy, stone box with no doors or windows: just one open archway leading into a dim hallway. Corin turned his head slowly, seeing that there were actually two more guards in the room standing against the wall behind him on either side.

Corin's back was aching, so he shifted his weight and discovered that his hands were bound. They were tied between him and the back of the chair so he couldn't lean back. Corin fidgeted against his restraints, trying to find a comfortable position. The anxiety became claustrophobia became terror. The room was dreadfully silent save his own panting breath. The three remaining guards didn't even look at Corin. They were just there: as cold and immobile as the stone of the walls.

The sound of footfalls lightly echoed down the hall.

Corin jerked and went rigid, noticing for the first time that his cheek was tender and swollen, and his mouth was filled with old blood.

With a presence of absolute authority, Elder Morten walked into the room. A guard followed behind him carrying a wooden chair. The guard placed it in front of Corin and Elder Morten sat. He slid the chair forward a little, so that now, even sitting upright, he was too close to Corin's face. Corin tried to sit up to get away, but his back was tired and weak and couldn't support him while pressing against the knot around his wrists.

The elder was no longer wearing his ceremonial robes, but a fitted military uniform of leather straps and plated armor that accentuated the mass of his chest and shoulders. His face was square, with harsh brow and jaw lines. His hair was clipped close to his skull, making his ears look huge and thick. They were framed by dark, square sideburns that almost looked false against his clean, sandy skin.

When Morten spoke, it was deep and friendly. It was the voice of an announcer, of a judge, of a king. It was the voice of someone who believed that they were better than you. And once you heard them speak, some part of you believed it too.

"I can't tell you how pleased I am to have you here." Elder Morten leaned back and casually rubbed an itch from his chin. "My guards have been looking for you for such a long time."

"Looking?" Corin blinked and scrunched his aching face. "Why me?"

Morten threw up his hands from their lazy perch on his thighs. "Well, we weren't looking for *you* in particular, but you turned out to be the one. You are Lorenzo's little brother, correct? Marcus' youngest son?"

"Y-yes…" Corin felt his voice stutter when he spoke, but he couldn't help it. "Why would you have been looking for me?"

"Still keeping up the act?" Morten chuckled to himself and sat back, gently folding his legs. "Well, that's alright. If it brings you comfort. I suppose you'll have precious little comfort in the future. But you should know that I am *not* a patient man."

He cleared his throat and leaned in very close to Corin. "How many of you are there?"

"W-what?" Corin's head wobbled in fuzzy confusion. "What are you talking about?"

Morten signaled to the guard at his right with a quick glance, and the soldier struck Corin with the back of his hand. The balls of his knuckles sank deep into his cheek, and the blow was so hard that the sting came after. Corin didn't scream, but he gasped for breath as he tasted fresh blood in his mouth.

Morten's face did not move or flinch or frown. He stared carefully at Corin with a bright look that seemed as if it might break into a smile at any second.

"I warned you, son. I have no time for patience. Not when my city's security is at stake. How many of you are there?"

Corin's body trembled and his voice with it. "I don't understand what you're asking…"

The guard slapped Corin again. He felt blood and spittle slip helplessly down his lip.

"You're so right, young man. I should be more precise. How many more *traitors* are there?"

Corin was afraid to speak, afraid he would be hit again. He looked up at Morten, asking the question with his eyes.

Morten sighed. "You are young. If you cooperate, you need not be hanged with the others. Perhaps you did not fully understand what you were doing. I might be persuaded to suggest to the council that they take mercy upon you if you tell me what you know."

Corin swallowed hard against the copper taste in his mouth. "What is it I'm supposed to have done?"

The guard lifted his hand to strike again, but Morten stopped him with a quick twitch of his hand. He leaned in close to Corin, his weight resting on his elbows on his knees, his nose nearly brushing Corin's.

"I can tolerate ignorance, young man, but I will not tolerate mockery. Ask another obvious question like that, and I will have my guard loosen your tongue with something a bit more robust than the back of his hand."

Morten studied Corin's face closely, expecting him to confess or weep or beg, but Corin just sat there, too confused and afraid to open his mouth. A few silent seconds passed, and Morten looked at the two guards behind Corin.

"Do it."

The guards grabbed Corin under the arms and lifted him up from his seat. A third guard came forward and hit him hard in the belly. The blow made Corin feel like he would vomit and defecate all at once. He groaned in a high, strained voice as tears parted his eyes and pursed his lips. The pain writhed deep into him, making him sick and weak. The guards flopped him back onto the chair, almost breaking his tail as it twisted in unnatural angles.

Morten stood, his hands clasped behind his back. He walked around Corin, staring at nothing but the wall.

"Today, not long before sunset, our guards at the southern gate were attacked," Morten explained. "First, they were attacked by your brother, who was trying to persuade them to disobey direct orders. Multiple witnesses have confirmed that a large, outlander creature was smuggled through our gates among an entourage of its fellow savages. This beast was clearly trained and made its way to the central tower where it proceeded to steal the sun gem. When the gem was acquired, your snake of a brother then mounted the beast's back and attempted to deliver it to the savages beyond.

"Witnesses also tell me that *you* stole a military laharto and attempted to escape the city with your brother. People have died because of this treachery. You have brought terror to this city, and it is my belief that terror alone was your purpose. Terror enough to shake authority in our system. Terror enough to rouse sympathy to the outlander cause. Terror enough to convince a squabbling mass of confused citizens to believe in the backwards superstitions of an antiquated age of *barbarism!*" Morten's voice was rising, fresh spittle fleeing his lips as he roared. "*This*, I will not stand for! I understand perfectly well what it is you are trying to accomplish! What I do not yet know is who else have you been working with. *How many more traitors are there in our ranks?*"

He came in front of Corin and grabbed his chin, forcing him to stare up into his eyes. Corin tried to speak. He tried to tell him that it was all wrong, that he was innocent, and that he and his brother had only been trying to save the city from the beast's attack. He tried, but his throat felt hot and swollen, like he could choke and drown under his own flesh. Morten waited for a moment, and then turned from the room.

"*Take him to a cell*," he barked.

Again, Corin was wrenched to his feet and dragged out of the room. He tried to move his legs fast enough to keep pace with the guards, but he was dazed and broken, and the bare knuckles of his toes scraped against the gritty stone floor.

He was taken down empty, colorless halls with lit candles illuminating meager stone alcoves every four meters. They descended flights of stairs, and the stone at his feet went from sandy and dry to cold and damp. The hall turned, and Corin was facing a row of prison cells. Iron bars were lined up on either side of the hall. Each cell was divided from the others by a thick stone wall. As Corin was carried down the line, he could see through his puffy eyelids that most of the cells were occupied. All of them were outlanders: tired, dirty farmers. It was hard to say, but Corin thought he recognized some of them from the incident at the southern gate.

Near the end of the hall, Corin was taken to an empty cell. A guard unlocked and threw open the metal door while another slid the rope from Corin's wrists. With his hands occupied with the rope, the guard kicked Corin's lower back, knocking him to his knees in the cell. His kneecaps cracked against the cool stone, and the cell door was slammed shut just behind his head. Corin slumped to the side of his thigh, pulling weight off his knees. The cell was barren save a pile of hay in the back corner, and a waste bucket on the opposite side.

And Corin wept.

* * *

CLOSE TO AN HOUR MUST HAVE PASSED, BUT STILL Corin lay there on the floor where the guard had thrown him, too shocked and exhausted to crawl to the hay. His throat was raw and tight, but he had no tears left. Eventually, the sting of the cold stone became too painful and he shambled to his toes. He limped over the hay pile, the pain in his knees spiking with each step. He collapsed to the moldy mound and tucked in his legs and tail so that none of his skin was touching the stone. The sandy walls felt strangely warm in comparison, and Corin was certain that he would be asleep any moment.

But the silence of the cell was interrupted.

Somewhere down the hall, an outlander struck his palm against a wooden pail. The sound was dull and smooth, like the thump of a box being unloaded from a cart. He struck it once, twice, and then he found a rhythm. Calm and steady as footfalls, the sound thumped along the stone walls.

And then another outlander joined in.

And then another.

Soon, the simple sound of the improvised drums was matched by a hum. The prisoners' smoky voices rose up like a swarm, buzzing through the sandstone walls, through the very chill of the cells. The hum was high and dusty and atonal, but not in an ugly way. It didn't really seem like the outlanders were trying to find a pitch; they were playing with the sound.

Testing it.

Stretching it.

Searching out its possibilities.

Their voices shook and warbled like a tree filled with singing birds. Each one was proud and unique but somehow still a part of the greater whole. Their hums became a chorus, and their voices flexed and slipped into a haunting, mourning, playful beauty. Not quite a melody, though… nothing that restricting.

And then, when the sound had grown to mesmerizing immensity, one of them started to sing.

"Ay ah-ah, miren chicos! Ay ah-ah miren chicos!"

The other outlanders repeated the chorus for every line, building onto it with their own varied voices and lyrics, but their embellishments were always appendages to the original. Corin found that he was intoxicated by the drums, and he noticed that the steady, single beat was now doubled up: like the *bump, bump* of a heartbeat.

> *"Ay, I am of the other side! Ay ah-ah, other*
>   *si-ide!*
> *"Ay ah-ah, miren chicos! Ay ah-ah, miren chicos!"*
> *"Come my children, see the light! Ay ah-ah, see the*
>   *li-ight!*
> *"Ay ah-ah, miren chicos! Ay ah-ah, miren chicos!"*
> *"Ay, dark clouds roll in with my drum! Ay ah-ah, with*
>   *my dru-um!*
> *"Ay ah-ah, miren chicos! Ay ah-ah, miren chicos!"*
> *"Come listen to the ancient sound! Ay ah-ah, ancient*
>   *sou-ound!*
> *"Ay ah-ah, miren chicos! Ay ah-ah, miren chicos!"*
> *"Ay, oh that I could fly away! Ay ah-ah, fly*
>   *awa-ay!*
> *"Ay ah-ah, miren chicos! Ay ah-ah, miren chicos!"*

*"And hear the voice beyond the plains! Ay ah, beyond
the plai-ains!*
"Ay ah-ah, miren chicos! Ay ah-ah, miren chicos!"

Corin looked out over the cell, clutching his torso for warmth. He couldn't see any of the outlanders, but it felt like they were all staring straight through the stone walls at him, like their song was directed to him alone. It hoisted up his soul, lifting his weary heart straight out of his shivering, aching body until he was no longer bound to the pains of mortal life.

Strangely, this experience did not feel surreal at all. It was like the highest pinnacle of an impossible dream, the part that feels real even after you're awake. This moment, this weightlessness, felt more vivid and clear than anything he had ever felt. Perhaps he was going mad. Perhaps his fragile mind was coping with the suffering. Perhaps it was because he had never been in this much pain before.

But, no… that wasn't true at all.

Corin remembered then how he had felt out on the plains. How the beast's black blood had crippled him. He remembered that burning ice in his veins, the shards in his intestines, and the torture it brought to his mind.

This was nothing.

There was *nothing* these guards could do to match that suffering.

With that terrible thought, Corin realized just how pampered and painless his life had been. He had never broken a bone, he was rarely ill, and he had never been a particularly daring child. Adahy had gotten hurt all the time while they were growing up. He was the one who fell off of rooftops or snuck into corrals of angry lahartos. Corin was the nervous little boy who watched and cried and ran for help when his friend fell too far. He had probably experienced more pain today than he had felt in his entire, pathetic life.

The outlander chant relaxed back into a cloud of cries, then a hum like wind through grass, then that tired, steady heartbeat against the wooden buckets. Corin felt his mind slip back into himself, the cold snatching up his awareness again.

But it wasn't so bad this time.

Corin let out a long, trembling sigh and studied the world around him anew. He noticed that at the end of the hallway, there was a single, round window. It was open to the night air, with no glass filling the cross of iron bars inside it. Through the window, Corin could see the gentle golden light of the shield. Beyond it, the storm parted for a moment, and the shallow sparks of stars filtered down to him.

With a sudden, yet comforting shock, Corin felt the voice from within speak to him again. It was that same foreign, yet intimately familiar, voice he had heard on the plains.

Things have finally been set in motion, and what is done cannot be undone. The sum of ten thousand past ages has been placed upon your shoulders. But first, you must rest, child. You will not die in this cell.

The thought came and went, like a warm beam of sunlight falling over his chilled, shadowed skin. Apparently, his sore throat had some more to give, and Corin cried silently and abundantly as he leaned against the soft, sandstone of his cell. But this time they were not tears of pain.

In a few seconds, exhaustion had taken him, and Corin was asleep.

CHAPTER 25

FRIENDS ON THE INSIDE

ORIN AWOKE TO THE SOUND OF A CELL DOOR screeching open. He jerked and thrashed to cover his face, cowering in fear in the filthy corner of the stone room.

But the sound wasn't what had scared him.

He had had that dream again: black clouds boiling over the plains. A turbulent sky with lightning so bright and hot that it painted the world pink. Something wicked writhing behind the storm, its mass obscured by the wall of clouds. Those clouds were closer than before, and they were moving toward him faster and faster with every dream.

He tried to swallow, but his throat felt as stiff as tanned baca hide. His eyes ached as they cracked open to his cell. It hadn't been his door that had opened. He could hear the soft scrape of someone else being dragged away down the hall.

Corin's body yearned for more sleep, but his mind was too alert, like the frantic attention of a cornered animal. He had rolled his sleeves down sometime in the night, and now he tried to pull his chilled fingers inside the cuffs, stretching his shirt tight up against his neck and exposing the small of his back. The storm's gale had long since passed, leaving only the cool of morning, but it was still too cold for a telak's liking.

Corin glanced up at the window at the end of the hallway. There was very little light, but he could tell that night was shifting into the first glimmers of dawn. He stretched and found that there was not one bloody centimeter of his body that wasn't sore and stiff. All his joints screamed and popped and crackled their protests as he moved up to a seated position.

He didn't know why, but Corin suspected that he didn't have much time left to himself. With the new day, he guessed that the guards would soon come to beat and question him anew. This might be his only chance to prepare an intelligent response, something he could have ready when the pain made him blurt whatever was on the tip of his tongue.

But what could he say to them?

What did they want to hear?

And where under the *scorching summer sun* was his grandfather in all of this madness? Had the old man abandoned him? More likely he was in a cell of his own, Corin realized. It was clear that Morten believed Lehonti was some kind of mastermind behind the beast's attack…

And then a thought suddenly drifted into Corin's mind. A small, terrible, reasonable thought: What if his grandfather was wrong?

Like a pebble that shifts a rockslide, the doubts came tumbling down on him. What evidence was there that the demons had actually returned? What evidence was there that they had ever come in the first place? Maybe Morten was right. Obviously Corin knew he wasn't a traitor or any of that rubbish, but maybe what he'd seen had actually been an elaborate hoax of some kind. Maybe they were caught in the middle of a conspiracy. A power struggle with the outlanders, perhaps? That was what Morten seemed to think, at least.

It was a trail of thought that quickly came to a dead-end.

With force far greater than any of his fleeting doubts, the memories came back to him: the beast, the pain, the voice, the light… How could he possibly doubt? After what he had seen on the plains, after the pain he had felt burning through his blood, after the voice he had heard echoing through his mind, what room was there left for doubt? Corin laid his head back against the sandstone wall and closed his eyes. No, the only rational explanation was his grandfather's.

That, Corin thought with a grimace, *or I'm losing my mind...*

Was he losing his mind? Hearing voices was... Well, it wasn't good. Corin didn't *think* he was going mad, but did anyone? How were you supposed to judge your own sanity? Especially when what you knew to be true was objectively insane to everyone around you? Corin groaned and rubbed at his tired, greasy face. He needed to focus on what he could control, and the state of his sanity was decidedly out of his control. He was going to have to assume that he could trust what he had seen and go from there.

So, what *had* he seen?

Well, first off, Corin had seen a demon. He could accept that as fact, couldn't he? The black blood, its rotten flesh, a living being as cold as death... there was no denying it. That creature couldn't have been some trained outlander beast. No telak was responsible for that monster.

Second, he had seen the mural.

Corin didn't care how many years of planning could have gone into it, that tiled floor was *too elaborate* to be a hoax, and it was too complicated to be art alone. That was history, and history was true. If the story was true, then that meant all of Centile was in great danger. If the demons had returned, then it was only a matter of time before the world was overrun with them. It meant that the sun gem's shield was the only real defense Centile had. Sure, the guards could probably kill some of the creatures, but hordes of them? Armies of monsters that felt no pain?

There was no chance.

Corin looked back out the window. The morning's light was starting to fill the horizon now, and the shield's glow was easing from its transparent nocturnal shine to the white, frosty haze of dawn. The significance of the golden barrier struck him. His ancestors had known this day would come, and they had left their children the best protection they could. Something that would never be destroyed or abandoned, even if its true purpose was forgotten to myth and song.

It was ironic; Corin had just been questioning the shield's worth. Not a full day ago it had seemed unnecessary and outdated. Just another way for the inner district to flex its superiority over the plains.

Now he believed it might be the only hope for his species.

Hope… Corin rolled the word around in his mouth, trying to find a place he could chew it so that it didn't taste quite so bitter. There was a third thing Corin had seen. Well, not *seen* exactly… More like *felt* or *heard.*

Hope was the one word that he really didn't want to pull up to the front of his mind, but with nothing else to distract his thoughts, it was inevitable. He knew that, somehow, he was Centile's only hope. He didn't know why, but he knew that this had all become his responsibility. Somehow, *he* had to stop this, just like Vallin had done three hundred years ago.

That was the thought that destroyed Corin. That was the thought that made him weep.

He felt with a burning certainty that if Centile were to fall, if his people were killed, if the world was lost to darkness, the blood of that calamity would surely be on his trembling hands.

Corin leaned his head forward and ran his shaking fingers through his hair, letting them tug at the grit and greasy roots. How? How was he going to do this? He knew in his bones that he had been called to do *something*, but he had no idea what it was. He picked through his brain, reliving each moment, trying against his better judgement to find some clue.

And then he thought about the mural of Vallin kneeling down before the crystal. He pictured his ancestor holding the golden sword filled with glorious, inspiring light. Was that the answer? The sword was at the center of everything, wasn't it? Hadn't Vallin survived the demons by channeling its light? Hadn't it been what saved them before? According to the legend, it was the *only* object that caused those monsters pain. It was the tool Vallin used to destroy the demons at their source.

Through the window, a crimson flag caught Corin's eye. As the sky continued to brighten, Corin could see the banners of Centile hoisted throughout the city. He saw the yellow insignia: the golden sword shrouded in the sun.

There it was.

The answer was all around him in plain sight. If the tower was built to make the people remember, then surely the founders of Centile would have preserved other clues. The emblem of Centile was the sword of Vallin. It had to be.

It seemed impossible that he had never known the flag's true meaning, but that must have been the truth. The crest of Centile must have been designed to depict the golden sword of Vallin burning with the sun gem's light, but that knowledge only brought more questions. Where was the sword? How could he find it? Once he found it, how would he use it? As he pondered his future there in that frigid cell, Corin realized just how clueless he was.

* * *

THE SUN WAS CRESTING THE ROOFTOPS WHEN THE SOFT echo of footsteps lighted through the hallway. Corin knew that this was it. They were finally coming for him. He shifted from his seat to his toes, crouching with his first knees tucked tight against his chest, staring at the cell door in anticipation. Two guards stepped in front of his cell…

…but they were accompanied by Elder Lehonti.

"Grandfather?" Corin bolted upright, overwhelmed by the shock of the sight. "What happened? Why are you here?" For a moment Corin was certain that the old man had been arrested as well,

but the thought was silly. The guards would never take him here, not in the same cell or even the same hall as Corin.

The old man chuckled. "It seems I still have some friends on the inside, my boy! Quickly, come here and we'll…" Lehonti paused mid-sentence, his eyes falling and darkening. "Corin, let me see your face."

Corin stepped slowly to the iron bars, for some reason ashamed of what had been done to him. Lehonti studied his grandson's bruised and bloody features, and hatred bloomed across the wrinkled corners of the old man's eyes. It was a hatred far greater than Corin had believed his grandfather was capable of.

"Morten did this to you?" Lehonti swore under his breath.

Corin ignored the question. His mind was too desperate for answers. "Grandfather, what are we going to do? How long do they plan on keeping me in here?"

The elder took a deep, shuddering breath and coughed into his fist, more to clear his mind than his throat. "You have a hearing in Elder Baltista's office this morning. The other elders are gathering there now."

"A hearing?"

"Yes, but just a preliminary one," Lehonti said. "Our laws always afford the accused an opportunity to present their case before the chief judge if… well… if *certain punishments* are being considered. It is then Baltista's job to determine credibility of the accusations presented and to hold a vote on whether to proceed to a formal trial There is a strict procedure to be observed in such matters, you see…" And the hatred flared back through Lehonti's eyes. "Though it seems Morten has taken the law into his *own*, soiled hands. Corin, tell me what happened last night. What did they do to you?"

"I…" Corin shrugged. "Honestly, I don't remember much. Morten thinks you staged the attack on the city, that you're working with the outlanders. He kept asking me how many more traitors there were…"

"And he beat you when you didn't answer?"

Corin nodded. "His guards did."

With a sudden flush of fear, Corin's eyes shot to the guards on either side of his grandfather. The old man looked puzzled for a moment and then followed his gaze.

"*Ah*, yes. I am sorry, Corin. You have no need to fear these two." Lehonti shook his head in annoyance. "Baca chips, I'm getting old… I should have introduced you first. This is Selina, and I believe you may have already met her brother."

Corin nodded a greeting to the guard at his right, and she nodded back. With her frame obscured by armor, Corin hadn't even noticed that she was a woman. She had a beautiful tan face, with a soft round jaw and dark, harsh eyes. Her eyebrows were as thick and black as a winter's night, and boldly defined a sleek forehead. Her dark hair was pulled back into a tight bun, and her whole demeanor was somehow both gentle and severe. Corin had the impression that she was a woman of fierce loyalty; the kind of person you could easily trust, but whose trust it was *not* easy to earn.

Corin glanced left at the other guard and was surprised to find that he *did* recognize him. He was certain he knew this man's face, but from where? His jawline was wide and much harder than Selina's, but the two shared the same dark complexion, round nose, and bold eyebrows. Siblings, clearly. He was a masculine mirror of the other, though his features were much kinder. There was a soft humor behind his attentive stare, like he could find anything in the world mildly amusing.

"How… how do I know you?"

The guard smiled broadly. "Name's Darrow. Ring any bells? No? Well, you probably didn't hear me last night… Seemed a little *frantic*, you did." He stopped to chuckle. "But you still took the time to save me! Mighty grateful for that. Me and that little girl both."

The memory came back in an instant. This man was a friend of Lorenzo's. He had been there during the attack, he had seen Lorenzo riding the beast out of the city, and he had been healed by the sun gem.

"It seems we have some friends on the inside!" Lehonti smiled at his grandson. "Thanks to you, Corin. Darrow sought me out when he heard that you had been arrested. He has offered us his help, and I fear we may be in desperate need of it."

"My sister as well!" Darrow thundered. "After what you did for me… I don't have a *bloody clue* what happened, but I'm betting you and Elder Lehonti have the answers. He's tried his best to explain it all to me, but…" the guard shrugged.

"But his skull was too *thick* for the history lesson," Selina finished.

Darrow's rumbling laughter felt both immensely comforting and wildly inappropriate to Corin.

"Yes, well… More's the pity." Lehonti faked a quick, uncomfortable chuckle, before he turned back to his grandson. "Corin, listen to me. We don't have much time to speak before the hearing, but there is a lot you need to know. Darrow and Selina believe they may have," his voice dropped to a whisper, "a way to get you out of here!"

Corin blinked. "Get me out? You mean, *breaking* me out?"

"*Shh!*" the old man hissed as he glanced back down the hall of cells. "Yes. Tonight. Morten has wasted enough of our time as it is. He's lost his senses, and I truly don't know what that baca-brained brute might be willing to do…" Lehonti sighed, his miserable eyes combing through the archives of his mind. "He's been waiting for an opportunity like this for *years*, Corin. He's going to use you as an excuse to centralize his power. I'm sure of it. If we don't get you out now, you may be stuck in this cell until it's too late."

"Too late? What do you…" Corin muttered and then realized he didn't want the answer to that question. "Never mind. Where would I *go?* I can't just go back home!"

"No, my son. You would not be able to stay within the city's walls until things… change." Lehonti swallowed and shook his head. "No… I'm sending you to stay with Adahy's family. They don't know you're coming, but I'm sure they'll see the necessity. Yesterday I promised Adahy I would pay a visit to his father, Mohe.

That should be a sufficient alibi… I will meet you there as soon as I can, but… Well, the *important* thing is that you will be safe there for now. Far from Morten's influence."

Corin nodded. He didn't like the plan, but he knew it was necessary. He knew everything was going to be different now. His dream kept growing clearer and closer. There was a storm on the horizon, and it was just a matter of time before the lightning struck.

"My boy," the old man whispered, "there is one more thing. I'm sure you've pieced it together by now, but you have a job to do. You understand that, don't you?"

Corin tried to speak or nod or do something to acknowledge the old man, but his tongue was so very cold… his mind, too.

"Vallin was chosen to save our world, and to destroy the demons at their source," Lehonti said, slipping back into his lecturer's voice, "but our ancestors knew this fight wasn't over, and for years I have somehow known that my days would see it return. I have spent a great deal of time thinking about what happened to you on the plains yesterday, and–"

"*Sir*," Selina gently interrupted, "we do need *to leave* soon. The council will expect us to be prompt, and I think it wise to try to avoid suspicion."

Lehonti nodded. "You're right, but I need to explain this first." He turned back to Corin. "My boy, you must understand what is being asked of you?"

Corin's eyes drifted back to the open window. "I think I'm starting to."

Lehonti grimaced as he spoke. "You must use the sword of Vallin to destroy the demons' source once more. I'm certain you know that, but there is something else you do not yet know. I tried to tell you yesterday, but my story was… cut short. We *have* the sword, Corin. Our family has held the sword for the past three hundred years. A kind of birthright, you might say. Each of us have held it and examined it, passing it from father to son, but no one has been able to bring back its light. Over the years, your father and I tried *everything*. He would deny it if you asked him, but I'm certain that is the reason he went into bladesmithing in the first place. For years he toiled with the sword until he finally lost hope that–"

"*Sir*, Selina's right..." Darrow pressed.

"*Yes, yes! Alright!*" Lehonti growled. "What rubbish! *Fifty years* of trying to get this story out... Anyway, I know this is not what you would have liked to hear, my boy, but you must succeed where the rest of us have failed. I'm sending you to stay with the outlanders so that you will have time and peace to work with the bloody thing. You may have months, or you may only have hours, but either way the demons are coming, son. They *are* coming. When that time comes, we will have to pull the entire population of the plains all back behind the shield and you'll have to lead us into battle."

Corin found that he could do nothing but blink. "Battle? You think... *Battle?*"

"We have no other options, Corin!" Lehonti reached through the bars and wrapped his wrinkled fingers around Corin's shoulders. "Once you've learned how to bring back its light, we will be able to lead an attack on the source! You must do as Vallin once did. Tell me that you understand what I'm saying to you, son."

Corin nodded weakly, his guts writhing.

"I need you to *tell* me you understand!"

"Okay! I understand, Grandfather."

Lehonti nodded, and turned away, muttering his frantic plans to himself. "So much to do. I'll need to meet with Marcus again. Yes... Yes, I'll have to go there next. He still has the sword stashed away somewhere in that *rat's nest* he calls a workshop. After the hearing... yes. That will do. Then I'll start the vote of no confidence... Yes, up all night, but..." He turned back up to Corin. "After that, you'll be on your own, I'm afraid. Well, I suppose not *entirely* on your own." Lehonti motioned to Darrow and Selina. "These two extraordinary friends will watch out for you in my stead. If I travel back and forth too much, I fear it would risk exposing you to Morten, so I'll stay in Centile and try to talk some sense into the other elders. We need to start gathering food and water now..."

The old man turned back to his rambling as the weight of leadership bent his back.

"*Sir...*" Darrow's voice was tight with anxiety.

"Yes, yes! I'm quite aware of the sun-scorched time!" He twirled away in a flourish of gold and orange cloth. "Take care of my grandson, you two!"

With that, the old man hurried down the hall before Corin had time to say a word.

* * *

THE THREE STOOD IN SILENCE AT THE IRON DOOR FOR A rather long, arduous moment. Corin was too overwhelmed to speak. Darrow and Selina held their positions with the practiced patience of professionals, occasionally glancing out the open window or down the hall. Selina noticed Corin's confused expression and leaned forward against her spear and smiled at him.

"We need to give Elder Lehonti some time to beat us to the council. Don't want it looking like he was here with us, you know?" She winked for emphasis.

"Oh." Corin nodded. "I guess that makes sense... So, what happens now?"

Selina smiled and glanced out the window again. "Now? Now we... well, what do you think, brother? Has it been long enough?"

Darrow nodded. "I think so. Might be suspicious if we dragged our tails any longer."

Selina's charming face grew stern and frigid as she turned toward Corin.

"Alright then. Listen up, *tenderfoot*, we only have one shot at this. Darrow managed to get us assigned as your escorts, but we have to be *convincing*. You can't act like you know us. We will yell in your face. We will hit you. We will insult you, and you are going to have to take it until we leave the hearing. Is that understood?"

Corin nodded in silence. His mind was stretched so thin that Selina's sudden change in tone brought it close to snapping. Corin felt sick and swallowed down the stomach acid in his throat, trying his best to keep his head upright.

"Hey, hey, hey. Hold on there, tenderfoot." Her voice was sweet again. She reached through the bars and placed a calloused hand on Corin's cheek. "Listen, this is only until we get through the hearing, alright? I *promise* you, we are your friends, Corin. You can trust us."

Corin couldn't keep his hands from shaking. He knew it wasn't true, but he felt like it had been weeks since anyone had been so kind to him.

"Why?" Corin whispered. "Why are you two doing all this for me?"

Selina's smile brightened, and she motioned to Darrow. "Because you saved my baca-brained brother!"

Darrow nodded and produced a set of rusty keys as he spoke. "*And* because we believe in you."

He slid the key into the lock and opened the door with a morbid screech.

"Well, actually…" Darrow said thoughtfully. "*Selina* believes in you. And I believe in Selina. She's always had this gift, you see, about judging people. I told her what you did for me, and *boom!*" He snapped his fingers. "She knew we needed to go see Elder Lehonti."

Darrow's rumbling chuckle rattled through the iron bars. Corin stood motionless, peering, but not walking, through the open door.

Darrow smiled warmly at him. "So, kid, do you trust us?"

It seemed like such a simple question, but Corin did not know how to respond.

Selina stepped into the cell and leaned her spear against the wall. She placed both her hands on Corin's shoulders and looked into his eyes. Corin involuntarily glanced away.

"Hey, look at me, kid. Listen. I *promise* we are here to help," she said. "We believe in you, tenderfoot. Can you also believe in us? Can you believe in me?"

Corin looked back at her. Her eyes were piercing but sincere. Corin sighed, feeling so much pain and fear escape with that one, warm breath. His eyes glassed over, and he felt the heat in his sinuses warm as he sniffed back tears.

"Alright. I believe in you…"

Selina's smile was pristine. She grabbed her spear and trotted back out into the hallway. Corin stepped through the door and Darrow jerked him around and began binding his wrists behind his back. It was rough, and it hurt, but Corin trusted them. He *had* to trust them.

"Okay," Darrow said, "here's the situation. Elder Lehonti predicts two possible outcomes of the hearing. The first is that the council will decide there is insufficient evidence to send you to a full trial but will hold you under monitored house arrest until they can determine the beast's origin. The second, and *more likely* scenario, is that you'll be taken to a permanent holding cell at the basement floor of this building until a formal trial is scheduled several weeks from now. Either way, you're out of here tonight. If the council decides to detain you again, Selina and I will ensure you are placed in the *correct* cell," he winked at Corin, "and we'll lead Marcus in to retrieve you. We'll meet up again as soon as we are able and escort you out of the city to the outlander village."

"Wait," Corin muttered, "you said my *father?*"

Selina nodded. "That's right. It was *his* plan for us to break you out."

Corin tried to wrap his mind around the thought of his father intentionally breaking a law, but he was shoved down the hall before he could process the absurd idea. It didn't take much effort for Corin to act appropriately timid toward his escorts.

"Enough talking, let's move!" Darrow yelled out against the back of his head, obviously loud enough for the other prisoners to hear.

There was the quick sound of curious ears scurrying away from their bars in response. Together the three of them marched past the rows of cells. Corin could feel set after set of weary outlander eyes following him down the hallway. They had heard everything, and they were keen to the two guard's antics. Corin tried his best to not meet their eyes as he was shuffled away, but the pull was too great. They smiled and bowed their heads as he passed. Someone down the hall even started thumping away on a wooden pail.

Corin's heart groaned as he sensed a very distressing feeling emanating from their worn, somber smiles…

He could feel their hope.

CHAPTER 26

THE HEARING

DARROW AND SELINA LED CORIN THROUGH A side door into a cramped alley and out into the tower plaza. Centile's streets were filled with the typical flurry of crowds and carts. All around him, city life pressed on. Stubborn and proud and oblivious.

The air was thick and muggy, but the sun was drying things quickly. Stands were being wheeled into place, bread was being baked, and well-dressed district officials rushed along the cobblestone, somehow late before the day had even begun. Nothing seemed out of the ordinary, except for the extra guards placed at intervals along the plaza's perimeter. Corin looked back over his shoulder, trying to determine which building he had been held in.

Selina was quick.

She struck her knuckles across the back of his head, sending a muffled thud echoing through his skull.

"Eyes forward, traitor!" Her voice was so different, so void of compassion. It seemed impossible that this was the same woman he had been speaking with minutes before. Corin stumbled from the blow but recovered before he tripped. He knew she meant him no real harm, but he still found himself slipping back into timidity, wanting only to do whatever it took to not be hit again. He kept his head down,

letting his eyes glance around the crowd without the aid of his neck. He didn't recognize any of the telaks here, but their eyes all lingered on him with a practiced disdain.

It was in that moment that Corin began to understand a concept that Adahy had been trying to explain to him for years. Just yesterday he had been one with this crowd. He had held the same rank as them, the same privileged capacity to look down on another telak with no consequence. From this new perspective, Corin understood that it didn't really matter *why* they looked down. Some watched him with pity, others with contempt, but the effect was all the same. He was below them, wretched creature that he was. He was an object of scorn and sympathy. He was somehow less than them, yet he had been one of them only hours before.

Amid the shocked gasps and bitter glares, what hurt the most were the telaks who pretended they did not see him at all. He could feel their gaze as they approached, and he could feel it slip away. They stole glances in passing, but always with shifting eyes mounted on rigid necks. He was being held up bare and exposed in the center of the crowd, and yet they purposely looked away from him. Purposely chose to not acknowledge his plight. None of them questioned his guilt. None of them pitied his pain.

They were just bystanders, and bystanders just watch.

On the far side of the plaza, Corin was taken down a wide and busy street. The walls here were ornamented with extravagance, every surface covered with clean cuts and vivid hues. Tiny statues were carved right out of the blocks and pillars, simple yet beautiful reliefs of warriors marching in the sun, sheaves of grain thrashing in the wind, and carts of produce caravanned across a vast, mountain-crested horizon. The bricks were polished, and the cobblestone was swept. There were no merchants or bakers here, just tall, stern faces and slick, tight tunics. Here the bystanders didn't even *pretend* to not notice Corin. They were so wrapped up in the movement of commerce and accounting that they barely noticed the street beneath them.

"'ey, Darrow!" A gruff voice called out through the clamor. "This 'im?"

"Hold traitor!" Selina's voice was cold and clear.

Corin felt a spear shaft crack against his lower back, and he fell to his first knees before he could see where the unfamiliar voice had come from. He gasped for breath at the jolt of the street on his bones, but he kept his eyes fixed on the cobbles. Several pairs of legs meandered toward him through the crowd, spear shafts gently tapping the street with their steps. Corin glanced up and immediately regretted it. Three male guards were staring down at him, leaning forward right into his air. The one off to the right kicked Corin's thigh.

"Oy, look at me, filth."

Corin felt his brow quiver, but he lifted his face to the man's scorn. The soldier smiled and tilted his head.

"Yeah, he looks like one o' them leather skins, alright. You can see it in the eyes. They've got them scared, animal eyes, like a baca 'bout to be slaughtered."

Corin tried to look away, but another guard caught his chin and wrenched his head forward. This man's face was not smug like the other; it was simply cruel.

"I want you to know what you did to me, traitor." He stared silently into Corin's eyes for a moment, waiting to feel Corin's fear chill his cheeks. "My best friend was watching the gate when you and the rest of those leather skins let in that beast. He's dead. Your brother rode that filthy animal right into him. Knocked him against the wall and cracked open his skull. My friend is *dead*, and *you're* still here."

The guard spat into Corin's face. Stale and sour, the foam stung his eyes.

"Sun-scorched snake." The guard stood up straight again, staring down with iron contempt. "I just hope the elders have the sense to take your life for his."

Corin felt the spear shafts prod against him from behind.

"On your feet." Darrow's voice quavered in pain, but the other guards misread its source. They watched Corin clamber up, his bound arms pressed awkwardly against his back. They each spat at him as he passed. The frothing gunk hit his chest and cheek, slipping down his neck. The guards nodded to Darrow and turned back to their post.

* * *

CORIN WAS URGED DOWN THE STREET TO A BUILDING more decorated than the others. A broad, curved archway of sandy stone was adorned with a spread pair of carved, eagle wings. Below each wing was a simple yet regal sculpture of a young telak, his hands resting on the handle of a sword. The sword was comically long and broad, with its tip resting on the ground at his toes. Behind each sculpture was Centile's sun crest surrounded by flowering sheaves of grain.

If it hadn't been for the events of the last day, Corin never would have known that he was passing by the face of his ancestor.

They ascended several polished stone steps into a broad hall of smooth pillars and rows of wooden desks. The roof was high and vaulted with a massive glass window in the back that lit the whole hall. The floor was a patchwork of black and white stone and cluttered with small crowds, all deeply engaged in absent-minded gossip. Guards moved swiftly between the huddles, sometimes dragging outlander prisoners. The clamor was immense as hundreds of voices slapped against the stone at every angle. The whole room had the paradoxical aspect of both a decorous cathedral and some primordial cavern. The men and women in here were academics, but they were also hunters. This was the hall of the high court of Centile, and its dusty tables had seen more excitement these past few hours than they had ever known.

Darrow and Selina guided Corin through the crowds. Ahead there was a large desk with a row of telaks seated behind it. Lines were shifting and being formed before each one, but there was one line on the end that was far longer than the rest. Darrow and Selina brought Corin to the front of it and shoved him against the desk with a piercing *clack*.

The woman at the desk jumped in shock, her conversation rudely cut off. "*Excuse me*," she scoffed, "but you are going to have to–"

Darrow spoke loudly over her complaints. "High priority prisoner delivery being brought to the council of elders. Don't make them wait."

The line went silent, and the woman nodded quickly, her mouth slightly ajar.

"Oh, of course! Yes, I have the paperwork right here." She held out a document and a dipped pen to Darrow. He signed quickly and jerked Corin to an empty stairway beyond. As they walked, Corin stole a glance at the line. It was composed solely of guards pulling ragged, dirty farmers along the floor. All of them were outlanders, easily labeled by their gaudy, colorful attire. Their faces were dim and fallen, and all of them were anxiously watching Corin. He saw himself in all of them, that painful desperation to not be hit anymore.

The steps coiled in a tight loop around a central pillar, taking the stairway somewhere directly above the main hall. It was cramped but private.

"Stop for a moment." Selina's voice was almost a whisper. She turned Corin around facing him down at her. Her eyes were red, and her mouth was pursed in displeasure. She pulled a small cloth from a pouch at her hip and stretched out her knees to be at eye level with him. Gentle as a mother, she began to wipe the spit from his face and neck.

"Now listen," she said, "it is not going to be quick or pleasant in there, kid. Elder Morten is determined to place blame. He's hoping to excite the council to military action against the outlanders. Remember, whatever happens, whatever their decision is, *you are getting out of here today*, you understand me, tenderfoot? This is just another unpleasant step in the process. Stay strong, and don't lose hope."

She smiled and placed a hand against his cheek. Corin felt like weeping, but there was nothing left to weep. His eyes were dry and tired. Instead he forced himself to smile and turned back up the stairway. Darrow was staring down at him, his arms folded.

"You ready, kid?"

Corin nodded, and they climbed the remaining steps together.

* * *

AT THE TOP OF THE STAIRWAY, THE DOORWAY OPENED into a long hall with wooden doors positioned along the outer side. At the far left end was another round window, exactly like the one in the main hall, but in miniature. Darrow and Selina took Corin to the left, walking toward the window. Unlike the hall below, this floor almost felt still. Somehow its silence was emphasized by the dull roar below rumbling through the floor. At the end of the hall, there was a set of double doors with two guards waiting on either side.

Upon their approach, the guards cracked their spear shafts against the floor and without a word opened the doors. Inside, the room was buzzing with hushed whispers. Grunts of approval and sighs of condescension were all cut short upon the prisoner's entry.

No one stood, but everyone stared.

The room was an office of some type, but much larger than Corin had expected. It was filled with rows of wooden chairs. Desks and tables lined the far wall. There was another massive stained-glass window in this room, this one shaped like Centile's sun crest. On the floor, there was a woven rug of the same shape. A large desk was placed at the rug's tip facing the massive window. Outside the sky was bright and clear, but the room still felt dark and musty.

Seated at intervals around the rug were the six elders of Centile. Behind the desk was Elder Baltista. His silver robes were haphazardly draped over his shoulders, clearly placed in a hurry. His desk was bare save an iron cup of water and a small stack of papers. He motioned to Darrow and Selina, and without a word Corin was shoved into a wooden chair at the edge of the rug next to his grandfather.

Corin glanced to his left. Lehonti shot him a fake smirk and gently slapped his grandson's knee. "It's going to be alright, my boy."

Morten was seated directly opposite from Corin. He was busy talking with Elder Aldren at his right. Corin had never been especially fond of the chief captain, but now he felt a warm hatred haze through his blood. This man was toxic arrogance and unchecked power. Corin found himself glaring at Morten, no longer timid or hurt. He dared him to turn his head, dared him to meet his gaze, dared him to look upon his bruised flesh.

But Morten could not be moved. He either didn't notice Corin or was deliberately letting him stare in vain. Either seemed plausible.

Corin turned away in frustration and noticed a small crowd in the corner. In it he could see several guards and some of the elders' wives. At the edge was his grandmother. Maria offered him a tear-streaked smile and Corin sighed at the floor, unable to find the tenderness to greet her in return.

At the clearing of his throat, all eyes turned to the telak seated at the front desk. Elder Baltista was a slender man, with a long, pointed chin and clipped, black hair. He was old enough to have some silver streaks accent his ears, but his face was full and youthful. His bottom jaw protruded slightly as he spoke, pulling the skin on his cheeks too tight against his skull and giving him an unwarranted abrasive look. Despite this, he gave the impression of civility and intelligence.

"Alright, let's proceed." He coughed and cleared his throat again, glancing at the ragged, tan papers before him. "As you all know, this is a preliminary hearing requested by Elder Lehonti to evaluate the veracity of the accusations placed against his grandsons: Corin and Captain Lorenzo. The proposed charges include treason against the Council of Centile, conspiracy against the city, theft of the sun gem, instigation of terrorism and insurrection among the outlanders, destruction of property, murder, and several other indirect charges of blatant disregard for the lives and safety of Centilean citizens."

With each item on the list of atrocities Corin felt his mouth and stomach sour. It didn't seem possible that so many terrible acts could actually be attributed to *him*. Elder Baltista paused, staring blankly at the page in his hand and passing his tongue against his teeth. With a start he looked up again at the elders, intentionally avoiding eye contact with Corin.

"Due to the severity of these accusations and the irregularity of the crisis, I believe it is appropriate to review the events of the incident as we understand them. Captain... Felipe, is it?" Baltista motioned across the room. A guard with a large, decorated frame stepped forward.

"Yes, sir." His voice was soft and terse.

"Captain, would you mind recounting for the council the events you shared with me this morning?"

The guard nodded. "Of course, sir."

He stepped to the side of Elder Baltista's desk and clasped his hands behind his back. His eyes were dark brown and completely empty. He seemed to be speaking straight through the window at the far end of the room.

"Sir, yesterday evening, some time before sunset, I received intelligence that a large caravan of farmers had been seen approaching the city to seek shelter from an upcoming storm. I received orders from my superiors to restrict transit through the southern gate. I have been informed by my subordinate officers that Captain Lorenzo and his brother were present at this event and caused some minor disruption before the caravan arrived. The reports on the following events have… *varied*."

Elder Baltista nodded and motioned to Felipe. "I understand. Please proceed, Captain."

Felipe nodded and cleared his throat before continuing. "At some point during the passing of the caravan, Captain Lorenzo became hostile, attacking several guards before he was detained. The cause of this outburst remains unclear, but it seems the dispute was in regard to security protocol, and whether or not a cart from the caravan required additional scrutiny. It was at this point that a large, unidentified creature was discovered to be hiding in the wares of the cart in question. The creature became immediately hostile and attacked the surrounding guards before leaving, presumably toward the central tower. Witnesses have confirmed that both Captain Lorenzo and his brother were unharmed by the creature and pursued it in haste. Witnesses have also confirmed that these two unlawfully acquired military weapons in their flight, and the younger brother was later seen in possession of a military laharto.

"Multiple witnesses throughout the city have confirmed that this unidentified creature was somehow able to ascend the central tower and steal the sun gem, thus disabling Centile's shield. Our guards have also reported that Captain Lorenzo was then seen *riding* this creature out of the city, followed closely by his younger brother. From here on the testimonies dissipate into wild speculation until the sun gem was returned to the tower and the shield restored. At this point, Elder Morten accompanied a platoon to investigate the central tower where the present suspect was discovered and arrested in the presence of Elder Lehonti. He was then brought in for questioning and containment. That is the entirety of our official report, sir."

"Thank you, Captain. You are dismissed." At a wave of Elder Baltista's hand, the guard turned from the desk and returned to the crowd in the back. As he passed, Corin caught a glimpse of the soldier's eye bearing down on him. It held nothing but derision, like the man had just bitten into something very vile.

Elder Baltista cleared his throat again, staring at the papers in front of him.

"Ladies and gentlemen, I want you all to know how deeply disturbed I am by this account. Those of you who know me will also know that it takes a lot to rattle my composure. I pride myself in being a man of placid temperament, but I am struggling to see anything but grief and guilt in this sun-scorched story… I have, admittedly, been shaken to my very bones.

"This is the first attack on our city in the entirety of our recorded history. We have had minor skirmishes with marauders, some of them even resulting in guard casualties, but *never* have we seen this level of violence and terror. Never have we seen the blood of innocent citizens spilled on our streets." He rubbed at his eyes as he gestured toward Corin and his grandfather. "As such, I am eager to understand with certainty the complexity of this issue, and it is with great hope, and even greater anxiety, that I now allow Elder Lehonti to address us in defense of his grandsons."

A brief whisper fluttered through the crowd in back. It spread up through the elders and ended with a hundred eyes on Corin. Lehonti leaned forward to his grandson and, in a strangely playful gesture, wrapped his knuckles against Corin's chest. He glanced up at the old man's wrinkled cheeks. They were warm and calm, as if he couldn't feel the stares of the crowd. He stood, adjusted his robes and turned gently toward the half circle of elders.

"Ladies and gentlemen," he briefly motioned to the crowd beyond before turning back to the chairs before him, "elders of Centile… I too share Elder Baltista's horror and concern. A choice has been viciously thrust upon us."

He turned back to Baltista's desk, speaking as if the two elders were alone. "I greatly appreciated your remarks, good brother. Especially the final point you so *eloquently* mentioned. This is the first attack on our great city."

Lehonti turned back, pacing slowly forward until he was standing at the center of the rug. "This is indeed the first attack on our *city*, but it is not the first time innocent blood has been spilled on *this ground*."

Lehonti stared at the elders for a moment, giving them time to process his words. When he spoke again it was with a voice filled with sorrow and concern, a pacing passion that urged him to circle the room.

"My dearest brothers, when our ancestors established our council, they created five positions that could govern and manage the affairs of Centile. When it came to the daily concerns of commerce and society, these positions were sufficient... and yet they saw fit to create a sixth position. My position. I am *He Who Remembers*. It is my role to not forget the lessons of the past, or the horrors of our history. There is a reason our city is guarded by the sun gem's shield. There is a reason the founders of Centile built our city around the central tower, why artists and craftsmen spent years placing the tiles of the great mural. Gentlemen, our world has *once more* come under attack."

Lehonti stopped walking, one hand clenched behind his back. He glanced past the elders at the crowd in back. "Captain Felipe, if I may?"

The crowd shuffled in confusion and Felipe stepped forward, silent and somber. "Sir?"

"Captain, you are experienced with life on the plains, are you not?"

Felipe nodded. "I am, sir."

Lehonti raised a hand toward him. "Please, tell us a little about your experience."

Felipe was puzzled but obedient. "Well, sir, I have been managing the city patrols for the past year, escorting caravans of farmers and tradesmen and managing the security of the inner wall. Before that I ran four tours on the eastern roads to Dawn's Harbor and seven more along the southern paths to the mountain mills."

Lehonti stared gently at the captain as he spoke. "And, would you say that you are a man of expertise when it comes to life on the plains?"

Felipe cleared his throat. "Well, perhaps not *expertise*... but generally, yes. I would say so, sir."

"And in all your years of duty, all that time spent on the plains, have you *ever* seen anything like the creature that attacked Centile yesterday?"

The crowd was very still, and Felipe's brow glistened. "No, sir. I have never seen anything like that monster in my life."

"An honest answer, Captain." Lehonti nodded in agreement. "And I thank you for it. *No one* has seen anything like it on the plains, at least not for the past three hundred years. Based on your extensive time beyond the walls, do you believe it is a *reasonable assumption* that a species of enormous creatures like that has been roaming the wilds for three centuries, and that we telaks have simply failed to discover it until now?"

The room was very silent, and Felipe didn't seem to know how to respond.

"Captain?" Lehonti pressed. "Your opinion, if you please."

Felipe cleared his throat and readjusted his stance. "I suppose not, sir. But I do not think that my own experiences are at all definitive."

"No, of course not, Captain. But what is deeply significant is that your personal expertise is in perfect harmony with our city records."

Lehonti turned away from the guard, looking back at the elders. "Our patrols have never reported a creature of similar size or shape. The many tribes of outlanders, who are intimately familiar with the fauna of the plains, were equally perplexed by this animal when they saw it burst from its hiding place. It may interest you to know that an *outlander farmer* was *murdered* to provide the creature passage into the city. His name was Takoda. Not that any of you will remember that. Not that any of you care. He made his living growing hay for our city's bacas. Something attacked him on the plains as he was seeking shelter from the storm. Something slit his throat and drove a stake through his chest, pinning him upright so that his cart would blend in with the caravan. It was done, it seems, so that we would think the caravan was responsible for the monster skulking among them. A monster that *none of them* knew was there."

Lehonti paused and studied the elders. All were watching him attentively.

All but Morten, who seemed far more interested in cleaning his fingernails.

Lehonti sighed and glanced out the massive window. "And it worked. Our city scares too easily. We have grown slow and dull. Overly confident in our spears… And the great lessons of the past go entirely forgotten.

"The truth is, my brethren, that we *do* have records of this creature. Not records in ink, or even spoken word, but a record just the same. A creature, nearly identical to the one seen yesterday, was painstakingly portrayed in a thousand tiles at the heart of our city. Just a few meters from this spot, on the floor of the central tower, an artist spent what must have been weeks crafting the image of a six-legged, woolly beast with large, empty eyes and curled horns. There are few who have seen this image because this council *foolishly* chose to bar the public from viewing it. They argued that the story of Vallin was mere *superstition*. They claimed it was a *dangerous myth*, concocted by ancient, feeble minds. They said it was a story that would *confuse the masses*."

Lehonti's sad, pleading eyes drifted over the elders. "Gentlemen, I ask you… can you still hold to such a decision?"

He was silent for a moment before shaking his head and continuing. "The ancient stories speak of a race of beings that bled black and felt no pain. A race of creatures that feared the light of our city's gem, that would do anything to be rid of it. After what we have all seen, can you sit here and *still* doubt their existence? The stories speak of a source, a twisted mass of crystal vines that spread across the plains, that belched forth horrible demons onto our lands. My grandsons followed that black beast across the plains, trying desperately to stop it. They hacked and stabbed its flesh, finally bringing it down at the foot of *this very source!* My grandson, Corin, described this to me without ever having seen the source depicted on the ancient mural! My friends, what are the chances that a young man his age could *invent* a story that has been tiled on the floors of our city? Was that not the purpose of shunning the public from this mural? To ensure that the youth could never be influenced by the *superstitious nonsense* of the past?

"I ask you, friends, even if he had somehow learned this story, even if he had guessed the details, or snuck past the guards into the mural's hallowed hall, what would be his motive? What could he possibly have to gain? My grandson watched that wretched creature rise from its own gore and brutally take his brother... my dear Lorenzo. *Captain* Lorenzo."

The old man's glistening eyes spilled over in a single, silver streak. "Can you truly doubt this young man's story? When that foul creature took his elder brother, my grandson mustered the strength to bring the sun gem home! To *defend our city* from the hell that he witnessed firsthand! And this is his thanks? His only crime was being present at the tower when Morten and his guards arrived looking for someone to blame. Corin's actions were not only *innocent*, they were *valiant!*" Lehonti growled. "Those of you who knew Lorenzo knew that he was a man of honor. A man of *passion*, perhaps, but never was there a more loyal Centilean than Captain Lorenzo. He gave the whole of his life to guarding our city. And now... now he has given it all anew. Is this how you will thank him? By cowering in the shadows of your offices while you spurn his name? By laying blame on the innocent? Those who have already suffered so much? By weaving a story of conspiracy that *circumvents* the truth of our heritage and *blatantly* denies the facts? Is this how you will honor my grandson's name?

"I have not come here today to sway a popular vote. I have not come to play a political game. I have come to urge you to look past your fears and to see *reason*. I have spoken to you plainly because our way of life, our very *right to live*, has been threatened. The demons have returned, brothers. They are testing our strength. And… I fear that they have found us to be weak and divided."

Lehonti shook his head in disgust and motioned to the stand. "I will say no more. I am free of your blood."

Without another sound or gesture, Elder Lehonti took his seat by Corin. The room was silent, and a sour flavor filled the air, scratching the backs of everyone's tongues. Corin stared up at his grandfather, but the old man's eyes were absently fixed on the rug at the center of the room.

CHAPTER 27

SUPERSTITIOUS MADNESS

ELDER BALTISTA REMAINED MOTIONLESS FOR AN uncomfortable length of time. His eyes were dark and cold, and his shoulders seemed to be hunched in pain. He did not speak, nor did he acknowledge any of what Elder Lehonti had spoken. He simply cleared his throat and motioned to Elder Morten.

Morten smiled at Baltista's gesture and rose swiftly from his seat. He was not wearing his robes. Instead he was clothed in the same military uniform Corin had seen him wear the previous night. He pulled down on the edge of his shirt and squared his shoulders.

"Well…" he said with a chuckle. "That was truly something, wasn't it? Some interesting ideas have been sold to us, haven't they? Some *colorful* ideas, wouldn't you say? It appears that Lehonti would have you pluck out your own eyes and tear off your own ears, doesn't it?"

He swooped quickly across the rug, calling out to the crowd in back. "Really, doesn't it, though?"

He turned back to the half circle of elders with eyebrows raised in concern. "My dear brothers of the council… I never imagined I would see the day when *myths* and *magic* were held up as *evidence* in a hearing. All while testimonies of sound and sight are cast aside. But I suppose that just goes to show how far we still need to come as a city, doesn't it? Let me make my position abundantly clear, because it appears that our debate has descended to an evaluation of this superstitious madness. I love the story of Vallin. It is a golden tale of courage and strength. It teaches us about the unconquerable power of the Centilean spirit, and the need to fight when evil rears upon us. But, my brothers, *it is an allegory*." Morten drew out those last four words in exaggerated emphasis. He smiled in mock affability before continuing.

"To lay faith on such a story is to deny what is right before our very senses. Lehonti's obsession with the legends of the past has *blinded* him to the present. He does not see beyond the pages of his books. And now..." Morten stepped close to Corin, bearing down on him with immense scorn and condemnation, "he has begun to corrupt the simple minds of our fragile youth..."

Morten clucked his tongue and folded his arms, staring absently across the room, as if deeply moved with pity. "Brothers of the council, I had hoped it would not come to this, but I believe that drastic action is needed to ensure the safety of our city and its citizens. My guards have repeatedly found evidence of rebellion on the plains. Those leather skin traitors are amassing an army just beyond our borders. I can't say I fully understand their intentions, but their aggression has been plain as the sun. The outlanders have been attacking our patrols, stealing from our private stores, and conspiring with clear, malicious intent. Just yesterday, moments before the ceremony, a whole tribe of those savages staged an attack on our southern baca corral! They sent a stampede crashing through our city, nearly killing four guards in the process, all as an apparent distraction to their greater plot.

"As we have sat in tolerance and stupor, their crimes have grown more and more aggressive, and now they have scrounged up a monster of a weapon, probably just some ordinary creature from the distant north, but *trained* to attack our city. Contrary to the lunacy of mythology, reason tells us that this creature was an animal from beyond the plains, trained to infiltrate our city and leave it defenseless. Nothing more. Nothing less.

"But how? How, you may ask, could a band of filthy leather skins have developed such a sophisticated plan? Is it not obvious, my friends? It is because they were not alone. All it took was one senile old man. An old man who *literally* interpreted a *symbolic* story. An old man who mistakes art for history. An old man who has let power get to his head. An old man who corrupted the vulnerable minds of his two grandsons. An old man who believes he is a descendant of the founder of our city, and thereby destined to rule over us all in self-righteous splendor.

"Gentlemen, this is a *scare tactic!* As a man of military discipline, I have learned to see past the enemy's bluff. He is playing off your fears, and your superstitions. Do you want to know what really happened? *Lehonti* staged this attack. He has been seeking for decades to bring back the traditions of the past, to stomp out progress. He has been scheming with outlanders. His own son *married* one of those leather skins, shaming his family heritage and costing him his potential seat on our council. And now they live in exile in the slums of the southern district. Can you not see the obvious, my friends? This is a family of *traitors*. I was foolish for trusting them for so long. I even appointed that snake Lorenzo as a captain in my guard. I have paid dearly for my naivety, and I ask you all not to share in my error."

Morten straightened his back and cleared his throat, letting his words rest on the anxious minds before him. He motioned to Captain Felipe. "As has been clearly proven by our good captain's account, this beast was trained by the outlanders, and it was smuggled into our city among their filthy carts. Lehonti's grandsons were conspirators in the attack, purposefully waiting at the southern gate, leading the dumb beast all the way to its goal. Using this beast, they stole our gem and threw our city into chaos. You see, brethren, a city in chaos is a city that can be controlled. A panicked city is a city that will *believe a myth*. It is the type of city that might dissolve its council and appoint a senile, old man to lead it in the stale ways of a ludicrous cult of the past.

"Lehonti claims that the beast was a *demon* because it resembles an image from an ancient mural. Wouldn't the ancient artists have looked to *real creatures* as inspiration for their fictional horrors? He claims that his grandsons were innocent saviors of the city. Is that not exactly what he would wish for you to believe? He claims that Lorenzo died a martyr, slain by a demon. So, I ask you, Lehonti, *where is the body?* If, as you say, your grandson is not currently at large among the outlanders, rallying a second strike on the city, then *where is his body?*"

Morten had stopped before Lehonti, staring intensely at the dropping back of the old man's grey head. Morten shook his head in disgust before wandering back to the center of the room.

"Gentlemen, it is my proposal that Lehonti be stripped of his rank, and that his *pointless* position in the council be dissolved. It is also my proposal that this senseless squabbling be put to an end, and that we act swiftly to crush this outlander rebellion before it brings any more death to our streets. My guards are clever, and they are strong. With your approval, I will lead them beyond our walls where we will avenge our dead and restore peace to the plains in a matter of days. Open your eyes. Recover your senses. Our fate lies in our own hands, not the senile fantasies of a madman."

* * *

MORTEN TOOK A STEP BACK AND BOWED TO THE council before returning to his seat. The crowd was no longer silent. Hushed whispers quickly rose to agitated phrases and grunts of approval. The crowd of guards in back seemed especially moved by Morten's words. Elder Baltista raised his hands for silence, and the din died reluctantly. He looked distressed, pained by all that had been spoken.

"Elders, our laws forbid that I should vote in this matter, therefore the weight of this decision falls upon a majority vote of you five. Sheig, Duarten, Aldren, I offer you the floor to discuss and question the statements made before we bring this meeting to a vote. Elder Sheig?"

The elder in lavender robes leaned back in his chair, stretching his arms forward against his knees. He was a younger man with chestnut hair and a hard jaw with a surprisingly weak chin.

"Elders, I'm not sure there is much left to discuss or question. As director of commerce, I have personally seen the barbarity of the plains. Our patrols are regularly hunted and harassed, and our wares are stolen on our doorsteps. Look to yesterday's incident at the southern baca corral if you still doubt it. I just think it is ignorant to pretend this will not escalate into a military conflict with the outlanders. This most recent attack proves that there is too much at stake.

"Now, as for Lehonti's claim… it is something I simply cannot accept. Songs must remain songs. We cannot allow ourselves to act out of fear of some fiendish myth. Our city is a city of reason and progress, not magic or superstition. We sealed that mural from the public for good reason, and it is time we banished this backwards ideology from among us. I concur with Morten's call of no confidence in Lehonti, and I too believe that his position should be abolished."

Once again, the grunts and cheers of guards burst from the crowd beyond. Morten smiled and placed a firm hand of approval on Sheig's shoulder. Baltista silenced the room with considerably more difficulty this time, and then motioned to Elder Duarten.

Duarten didn't respond quickly. The minister of education sat back lightly in his chair, his legs folded high on his first knee, and his arms folded high on his chest. He was not wearing his blue and silver robes, but was instead neatly dressed in a tight, white shirt with silver buttons and no collar. It was tucked into long, grey pants with white stitching and white cuffs. His long, black hair was tied back into a loose bun, and the nostrils on his pointed nose were subtly flared in displeasure.

"Elders… there is something more to this discussion that greatly distresses my mind," the young elder said. "For some time, I have been watching the several districts of our city with concern. We are *divided*, gentlemen, and this division has been demonstrated in our conversation here today."

Duarten leaned forward, resting his elbows on his knees and his chin on his fists. "Our culture is developing a great schism, and that schism seems to be increasingly geographic. We have developed rich and poor, weak and powerful. Those within the wall, and those without. No group is lower in this social structure than the outlanders. They are a vulnerable people, stripped of any say in our political process. Who is to be *their voice* in this debate? Do they not deserve a chance to defend themselves before we rashly declare all-out war on them?"

Duarten sighed deeply and leaned back. "We have become arrogant in our success, brethren. We are too sure of our assumptions and give too little thought to those who will suffer at our hands."

He paused and glanced across the room. "Morten, Sheig, I have a question for you. Each of you has mentioned magic, have you not? My question is simply this: What is magic, if not Centile's shield?"

The room was silent. Morten chuckled in hesitation but spoke up first. "It is a testament to telak ingenuity. It is a gift from our predecessors, something we must defend and protect."

Duarten nodded and raised his hand. "Yes, yes, but how can you say the *story* of Vallin is magic, but the *gem* is not? What makes one miraculous occurrence magical but another commonplace?"

Morten smiled and nodded. "Duarten, I see your point, but I fear I must disagree with you. The sun gem is a part of our daily life. It is *real*, it is *tangible*. I don't need to understand it in order to see it. It was built by our ancestors as a gift to us. We do not need to explain it in order to respect it."

Duarten tilted his head slightly to the left as he spoke. "So, it is not magic because it was built for us by our ancestors? Because we can *see* it?" Duarten rubbed his thumb and forefinger against his temples. "Do you not see the flaw in this logic? Brother, this is dangerous thinking…"

"Dangerous?" Morten scoffed. "My friend, what's *dangerous* is–"

"Now, hold on a moment. You've had your chance." Duarten raised his hand and voice as he spoke over Morten. "This *is* dangerous. We are basing city policy off assumptions. Assumptions that we cannot even *pretend* to explain or justify. We have no clue how the sun gem works. We simply know that it does. It was built by the same *superstitious ancestors* that built the great mural. Read the ancient texts, friends. Our ancestors clearly believed the demons were real. They claimed the sun gem was our only defense against them. How can we be so hypocritical as to take only *pieces* of the story? History is not some banquet where we pick and choose what to place on our plates.

"Now, I'm not sure I believe *all* the old stories. I'm not sure I can fully support all of what Lehonti has said. But I do believe that this is a far more complicated issue than most of us are willing to admit. I can see the ancient mural as plainly as I can see Centile's shield. We cannot dismiss our city's history simply because we no longer see it unfolding around us. I stand with Lehonti for two reasons. The first is because I fear this line of thinking will lead to oppression: first to Lehonti's grandson, next to the outlanders, and eventually to all who dare to disagree with this council. Second, I feel Lehonti's point deserves further inquiry. Perhaps the ancients knew more than we do. Perhaps we are not as *advanced* as we would like to believe. If they were willing and able to build the tower with its shield, then isn't it at least *plausible* that there is more to their stories than we are choosing to accept?"

He shrugged and went to say more but paused. "*Bah...* I've said my piece."

Duarten sat back and glanced across the room. Morten's face was bitter and annoyed, but the chief captain held his tongue.

All eyes fell next on Elder Aldren, a feeble old man with a thin body and deep wrinkles. His brown hair was dimming to grey and bound in a thick braid that draped over his green and yellow robes. He sat very still and very erect. When he spoke, his voice was soft but firm.

"Brothers... I have always been a simple man. In my time in this office, I have worked extensively with the outlanders to produce the wheat that feeds our city. I have not concerned myself with the cares of politics and history for many years..."

He paused to cough into his clenched fist. When he finished, he quickly scanned the other elders and frowned. "That having been said, I too have noticed a great disturbance in our way of life. The marauders have become bold and restless. We have lost crops and land. Our stores are always under threat of raids... I don't wish to remove our dear brother Lehonti, but... I think Morten may be right. This attack on our city has shown just how bad the plains are becoming. Perhaps Corin should be retained until this situation is figured out. I believe Morten should be allowed to investigate the outlanders and... perhaps use force if necessary."

Aldren relaxed back into his seat, as if his speech had required great effort to deliver. The whispers began again, quickly filling the office. Corin shifted in his seat, chills shooting through his intestines. He watched Elder Baltista shuffle the papers before him and run his eyes across their ample lines. Once more he raised his hands to the crowd and waited for silence.

"Elders... I thank each of you for participating today. Since this is only a *preliminary* hearing, I have no qualms against sharing my thoughts on this issue. Before you vote, I want each of you to know that I stand with Lehonti. At least in part. I firmly believe that any path that leads to violence should be a final option. I believe there is insufficient evidence to accuse this young man, who may very well have been a victim of cruel circumstance. Furthermore, I believe that there is wisdom in Elder Duarten's admonition that we must not allow our overconfidence to excuse our hypocrisy or cause us to dismiss the past. But I hold my peace. I will honor whichever decision this council makes today."

Baltista cleared his throat and leaned forward, his forearms resting firmly against his desk. "All those in favor of releasing Corin and clearing him of all charges, please indicate."

Corin glanced up at the elders. Duarten and Lehonti raised their hands. He expected as much, but still his heart sank.

Elder Baltista nodded. "All those in favor of retaining Corin for a formal trial, please indicate."

Morten, Sheig, and Aldren raised their hands, and the crowd stirred to commotion. Elder Baltista briefly bowed his head and stood.

"Seeing as the suggestion that Elder Lehonti's position be dissolved is *far* beyond the scope of this meeting, this council will vote only on the temporary fate of the accused. It is the decision of this council that Corin will be retained by the city guard. Evidence will continue to be gathered and evaluated, and Corin will await a formal trial at a date yet to be determined. For the time being, the city guard will maintain its *present course* in defending, patrolling, and monitoring Centile and the surrounding land. We will evaluate the proposal that increased military action be required at a future date in the event that more substantial evidence is presented, specifically linking yesterday's attack to outlander conspiracy. Guards, please escort Corin to his holding cell. Brethren, you are dismissed."

In a swirl of white and silver, Baltista stood from his seat and briskly walked to a door at the back of his office. The crowd in back meandered to the half circle of elders, and Darrow and Selina pulled Corin from his seat and back toward the hallway behind him.

"You should be *ashamed* of yourself."

A woman's voice penetrated the clamor, and Corin turned in time to see his grandmother, Maria, slap Morten in front of the whole crowd. The room exploded into commotion, but the double doors were quickly shut behind Corin, and he could no longer hear or see what was happening beyond.

Corin tried to walk, but his legs were giving out beneath him. Darrow and Selina felt him drag and hoisted him higher onto their shoulders. They were swift and silent, pushing their way past swinging doors and muttering crowds. Corin's mind was aware of everything, but he retained none of it. Somehow, they had made their way back into the sunlight, and across the central plaza. Somehow, they had entered into the guard's permanent holding cells, and somehow Corin had once again been brusquely thrown behind iron bars.

Darrow and Selina did not linger. The door was closed, keys were exchanged, and Corin was forgotten to a bland floor of stone and straw.

"The elders have decided to hold the prisoner here. You are to guard him until you receive further word. I'll be back before sundown to relieve you," Darrow muttered in the distance.

"Yes, Captain."

Without another word, Darrow and Selina left the prison block. Corin had understood Darrow's words. They had been meant as a comfort. He would be back for him. Before sunset tonight they would be back for him. With some simple hope in his heart, Corin turned to inspect his cell. It was nearly as barren as the other. Along the far wall was a small woven shawl, folded neatly on the straw. The walls were solid stone except for a single, grate along the back of the cell letting in a terrible draft. It must have been used to drain water when the guards mopped the cells, but right now it only served to nip at Corin's toes.

Corin unfolded the shawl and wrapped it around his shoulders, pulling it over his tail as he slid into a seated position against the wall. He became painfully aware of just how long it had been since he had last eaten. He folded his arms tight across his knees and pressed his forehead against his arms.

There was nothing to do now but wait.

PART FIVE

WHEN HER WAVES DO ROAR

CHAPTER 28

SEA OF SICKNESS

OLENKA AWOKE FROM A DEEP, DREAMLESS sleep, the kind of sleep that makes you question whether you had slept at all. The sand was damp beneath her side, and the sky was lit only by the sparks of a million stars streaking across the great cosmic canopy. Diwala's hand was placed against her back to wake her. Olenka shifted to a seated position and wiped the grit from her cheek.

"It is time," Di whispered.

Olenka nodded and rammed her face into her hands. "Alright. Go call the pod. I'll wake Mari."

Diwala nodded and stood softly, walking gently back to the water. Olenka didn't move for a moment. She braced her forehead against her palms and tried to exorcise her bursting headache through will alone. They had ridden all day yesterday and straight through the night, only stopping once to eat and once more to rest. It was dark when they finally lay down on the beach, and it was still dark now that they were getting up. When they first came to shore, they weren't even sure if the plalomas would return, but their exhaustion was too great to continue.

Olenka stood, her balance very poor, and tripped her way over to Mari. Marikit was curled up tight in a little hollow on the beach made by the tide washing away the sand around her. Olenka crouched down and patted her shoulder.

"Mari?" she whispered. "Come on, sister. It's time to get back to the pod."

Marikit jerked awake and gasped. Her eyes were bloodshot and wide, and half her face was painted tan with beach muck.

"Oh, what? The pod?" She shifted onto her right elbow but didn't sit up.

"We need to leave now, Mari."

"*Ugh...*" Marikit closed her eyes and threw back her head. "But I *just* fell asleep..."

Olenka chuckled, suddenly feeling a little less sorry for herself. "We all did. It's still a while from morning. But we can probably reach Ka Jiya before sunrise if we leave now."

Mari sat up and pulled herself into a ball, her face pressed against her knees. "*Uhh... Kay Kay, everything hurts...*"

Olenka sighed and sat down next to her. "I know. I still can't feel my fingers yet."

"*Right?*" Mari's head bolted up. "How in *Heaven's name* is anyone supposed to hold on that long? The drag alone is enough to rip barnacles free, but then they see a school of fish and start flipping around after them! Kay Kay, it's a *nightmare!*"

Olenka laughed, loud and hearty. "But I thought you were dying to ride plalomas."

Mari sighed. "Ugh, no. I'm dying *from* riding plalomas," she whimpered. "When we get back to Sotay I'm going to sleep for a week straight, and there's not a buwisit thing you can do to stop me."

Olenka smiled and watched Diwala wade out into the surf and blow her shell whistle. The moon had set long ago, but the sky was still bright and dazzling without it. Olenka loved the look of the sea at night. Its surface was black and mysterious, all the subtle ripples and waves dancing together in the meager light. She pushed herself to her fins and offered Marikit a hand. Mari scowled, but took the help.

"*Uhh...* Uzai sand..." Mari complained, stretching out her back. "I miss my bedroll."

Olenka nodded her agreement, but her mind was elsewhere. They were very near Ka Jiya Island now, and she had to keep her thoughts clear.

They were undoubtedly close to whatever had happened to the last crew...

There was a flutter in the tide, and Olenka watched their three plalomas scampering up to them just past the shore in the darkness.

She smiled and pulled on Mari's arm. "Come on, they're here."

Mari grumbled and fussed with her hair. "Alright, I'm coming. Just, not very quickly..."

Olenka laughed and hiked out into the surf. Diwala was gently stroking the side of her mount.

She turned and smiled softly to Olenka. "We need some fish for them, do we not?"

Olenka blinked and then glanced around. "That's right, huh? I didn't even think about that. Did you see anything around here?"

Diwala nodded absently but was too busy smiling and cooing to her plaloma. "Thank you for coming back to us, Yashiro. We will find you some fish, yes?" She turned to Olenka. "I am sorry, I believe I saw a school along the sand bar just down the shore. Would you mind spearing them their breakfast?"

Olenka nodded. "I don't mind, but it looks like he might let you ride him without it, Di."

Diwala nodded as she petted Yashiro. "You are right, but they were out all night alone. I do not want to risk weakening our bonds with them. We are too far out at sea to easily swim away from here on our own. We need them, and they need to know we appreciate their services to us. Huh, Yashiro? You need to know we appreciate you."

The plaloma buzzed in delight as Diwala rubbed his snout.

Olenka rolled her eyes but unfastened the straps at her chest that cinched her spear to her back. She reached over her shoulder and grasped the weapon's thin handle and slid it over to her front. Olenka twirled the spear and then let it rest along the crook of her elbow. It was short and sharp and serrated, designed for maneuverability in the water. Typical hunting spears were long, wooden poles with a wide head filled with sharpened prongs to ensure the animal was hit. Sirena only carried short, metal spears no longer than the length of an arm. They were weighted and thin, with a jagged blade that widened smoothly into the handle. It wasn't the optimal tool for hunting, but if you were skilled enough to make a living as a sirena, then surely you could catch yourself something to eat with a short spear.

Olenka slid into the water, letting the crisp burst chill her nerves awake. The sea was terribly dark, but also beautifully clear. She followed the meager curtains of light, gauging depth as she watched them flex in the gloom and brush the sandy floor.

She quickly came to the sand bar and lifted up onto her fins. Ahead, there was a decaying branch in the water. The perfect shelter for small shore fish. As gently as she could, Olenka pressed through the water, trying to approach the branch unnoticed. Finally, she saw her quarry. It wasn't much, but from her angle she saw the subtle shimmers of turning fish in the starlight. Olenka lifted the spear, resting the shaft along the palm of her left hand and gripping the blunt end with her right. She guided the blade smoothly along the surface, aiming below her target to compensate for the bend in the water. With a decisive thrust the blade shot into the sea, pinning the fish against the silt.

Olenka stepped quickly and pulled the blade from the sand. The fish skewered on the end thrashed and squirmed, flaring out its frills and gills. She slipped it off the blade, cracked its head against the branch, and tossed the fish onto the sand bar off to her side. She repeated the process until she speared her third fish. Once the last one was collected, Olenka trudged up onto the sand bar, lanced the other two next to it, and swam back to the pod.

Mari was up and moving now and, judging from her crouched, adoring posture, she seemed to have forgotten her newly acquired distaste for plalomas. Olenka chuckled, whistled to get

Mari's attention, and then tossed her a fish. Mari caught the fish, paused to study it...

...and then she screamed.

The sirena jumped back, jerking her hand around and splashing it into the water. Olenka chortled and stomped closer.

"Are you kidding me, Mari? What could you possibly be scared of?"

Marikit glanced up at Olenka and then back to her hand. Her eyes were wild and shaken. She frantically rubbed her palm against the grit of the sand, like she was trying to scrape something from her palm.

"There was something on the fish! Like *a worm!* It tried to bite me..." She flipped her hand over and over, flexing her fingers.

Olenka chuckled. "You probably just hit one of the spikes on its fins."

Mari shook her head and glanced around in the water. "I don't know..."

Diwala stepped forward, suddenly tense and very alert. "Olenka, look at the plalomas."

Olenka scrunched up her skeptical forehead but walked over to investigate the pod. She stood next to Mari and Di and could see the fish drifting limply to the sea floor, exactly where Mari had dropped it. The plalomas had cautiously approached, and were circling around the carcass, but none of them ate it.

None of them would even touch it.

"That is odd," Olenka muttered. "They're not poisonous. I just caught a couple blue bakkos. Do you think they mind the spines?"

Diwala was very still as she spoke. "*Look.* Watch it closely."

Olenka and Mari leaned in, trying to see the fish in the limited light. It was hard to tell with the rippling water, but it almost looked like the fish was still breathing, like its gills were still fluttering with life. Olenka glanced up at Diwala, but her sister's gaze was fixed on the shuddering corpse.

Suddenly, the fish moved. Or, rather, something *on* the fish moved. All three sirena jumped back. Through the water it looked like there was something *in* the fish's gill, something waving in the water against the current.

Diwala turned to Olenka. "You have more?"

Olenka nodded and held up her spear.

Diwala turned and motioned for shore. The other two followed her up onto the beach and Di unsheathed her knife.

"Throw another one down onto the sand," she ordered.

Olenka nodded and slid another fish off the spear, pinching it tenderly by the tail. The fish slid onto the beach, inert and silent. Diwala crouched down and slit a long cut across the creature's side. She sat there very still, all except for her knife softly turning in her grip.

"Di," Mari whispered, "what are you…"

Diwala held up a hand to hush her, her eyes never leaving the fish. Suddenly she straightened. "*There!* Look now, do you see it?"

Olenka had to strain in the darkness, but she could see it. A thin tendril of black was coiling out of the fish's open wound. It slid around the split in the skin, feeling its way across the scaly surface. Another coil slid out from the wound beside it, reaching and feeling out along the fish's belly. With this putrid sight, the unpleasant memories washed back over Olenka. She saw the black tendril crawling down her knife in the samay lawa. She saw it thrashing in sickly spasms in the water all around her. She remembered it seeping out of the gutted belly of the mad shark.

"It is the same sickness," Diwala muttered.

Olenka stepped back, and then quickly wiped the remaining fish off her spear. She held the shaft up to the night sky, trying to discern any splotches or movement on it.

Mari stepped closer, peering over Diwala at the fish. "Sickness? You mean like the shark?"

Di nodded. "And likely whatever drove Krit's siokoy mad. We must be very close to Ka Jiya. Olenka? What do you think?"

Olenka threw her spear straight into the sand, hoping the coarse grains might scrape off anything she had missed.

"I think we need to hurry."

* * *

THE NIGHT BEGAN TO ILLUMINATE AROUND THEM AS they rode, a thin orange glow just seeping over the horizon. The plalomas had been compliant enough and had allowed them to board without their usual snack. It was almost as if they understood the severity of the situation.

Olenka tried to think as the water coursed over her, but all she could do was worry. Whatever had infected the fish seemed to be exactly what had poisoned the mad shark. It was unlike anything Olenka had ever seen in the Great Sea. It moved and behaved almost like a parasite, but it was somehow a *liquid*. She had seen it spill out of the shark's gut in great drops and puddles. It didn't make any sense, but no matter how much she clawed for a reasonable explanation, she could not deny what she'd seen...

...just like she could not deny her dream.

As the sun filled the sky, Olenka sped forward on her plaloma and signaled to Diwala to head for the surface. She nodded, and the crew burst out into the salty, morning air. Olenka breathed deep and shook her face. She sat up straight on the plaloma and took note of her surroundings. Off slightly to the left was the green skyline of their destination. Di and Marikit pulled up beside her, staring out across the horizon.

"Is that it?" Mari asked, holding her hand to her brow.

Olenka nodded and squinted against the sun rising to her side.

"Why have you stopped us out here?" Diwala's voice was gentle, but tense. Mari didn't seem to fully grasp the significance of their discovery on the beach, but Diwala understood the implications of a sea of sick, mad fish. She had seen the shark, same as Olenka.

"We need a plan," Olenka whispered.

Diwala nodded. "I agree. Do you have one?"

"Maybe…" Olenka's face scrunched and fell as she thought. They were too far from Ka Jiya to see where the reef was, which meant they would have to spend more time searching.

And more time searching meant they would be more likely to…

"We need to find that reef quickly and start combing the sea floor. I don't want us over there any longer than we have to be." Olenka swallowed and fidgeted with the spear straps on her chest.

Diwala glanced to Marikit and then back to Olenka. "And what if we are attacked?"

Olenka smiled bitterly and patted her ploloma. "Then we make for the beach."

Mari paled at this suggestion. "But, what about the pod? We just *abandon* them?"

Olenka shrugged. "They made it through the night. They will just have to make it again."

Marikit did not look satisfied with this answer, so Olenka swiveled around to speak with her directly. "Mari, listen. You didn't see what Di and I saw in the samay lawas. If that crew was attacked by more mad sharks, then we simply don't have the strength to take them. We'll be lucky to make it to shore with all our fins intact."

"But you two *did* take it, Kay Kay!" Mari's voice was reassuring, but painfully naïve. "You two killed the shark and made it out of there without a scratch."

Olenka sighed. "Yes Mari, we killed *one* shark. Just one. And we ambushed it, and we coordinated our attacks, and we baited it up onto the docks, and that *one buwisit shark* still almost killed us. It was out of the pool, flopping on the dry deck, and it nearly chased us down, Mari. Can you imagine what two or three could do? Especially out here in the open water?"

Diwala shook her head and stared out across the vast horizon. "Perhaps they will no longer be here." She turned back and glanced at Mari and Olenka. "It is unlike a shark to stay in one place for too long. They will hunt if there is food, but then they move on to choicer feeding grounds when it is depleted."

Olenka shrugged with her hand panning the horizon. She leaned back, squinting her eyes out toward the distant smear of the island.

"We just have to assume that the threat is still present," Olenka said. "All of us need to be on guard the *whole* time we're out there. It's going to be a long salvage, but we need to stick together on this one. No fanning out to cover more ground, is that understood?"

Diwala and Marikit nodded, and the crew straightened the pod out toward the island.

"Do you see that dip in the tree line off to the right?" Di asked. "Looks like a freshwater river emptying from the center of the island. I suspect that a reef could not grow on the eastern bank by that river outlet."

Mari nodded. "So, we'll start on the western bank and work our way around the island?"

"That's good enough for me," Olenka whispered.

With a quick gesture and some deep breaths, the three sirena and their mounts slipped out into the water, diving a bit deeper than normal to avoid the glare of the rising sun. The water was particularly cold and murky, and visibility was very low in the green haze. Particles of drifting plant debris further obscured their sight.

The plalomas were unusually silent and reserved as they approached the island. They did not click or play or chase fish, and they even began to resist their riders. Again and again, the pod would shoot forward at their commands only to flip around, heading back out for the open sea. The plalomas grew increasingly belligerent, and the crew grew increasingly impatient the closer they swam to shore.

But they pressed on.

Through the murky water, the sea floor finally came into sight. The ground was patched with thousands of rubbery, green weeds and hundreds of rocks coated in a fuzzy, brown layer of scum. Olenka shook her head in frustration. Terrain like this would be difficult to search. The algae coating the rocks could very quickly creep across a foreign surface, and the bleary water limited their range of search to only a couple of meters in front of them. They would need to hurry. If the salvage wasn't already buried in muck, then it would be soon.

Olenka clicked in the water for her mount to speed up, but Akia refused. Olenka clicked again and patted the ploma's head. Again, Akia would not speed up. In fact, the stubborn creature slowed down, and began drifting away to the right. Olenka looked around in frustration. The whole pod had gone still. Diwala and Marikit were likewise trying to coax their rides along, but to no avail.

Olenka could take it no longer. This was potentially the single most important job of her career as a sirena, and she was not about to let some stubborn city fish ruin it for her. She clicked again, but also smacked her heels into the ploma's sides.

Akia jerked and thrashed but sped forward. At first, Olenka was pleased with the results, but then the ploma veered straight down into the water. Olenka felt the pressure rise and the temperature fall, and without warning, Akia twisted onto her back and crushed Olenka against a rock on the seafloor.

Olenka coughed and had to suppress her instinct to gasp as the wind was beaten out of her frame. Her vision flashed a blur of light and streaking shimmers, and a profound thud burst against her skull. Dazed at first, but soon lucid in her fury, Olenka shoved off the rock and pursued the vindictive beast up to the rest of the pod.

Mari and Diwala had already pulled up to the surface when Olenka burst through the swell, panting wildly. *"That buwisit fish!"*

Marikit looked confused and concerned. "What happened? Did you fall off?"

Olenka gasped and shook the drops from her face. "No! I did not *fall off!* That uzai beast *rammed me against the rocks!*"

Diwala nodded and smiled. "Did you disrespect her?"

Olenka scoffed. "What, are you *serious?*"

"Absolutely," Di snipped. "Father Decha warned us, did he not? The plalomas serve those who respect their power. Perhaps you did something to offend Akia?"

As if on cue, Akia bobbed to the surface, gingerly circling Diwala. Olenka glared and rubbed the aching back of her head. "You know what? Whatever. That stubborn fish can do whatever it wants. *Tattered sails*, I'll probably be faster on my own anyway. The way she's dragging her fins…"

Marikit smirked uncomfortably and leaned back. "You do have a point. I think something's got them spooked."

"I agree." Diwala turned her eyes to Ka Jiya. The island was not far, and the shoreline was now clearly visible. "Perhaps they are trying to warn us–"

"No," Olenka interjected, "we *need* to stick to the plan, not get scared off. We have a job to do and no time to waste. We've come too far to give up before we've even started searching. I'm heading down. We're probably in the right spot now. If the reef is off to the west, and the river empties out just ahead of us, then this was probably the last crew's path off the island, yes?"

Diwala and Marikit nodded but stayed silent. This was how things went with the crew: Mari and Di were there to advise and support, but Olenka was there to push them when it seemed impossible. She had taken this role many times before, and it had not failed them yet.

Not *badly*, anyway…

"Okay, then…" Olenka said. "Mari? You come with me. We'll dive down together and search in a straight line toward the river. Keep about a three-meter spread between us. Just close enough that we could signal to the other. Di, since you're riding the big one, you stay topside with the pod. Follow along our trail as best as you can from the surface. I doubt you could help us much with searching for the cargo, but keep an eye out for anything... *unfriendly*, okay?"

Diwala dipped her head and called for the other two plalomas. Olenka took a deep breath, and she and Mari descended.

CHAPTER 29

THE BLACK POD

THE HAZE IN THE WATER WAS OPPRESSIVE. Olenka kept glancing around behind and beside her, unable to see or hear anything. It felt like being trapped, like she was back at the bottom of the sea in that buwisit kaizo bell. She tried to take stock of the moment but found that every sense she isolated only cast messages of fear, not comfort.

Eventually she pulled her spear from off her back and swam with it against her thigh. It was a nice amenity, but, more than anything, it provided her something tangible and familiar to fidget with. The seafloor around the island was bleak and would have been unsettling under *any* conditions. But now, while they were following the morbid path of a fallen crew, every dark shape in the murk took on macabre malevolence.

The closer they got to shore, the more crowded the scummy sand became. There were no fish or crustaceans anywhere to be found, but the underwater rock formations grew in complexity, and dense patches of driftwood created natural walls and nets to catch debris and block the sirenas' views. Not long into the search, Olenka heard the distinct rumble of the river draining into the sea off to their right. The water on her face testified to the decreased salinity. As soon as the river's mouth came into sight, Olenka caught Mari's attention with a wave, and the two doubled back on their path toward the unseen reef beyond.

Olenka swam very close to the bottom. It was unlikely that they would miss cargo or wreckage if they came upon it, but she worried that they might be passing over clues in the muck. If a trinket had fallen from the crew's banca, an oar or a knife perhaps, it might help the sirena identify an area to search with greater care. In water this foggy it was not improbable to miss a sunken banca five meters from your face. Olenka pulled at the kelp and sea fronds beneath her as she swam, trying to uncover whatever they held.

A white gleam caught Olenka's eye.

At first it appeared to be the inside of a shell, but that was unlikely in such a barren patch of sea. Olenka pulled up to the rock that held the shimmer and brushed her hand across it. To her delight, she found it was a coin: a single, silver barya partially obscured by the encroaching scum of the rock.

Olenka picked up the token and waved it to Marikit who noticed the movement and kicked over. Olenka held the coin to her and twirled her hand around the area above her head. Mari nodded and the two panned out from that spot, widening a counterclockwise path away from the rock where the coin had been found.

Olenka felt her spirits start to lift. A coin like that had to have been from the missing crew. In a tidal area like this, with a river feeding into it no less, there was no way a coin could have stayed perched on a rock for more than a few days. If it hadn't been for all the scum clinging to its surface, it probably would have been lost to the silt long ago. This had to be the area to search. The cargo may not be close, but at least they knew it was down there somewhere. A thrill of eager joy shivered through her fins…

…and a bright, horrifying sound filled the water.

Olenka paused and stabilized herself upright in the water. She had no idea where the noise had come from. Even the general direction was ambiguous in the muffled, echoing green. It had been very clear, but not very loud. In fact, she might have missed it had it not been the *only sound* she had heard beside the river.

She kept very still and scanned the area around her. She could barely make out Mari's silhouette in the distance, just as frightened and rigid as her own. Olenka swam out to her. Mari's face was pale, even for a Bantay Tubig. Her spear was drawn, and her eyes were darting around the darkness. Olenka pressed her back to Mari's and joined in the search, but there was nothing to see. Aside from the ghostly shadows of rocks and sunken branches, the world around them was a solid smear of oily green and cloudy grey.

Olenka twisted around and tapped Mari's shoulder. The scared sirena jerked but looked her way. Olenka pointed up to the surface, and Mari nodded her agreement. It would be good to go topside. Diwala might have seen something but been unable to warn them. They had been so excited about discovering the coin that neither of them had been paying much attention to their surroundings.

As the two kicked up toward the surface, another call sounded out through the deep.

It was louder this time, but still bright and gentle. It was something between a scream and a song: a sinister sound made all the more terrifying by the playful tones that carried it through the unseen shadows. Olenka and Marikit froze, bobbing stiffly in the current and staring directly into the void that unmistakably bore the cry. There was something out there, closer than before, and it was calling into the water.

Whatever it was, it was searching.

Olenka gripped her spear and slowly swiveled her head from side to side. She hoped that if they stayed still whatever it was would dismiss them for flotsam and pass them by. She scanned the water over and over, but there was nothing, just curtains of light filtering through the gloom.

And then she saw it.

It was a blur in the distance, nothing more, but it was approaching. There was no shape to it, just color. It drifted in the murk, barely discernible. The call came again, piercing and direct this time. Olenka and Marikit both cringed at the sound, and the thing beyond seemed to respond to their movement. Its shape grew, approaching in a slow drift.

Its bulbous outline became more defined, and Olenka realized that it was not actually approaching slowly at all. It was colossal: massive enough to hide its speed in the haze, to disorient its prey by the sheer immensity of its girth. Its outline was clear now, the round face and three protruding fins of a plaloma, but larger…

So much larger.

Olenka smacked Mari's arm, and the two tore off into the sea, frantically kicking their way to shore. At least they *hoped* it was the way to shore. The cloudy deep had hampered their sense of direction, and, in their panic, they hadn't had time to properly gauge their surroundings.

Olenka glanced back and saw the beast bearing down on them. It was impossibly fast and growing larger and clearer every instant, its massive tail pumping through the foggy brine with monumental force. Olenka gazed ahead through the water. The shore was nowhere in sight. It didn't even look like the seafloor was approaching.

Trapped…

Olenka felt the spear still in her grip. She shot a glance toward Mari who looked back in distress. Being trapped was the one feeling Olenka simply could not tolerate under any circumstances, no matter how big the buwisit fish was.

She kicked down hard and twisted up into the water above. Mari flipped around after her in confusion but quickly shot off to the side. Olenka, however, dove straight for the fight. The creature was almost on them. The shape of its body was clearly visible now: like a dark, gargantuan ploma, but with a short, round snout, and a vicious maw filled with dozens of pointed teeth. Its body was black, with confusing patterns of blotchy white flecked along it. Olenka had no time to study the minutia of this mysterious creature, but there was one detail that sank itself deep into her mind…

This creature was infected.

Waving from wounds along its flesh, and seeping out of gaps between its teeth, were the black parasite's tendrils. The same sickness in the shark at Sotay. The same sickness in the fish at the beach.

The beast gaped open its mouth, coursing through the bleak haze at blinding speed. Olenka kicked hard and twisted ahead. She punched her arm forward with all her strength, letting her spear fly as she tucked her head down under the creature's attack. The spear sank straight into the giant's mouth, piercing the beast's cheek and bursting out the side of its neck. Just like the shark, and just as Olenka had feared, the leviathan felt no pain. The sick hunter's jaw grazed Olenka's hood and snapped shut as it passed.

Olenka wasted no time. She pulled her knife from its sheath and swam after the beast, trying to keep herself too close to its flank for it to turn and attack her. Mari seemed to share her idea and pulled up next to Olenka.

The monster's movements were not as spastic as the sick shark's had been, but it still swam with unnatural speed and chaotic courage. The black ploma pulled away from them in a sudden burst of speed and jerked its body around with horrible efficiency, ready to rush the two sirena. As it crashed forward, Olenka heard its deafening calls piercing the darkness once more, the shrill, playful song wailing from the monster's maw. But a horrible realization struck her.

The sound wasn't coming from *this* creature at all…

She looked about in panic, only to find her fears heighten. There were more shadows racing toward them in the water. It was all in a frantic moment, but Olenka counted at least three more smudges pressing through the green gloom.

She flipped her head back around and saw the first brute still bearing down on them, bare meters away, the black coils in its mouth excitedly rippling against the drag. In that moment, everything seemed to fall into perspective for Olenka. It was a moment of sunken horror, pulsing adrenaline, and a mind crumbling away from time. The sea slowed and stilled, and Olenka found herself floating not only in the water, but in time itself.

What has happened to me? Why am I here?

What an intriguing question. Olenka considered the possibilities and concluded that she was here to die: to die at the sides of her closest friends. To die because she was no longer strong enough, or perhaps *important* enough, to live. She could accept that.

This felt like a good end. A sirena's end.

But, if I'm about to die, why would I have dreamed of the future? A future that clearly reaches far beyond this moment…

It was a fair point. Her dream had already begun to unfold before her. How could it possibly end now? There was more. So much more. She couldn't exactly remember any of it in this painful, surreal moment, but it was there all the same. Packed away in waxy, waterproof wrappings. Ready to be remembered when it was needed. Somehow, these thoughts all ebbed and meshed and combined into one, simple idea of such singular importance that it shook Olenka to her soul.

I am going to get out of this.

The crashing sound of speed in water broke upon Olenka's ears as she felt the tides of time sweep her away once more. Two trails of bubbles shot out in front of her. The charging black monsters were distracted from their targets on either side of the sirena. Olenka blinked in dismay as she watched a plaloma flash its fins before the infected creature bearing down on her, leading it off toward the surface.

The pod twirled back around, jerking past the snaps of rancid, parasite-ridden jaws, and Akia and Hoshay rammed themselves hard against Olenka and Marikit. The smooth, sweet noses of the mounts were like fists to their guts, but neither of the sirena dared cast a dark thought. Olenka shifted herself along Akia's streamlined body and gripped onto the harness, slipping easily back into a riding position as the plaloma burst onto the surface. She glanced around and saw the pod of black beasts converge in the gloom and erupt out of the water behind them, enraged and disoriented.

Olenka barely had time to breathe and get her bearings. From beside her, Diwala called out a single, pointed word over the spray.

"River!"

The plalomas dove once more. Olenka looked back and saw one of the infected monsters swerve her way. Akia barely twisted away from the attack and breached the surface to escape. The two flipped through the air again and splashed down just out of reach of the giant, black plaloma's teeth. In that passing instant, Olenka sucked in a deep, filling breath, and scanned the horizon. The river was ahead, slightly off to the right. The plalomas seemed to be heading there naturally, but the mad pod was closing in on them too quickly. Olenka had an idea to buy them some time. The black brutes could beat their plalomas for speed, but maneuverability…

She clicked in the water and guided Akia farther off to the right. The plaloma miraculously obeyed, and they swiveled away from the pod. The beast behind them followed. Olenka pulled her blade up to her arm and cut a simple slit along the back of her forearm. It was not deep or overly painful, but the drag of the sea sipped out the wisp of blood in a clear, red stream. Olenka heard a chorus of haunting calls respond, and the whole collection of black smudges in the distance changed their course. Her plan was working, but Olenka did not rejoice.

Please trust me, Akia, Olenka pled in her mind.

Olenka clicked and jerked back on the harness. The plaloma squealed in fear but flipped a perfect vertical turn. Together they drove straight back into the faces of the approaching black pod. There was no time to think, only to react. The first beast charged straight at her, but Akia jerked aside just in time. Two more creatures were right behind it and came at her from either side. Rider and mount swerved down and to the right, passing between the jaws and fin of one of the approaching creatures.

The other monster twisted harshly to follow and sank its teeth into the flank of the other.

Black coils squirted out into the water from the new wound, and Akia shot away toward the surface. Olenka was grateful. The squirming parasites frightened her *far* more than the monsters they infected. Akia burst out into the air and Olenka saw that they were still on course. The river was only fifty meters away. With any luck, they'd–

The fourth monster punched up from underneath.

It rammed Akia with the back of its head, launching her and Olenka up over the surf. The plaloma flailed in fear, and Olenka held on with her full body. They crashed back into the water to find the beast facing them. Akia swam straight for the seafloor, skimming the silt. The black plaloma followed but was unable to react in time as Akia pitched herself back up toward the sky. The monster crashed into the rocks and mud below, and Akia and Olenka began to sprint.

It was unclear how close the other three beasts had gotten during the maneuver, but Olenka could feel them coursing through the water behind her. She had no time to turn and check, the river mouth was just ahead. She had hoped it wouldn't come down to this, hoped Akia's acrobatics could have bought them some more time, but they were in a mad dash to the river. The entire attempt had been boiled down to this one, bleak moment of speed, a race against creatures far quicker and more powerful than her or Akia.

The mouth of the river came into sight through the haze. Thick current cuts adorned the seafloor, and the plants were all pressed down onto their sides. Akia pulled up with the ground and slipped into the fresh water. The adverse flow slowed her down, but she kicked with immense force and threw the two over the lip and into the wider river base.

But there was no moment of peace or celebration.

The black pod collided with the river mouth and fought their way into the pool. Akia jerked in fear and took off down the river. The water was almost transparent here, and Olenka could just make out the shapes of the other riders far ahead. She clicked for speed, but Akia was already swimming at her limit. As the water grew shallower, Olenka's face and torso breached the surface. She looked over her shoulder and her heart dropped into her stomach.

The entire black pod was crashing toward them.

The monsters had seemed immense *in* the water, but out on the shallow river their enormity didn't seem possible. Each one was easily five times the size of a plaloma, and there was a pod of four of them. The wretched things barreled and burst through the shoals, carving into the mud banks and ripping up the brush and trees around them.

Olenka blinked and swallowed. She was out of ideas, out of time, and quickly running out of courage. She could see Di and Mari in the distance, their heads and shoulders just peeking out over the surface. They were glancing back at the black pod's din as well, their faces anxious and broken.

They were all trapped again.

Upriver without the room to escape or turn or fight. Olenka placed her cheek against Akia's fin.

"Thank you for saving me, dear sister," she muttered miserably into the incoming spray. "I'm sorry I couldn't repay the debt…"

But as Olenka turned her head to embrace Akia, she saw something she did not expect. There was a young man standing on the shore; except, he wasn't really *on* the shore. He was standing on a metal catwalk hanging *over* the shore which was suspended from the trees. The man's face was steeped in horror, and his eyes were desperately shooting around the turmoil in the water. Olenka sat up and saw that there were many others positioned in similar gawking stances around the river, and there was just as much metal walkway around them as well. It was unlike anything Olenka had ever seen. Iron seemed to dress every surface, confusing the lines of land and tree.

There was a great clamor on the shore, and dozens of voices screaming out panicked instructions. Above them all came one clear command.

"Close the dam! Hurry!"

Olenka's eyes and ears perked up. There was a terrible metallic screech, and an immense change in the river's current. Ahead, Olenka could see a massive wall of iron. No, it couldn't have been a wall because it was *moving*. It was a gate, and its doors were closing.

"Akia, my sister, this may be our only chance!" Olenka called out over the roar of the water. "Swim like you've *never* swam before! Swim like *yokai* are at your fins!"

Olenka clicked her tongue over and over, and somehow Akia found the strength to respond. They began to close the gap to their pod ahead, and the three plalomas shifted into a single file line. The opening in the gate was narrowing as two imposing iron doors folded in. The condensed water streamed out with vicious force, and the three plalomas cried out in desperation.

"Come on! You can make it!"

Olenka looked up to see a young Bantay Tubig waving and calling out to them. He was leaning off the edge of the gate and pointing to the narrow passage. The pod pushed with everything they had, and with just enough space to pass, they managed to slip through the closing doors. Akia cried out in pained chirps as the metal edges scraped along her fins and the sides of Olenka's legs. The pod erupted out into the deeper water as the gate screeched shut behind them.

The plalomas fanned out to the shallow bank. Olenka jumped free of Akia and tried to stand but stumbled into the water. She stared back at the gate and saw dozens of siokoy screaming and jumping from its edge into the deep water beside them. There was an overwhelming blast of sound and pressure as the black pod slammed into the metal barrier like a tsunami of flesh and black, putrid blood.

But the iron doors held.

Over and over the monstrous plalomas beat themselves into the dam, bending and denting its surface, but the divide remained. Finally, to the sound of cheering siokoy, the brutes retreated.

Olenka scrambled to her fins, panting in rigid fatigue. It felt like all her throbbing muscles had stiffened at once. Mari stood in the shallows, panting and clutching at her stomach. Diwala was still in the water, staring out at the gate. Her face was bright, and her mouth was wide.

"What *a ride!*" Diwala screamed, her tattooed arms shooting up triumphantly into the air. "*Ha!* Heaven above, Olenka, you sure found us a job! Oh, that was a hunt never to be forgotten, eh? It is not often that I am rooting for the success of the prey!" Her eyes and voice were wild and unrestrained.

Olenka walked up and punched her in the arm. "You're a buwisit *lunatic*, did you know?"

Diwala smiled and laughed and pulled Olenka into a powerful embrace. They then tackled Mari, who seemed too shocked to speak or protest. They hit the shore and collapsed, laughing in staggering relief.

Just overhead, there was a metal walkway. A large siokoy was standing above them. His head was shaved, and his arms and chest were covered in dark leather pads bound together with metal clasps and studs. His arms were thick and bulky, unlike the typical lean musculature of the Bantay Tubig. He held out a worn, calloused hand with cracked nails and receded webbing.

Olenka glanced at Mari and Di, but then took the man's help. With ease, he hoisted her up onto the walkway. He chuckled and scrunched his ample brow, which Olenka was surprised to see held the delicate lace of a *kataw*, not the sharp points of a siokoy.

"Welcome to your graves, little sisters," the burly kataw said.

Olenka's face fell in disgust. "Is that a *threat?*"

"Threat?" The kataw laughed in long, jaded bursts. "No, no. No threat. Lightning upon that chum. Just a guarantee we have all learned to accept around here. *No one* leaves Ka Jiya."

CHAPTER 30

THE PLIGHT OF KA JIYA

THE CROWD DESCENDED QUICKLY THEN, overwhelming Olenka with their barrage of questions. Most were excited, even delighted to see them. They thronged the sirena with the lingering adrenaline of the chase. Others, however, screamed out threats and curses, shoving their way through the buzzing crowd and pointing angrily at the gouged gate. Olenka stepped back, debating whether or not she should jump back down to the pod and river below.

"Quiet! All of you!"

A powerful voice, full of age and soot, cracked out over the roar. The crowd went silent as a large, elderly man stepped down a metal stairway onto the catwalk. He was dressed in a thick leather apron, with plates of metal bound into the cloth. He had a large tattoo that curled around his cheek and across the back of his shaved skull, and a metal walking stick propped in his hand. His skin was weathered and dark: the skin of a man who had long since forsaken the sea for the fires of craftsmanship.

"Master Taro." The man who had pulled Olenka up onto the walkway turned and bowed to the old man.

The master leaned forward on his staff and studied the dents in the metal dam. "*Naraka's jaws*, Masato… What has happened here?"

Masato turned and motioned toward Olenka and her crew. "Master, these three sirena outran the devil pod! They came straight up the river on plalomas. We were barely able to close the dam in time to save them and their mounts."

"Sirena?" Master Taro grunted in amusement before turning his attention to the crew. "And who would be so foolish as to willingly come to our island?"

Olenka cleared her throat. "Our crew came up from Sotay. We are on the errand of the monks of the Lunsod sa Dagat to retrieve the armor of the ancient hero."

The whole crowd around them cracked and sputtered in scorning laughter, and Olenka glanced around at the bitter faces, displeasure building in her gut and shoulders.

Marikit bowed her head and stepped to the edge of the walkway. "Please, sir. We mean no disrespect."

Diwala followed suit. "We have simply come to salvage the armor from the wreck offshore."

Masato laughed and offered his hands to Mari and Di. "Is that so, little minnows?"

Master Taro shook his head as Di and Mari were hoisted up onto the metal walkway. "You three have come a very far distance for nothing, I am afraid. Far better you had elected to die in your own waters."

Olenka cocked her head as she spoke. "What are you saying?"

Master Taro offered a passing smile to the sirena, and then scowled at the crowd. "All of you, return to your posts! And someone, pull those poor plalomas out of the river and into the tank. Masato, would you be so kind?"

"Yes, Master." Masato bowed again as he turned to a nearby youth. "Eiji, you man the crane!"

"Whoa, cut the sails, old man!" Olenka stepped up as the crowd began to disperse. "You touch our pod and you answer to me."

Master Taro smiled at her rough tone. "If you care at all for the safety of those creatures, then you will let us take them out of the river. I cannot keep a foolish crew from risking their lives, but I will not have the blood of innocent plalomas on my hands. They are stained enough as it is."

Olenka turned back to Diwala and Marikit who each looked equally concerned.

"It's alright," Masato offered. He jumped down and held a hand out to stroke the timid plalomas. "I won't let anything happen to them. Trust me, sisters. If we don't get them out, they'll be devil fish by dawn."

Master Taro nodded and gestured up the stairway. "Come, and do not fret. It seems we have much to talk about."

Olenka frowned in skepticism. "You're *sure* your siokoy can move them safely?"

Master Taro stopped and turned in his tracks. "My dear, they may not fit your expectations, but all who live on Ka Jiya are *kataw*, and sirena like yourselves would do well to remember it."

The old man continued up the stairs. Olenka scoffed and shook her head as she climbed. "You are what you *do*. Kudori has nothing to do with it. I know thugs when I see them."

Taro raised his eyebrow and glanced back as he walked. "An interesting perspective for one of your standing. What would *you* know of such things?"

Olenka rolled her eyes and leaned over the nearby railing on the walkway, letting Mari and Di catch up. She pulled off her hood covering her kudori and squeezed the water from it. The trees were dense through here, and great puddles of rainwater had accumulated in the tangles of their roots. Olenka shook out her matted hair and stared down at her reflection.

"I know more than you would guess."

She pushed off the railing and glared at Master Taro down the walkway. "So, I assume you're in charge around here. Taro, wasn't it? What is it that you believe we need to talk about? To be perfectly clear, I'm really in no mood for a lecture from another arrogant kataw."

Master Taro's hard grimace broke into a smirk. He gazed up at Olenka's kudori and then chuckled. "Is she *always* like this agreeable?" he called back to Di and Mari.

Diwala nodded gravely as she pulled off her hood. Mari smiled and mouthed *always*.

Master Taro laughed and took a couple of hobbling steps over toward Olenka. "Well, I like her. She reminds me of myself in my youth. Trust no one. Question everything… Honorable traits, if *bridled* properly."

The old man smirked and leaned against his cane. "Little sister, do you know how the Bantay Tubig gained their caste system?"

Olenka scowled. "What could that *possibly* have to do with anything?"

The old man cocked his eyebrow and shrugged. "Perhaps nothing. And perhaps everything. Either way, you didn't answer my question."

Olenka folded her arms, trying to hide her mild intrigue. "I guess I haven't heard that particular myth."

"Hmm… I'd thought not." He winked and walked to the railing next to her. "It's not a story the faithful would have told you. You see, centuries ago, when the ancient hero first found our people, they were deeply divided. They all shared and defended the light of the Pa Naing, but that was about the depth of their fidelity. They were all separated into distinct, squabbling tribes, each with their own nonsense beliefs and traditions and religions… *Bah*." The old man grimaced before he continued. "They were certainly a great force, but their division made them weak against the yokai. Our ancestors didn't even speak the same *language*. Can you imagine that?"

The old man paused to shake his head and clear his throat. "So, the ancient hero, in his great, military wisdom, unified our people, and gave them all tasks and duties for the greater good. Some were called to lead the armies, while others were made into warriors or farmers. We here at Ka Jiya, however, were sent to learn from the great craftsmen of the mountains."

Master Taro smiled and placed his fingertips against his forehead. "You might be wondering how *these* got involved, hmm? Well, after the hero's departure, the church began to assess the divisions in the people. They determined that all who were chosen for a certain task bore similar patterns in their kudori. The practice was refined to an art, and now all Bantay Tubig believe that their fate is determined by silly scribbles in their skin." The old man chuckled but drew his face into a serious glare. "But don't you go telling any of those monks down there that I said that. I'm perfectly content to let them go on believing that we are undeniably their *Heaven-sanctioned equals.*"

Olenka stared into the old man's wrinkled eyes, trying to make sense of him. "Why are you telling me this?"

Master Taro grinned. "Because I thought you'd enjoy hearing it. Or perhaps it's because I like questioning the system. Or maybe it is simply because I am growing old and senile and have far too many stories schooling inside me and far too little time to share them."

Olenka sighed and clasped her fingers together. "Well, this might come as a surprise to you, but I was raised kataw. Both of my parents are members of the church clergy, and I am sure I've heard most of your waterlogged stories *ten times* over."

The old man's voice was loud and bright. "But of course! How could you have been anything *but* kataw with a kudori like that?"

Olenka spat into the mud. "By choosing not to be."

Diwala stepped up to the railway, looking stiff and annoyed. "Master Taro, we do not have time for stories, and it seems to me that you are deliberately wasting what little time we *do* have. Our mission must be concluded before the Sacrament of Light. That is just a few days from now. What is it that we need to know about this island?"

Master Taro turned slowly toward Diwala, studying the expression in her face. "All you need to know, little shark, is that no one can leave Ka Jiya Island. You best forget your haste. And forget your *buwisit mission* while you're at it."

Olenka's face drew tight in suspicion. "Hold up a moment… You just told me not to tell the southern kataw of your beliefs. Why would you say that if no one can leave the island?"

Master Taro waved off her remark. "I assure you it was a slip of the tongue, little sister. You are more than welcome to *attempt* to leave. No one's stopping you. I just doubt you'll make it past the reef. We have been trapped here for months."

"Trapped?" Olenka stepped forward. "By what? That pod of sick plalomas?"

Master Taro smiled bitterly as he spoke. "Yes, by the devil fish. You escaped the greatest of them moments ago."

Mari shook her head. "Whoa, wait. Are you saying there are *more?*"

Master Taro nodded gravely. "There are as many devil fish out there as there were fish to infect. We have been studying the phenomenon for almost a year. Some of our fishermen began reporting a mysterious illness that was tainting the fish. We experimented with it and discovered that it spread rather quickly and aggressively, but only through the mouth or bloodstream. We have no idea where it came from, but everything in the waters around Ka Jiya is infected, no matter how big or small. That's why we are removing your plalomas from the river to a contained tank of clean water. It was only a matter of time before they ate something contaminated and were lost to the infection as well. Our own food supplies have been almost entirely depleted. In our rationing, many desperate, hungry kataw have turned to the meat of the devil fish." He rubbed at his eye. "We have lost quite a few to the parasite…"

Master Taro looked away into the forest. It was as if he had forgotten that the crew was there. He was reciting the story to himself more than anything, like a tragedy that must be confronted in order to be accepted.

"A couple of months ago," the old man continued, "the situation became much more severe. The sickness spread to bigger predators, driving them mad..."

Olenka nodded. "Like those black plalomas that almost killed us?"

"Yes." Taro nodded his head in sorrow. "But they are not plalomas. They are called ku jira, and they were our most precious friends and allies on this island."

Mari scoffed and pressed her fingers into her tired eyes. "Yeah, they seem like a *really loveable* bunch."

Master Taro nodded sadly. "It is reasonable that you would hate them, but the ku jira were not always what they are today. They are naturally affectionate creatures, and insatiably curious. They are smarter, stronger, and faster than any plaloma, but that makes them impossible to control or train as mounts. So, our ancestors started a tradition of *paying* the ku jira for their work. We would give them a meat offering, and they would help us fish or haul loads for us to shore."

Diwala looked puzzled. "Without riders?"

Master Taro nodded and smiled. "I know it sounds like chum, but it is the truth. We would attach straps to cargo rafts, and they would haul them to the mainland with their teeth. We became quite dependent on them, actually and, well... losing them has all but cut us off from the peninsula. The few ships we had at port were destroyed by the ku jira pod as well. We could not have been less prepared for this tragedy..."

Olenka glanced around, searching for the sun through the trees. "So, is that why you're trapped? There are no ships that can take you to shore?"

Taro nodded as he spoke. "That's *part* of the problem, but the ku jira themselves pose a far greater threat. The pod attacks anything that breaks the coast. I've never seen anything like it. They were such gentle beasts, but now... nothing escapes the island. We could try to swim to our kin on the Bharatian Peninsula, but it would be a slaughter. Boat or otherwise, nothing is fast enough or strong enough to get us out of here. We should have evacuated months ago."

"So," Olenka thought out loud, "if they were destroyed…"

The old man shook his head. "We've tried *everything*. It just isn't possible. The devil fish feel no pain, and maiming them hardly slows them down. Nothing even *scares* the brutes, much less kills them. Even our most skilled warriors–"

"We will do it." Diwala stepped forward. "We have killed one before."

Taro looked up with naked skepticism. Olenka nodded toward Di. "It's true. An infected shark was captured down off Sotay for the samay lawa fights. We killed it for the proprietor. It wasn't easy, but it can be done."

The old man shook his head. "Well of course it *can* be done, but that does not mean it *will* be done. Nothing can stand up to the ku jira! Their strength and speed are unparalleled."

Diwala glared at the kataw. "You doubt our skill?"

Master Taro stood a hair straighter, but he didn't speak immediately. He chuckled a little, but his features melted from humor to confusion. He panned across the faces of the crew, evaluating their rationality. "What *exactly* are you three proposing?"

Diwala shrugged and laid a tattooed arm on Olenka's shoulder. "I believe it is pretty simple, is it not? You are trapped on this island by fierce beasts. You need hunters."

Taro chuckled. "And you three are volunteering?"

"Yes." Diwala's voice was firm and resolute. Olenka and Marikit smiled and nodded with her. Diwala tapped the sharp, jagged lines of her forehead. "Unlike *some*, there are those of us who choose to embrace the fate that Heaven has given us."

Taro cocked his head and scratched his chin, unaffected by the sirena's salty comment. Taro's eyes were heavy with cynicism and doubt, but there was hope there too, glimmering in the shadows. It was a hope that he was almost tempted to embrace.

"And how would *three sirena* rid us of a pod of mad ku jira?"

Olenka shrugged. "Show us around and we'll put strategy to our courage. What have you learned? What have you tried? What resources do you have?"

Master Taro shook his head and grumbled. "I suppose there's no harm in showing you…"

CHAPTER 31

IRON SIDES

THE CREW WAS LED DOWN A MAZE OF METAL walkways, all suspended from the trees or built across stray boulders on the jungle floor. It was some kind of iron wharf, and it ran right through the thick of the forest, branching off to dozens of metal huts and platforms hidden in the foliage.

Olenka glanced over the scene in awe. All around them the area was completely obscured by ancient trees. Due to her life on the sea, limited line of sight was often distressing for Olenka, but she found these green guardians oddly comforting. Given the circumstances, perhaps it was for the best to have a barrier between them and the water. This strange iron pier could have been as close as ten meters from the beach or as far as a hundred. They never would have known the difference.

The walkways widened and converged on a large, crowded platform. The craftsmanship was striking to Olenka. She was used to the southern Bantay Tubig's architectural dichotomy: either the rickety docks of Sotay or the gaudy halls of the underwater city. The structures here were painfully practical. Buildings were boxy, barren, and sturdy, and the platforms were remarkably solid. Hammered studs and wrought iron guardrails were the only decorations among the soot pits, anvils, and bent backs of the despondent Ka Jiyans. Many of the island's kataw just seemed to be lying around, mindlessly waiting for death or rations.

And their eyes carried such sorrow…

The edge of the platform was lined with huge warehouses and shops, and, as far as Olenka could tell, everything larger than a table was made exclusively from metal. The buildings were all equipped with enormous, open doorways looking into the massive tools and furnaces beyond. It was all incredibly advanced compared to anything she had seen in the southern towns. Even the great Lunsod sa Dagat did not possess machinery of this quality. Many kataw crowded the platform, but despite the array of tools and supplies, none were engaged in any kind of meaningful activities.

"What is this place?" Olenka asked.

Master Taro looked at Olenka and chuckled. "This is our way of life, little sister. These are the workshops and furnaces of Ka Jiya. This is where we build and melt and polish the wonders of the sacred city."

Olenka looked around at all the empty, hopeless faces. "No one is doing anything."

Taro nodded. "I cannot blame them. We have lost too much."

Marikit grimaced. "So, what? You're all just going to *wait here to die?*"

Master Taro shrugged. "Perhaps."

Mari's face contorted in horror and disgust. She looked around at all the broken lives, listlessly drifting to their end.

"This is madness," she whispered.

The old man nodded in grim amusement. "These are mad times, little sister."

Marikit glared up at Taro's face, her eyes glittering with contempt. "What kind of a leader are you? How could you just sit back and let this happen?"

Master Taro laughed and braced himself against his cane. "And what would you have us do? How would *you* lead my people?"

"I would have them fight!" Mari stepped back, gazing out over the platform. "How could they have given up so easily? How could *you* have given up on them?" She stared accusingly at Master Taro, stretching out her hand to the kataw.

The old man shook his head. "Mind your tongue, little minnow. Do you think we haven't done all we could? Do you really believe that we haven't all broken our backs trying to free ourselves from this miserable prison? Sometimes, you must learn to accept your fate in order to truly be at peace with the world."

"What a rotten load of chum," Olenka whispered.

Master Taro turned to Olenka, glaring his annoyance. "Excuse me? Just who do you three think you are?"

Diwala leaned back against the platform's railing. "I believe we already told you. We are the hunters who will save your sorry souls."

Master Taro looked frustrated and offended, but he remained silent. Olenka stepped up to him and looked directly into his eyes as she spoke. "You said you've tried everything? Well, show me."

Master Taro grimaced but sighed. "Come with me."

The old man led the sirena across the platform to the largest warehouse. There were no workers inside, but the building was filled with equipment. The long hall and high rafters ran for more than a hundred meters, all packed with hammers and clamps and piles of scrap. Taro gestured to a large line of spears and harpoons resting against the closest wall.

"At first, we simply tried to arm ourselves. We sent out several crews to hunt the ku jira, but none of them returned. Our efforts just served to deplete our supplies and wreck our ships."

He looked away from the wall and gestured to the back of the warehouse. There was a massive opening leading out into a gated inlet, completely obscured from the platform by the trees and the building. Floating against the docks, and partly shaded by the warehouse, was a massive iron ship.

The old man trudged down the length of the warehouse. "When *aggression* failed us," he growled, "all our efforts turned to escape."

Olenka stared at the ship, puzzled. "You built a *metal* boat?"

Master Taro smiled and nodded. "We built two, in fact."

Mari stepped up, staring with Olenka. "But... how does it...?"

"How does it float?" Taro chuckled and marched out onto the dock, gazing at the iron ship. "Little sister, have you ever dropped a cup in the water?"

Marikit frowned but conceded. "Yeah."

"And what happened to it?"

Mari shrugged. "It sank."

Master Taro nodded. "And did you ever study *how* it sank? *Why* it sank?"

Mari laughed. "No, of course not! Why would I?"

"Hmm..." Master Taro nodded. "You would not have done well on Ka Jiya. You see, we *did* study it. That's simply what we do. We take nothing for granted. We discovered that there are two ways to make something float. First, you can build it out of a material that floats, like wood. Or, second, you can fill it with air. You see, if you place a cup faceup in the water, the air inside will keep it floating for a little while so long as the edges of the cup are high enough. Fill it with water, however, and the cup will sink immediately." He motioned to the ship behind him. "This is our cup. Despite its immense size and weight, we have captured so much air inside that this ship floats. Quite well, I might add."

Olenka stepped up to the ship and placed her hand along the metal wall. "How thick is it?"

Master Taro chuckled and clacked the end of his cane against it. The whole boat boomed with a resonating echo. "I know what you're thinking. It was exactly what *we* were thinking when we built it. Sadly, the walls are not thick enough, and the ku jira can still pierce their sides and sink them."

Diwala frowned. "You know this?"

Olenka shook her head in sorrow. "He said they made two, remember?"

Diwala breathed in for a moment of clarity, but then nodded. "I am sorry."

"Me too," Master Taro whispered as he sat down on the dock, his back pressed against and sliding down the warehouse wall. "It was all my fault… These ships were our last hope, and they failed us. We lost almost sixty souls in one evening. That was half the population of the entire island, you know… The ku jira were relentless. They rammed the ship over and over until the hull split along the welding. No one made it back. They didn't even have time to get the buwisit steam going."

Olenka lifted her head and stared down at the kataw. "Steam?"

Master Taro nodded. "That's right. These ships move by steam."

Marikit giggled and shook her head. "What are you talking about? *Actual* steam?"

The old man nodded and pointed his cane at the side of the boat. "Do you see that waterwheel on the far side of the ship? The wheel's paddles are what propel the whole boat. We built a compression chamber in its lower level that moves the axle attached to the wheel. It's quite simple, actually. We use something very similar in our–"

"Wait," Olenka interrupted, "what did you mean when you said you couldn't get the steam *going?*"

The old man shook his head in frustration. "Okay, listen you three. We burn coal to heat a tank of water in the belly of the ship. Make sense? The steam then rises from the tank through a pipe to the compression chamber. There is a paddle wheel inside the chamber attached to the one outside the ship by a metal beam. The steam turns the inner wheel, which turns the beam, and the outer wheel spins to paddle the ship forward. It's simple, but it takes time to get the steam hot enough to get it to work."

"So," Olenka whispered, "what you're saying is that you just needed more *time.*"

Taro shrugged. "I suppose…"

"And how fast does this ship go once the steam is hot enough?"

"Well, we designed them to be pretty fast. I'd say at least…" Master Taro stopped and squinted up at Olenka. "Wait. Oh, no. I see what you're getting at. *Forget it*."

Diwala looked confused. "What? I do not understand."

Olenka smiled and turned to Diwala. "We can do this. If we can find a way to distract the black plalomas for long enough then the kataw can get their ship moving quick enough to escape." She turned back to Master Taro. "Am I right?"

The old man nodded and then groaned deep in his throat. "In *theory*, yes… Our hope was that the ships would be strong enough to handle the ku jira's attacks until we could outrun them in the open water."

"Right!" Olenka shouted excitedly. "But that was where you all failed. Your ships weren't strong enough, but who's to say they're not *fast* enough? All we need to do is find some way to lure the black plaloma pod away long enough to get your metal ship up to speed."

Master Taro rolled his eyes. "Oh? Is it so easy? And how do you plan on distracting those brutes? Any of you willing to be the bait?"

Marikit shook her head and stomped up next to the bitter old man. "You know what?" she snapped. "I've had just about enough of you and your uzai attitude. Tattered sails, are you going to keep sulking like an angry pup, or are you going to get off your lazy fins and help us?"

Master Taro chuckled to himself quietly. "How can you three still be so determined? You *saw* them out there! You've seen what they can do… and yet you've all found courage to face them. How? Why?"

Olenka crouched down next to the old kataw and offered him a hand. "We do what we must for each other. As a crew, we all pull our weight, and sometimes that means being the voice or courage when the rest of the crew is ready to turn fin. We find the courage to go on because we care what happens to each other."

Diwala nodded and crouched down beside Olenka. "When you forget your own suffering and listen to the pain of those who are near you, you will surely find the strength to protect them."

Master Taro grunted and rubbed his eyes. "I still think you buwisit minnows are naïve, but… why not? What is there to lose?"

Diwala smiled as Taro took her and Olenka's hands and let the two sirena hoist him to his feet. Diwala clapped his shoulder. "It is better to die a shark's death at sea, than to dry up like a fish on the sand."

"Go out with a bang, huh?" Taro chuckled then stopped, his eyes drifting as he nodded his head. "You want something to distract the ku jira? I can't believe I'm doing this, but I think I've got *just* what you need."

* * *

THE OLD KATAW TOOK THE CREW TO A DIFFERENT warehouse across the platform. It was a smaller building, but it was packed with even more supplies. Barrels of various sizes, all marked with foreign symbols, were stacked up against the far wall. Inside, there were a series of tables and furnaces situated in an assembly line of workstations. Master Taro hobbled quickly down the row, evaluating the equipment on each table: shaking jars, sniffing strange substances, tossing around complex tools as he cursed and grouched.

"Where in the crushing depths did I leave that buwisit…" he muttered as he walked. He tossed a few jars to the side, letting them shatter on the iron floor. Finally, he stepped back and smiled, holding a small jar in his hands.

"Here we are, little sisters! Any of you know what this is?" Master Taro turned to the crew and held out the little container. It appeared to be filled with black sand.

Olenka shook her head. "No, but are you going to tell us?"

"This," the old man said with bursting pride, "is *whu yao*, the ancient fire medicine of the mountains."

Olenka scrunched her face in confusion. "The fire what?"

She glanced to Mari who was obviously just as perplexed. Diwala, on the other hand, had taken on a reverential awe, like she was basking in Heaven's glory itself.

"How is this possible?" Diwala stepped forward, reaching for the jar. "The recipe for whu yao was lost hundreds of years ago!"

Taro chuckled and gently handed the precious container to Diwala. "Not lost, little sister, merely hidden. After the death of the ancient hero, the kataw on Ka Jiya decided that the recipe was too dangerous for the rest of the world. We keep it now for mining purposes: to dig quickly and crack our way through solid stone. Aside from the giants of the mountains, we are the only ones skilled enough to craft it."

Olenka stepped up to Diwala, muttering the foreign word. "Whu yao?"

Diwala nodded and delicately sniffed the powder inside. "Yes. It is an ancient recipe. A blend of stone powders that can cause great destruction."

"How?" Mari asked, stepping up to peer into the jar.

Master Taro reached for the powder. "Here, I'll show you."

The old man took a pinch of powder from the jar and placed it in a little pile on the metal floor. He grabbed a device from the nearest table and clicked it in his hands. There were two prongs: one that held a black stone, and another that scraped across the stone as he squeezed. The stone sprayed a cascade of sparks each time the other prong scratched its surface. Master Taro leaned down and clicked the sparking device over the small pile of whu yao.

Olenka jumped back as the powder blazed into a flare of blinding light. It burst up suddenly, a rapid puff of white smoke and streaking embers. The flame sizzled and then died down very quickly, leaving nothing but a grainy, black stain on the floor.

Diwala shook her head in amazement and breathed in the chemical scent. "*Remarkable...*"

Marikit frowned. "*That* was it? It just burned! Dried reeds do the same thing!"

Olenka nodded. "I don't understand what's so dangerous with this."

Master Taro grunted in frustration. "You two really don't use your eyes, do you? Did you not see *how* it burned?"

Olenka shrugged. "I mean… it was *fast*, I'll give you that."

The old man studied her for a moment, and then turned back to the table. "Perhaps I am being too hard on you. You see, the true potential of whu yao comes when you add *pressure*." The old man rummaged around the cluttered desk and produced a metal sphere. He twisted a section off the top and poured the entire jar of black powder down the now open mouth.

"What's your name, by the way?" Master Taro motioned to Di as the fine powder tumbled into the metal case.

"Diwala," she declared.

Taro nodded. "Diwala, eh? Well then, Diwala, would you be so kind as to fetch me that barrel of water over there?"

Di turned and saw the barrel sitting by the closest furnace. She grabbed it around the lip and slid it awkwardly toward the master.

"Not too close, now, if you please," Taro said.

Di nodded and let the barrel sit about two meters away from the table. Master Taro tightened the lid back down on the metal sphere and brought it and the sparking device over to the barrel.

"Now then, if you *contain* the whu yao in a tight enough space, then it has nowhere to go when it burns, but it will burn all the same. You there, what was your name?" He pointed to Marikit.

She stepped to the barrel cautiously. "It's Mari."

"Mari. Tell me, what did you notice about the *way* the whu yao burned?"

Marikit sighed and shrugged. "I don't really know. It was quick, like Olenka said… I was surprised that such a little pile of powder could make such a large fire."

"There." He smiled and pointed at her. "Exactly. Not only does it burn quickly, but it *expands* at an alarming rate. Here, come help me light this."

Mari stepped forward, clearly a little nervous. Master Taro handed her the sparking device and pointed down at the edge of the metal sphere. "Look here. Do you see the fuse?"

Mari nodded, and Master Taro grinned wickedly. There was a second metal clasp on the sphere that spanned the circumference of the shell. Underneath the clasp was a long wick. He lifted the tip away from the metal with his finger and placed it against the stone at the end of the sparking device.

"When I say go," Taro said, "I want you to light it and get out of the way, got it?"

Again, Mari nodded quietly. The old man adjusted the wick and looked over the device's latches one last time.

"Okay," he said. Mari clicked the device and jumped back out of the way, staring intently at the unlit wick.

Master Taro laughed and shook his head. "It might take a couple of clicks, sweetheart."

Olenka chuckled. "You're not *nervous*, are you Mari?"

"Clam up," she grumbled to Olenka. Mari leaned back in over the barrel and clicked the device. She clicked it again and again, and finally, with a quick hiss, the fuse lit. A thin line of white smoke plumed out from its tip.

"Okay!" Master Taro exclaimed. "Once it's lit, you've got to hurry." He closed the clasp over the fuse and cinched it down, encasing the flame in a small pocket of air. Once it was all contained, he dropped the sphere into the barrel and stepped back to the worktable. The crew stood there, nervously staring.

Nothing happened.

"Huh, might've smothered the flame before it got past the clamp." Master Taro folded his arms in disappointment. Olenka stepped forward, curiously stretching out to try and see into the inert barrel.

With a deafening crack, the barrel burst.

There was a brief flash of orange light, and the water in the barrel surged up and out. Olenka took the full blast of water to the face and fell back on the metal floor with a shriek.

Master Taro bent over himself laughing. "You didn't believe me, did you? *By Heaven*, what a nice bang!"

Olenka coughed and spat the wet splinters from off her lips. *"Naraka's jaws! What was that?"*

Diwala stepped to Olenka's side and lifted her to her feet. "That was what makes the fire medicine so dangerous. Truly incredible…"

Olenka wiped the grit and wood from her face and coughed again. "Wow, those little shells don't mess around…"

Master Taro shook his head. "No, they don't. We use those little waterproof shells for cracking open mineral veins underwater. The fuse stays dry under the clamp, and there's an air pocket contained within the metal wall that gives them just enough air to burn to the whu yao packed inside."

Mari stepped up to the barrel, inspecting the carnage. "But why did it *explode* like that? It was so strong…"

Master Taro held up another empty metal case from off the table. "It's because of this. The metal shell contains the powder's fire. As it tries to expand, the pressure builds. If the metal is too brittle, then the powder flares out of whatever crack or weak point it can find, and there's no explosion. If there's not enough powder, it burns but does not break through the metal. We've spent *years* trying to perfect this balance, and now we've been able to craft the most efficient and powerful blast."

Olenka stared at the metal shell for a long time, then she glanced back at the burst barrel. "This could work, couldn't it?"

Diwala smacked her arm down around Olenka's shoulders and cracked an immense smile. "It will be fun either way, yes?"

CHAPTER 32

HOPE OF THE CAPTIVES

MASTER TARO MOVED QUICKLY, SHUFFLING out of the warehouse and onto the platform. Just outside the entrance several kataw were lounging on a pile of cloth tarps leaned up against some wooden crates. One unfortunate young man was sleeping a little too close to the warehouse opening.

The old man hobbled up and whacked his unsuspecting victim with the cruel, blunt end of his cane. The kataw jerked awake, grabbing at his bruising arm.

"Ah! You waterlogged piece of… *Master!*" The young man whipped up to his knees and bowed deeply, placing his forehead against the back of his hands on the metal floor.

"Hmm," Taro mumbled. "Boy, I need you to run me an errand. You and the rest of this pile of urchins." He rammed the end of his cane into the gut of another unwary grunt to punctuate his command.

The second kataw yelped and sat up, clutching at his stomach. He shot out an angry glance that froze in surprise. The first young man nodded and stood.

"Anything, Master. What do you need?"

Taro smirked as he spoke. "Gather everyone to the platform. I don't care what they're doing. If they've got a pulse, I want them here immediately. Is that understood?"

The young man bowed and quickly roused the rest of his companions. The group stood, trembling with fatigue, but obediently rushing off along the metal pathways. Master Taro turned his attention back to the crew of sirena.

"Well, that's that then." The old man shrugged and leaned forward on his walking stick. "You've convinced *me*. Let's see how you do with the pups."

Olenka's face scrunched in confusion. "With the pups?"

Master Taro nodded. "That's how things are done here on Ka Jiya. No single man is truly in charge. Everything is decided by a vote."

Marikit stepped up. "Are you saying that we have to convince all of these gutless guppies to support our plan?"

The old man shook his head. "Not all of them. Just *most* of them."

Mari glared. "But that doesn't make any sense! Can't you just *make* them agree?"

Master Taro laughed. "Make them? You suggest that I *force them* to save themselves? My dear, I am only their *master*, not their *king*."

Olenka folded her arms and watched as several kataw boys began to trickle onto the platform. "What exactly does that title mean, then?"

The old kataw smiled gently. "It means simply that. They are the learners, and I am their master. Ka Jiya is a unique place, little sister. It's not really a city so much as a school. Young apprentices are chosen from our sister colony on the Bharatian Peninsula and ferried to the island for training. Most of the kataw here are under twenty years old. They come, they work, they learn, and then they leave. I select a few of the more promising students to remain here with me, but most of them do not stay any longer than two, maybe three years."

Olenka nodded. "Is that why I haven't seen any women or children here?"

The old man nodded. "Exactly. All of these young men have come seeking to learn the techniques of our ancestors. And thus, I am not their ruler, young sirena. I am simply their teacher. We work together on this island, and nothing is decided without the consent of the whole. In contrast, however, what the majority agrees to is absolute. If you can convince most of them to follow you, then all will follow you without question."

"An interesting system," Diwala stated with a nod. "But why do you not take female apprentices?"

The old master frowned. "I suppose it is just tradition. I've never heard of any young women who *wanted* to be trained."

"Have you ever *asked* any?" Diwala's words were uncomfortably candid.

The old man seemed perplexed and a little defensive. "Is there something troubling you, huntress?"

Diwala shrugged. "I suppose I am just trying to understand a new culture. It seems odd to me that you would allow genitals to restrict someone's fate but deny Heaven's mark in their kudori."

The old man laughed. "Well, you certainly don't hold anything back, Diwala. If you fight the way you speak then we all may just find our way off this pile of rocks after all!"

Olenka chuckled to herself and shook her head. She had some thoughts on the matter, but the crowd was growing, and her mind was consumed with planning her impending speech. How could she convince all these boys to take to the sea? Taro had mentioned the previous tragedy. It would require some serious persuasion to get them back out onto the water after that…

Master Taro stepped forward and whistled across the platform. In the distance, Masato waved. The kataw jogged forward and bowed. "Master?"

Taro lifted his cane and twirled it over the many young faces gathering around him. "Take roll, if you would, Masato. These three young sisters have a proposal that they would like us to take to a vote."

Masato nodded and drifted out into the crowd. He counted off the heads on the platform, and pointed out to the last group of stragglers trickling in.

"All fifty-three present, Master."

The old man ran his hand across his mouth and chin. "Fifty-three? Is that *really* all that are left?"

"I'm afraid so."

The old man shook his tattooed head but stepped forward and clanked his metal cane against the platform. "Quiet down, everyone!"

He paused for a moment, letting the anxious crowd hush and settle.

"It seems that *hope* has not completely abandoned us! Many of you were present at the river when these three sirena outran the devil fish earlier this morning. I have spoken with them, and I believe that they may be able to help us. This is Olenka of the southern kataw. Listen well."

* * *

THE OLD MAN STEPPED BACK, OPENING THE CENTER OF the crowd to Olenka. She looked up at all the faces around her. They were tired and thin. They were dirty faces that had long since abandoned purpose.

These boys weren't living; they were just surviving.

Olenka cleared her throat and stared forward. "As your master mentioned, my crew and I are sirena. We are warriors from the south. Hunters. We came here because we were hired by the monks to salvage the ancient armor. We didn't know about the situation on your island until we arrived. I am sorry for everything you've been through."

The crowd was drifting. Many of the young kataw were whispering to one another and shaking their heads. One up front openly scoffed, loud enough for the rest to hear. Olenka paused and stared at the insolent youth.

"Excuse me?" she said.

The young man glanced to the side and then at the three sirena in front of him. "Quit trying to soften us up. Just tell us your ridiculous escape plan so we can vote it down, alright?"

Several in the crowd began to chuckle. Olenka felt her volatile passions rising.

"What is your name?" Olenka asked through gently parted teeth.

"Jin," the young kataw sneered.

"Jin?" Olenka whispered. "Well, Jin, what do *you* think should be done?"

The young man chuckled bitterly. "Nothing."

Olenka nodded. "Nothing, huh? Interesting answer. Tell me, Jin, are you an empty shell or simply a coward?"

The young man stiffened and stepped forward. "What?"

"Oh, *deaf* as well!" Olenka smiled and stepped closer, right into his face, speaking as loud as she could without yelling. "I asked if you were an *empty shell* or a *coward*. Perhaps both?"

The young man reached forward and shoved Olenka back. She stepped back with the blow, maintaining her balance.

"*Shut up!*" he barked. "You don't know *anything!* You think you're better than us?"

Olenka shrugged. "Well... maybe just you."

The kataw shot forward, only to be grabbed by his peers. "*Get your claws off of me!*"

Olenka nodded, holding a hand up to the group. "Surprisingly, I agree with him! Let him go!"

The young men looked at each other in hesitation but loosened their grip on Jin. He wrenched his arms free, flinging their hands off his shoulders. He glared at Olenka, his eyes glistening.

Don't hurt him too much, Olenka thought to herself. *He's just scared and hungry.*

Jin shot forward, swinging wildly. Olenka ducked in between his blows, slapped her left hand against the side of his neck, and slammed her fist into his abdomen. Jin cried out in pain and fell forward onto his knees. He gasped for breath between staggered sobs and vomited onto the metal.

"Mari?" Olenka turned and motioned toward the young man. Marikit nodded, and crept forward, placing a hand on Jin's back. Olenka shook her head sadly but turned back to the silent crowd.

"I have never been a particularly *social* woman," Olenka stated flatly. "My crew and I have neither the time nor the patience to coax you all out of your fears. If you came here expecting a pep talk, then I promise I am going to disappoint you. The three of us are leaving this island. Whether you leave too is entirely up to you, but we do need your help. You see, as Jin was kind enough to demonstrate, you all do not know how to fight."

She paused to let the words ring, then she gestured to her crew. "But *we* do."

Olenka cleared her throat and stepped closer to the crowd. "Now please, don't misunderstand me. I know that we are not *better* than any of you. We have merely spent our lives developing different talents. I am not here to insult or embarrass any of you. In fact, I am *pleading* for your assistance. With our skill as hunters, and your skill as craftsmen, I believe we have what it takes to evacuate Ka Jiya. But this plan can only succeed if we work together." Olenka looked around at the pale faces. They were all young, and they were all scared.

"What do you plan to do?"

A kataw at the far end of the crowd had spoken. Olenka turned to him and casually locked her hands behind her back. "We are going to distract the ku jira while the rest of you escape in your master's iron ship. We'll fight them if necessary. Kill them if we have to."

Murmurs fluttered through the crowd. Olenka missed most of it, but she did pick out the word *foolish* being whispered somewhere in back. She remained silent, refusing to defend her statement. It had always been her opinion that the truth could speak for itself.

Finally, a much deeper voice broke the tension as Masato spoke up off to the left.

"How would you three accomplish this?"

Olenka motioned to the warehouse behind her. "We would use your whu yao shells, and whatever else we could gather. So far, the plan is that my crew will make a lot of noise and get the pod's attention somewhere east of the island. Once the ku jira are busy with us, you all would be free to launch the iron ship from the far port. We'll keep them distracted long enough for your ship to pick up enough speed to escape. The rest is on us. Whatever happens, you will make it back to the mainland."

Silence.

Some kataw looked around at each other, but many simply looked at their fins. Masato grunted and folded his arm loosely over his ample chest. "And you think you could hold their attention long enough for us to get the steam wheel going, huh?"

Olenka nodded. "I *know* we can. We've fought and killed sick creatures like them before. They react to sound and smell. Just leave it to us and worry about getting your ship out of the harbor."

"You've killed devil fish?" a timid voice asked.

Olenka nodded. "We have. They don't feel pain, but that doesn't mean they're *immortal.* You just have to know where to hit them, and you have to be quicker than their wild attacks. It's not like they're *yokai* or anything."

Whispers rose up again, and Olenka leaned back on her hips. "Listen, I don't know all the details just yet, but that's why we're coming to you. The kataw of Ku Jiya are supposed to be the most brilliant craftsmen among all the Bantay Tubig! Surely we can figure this out!"

Masato nodded thoughtfully. "How would we know when the ku jira are distracted?"

Olenka shrugged as she spoke. "Excellent question. Pitch us an idea. That's one of a dozen problems that my crew can't work out on our own. Let's work together to figure all this out!"

Olenka paused, waiting for someone else to break the silence. Eventually she rubbed her eyes and sighed.

"Listen, we really don't have time to sell this to you all. We barely have enough time to make all the necessary preparations as it is. But, tattered sails, just *think* about it… What could you *possibly* have to lose working with us? You have no way of feeding yourselves anymore, your master tells me that your rations have been nearly depleted, but you've built an incredible ship that just needs a little time to get going! You really only have two options. You can stay here and accept that you all, *without exception*, will starve to death. Or, we can work together to give us all a solid chance to change our fates. What I'm offering you is hope."

Olenka paused and watched the crowd. She wasn't sure what to expect from this broken group, but she believed that people would generally listen to reason when it was given to them. When no one else responded, Olenka stepped back and looked at Master Taro. The old man smiled and stepped up into the circle.

"Before we begin," the old man announced, "I want you all to know that I support these young ladies. They're sharks. Every one of them. I saw their talents this morning, and I see their courage now." He cleared his throat and raised his voice. "Alright! Let's put it to a vote, you suckerfish. All those *in favor* of the sirenas' plan?"

Many hands shot up around the crowd, including one from Jin's huddled mass next to Mari's lap.

"And, all those opposed?"

About ten hands tenuously rose, but quickly dropped back down in defeated submission. The old man nodded and smiled.

"So be it," he said. "Masato? Coordinate the groups. I need twenty kataw loading the iron ship with the last of our food and coal. Check the steam chamber as well. Make sure everything is sealed and running tight as a barnacle."

Masato bowed. "Anything else, Master Taro?"

The old man nodded and grunted. "Get another twenty working on finding these young ladies a reasonable vessel and loading it out onto the river. Have another ten more start gathering supplies for them: oars, baskets, harpoons, whu yao shells, anything they could need. You got me?"

Masato nodded, and then dove back into the crowd shouting orders.

Master Taro turned to Olenka and frowned. "Well, you convinced them. Rather harshly, but it worked. I just hope you three can live up to everything you just told them. Death is a pain that we all must confront, but shattered hope? That is a cruel thing indeed, sisters."

Olenka stepped past the old kataw, walking back into the warehouse. "I meant everything I said. To be completely honest, I don't think any of *you* should feel the least bit concerned."

Master Taro hobbled along behind the crew. "And why is that, little sister?"

Diwala sniffed and cracked her neck as they walked. "Because whether we live or die, the ku jira will be plenty distracted."

The old man chuckled and followed them into the warehouse. "Well, you said it, not me. What do you three say we try and improve your odds?"

* * *

THE OLD MAN GATHERED TOGETHER ALL THE SUPPLIES he could find. Piles of empty powder shells were dumped out onto the metal floor, and jars of whu yao were scrounged from every corner of the warehouse. Once the materials were collected, he knelt down on the iron floor and began assembly.

"Come on, you three." He motioned for the crew to sit on the floor beside him.

The sirena obeyed, and Master Taro nodded. "Alright, if you're going to be chucking these things into the ocean, then you should probably understand how they work." He grabbed a metal sphere and opened its main latch.

"None of these are armed yet, so you'll have to pour the powder yourself. See this opening in here? Check inside to make sure the fuse has run into the chamber. You want it to stick out about the width of your little finger. See that?"

He held the shell up to the light for the sirena to see. "Right in there, see? Once you're sure the fuse is in place, you need to fill the chamber with powder. Make sure you fill it all the way to the top. Any room you give it to expand will weaken the explosion, you understand?"

Olenka knelt down and inspected the bomb, then began assembling her own. Mari and Diwala followed. It was simple but tedious work. Master Taro was very picky and demanded perfection. The sirena were often scolded for wasting powder on the floor, or not cinching down the whu yao chamber tight enough.

Olenka glanced around at their growing pile of explosives. "Who *discovered* all of this, anyway?"

The old man smiled, his nimble fingers gingerly patting powder into the chamber. "Our tall neighbors to the north. Who else?"

Olenka shook her head. "It seems like *everything* comes from the tall miners."

The old man chuckled and shrugged. "I wish I could argue with you about that. They are truly an incredible race, but a little too sanctimonious for my taste."

Olenka glanced up from the fuse she was positioning. "Sanctimonious?"

Master Taro nodded. "Yeah, you know… They're the kind of group that makes you feel unworthy. Talking with them is always so formal. I don't think they mean to be condescending, or anything.

It just sort of happens. It's like they can't stifle their beliefs long enough to hold a friendly conversation with the likes of us lowly fish."

"Huh," Olenka muttered, "what *do* they believe?"

Master Taro paused from his work and wiped his forehead with the back of his hand. "That's hard to say, really. They aren't very open about their religion. I know that they refer to themselves as the Ju Ren. Means something important, I think… but, Heaven knows I've forgotten what. What else…" The old man leaned back and thought. "Let me see… It's been a tide or two since I've travelled that far. I suppose you could say that they believe in harmony."

Diwala asked, "Harmony?"

"Yeah, harmony. They're always going on about living at peace with everything else: never asserting control over another form of life, not disrupting nature. That kind of chum."

"And this bothers you?" Diwala asked.

Taro shrugged. "A little, I suppose. It should probably bother *you* more."

Di looked surprised. "And why is that?"

"Well, you three are warriors, right? Violence is *very* discouraged by their beliefs. I imagine you three would be downright heretics to them."

"Huh," Diwala muttered. "Intriguing. Do you know why that is?"

The old man reached up and rubbed his neck as he thought. "Well, they have a pretty unique perspective on history. The Ju Ren claim to be descendants of an ancient race of very powerful beings, long before the ancient hero ended the yokai calamity. According to their myths, this race invented wonders, and they built incredible cities that consumed the world. Eventually, they came to believe that they were more powerful than Heaven and stopped relying on the strength of the land and the sky and the sea. It's a little hard to understand, but they think those ancestors were somehow *responsible* for the yokai calamity, as if they broke the world with their actions and invited the monsters in. Some chum like that. So, now they live in solitude, and they hide their knowledge and discoveries from the rest of us. It's a buwisit shame…"

Olenka chuckled. "So, *that's* what really bothers you, huh? You're mad they won't teach you everything they know."

Master Taro smiled. "Perhaps. But what really annoys me isn't that they *won't* share their knowledge: it's *why* they won't share it."

Diwala frowned. "Why should that upset you? Everyone has reasons for what they believe. Why should their reasons be any less important than yours?"

The old kataw shook his head. "You probably wouldn't understand, little sister. You are a being of faith, not reason."

"Does one cancel out the other in your small mind?" Diwala said bitterly.

Master Taro scowled a little as he thought. "Well, it *shouldn't*," he laughed, "but it always does. Sure as snapped rigging, little sister, faith clouds things worse than any typhoon."

"In what way?" Di pressed.

The old man smiled and twisted around to face Diwala more directly. "Okay, I'll give you an example. Why is the ancient armor so important to those soggy monks?"

"It is a symbol of Heaven's victory over the yokai," Diwala declared, "and it is used in the Sacrament of Light."

The old man nodded. "*Heaven's* victory, huh? I don't remember *Heaven* doing any of the work. Well, either way that's correct. So, the next obvious question is why is the Sacrament of Light so important to them?"

Diwala spoke with a clear, dry voice. "It is our way of showing our remorse to Heaven. It is a ritual to remind us of our sins and to teach future generations not to repeat them."

The old man nodded. "I mean, that's all true, but that's a pretty watered-down version of it, don't you think?"

Diwala nodded. "I believe it is the *most important* reason for the ritual."

"Really? And appeasing Heaven's armies so that they won't send another calamity, *that* doesn't sound like the most important reason to you?"

Diwala chuckled. "Which is more important: the lesson or the punishment for failing to learn it?"

The old man laughed. "Spoken like a true disciple. Alright, well I'll tell you my problem with it all. *Why?* I'm not even really worried about *what*, I just want to know *why!* Assuming this was all true, why would Heaven have punished us so severely? The church teaches that Heaven is a kingdom of compassion, that all love trickles down from its buwisit throne. Why then would Heaven send horrors to murder its people? What sins were we punished for? What could we have done that was so offensive that all life was punished almost to the point of extinction?"

Diwala shook her head as she whispered. "You are a very bitter man, Master Taro. Why do you carry so much hate in your heart?"

Taro shook his head. "Not hate. Frustration. We live in a land of walls and secrets. Truth is kept hidden because of the myths of the past. And everyone clings to their beliefs so dearly, and with such buwisit certainty... Lightning on all that. Someone has to be wrong, don't they? The Ju Ren say that their ancestors brought about the yokai calamity by destroying the land, and the church says that Heaven sent the yokai to punish the world for its sins–"

"Can they not *both* be right?" Diwala interrupted.

Master Taro shook his head. "You're not even listening to me, are you?"

Diwala remained quite calm. "I have heard you. Perhaps you should hear me now. Why cannot both stories be true? Is it so hard to believe that the Ju Ren and the Bantay Tubig are both describing different sides of the same event? Perhaps the Ju Ren better understand the sins of our ancestors. Why do the little differences have to add up to such confusion? Is it not our job to seek the truth in all things? If you and your boys can ask why a cup will float, why will you not ask why history has produced two stories? I do not believe that the monks have all the answers, but I do believe that there is great truth in their teachings. Faith is not about rejecting reason. It is about choosing belief over doubt when the answers are unclear. To me it seems unreasonable that these two beliefs would have risen from nothing. There must be truth within each of them if we are simply courageous enough to seek it."

The old kataw nodded his concession. "I suppose there might be wisdom in your words, little sister. But, will you practice what you've just preached to me and admit that there is truth in mine?"

Diwala smiled. "Of course. The light of Heaven exists in us all, but the darkness of the yokai is ever present as well. None of us have all the truth, and none of us are completely free of error."

Master Taro grunted and returned to his bomb. Olenka stared at the old man and giggled. "You know, I have always prided myself on having a healthy skepticism, but you are downright *cynical!*" She turned to Diwala. "You remember all this next time you want to give me one of your sermons, alright? Do you see how much worse I could be?"

Marikit rolled her eyes and grumbled. "You know, all *I* see here is that I have filled eleven shells, and each of you have only filled five."

* * *

THE THREE SIRENA CHUCKLED AND HAD ALL BENT back to their work when a rapping at the metal doorway caught their attention. Olenka turned around to see Masato and a couple of young kataw standing in the doorway. They had a pile of mid-sized barrels between them.

"Master," Masato bowed as he spoke, "may I address you?"

The old man nodded and beckoned the group into the warehouse. Masato came forward and dropped down to his knees beside the sirena. He pulled a barrel in his arms around to his front. "I have been considering your words from earlier, Miss Olenka. I believe I may have a solution for your problem."

Olenka placed her shell on the ground. "Which problem are you referring to?"

"Coordinating the iron ship's departure with your attack." He gently patted the barrel in front of him, "The young ones uncovered a few casks of coal oil, Master."

Master Taro smiled and nodded. "That would work quite nicely."

Olenka was getting rather tired of being confused. She shot an expectant glare at Master Taro. "Coal oil?"

The old man reached forward and hefted the barrel toward him. "Another gift from our friends to the north."

"But what is it?" Mari asked.

"Well," the old man muttered, "I suppose you could call it liquid whu yao. It has a similar consistency to the oils found in beans and seeds and fish livers, but it is extracted from deep underground."

"*Ugh...*" Marikit whined as she rubbed her puffy eyelids. "Do you realize how little sleep I've gotten in the last few days? Will you *please* just explain how this will help us?"

Masato chuckled. "I apologize. It's just that coal oil has some incredible properties. Most notably, it can burn on water."

Olenka rolled her eyes. "*On* water? Nothing burns on water."

Masato nodded. "I'm being completely honest with you. If you poured a barrel of this out on the sea and lit it, the fire would be bright enough for us to see from across the island."

Diwala nodded and smirked. "Fire on water? That might even be useful for fighting the ku jira, no?"

She smiled at Olenka, but Olenka did not respond.

Fire on water...

"Miss Olenka?"

Olenka blinked and shook her head. Masato was staring at her with obvious concern. She cleared her throat and glanced around. "I think it's a great idea. How do the rest of you feel about it?"

Mari and Diwala nodded and glanced back at Masato. The burly kataw smiled and stood. "Excellent! I will have the barrels loaded onto your raft."

He bowed again and left.

Olenka reached for her forehead. Marikit scooted closer and placed a hand on her arm. "Hey, you alright, Kay Kay?"

Olenka smiled and lowered her hand as she mumbled. "I'm fine… I think my mind is just starting to drift a little."

Diwala nodded. "We need to sleep. We are in no condition to fight."

Master Taro grunted and yelled to a couple of young kataw outside the warehouse door. "You two! Drop whatever it is you're doing and come here!"

The young men did as they were instructed and placed the crates they were hauling down on the platform. They rushed up to Master Taro and bowed.

"I need you pups to go find someplace for these sirena to sleep. Make sure it's quiet and out of the way, can you manage that?"

"Yes sir," the kataw on the left bowed.

The old man nodded and turned to the crew. "How long do you need?"

Olenka shrugged and stood. "Come wake us when you're prepared to leave. We'll be ready by then."

Master Taro nodded and dismissed the group with a casual flick and went back to filling shells.

The kataw youths led the crew down a walkway toward the river. One hopped off the railing and guided them to a group of hammocks mounted in the secluded jungle trees. The sirena thanked him as he left. The crew did not speak as they selected beds. The day was still young, and the buzzing of insects pierced through the humid air. It was bright and hot, but the sirena were too exhausted to care. Mari and Di were out nearly as soon as they were horizontal.

Olenka did not fall asleep quickly, though. And when she did, she did not dream.

CHAPTER 33

STRENGTH TO ACT

"MISS OLENKA?"

Olenka's eyes shot open and her breathing paused. She looked around to find a young man standing at the side of her hammock.

"I'm sorry to wake you, miss, but Master Taro says that the ship is prepared to leave whenever your crew is ready."

Olenka propped herself up on her elbow and rubbed her eyes. She was completely awake, but her mind and body still ached with thrumming exhaustion, as if she hadn't slept at all. She blinked away the last crusts of slumber and studied the young man before her. He was probably around Olenka's age, maybe nineteen or twenty, but he looked *so young* to her. It was a thought that struck her with special, surreal significance. Here was a handsome young man, about her age, clearly very kind and polite, quite fit and attractive, and all she could think was how young he looked. She glanced down at her webbed fingers, flexing them in the dying light of evening.

"Miss Olenka? Are you feeling alright?"

Olenka smiled and glanced up at the boy. "I'm fine. It's just been a funny couple of days, you know?"

He laughed to himself and shrugged. "For us it's been a funny couple of months."

Olenka nodded. "I suppose it has."

The young kataw looked a little confused, so he bowed gently and turned to leave.

"What's your name?"

He turned around, surprised by her inquiry. "My name?"

Olenka nodded silently.

"My name is Eiji," he said.

Olenka smiled. "It's nice to meet you, Eiji."

He offered a timid smirk in return. "The pleasure is truly mine… Miss Olenka, may I ask you a question?"

Olenka shrugged in indifference. "Why not?"

Eiji looked down at the puddles between the trees as he spoke. "Why are you doing this for us?"

Olenka cocked her head in confusion. "Do we need a reason to help?"

Eiji chuckled. "I mean, *most* people would. *I* certainly would."

Olenka shook her head. "If you have the strength to act, then you are under obligation to act. It's as simple as that."

Eiji nodded his understanding, folding his arms over his bare, toned chest. Again, Olenka was struck by how young he seemed to her. In reality, he wasn't young at all, but a kataw man full-grown. Still, she just couldn't see him any other way.

"I suppose that's true," he muttered, "but it just seems like a rash path…"

"Have you seen what we are up against?" Olenka scoffed. "Rash is the only option left."

Eiji sighed. "Of course, I have… Please don't get me wrong, I understand how desperate things are, but… what about you and your crew?"

Olenka's expression morphed into a mild glare. "What *about* my crew? You don't think I know their limits? You don't think we can draw away the plalomas?"

The boy shook his head quickly, his words flustered and clumsy. "No! No, that's not it at all. I'm confident that you three will give us enough time to escape…. It's just, what happens to you once our ship leaves? How will you three escape? Even if you do somehow make it back to shore safely, you'll be trapped here. Same as we are now. It's like we're just passing our bondage onto you–"

"We are not planning on escaping."

Eiji spun around, startled by the new voice. Diwala had spoken from her hammock, her decorated forearm draped over her eyes.

"What?" Eiji whispered. He turned back to Olenka. "What does she mean?"

Olenka tried to smile, but she was too exhausted to force it. "We came here on a very specific job, and we're not leaving until we finish it."

The young kataw squinted in surprise. "The armor?"

Olenka nodded. "The armor."

"But… That's *madness!*" he cried. "How can you still–"

"What are you so concerned about, puddle pup?" Diwala rolled in her hammock and glanced out at the young kataw. "You all make it off Ka Jiya whether we live or die."

Eiji scowled. "That doesn't exactly make me feel any better," he spat. "This isn't right. We shouldn't just–"

"Run along now," Olenka muttered.

The young man looked up in surprise and then defiance.

Olenka raised her eyebrows to him. "The last thing we need right now is your concern. Go inform Taro that we will be with him shortly."

Eiji grimaced but bowed and trotted off down the metal path. Olenka sighed and placed her face in her hands, rubbing them briskly against her worn-out skin.

Diwala smoothly transitioned from lying to standing and stretched out her tattooed arms over her head. Neither of the two sirena spoke, nor did they make eye contact. Diwala stepped lightly to Mari and placed a hand on her shoulder. Marikit opened her eyes and sighed. She sat up and placed her hands on her hips, pushing down to stretch out her spine and shoulders.

Olenka did not move. She sat in her hammock, gently drifting over the jungle floor and staring at her reflection in a puddle.

"He looked so young to me…"

Diwala smiled but did not speak. She stepped to Olenka and held out her hands.

"Come."

Olenka looked up with an empty smile and grasped Di's webbed fingers. She pulled her to her fins, and Olenka pulled Mari to hers. The crew wandered over to the metal walkway and hoisted themselves up onto its surface. Olenka crossed her legs and stared up into the sky. There were many clouds streaking the auburn haze beyond. It must have been nearly sunset. Olenka looked back down and saw Mari and Di fold their legs to sit with her, the three forming a perfect triangle on the catwalk.

Olenka sighed and rubbed her cheek. "How are we feeling, sisters?"

Diwala swayed a little and shrugged. "I am tired, but I think I will be fine once we are out at sea."

Mari blinked a couple of times but nodded her agreement. "Same. Everything aches, but once we get moving I should be alright. Are you doing okay?"

Olenka grimaced. "I'm not really sure, you know? Honestly, I'm a little concerned with how *unconcerned* I am. Does that make sense? I feel like I should be more afraid…"

Diwala nodded. "Fear has a place, especially in our line of work. Why are you unafraid?"

Olenka leaned back on her palms and stared up into the trees. "I guess it hasn't really hit me yet, like I'm in denial. Or maybe it's shock. Maybe what's about to happen is *so* overwhelming that it's beyond my mind's ability to comprehend it…"

Marikit scratched her head. "Yeah, I'm with you. I keep thinking we need to reconsider the plan, but my heart just feels numb. Not afraid, but numb."

Diwala leaned forward and placed her hands together. "When I was just a little girl, my mother took me out to go fishing for the first time. She told me that I was not allowed to use a net or line, that my first fish must be killed with a spear. She said that other fishing tools turned killing into a game, and that killing was never a game. We wandered out into the tide pools where you can jump from rock to rock without ever even getting your fins wet."

Di chuckled at the memory and pensively tapped her fingers against her kneecap. "I remember running out onto the tall rocks where the tide was strongest, away from my mother. I told myself that there might be bigger fish there, but the truth was simply that I wanted to play, not hunt. I looked down between the rocks and I saw a fire-fish. Now, I had been told a hundred times to keep my distance from such fish, but I of course listened to *nothing* I had been told. The fish sat very still in the water, but it was farther than my spear could reach. So, I decided to squeeze down between the rocks, pressing my arms and legs against the sides. When I was down the crack, I shifted my weight to my legs only. It was very unstable, but I could hold my spear in place for the attack.

"Just then, a wave hit the rocks. It hit me hard and knocked me down almost to the water. I was very disoriented, but when I got my bearings I could see the fire-fish right beneath me. It was all puffed up with its spines flared out. You know how they do… I realized then that if I couldn't pull myself back up, I would die. If I slipped, even just a little, I would get a full load of the fish's venom in my chest and neck."

Diwala smiled and shook her head in wonderment. "Now, the most amazing thing happened then. I still remember it so clearly… I realized that I was not afraid. There was no time to be afraid, you see? My arms were too weak to hold myself steady any longer, and I only had one chance to push my way out. If I slipped, or if my strength failed, I would die… It really was that simple, so I made the choice not to die."

Diwala smiled and looked up at Mari and Olenka. "I felt afraid once it was over of course, once I was out of the little crack and back with my mother… but not *before* it happened, or *while* it happened. When I realized that it was time to act, then it was just time to act. Simple."

Olenka smiled and looked up at Diwala. "Thanks, Di."

She smiled back and pushed herself up to her fins. "We must see Master Taro now."

* * *

TARO WAS NO LONGER WITH THE REST OF THE KATAW in the iron ship. He and a small group had been finishing preparations for the crew's raft. They had hauled the boat out onto the water behind the dam in the river, ready to launch with the opening of the metal doors.

The raft looked a lot like a southern banca, but it was much larger and wider. The space in the middle was almost flat, and both sides were buoyed up with hollow, wooden pontoons as thick as casks of rice wine. All the preparations had been finished and the cargo tied down long ago, but still the old man ran up and down the vessel: checking the quality of powder shells, tightening ropes down over the oil barrels, and obsessively checking the blades of the harpoons.

As the sirena approached, Master Taro grunted and stepped off the raft and onto the walkway.

"Ah, you three got my message. You are here sooner than I would have expected, little sisters." He twisted back to gaze at the raft. "I hope we haven't forgotten anything."

Olenka shook her head. "Don't worry about us. I'm sure everything is perfect."

"Yeah, I sure hope so…" Taro frowned in thought as he stared at the raft. "What am I forgetting… Ah!"

The old man hopped down to a barrel offshore and grabbed three large metal cups from off its top.

"Here," he said, offering them to the crew.

The three sirena took the cups gratefully and swallowed their contents without question. It turned out to be a simple rice porridge cooked with too much water and not enough, well... anything else.

"I know it's not much," he muttered, "but it's more than anyone on Ka Jiya has had for a single meal in over a month. You'll need the strength more than any of us."

Mari stopped drinking and glanced around in shame. "Are you sure we–"

"Drink it," Diwala interrupted. Mari flinched, but swallowed a mouthful of the bland slime. Diwala rolled her eyes and then kept drinking.

Olenka sipped hers slowly, trying with immense difficulty to keep it down. It wasn't that she didn't want it, her limbs were very weak, and desperate for the nutrition, it was just that her stomach didn't seem to be working at the moment. It was like her body had channeled all its efforts away from her gut. Starting it up again now was almost painful.

The old man grunted approvingly as the crew drank. "Well, we've loaded up everything you asked for. Your plalomas are in the water tank just over the far bank. There's a latch on the side that will release them back into the river. Just, make sure everything is clear before you dump them." He paused for a moment, looking both confused and concerned. "You know, I'm really not sure what to say to you three."

"Okay?" Olenka glanced up and cocked an eyebrow. "Is there some kind of an *explanation* hidden in there?"

He chuckled and folded his arms. "It's just so unreasonable that a group of three little minnows is going to try to save the whole of Ka Jiya."

Diwala drained the last of her cup and then tossed it to Master Taro. "Three *sirena*. And we are not going to try. We will succeed, and you and your people will make it safely to the north."

The old man bounced the cup in his hands as he spoke. "If you three were under my authority, I would never let you do this." He shook his head and let the cup fall to the ground. "What happens when you run out of whu yao shells? What if you aren't quick enough, and the ku jira flip the raft?"

Diwala stepped past the kataw and onto the raft. "You talk as much as you worry, do you know that?"

Taro sighed in frustration. Olenka stepped up and playfully punched his arm. "Hey, old man. You just leave it to us, alright?" Olenka smiled warmly and tried again to sip her cup of slop.

Master Taro smirked. "You really do remind me of myself, sister. I know you can't see it now that I'm old and fat, but it's still the truth. You know something? I just realized that's probably the only reason I'm letting you three go out there."

Mari scoffed and tossed her cup aside. "Why, because you'd only trust *yourself* to go out there?"

"Not at all." The old man shook his head in slow, melancholy drifts. "It's because I know that nothing on the Great Sea could talk me out of it if our roles were reversed." He scratched his arm and looked back at the raft. "You three are still sure about this? Once we're gone, you'll be out there on your own."

Olenka handed him her half-full cup. "It's not your job to worry about us. It's mine. Your job is to make sure that all of those guppies get to the Bharatian Peninsula safely. Watch for our signal and don't delay your departure. No matter what happens to us, keep that ship moving."

The old man nodded but glanced up to the sky. "Are you three sure you're ready to do this now? There's no rush waiting until morning."

Olenka shook her head. "No. We'll never get the armor back to Lunsod sa Dagat in time if we don't hurry. Besides, the dark might give us an advantage. We might be able to hide from the pod before they spot us."

Mari smiled and hopped onto the boat. "Not to mention that you all need to see the signal. It will be clearer at night."

Olenka followed Mari up onto the raft while Di began loosening the lines holding them to shore. Master Taro snorted his distaste, but then hobbled up the iron stairs behind him to grip the dam's release lever.

"Listen," he grumbled, "if any of you *ever* need something from us, perhaps something built or repaired, don't hesitate. You come find us and we'll pay back this debt any way we can."

Olenka dismissed his words with a flick of her wrist. "Go. Your boys are waiting for you."

The old man yanked on the lever, bowed in solemn gratitude, and then marched off into the dying light of the jungle. The dam before them clanged and shifted, slowly drifting open with the strength of the river. Diwala loosed the last rope, and the raft lurched forward with the current. Olenka grabbed an oar and crouched down at the edge of a pontoon. Nothing had really changed now that the dam was open, but Olenka suddenly felt the weight of their risk pressing against her mind. She glanced around, ensuring she was close enough to all her supplies: harpoons, sparking device, torch, barrel of oil, basket of powder shells…

She sighed and stared out down the river as the raft floated through the battered iron gate. The sun was setting far off to her right, and the horizon beyond was a blending dissolution of vanishing light and color. The orange tips of the west streamed out on golden clouds that melted with the purple twilight. The sea shimmered on its surface but was dark as tar underneath. In the distance, the waves looked choppy but not strong. It would be fairly easy to spot the boisterous advance of the black pod.

"Okay," Olenka muttered, trying to find an appropriate volume for the moment, "let's go over the plan."

Marikit and Diwala both nodded, each leaning in to hear her voice over the clamor of the current. Olenka shifted her position to face them more directly.

"We know that they respond to sound and smell, particularly the smell of blood, so we need to be very careful with our movements…"

Olenka glanced around. They were closing in on the river mouth now. She turned back, hushing her voice. "Di, you've got the best arm among us. Would you mind?"

Diwala smiled weakly. "Not at all."

"Mari?"

Marikit nodded and held up a knife and a sparking device.

Olenka gazed back out at the sea and listened. She hoped this wasn't a mistake. She hoped that she wasn't leading her crew to catastrophe.

Why do you fret, child? You will make it out alive.

The thought came clear and gentle from within. It felt so alien to her, and yet so familiar. She sighed, and felt her sight start to glisten. It was true. In her heart she knew that she would make it through the night. There was more to come. What she feared, she suddenly realized, was whether her friends would be there with her.

"Kay Kay?"

Olenka sniffed and glanced back. Marikit was gazing at her with curiosity and concern. Olenka wiped her eyes and smiled.

"I'm fine," she whispered. "I just… I don't know what I'd do without you two."

Diwala smiled and tapped on her tattooed forehead. "Do not fear for me, my friend. I am anxious to *also* see our fates unfold before us." Diwala turned to Mari and gestured to Olenka. "She has already seen this night."

Mari's face softened, and she turned to Olenka. "By the sea…"

Mari went to speak some more but caught herself. She smiled and turned back to Diwala. "I don't want to know, do you?"

Diwala suppressed a chuckled. "Where would be the sport in that?"

Olenka realized how sour her mouth had become and she swallowed hard. "Let's just stay in the moment. I counted four mad ku jira last time, is that correct?"

Diwala nodded. "That is how many came down the river."

Olenka tapped on her barrel of oil. "Alright, then once all four are spotted?"

Mari and Diwala each tapped their drums of oil.

"Okay," Olenka whispered, "then no more talking until it's started."

CHAPTER 34

FIRE ON THE WATER

THE RAFT DRIFTED OUT OVER THE MEAGER RAPIDS of the river's mouth, and the crew began paddling, hoping to let the white water hide the sound of their approach. They guided the boat off to the left, letting it settle in the eddy caused by the river's flow crashing into the cold, rocky ocean waters. As soon as the current took, the crew pulled up their oars. The raft drifted and stabilized, sitting almost perfectly still about fifty meters from the river's mouth.

Olenka stood silently. She signaled for Diwala and Mari to keep still as she glared out across the sea. The light was dying quickly, and she wanted to wait for their vision to adjust to the darkness. She stared with resolute intensity, searching for the mildest sign in the swell. The waters were haunting in their silence, with only the gentle lapping of the tide against their raft's pontoons.

Finally, certain that the black pod hadn't heard them, Olenka turned to her crew and nodded.

Mari slit her knife gently across the back of her forearm and squeezed her wrist. She pumped her clenched fist and a dark trickle began to slip down to her elbow. Quickly, she grabbed a powder shell and rolled it up the line of blood, letting it smear across the bomb's surface. She then handed the weapon to Diwala who unlatched the wick chamber at the side and held it down to Mari. Marikit pulled a sparking device up to the fuse and cupped her free hand around it.

She clicked five times before the sinister hissing broke the silence. As soon as it did Olenka began counting in her mind.

Diwala bolted upright. She watched the fuse sizzle for a moment, and then tightened the clamp down over it. With a quick hop forward, and all the bursting force of her toned arms and chest, she threw the metal sphere into the distant inky swell.

There was a tight splash and then an uncomfortable silence.

Olenka whispered under her breath. "Six… seven… eight..."

A blast erupted in the distance, farther away than Olenka had expected.

Nine, she thought. *We have until the count of nine.*

Mari began dressing another shell while Diwala crouched down to help her. The whole crew was silent in their work, waiting for any response from the sea. Any reason to act.

Olenka was prepping a torch when she paused and squinted into the murk. She thought she had seen something, but it was impossible to tell for sure. The shimmering waves hid anything that didn't breach the surface, and it was entirely possible that her mind was just getting the best of her. After a few more silent moments to be sure, Olenka gestured to Di and Mari. Once again, the two lit a bloodied shell and hurled it into the distance.

As the water sprayed out from the explosion, Olenka saw a mirror image in her peripheral vision.

A series of spouts erupted from the sea off to the right. The whole crew had noticed, and they stayed still and low and tense. Diwala glanced at Olenka, and Olenka shook her head.

"Not yet," she mouthed. She couldn't tell how many there were. They needed to hold off a bit longer. Engage the pod all at once. The last thing they needed was an ambush in this darkness.

There was very little movement in the water, but Olenka could sense the black beasts coursing under the swell. She could almost feel them churning the sea beneath the raft. She knew that there were at least two nearby from the spouts, but two wasn't good enough. With a quick, pointed gesture, Olenka signaled the others to throw one last shell. The pair worked quickly, and Diwala tossed the explosive, aiming for the same spot as before.

The blast went off, and a chorus of agitated shrieks pierced the night.

The infected pod thrashed angrily about in the black water, flailing over one another and beating about the surface. This time it was obvious that there were four.

Olenka smiled. The plan was working perfectly. She turned to her own basket of shells and began to light another. This was their chance to even the odds. Olenka doubted that they could *kill* any of them with the whu yao shells alone, but maybe they could be slowed down. Four wounded ku jira would be more manageable than a fully functioning pod.

Hopefully…

The crew tossed shells as often as they could light them. Most of the bombs went off harmlessly in the water around the beasts, serving only to agitate and confuse them. Diwala's aim, however, was extraordinary. She held back a shell, gauging her target, and then launched the sphere into the depths. A ku jira emerged from the water, and the shell bounced off its bulbous head. The explosion was almost instant. The bomb had flung back about a meter before bursting above the breaching beast. The blast was bright and deafening, casting a violent array of sparks and flames down into the brute's rubbery flesh. The explosion decimated the creature's dorsal fin, and ripped shrapnel deep into its hide.

The mad animal did not flinch or howl in pain, but it did retreat. The light of the blast remained long after the explosion should have faded, and Olenka strained to see through the smoke. It seemed like the ku jira's whole back was on fire. How could that be? White hot flames were fuming up into the night, casting a strange violet light on the waves around the black pod as showers of blinding sparks shook free of the devil's snout.

And the beast thrashed. Not in agony, but in *panic*.

Almost the instant she noticed its plight, the ku jira descended into the depths. It was racing toward them now: their location finally revealed.

Olenka stood very still, but not out of fear. It was in concentration. What had she just seen? It felt as if something monumental had just occurred to her, but it had not yet made it to the front of her mind.

The shell exploded, and the creature burned, she thought. *Why is that important?*

The injured ku jira erupted from the swell, spraying a spout of water and bits of singed, rotting meat out into the salty air. The rest of the pod turned with it, bursting toward the raft with terrible force.

"*Now!*" Olenka screamed to her crew. The three sirena hurried to light their torches, mounting them in the gaps of the raft. Olenka knelt down beside her cask of oil and cut it free from the rope tying it down. Mari and Di continued to light and hurl powder shells, now with impressive speed and reckless abandon. The black pod raced forward, each bit of their journey punctuated by the blasts of shells in the water. Overwhelmed by this bombastic assault, the mad pod split off, racing around either side of the raft in a pincer attack. Mari and Di stayed on them, adjusting their aim as they went and forcing the brutes to keep their distance and give Olenka time.

Olenka pried the lid off the drum of oil and began to pour the greasy stuff into the sea. When it was finished, she tossed the empty drum aside and reached for her torch, lighting the signal for the metal ship to go. The oil caught and flared up underneath her. She jumped back at the burst of heat on her face and watched the oil blaze out in a swirling arch along the current. The whole world was suddenly bright and clear around her, and Olenka took a shallow bit of comfort in knowing that the kataw would certainly be able to see the signal.

And the thought finally came to her as she watched the oil burn across the water.

How could the creature's flesh be burning? Live meat doesn't ignite. It's filled with too much water, she realized. *Somehow, these monsters are flammable. Fire is their weakness...*

The pod was almost upon them, and their titanic movements were rocking the raft in wild dips and jerks. Olenka reached for a shell and lit it against her torch. A ku jira was approaching, madly sweeping through the water toward the raft. The beast charged at full speed, its putrid mouth spread open in a gaping, twisting array of ghastly, parasitic coils and jagged teeth.

Olenka stood her ground and timed her throw, sending the lit shell straight into the black beast's esophagus.

Seven... Eight... Nine...

The blast was immense, pitching the raft back, and stopping the creature with overwhelming force. The ku jira shrieked, spun off to the left, and went limp. The blast had cracked through the monster's skull and completely torn off its bottom jaw.

Olenka gazed in wonder at what she saw.

The dozens of black tendrils worming through the creature's flesh had all been ignited. Its mangled physiognomy was now perfectly illuminated with a blinding blaze as each black coil writhed in searing white sparks that cast an eerie, violet shine on the tumultuous waves. The creature was still and silent, but the black parasite within was a conflagration of motion and tortured spasms.

The ku jira's corpse sank lifeless into the waves, but the black coils continued to writhe in pain: glorious, merciless pain. It all made sense to her, then. The *ku jira* weren't flammable, the *parasite* was. Olenka was mesmerized by the sight, but strangely unsurprised by it.

I was shown this fire in my dream… she thought. *I was warned.*

A monstrous tremor rocked Olenka out of her mind as another beast rammed itself into the side of the raft. All three members of the crew lost their footing and fell back against the far pontoon.

Olenka grabbed Diwala's ankle and screamed out over the cracking wood. *"Light the rest of the oil! Burn the ku jira!"*

Diwala's eyes were bright with life as she pushed off the pontoon. She slipped her knife out of its sheath and grabbed the rope on the closest barrel. The attacking ku jira twisted away from under the raft, sending the crew tumbling again, but dropping the ship back onto the surface. The raft's beams had cracked from the attack, but they held.

With a single slice, Diwala split the cord around the barrel and rolled it down to Olenka.

Just as she caught the oil drum, a ku jira burst through the swell, crashing down on the front of the raft like it was beaching on a wooden shore. Marikit screamed as the monster's fin slapped down against her leg with immense force. Diwala was there in an instant, just as the raft began to shift and lift up from the brine. She grabbed a harpoon and wrenched it up from its stack. She ran with all her might at the ku jira, burying the blade deep into the creature's snout. The ku jira did not budge from the blow, but it shifted its attack toward Diwala, freeing Mari's leg.

Marikit screamed as the brute hefted its girth away, and she kicked off the black beast's blubber. She clawed for Olenka's hand, and she hoisted her away from the fray. Olenka had propped herself up at the raised tip of the raft, her heels wedged between the beams to keep from slipping into the ku jira's gaping maw. She pulled at the oil barrel's metal clasp, but her hands were wet and slippery, and she couldn't break the seal.

And then the attacking ku jira was joined by another.

The second monster erupted from the water and pounded its black mass onto the raft beside the other. Its mouth snapped over and over on the wet wood, slipping Mari closer to the edge with each jerking movement. Mari had clawed her way up to a torch and was lighting a powder shell that had been knocked from the basket. Without even bothering to seal the clamp over the fuse, she tossed the bomb down the spastic beast's gullet.

The monster didn't seem to notice.

Just as Olenka was able to pry open the clasp on the barrel, the shell erupted. The blast came from under the raft, forcing the animal's innards out into the sea below them. The beast did not twist in pain, but it bellowed in fury as the force of the explosion knocked it off the raft. The ship dropped and rocked, but the other ku jira held its position, still slipping its fetid mass down Diwala's harpoon shaft. Di roared into the brute's wretched mouth, the black coils within thrashing closer to her chest with each burst of momentum.

Olenka finally wrenched the lid off the barrel, oil sloshing up her arms and chest. She swung the container and threw herself forward. The oil pumped out in great gulps, drenching the beast's snout and throat. Olenka tossed the barrel straight down the monster's tongue just as Mari hurled her torch into its ragged jaws.

The effect was instant and overwhelming.

The fire flowered to gargantuan immensity, fully consuming the creature's head and flippers. The ku jira cried out into the night as a hundred tendrils of black squirmed and sizzled into crisp, white sparks that fed the inferno. The beast, or perhaps the *sickness* within the beast, thrashed in absolute agony, trying to free itself from the raft. With impossible force, it threw its head back, splashing into the inky sea and hurling ribbons of molten flesh and parasite out over the raft and crew…

…and a single piece pelted Olenka's shoulder.

Olenka screamed as the oil on her body ignited, and when her scream became very bright and resounding, deafening in the chilled wind around her, Olenka looked up to see the raft slap back down to the water's surface. The ship was thrashing wildly, the pontoons on either side crashing hard into the chaotic crests. All around her the sea was on fire. The waves of light flicked and jerked with the waves of water beneath them. Great crimson tongues flared around the boat, casting oily plumes of smoke that choked out the sweet, ocean air and obscured the night sky. The greasy black belched and smacked and tainted the clean marine sky that was no longer clean.

Mari and Di were frantically maneuvering around the boat, cutting cords off barrels and dumping oil into the inferno. The barrels fell right through the flames, dipping oblivion one brief, bobbing bow before drifting to obscurity below. Olenka felt smoke sting and blur her vision, twisting the light of the fire into distorted shimmers and dim sparks that smeared and stretched the colors around her that were suddenly much brighter than they should have been.

And she fell back into the water.

* * *

SOMETHING MORE POWERFUL THAN OLENKA'S MIND took control, and her body was suddenly numb to all sensations. Time slowed as she felt a force within her rise to the surface of her thoughts, and vivid memories of her vision returned to her. With perfect clarity she saw again the crushing tentacles of daiow ika, black veins pulsing under grey, rotting flesh, and the face of the ancient hero, drifting in the deep water.

Olenka's thoughts were swifter than her body, and it occurred to her that twice now her prophetic sight had been fully realized. She watched the flames on her vest douse to plumes of steam swirling through a barrage of oscillating bubbles, all of it moving much slower than should have been possible. She felt her lungs jerk and tighten, as her body entered the cold. The water was beautifully lit, a chilling white light streaking and swaying around her. She gazed up past the water and saw the ember plumes dancing on the lustrous surface. It was almost as if she were peering at it through shattering glass.

The water was filled with the piercing resonation of the bellowing beasts. Olenka's head drifted on her neck, staring out through the grey, foggy sea. A ku jira floated beside her: limp, lifeless, harmless. Its flesh was burnt and marred, and there was a deep crack running the length of its yawning skull. Long, thin stains of chalky white were singed into its inanimate flesh, the last marks of the poor creature's conquered illness.

But she was wrong.

The ku jira's flesh began to shift, and a pulsating coil of black teased its way out of the corpse. There was no fear in Olenka's heart. She was too exhausted for fear. She watched with macabre fascination as several veins of the oily plague bubbled to the grisly tips of the animal's torn flesh, converging and merging into an awful black sludge in the murk. Ripples of bulbous nodules rolled down the swollen protuberance, stretching its feeling, pointing, searching tips ever closer to Olenka's flaccid lips.

But someone yanked Olenka free of the tainted water.

As her face pierced the surface she gasped and screamed as her conscious mind rushed back to time and feeling and a frigid, fearful realization of what had almost happened. Marikit and Diwala were at her sides, violently hoisting her back up onto the raft. Olenka spun onto her back, frantically sweeping her hands across her arms and chest as she screamed. The skin on her neck and collarbone had been burned, but there was no sign of the black pestilence. She was still clean. Still not infected.

She wept and gasped and kicked back on the slick wood, sliding herself toward the center of the raft. All around her, the world was a blur of sound and light. The two remaining mad beasts were screaming into the night, eagerly stirring up the waters, but unable to pass through the fiery barricade. The flames had grown to dizzying heights that cooked the crew's skin and towered a meter above the raft.

Diwala and Mari rushed to Olenka's side, gripping her arms, and huddling together away from the flame.

"*What should we do?*" Mari screamed over the blaze. Tears were streaming down her terrified cheeks, a spark of hysteria convulsing just beneath her quivering brow.

Olenka trembled and wept with her sister, still feeling the black coil twirling toward her in her mind. She raised a shaking hand to her brow but clenched it. She shook her head and leaned forward onto her knees.

"What do we have left?" she yelled, and the roaring of the flames and the furious ku jira beyond nearly swallowed up her words.

Diwala swiveled her head to the crushed front of the raft. "It looks like one stack of harpoons and a handful of shells! Everything else was lost to the sea!"

"What about the oars?" Olenka tried to stand but stumbled helplessly into Mari's lap.

Diwala glanced around, squinting into the glare of the fire. "I see two," she called out, "pressed against that far pontoon!"

Olenka tapped on Mari's leg. "Go grab the oars! Di, gather up the shells!"

The two sirena split off across the wreckage. Olenka stumbled onto her side, landing on something sharp. She lifted up on her forearm to find a sparking device pressed against her hip. She crawled up onto her hands and knees and slid the tool into the pouch at her waist.

Mari rushed back first, gripping the oars with one hand and pulling Olenka to her feet with the other. Olenka steadied herself against her friend, slowly finding her balance. She leaned up against Mari's hip and took an oar. She propped herself against it and shook her head once more. The pain bursting through her skull was phenomenal. A blinding light was tightening around the edges of her sight in bright, blurry rings that crippled her balance and obscured her sense of direction.

"Di, grab us some harpoons! Mari, take the left pontoon! I'll paddle on the right!"

Marikit stared at Olenka in horror as she shrieked. *"What do you mean?* You want us to *leave* the fire?"

Olenka nodded and forced a reassuring smile. "That fire's going out sooner or later, and I don't like where that puts us… Let's give them something to chase! Get us back to shore!"

Mari's eyes were anxious, but she nodded and took her post. Olenka swiveled around to see Diwala cast a pile of harpoons at her feet.

"Di, if you get the chance, sink one of those straight into their skulls! Nothing but a killing shot, you got it?" Diwala nodded, and Olenka forced another grin. "Just keep them off us until we get to shore!"

Diwala hefted a harpoon into the crook of her arm. Olenka slid up to the pontoon and sank her paddle into the water, not bothering to signal Mari. The raft drifted, and the fire whipped out over their heads. Mari screamed as a flame twisted up her forearm, but still she paddled. The heat was cruel, and Olenka swore she could feel the burns bubbling up in the tender webbing between her fingers. She yelled out through clenched teeth, and in a few more excruciating thrusts, the raft cleared the inferno.

Olenka blinked away her tears and kept the oar moving as fast as she could. As they pulled away from the smoke, Olenka could see the shore coming into view. It was no more than twenty meters away, but those were twenty meters of complete blackness: an awful abyss that could be hiding thousands of parasitic tendrils.

The wall of flame behind them raged on, and the screeches of the two remaining beasts sounded frantic and confused. Olenka signaled to Diwala who popped open the clamp of a powder shell and lit its fuse on their one remaining torch.

A brutal impact rocked the raft.

Diwala fell back onto the deck, the powder shell careening into the sea with an impotent burst of bubbles that broke against the seafloor. One of the two ku jira had swum under the fire and was trying to flip the raft. It rose up from the deep, ramming its head against Olenka's pontoon. The raft snapped and creaked but settled as the monster dropped them back onto the water. Olenka's frantic eyes assessed the snarl of splintering beams and frayed ropes that used to be their raft.

One more attack like that and the deck would be flotsam.

Olenka knew she had mere moments to react before the ku jira circled back around. She tossed aside her oar, took up a harpoon, and screamed out behind her. *"Di! Light another one! Bring it to the pontoon!"*

Diwala did as she was instructed, but the raft lurched up beneath her as she sprinted to Olenka's side. The ku jira's head and back slammed up against the flimsy boat, right where the pontoon met the beams. Olenka gripped the harpoon with both hands and sank it into the monster's back. She yanked back on the shaft, splitting open a sizeable gash on its head.

"Now, Di! Before it dives!"

Diwala threw herself forward, plunging the sizzling bomb into the animal's wound. She jerked her hand back out, narrowly escaping the black tendrils closing in around the foreign sphere. The three sirena tried to run, tried to leap to safety, but the explosion was too quick. The shell burst, shredding both the beast's skull and the raft's beams into a shroud of tan and white splinters. Half of the boat folded over onto itself, crashing viciously into the crew as they plunged into the water.

Olenka hit the sea dazed and broken. Her sight was a swirl of flashes and glimmers and broken bits of wood. She kicked in the direction she believed to be up and felt herself collide with the sand of the seafloor. She clawed at the grit, trying to find the traction to flee.

There's still one more out here, she thought. *We have to get to shore.*

The current whipped up around her, cool and clean, and Olenka realized that she was swimming for the mouth of the river. She rushed forward in desperation. Perhaps the river's flow would keep the parasitic coils at bay. Perhaps she'd be able to—

And the final ku jira rammed into her legs and abdomen.

The weight of the creature's attack spiraled Olenka into the air, her body spinning limp and helpless, all her limbs stretched out like a sea star. She careened straight into the pool of the river's mouth. The impact of the fall slammed her against a jagged rock, and she felt the stone's point punch through the meat above her right shoulder blade. She screamed a flurry of bubbles into the clear river water as her own blood rose up like wisps of smoke around her. She thrashed ahead, feeling the thrill of adrenaline bloom through her tendons.

A massive wave shook through the pool as the black beast surged up into the river. The water rushed against Olenka, tossing her forward like flotsam caught in the surf. The monster pounded forward onto the shoal, crazed and consumed by the smell of Olenka's blood. Olenka slipped along the shallow water, trying to ride the beast's swell upstream. Her eyes shot around, searching for an escape, searching for shore, but she could only see the black beast writhing its girth towards her. The ku jira was so enormous that even digging its way across the sand it still was closing the distance to her at an alarming rate.

Just off to the right, Olenka saw the wrought iron poles of a kataw walkway. She suppressed the pain in her shoulder and twisted her body toward it, clawing at the water for speed. Just as she slipped under the metal, she felt the whole structure tremble. The water was ankle-deep now, and Olenka swiveled around under the catwalk. The ku jira crushed into the iron frame, bending it like wax. Olenka screamed, crawling back against the mud bank behind her. The metal walkway screeched as it caved in on itself, and the black brute bellowed. Rotten flesh peppered her face as the creature bit into the walkway and shook its head.

The beast's violence wrenched the walkway straight out of the sand, and Olenka heard wood snapping as the metal support beams burst from the ancient trees in the darkness behind her. The walkway broke and buckled under the monster's teeth, and the beast tossed it away into the water.

Olenka scrambled up the mud bank, now totally exposed…

"Get down!"

Olenka cast her gaze up into the trees to see Marikit and Diwala rushing through the jungle, harpoons raised over their shoulders. Olenka leapt forward, her stomach skidding across the dirt and sticks of the forest floor, her hands clapped down over the back of her head. The beast roared and tumbled up onto the beach behind her, its jagged maw bearing down on her fins.

Olenka twisted back, prepared to see the beast's mouth consume her fins.

Instead, she watched the harpoons sink into their mark. Mari's tore into the ku jira's neck, chipping into the creature's skull. Diwala's blade cleaved straight through the beast's eye, slipping deep into its head, and stopping the beast dead in the dark. It convulsed and something inside it seemed to deflate, but the black brute did not move again.

Olenka sat up, panting. She couldn't believe it, but it was over. The final ku jira was dead. She stood slowly, watching the creature's damp, still carcass glisten in the moonlight. There was no life in its eyes, no movement in its muscles.

But the animal's black skin began to writhe and shift.

Olenka crouched down and gaped at the remains. Hundreds of the oily, black curls were piercing their way out of the beast's body. They plopped out in rancid puddles, drifting and draining back to the river. From the ku jira's mangled eye socket, a tendril coiled out into the air, searching and feeling for a new host. Olenka reached for the sparking tool at her waist and held it up to the thing's pointed end. It felt forward, grasping at the metal fork.

When it touched, Olenka clicked the device's prongs together.

The minor scrape of sparks instantly erupted into blinding white. The filthy coil reeled back on itself, twisting in agony as it was consumed. The fire spread like a falling star, burning faster and brighter than a mound of whu yao.

Olenka stood and limped to Di and Mari, gripping at her gored shoulder. Marikit's face was streaming tears. She fell forward into Olenka's arms, and together they collapsed onto their knees and wept. Diwala stepped up beside them, her arms tightly folded across her chest.

There, in the violet light of the blaring flame, the crew watched the blight singe down to white, empty powder.

Epilogue

Beautiful Boy

THE BEAST'S LONG, WORN TEETH RIPPED THEIR way into Lorenzo's torso, popping through his abdomen with nothing but brute force. Blood bubbled up into his throat, drowning out his cries. With the crisp clarity that comes with catastrophe, Lorenzo saw the sun gem crash onto the grass of the plains, shatter, and then reassemble. Through billowing distortions, Lorenzo could just make out his brother's face, frozen in horror. Then, with impossible speed, Corin fell to his knees, then to his side, then there was a burst of light...

...and then he was gone.

The sky over the plains quickly raced from day to night. Storm clouds came, speeding across the horizon far too quickly to be real. The grass below was a blur of motion that smeared into a solid, coursing mass that made no sense to Lorenzo's tortured mind.

His eyes rolled away from the sight, suspended in a void of bending light and shadow. A curtain of oily haze whipped around him. Time, gravity, and all other sensations seemed to pull away. His mind was briefly lifted from his pain, and then the surreal vision ended.

But the nightmare was only beginning.

The woolly beast erupted through another wall of shimmering air, collapsing onto an immense platform of tangled, violet tendrils. The beast went limp, letting Lorenzo flop out onto his back. His diaphragm contracted, desperately sucking at the atmosphere, but his lungs filled with something rancid and disturbingly sweet. The greasy plumes of air filled his chest, burning with toxic acidity. The panic for oxygen quickly eclipsed the suffering in his gut as he choked and clutched at his throat.

He shot his eyes around in desperation and saw the sunken, glittering eyes of ten thousand devils staring back into his. His mind shrank, and his vision blurred, unable to comprehend the array of monstrous creatures before him. They stood in tight, organized rows with military coordination contrasting their wild spectrum of primal disfigurement.

Well, well... what a wondrous gift you have brought me.

The voice came from everywhere at once, assaulting Lorenzo inside and outside of his mind. Through the thick, putrid air, the young captain saw a web of black coils squirming across the crystal surface. A million inky vines twirled up from the marshy expanse beneath the demon army and descended on Lorenzo's helpless, failing body. They forced themselves into every cavity, burrowing into the wounds in his belly, and pumping into the corners of his eyes. Crimson panic raced through his mind as his veins swelled and burst.

Do not resist me, child. I can save you.

The voice echoed across his flesh, and the kind, foreign words brought no comfort. That pain... That indescribable pain. Lorenzo knew he would do *anything* to end it.

Save me, he thought.

And the voice heard him.

The black poison burned through his rigid frame and quickly eclipsed all sensation. His mind separated from his body. He felt his senses snap and recede. With them went the pain. His fear as well.

Be still, beautiful boy. I can bring you such strength. You need only trust me.

Lorenzo tried to struggle, exerting all his might to move, but his body remained inert. He was aware of something else filling his frame, suppressing his limbs. The feeling would have been madness, but the terrible dark voice had wormed its way into his mind as well as his body. He felt only a soothing feeling of joy brush across him, caressing his frail nerves with gentle, practiced empathy. It felt like a master stroking an anxious pet. Despite his pride and horror, Lorenzo relaxed.

There, child. Good. Very good. Now, embrace your liberation. Feel my strength.

The pressure in his mind receded, but not fully. Just enough to give him control of his limbs. Lorenzo opened his eyes, and stared up at an overcast, charcoal sky. He blinked out of habit, not necessity. He stood effortlessly, feeling the tethers of pain and fatigue fall to his feet. They were an old, tattered garment that he had outgrown.

He looked down at his hands. His flesh was pale, and his veins were black and bloated, but he had never felt more alive.

Come, beautiful boy. Come to me, my most impressive warrior.

THE END

<u>GLOSSARY OF TERMS</u>

THE TELAKS

BACA: Quadrupedal herd animal common to the plains of Centile. Prized for its milk and hide, though occasionally used as a beast of burden for transport and agriculture. Unlike their milk, baca meat is often discarded by the strictly vegetarian Centileans who most often use it to feed cyoves.

BRILLO: Derived from "brilliant." Outlander slang for Centilean guards. References the metallic shine of their armor.

CENTILE: Largest city on the vast plains of the same name; founded by Vallin nearly three hundred years ago. While there are some additional towns and outposts (most notably Dawn's Harbor far to the southeast), Centile City is the undisputed cultural and economic hub of telak society.

    The city is built around Vallin's Tower, an enormous structure that houses the Sun Gem which powers the canopy of golden light protecting the tower plaza and the city's inner district.

CYOVE: Fearsome canine mounts used by the Centilean guards. Cyoves are incredibly fast and strong, and highly valued for their prowess in both mounted combat snd transport. Covered in bristling hides of tan and brown fur, they blend easily into the golden grass of the plains.

LAHARTO: Burly lizards used for hauling carts. Lahartos are covered in a thick, scaled hide that ranges from dark red to light brown. They have wide mouths with blunt teeth, snub tails, and yellow eyes. While stout by comparison, lahartos can match cyoves for speed when given the opportunity on the open plains.

OUTLANDER: Term used to describe telaks living outside the districts of Centile. While biologically identical, there are stark cultural and linguistic differences between outlanders and Centileans. Prejudice is common on the plains and has led to significant military disputes in the past.

TELAK: Bipedal race that inhabits the western coast of the Great Sea. With dark, tan complexions and an affinity for heat and sunlight, telaks are uniquely suited for life on the plains.

Telaks have long, pointed ears and thin whiplike tails that end in a collection of barbs. Bound in a tight club until adolescence, the barbs separate and bloom out as telaks reach maturity. The tips become curled and brittle with old age.

The most pronounced physical feature of the telaks, however, are their long, digitigrade legs with their distinct "lightning bolt" shape. Thighs run to an initial set of knees which bend back to a second set, giving telaks an almost bird-like gait. This is further emphasized by their feet, which consist of four muscular, load-bearing toes.

WALLIE: Outlander slang for citizens of Centile. References the city's wall and those who choose to live behind it.

THE BANTAY TUBIG

BANCA: Small, pontooned sailboat. Unlike "barges" (a term used generally to describe all large, seaworthy vessels) or "riverboats" (typically long, flat, sail-less cargo vessels used for shipping along jungle streams), bancas are compact and swift ocean vessels. They have a base canoe holding a bamboo mast with full-batten sampan rigging, and typically one support pontoon mounted to the starboard hull, though some have two. Bancas are often used by sirena and siokoy crews to quickly travel up and down the coast.

BANTAY TUBIG: The semi-aquatic race living along the eastern coast of the Great Sea with a deeply religious, collectivist culture divided into a strict caste system. Settlements range from the southern coast of the Bharatian Peninsula, through the eastern mangrove estuaries and jungle rivers of the Padmaputran River Basin, and down the southeastern coast to an archipelago known as the Southern Isles.

    The Bantay Tubig are marine mammals, capable of holding their breath up to fifteen minutes at a time. Their fingers are webbed to the first knuckle, and their feet have evolved into short, graceful fins, capable of both walking and swimming. They are hairless (save the top of their heads) and their bodies are counter shaded: dark, slate blue down the back and sides, and a light, creamy shade covering the belly, inner-arms, inner-legs, and most of the face.

BARYA: Bantay Tubig base currency. One hundred silver barya (also known as "silver scales") are worth a single gold barya.

BHAI: Bantay Tubig micro-currency. Ten bhai are worth a single silver barya. Copper Crabs are used instead of Bhai in most inland settlements. No form of micro-currency is accepted in Lunsod sa Dagat.

BHARATIAN PENINSULA: Vast northern peninsula, the southern coast of which is populated by Bantay Tubig. Bharatian settlements border the northern mountains populated by the reclusive Ju Ren, and are therefore a trading hub for exotic mountain materials and northern novelties.

BUSHI: The elite warriors of Lunsod sa Dagat. The bushi are not a caste of their own, and members may be recruited from any caste besides the ugkoy. Typical bushi garb includes a body suit of scaled armor, ornamented shoulder pads and thigh coverings, and a large, shafted weapon, usually a spear or halberd.

BUWISIT: Moderate expletive commonly used among Bantay Tubig lower castes. Roughly translates to "unlucky" or "annoying." The term has vague associations with being struck by lightning.

FIRE-FISH: Species of venomous, quilled fish found commonly up and down the tropical eastern coasts of the Great Sea. Because of their gaudy, barbed appearance, as well as their potent, painful venom, fire-fish have often been associated with strength and courage in Bantay Tubig astrology.

GREAT TRENCH: Immense submarine trench running along the western borders of Lunsod sa Dagat. Because of its incredible size, as well as its bleak, foreboding appearance, it has long been associated with the Jaws of Naraka: the legendary gateway where the ancient armies of yokai first emerged.

HIHI'IROKANE: Sacred metal capable of channeling the light of Pa Naing. A lump of hihi'irokane can easily be mistaken for polished silver when not illuminated, but it is heavier than comparable portions of other metals. Little else is known about the sacred ore except that it is incredibly rare and precious.

The kataw of Lunsod sa Dagat teach that hihi'irokane was a gift sent from Heaven to protect the Bantay Tubig during the Yokai Calamity. The metal is also rumored to be capable of housing the souls of the dead. The altar and wall etchings of Pa Naing are made from molten hihi'irokane. Bantay Tubig legend states that the ancient hero's sword and armor were likewise crafted from this sacred ore.

KA JIYA: Enormous, isolated island found just south of the Bharatian Peninsula. Home to an ancient clan of blacksmith kataw said to have originally been trained in their secretive arts by the great Ju Ren smiths of the past. The Ka Jiyan kataw are credited with having crafted the ancient hero's sacred armor and are commissioned with its annual upkeep before the Sacrament of Light. Most of the holy city's metallurgical wonders, including Pa Naing's altar, wall etchings, and the Temple of Light itself, are all due to the skill of Ka Jiya's smiths.

KAIZO: Gender neutral term synonymous with "pirate."

KARAFURU REEF: Rich, barrier reef that runs along the southern coast of Sotay Wharf toward the isle of Lunsod sa Dagat.

KATAW: The highest caste of the Bantay Tubig. There are two clans of kataw: those who dwell in Lunsod sa Dagat (commonly referred to as "city fish" by the lower castes), and the blacksmiths of Ka Jiya. Kataw bear the most intricate kudori patterns, distinguished by their thin, delicate swirls and dots (sometimes referred to as "holy lace").

KROK CAKES: Common bar food. Fried cups of mashed rice, typically filled with fried shrimp or brook minnows, sliced white-flower chives, and finished with coconut syrup.

KUDORI: Pattern formed along the brows of all Bantay Tubig, used to determine caste. Often referred to as "Heaven's mark." The countershading of Bantay Tubig smoothly fades from one color to another in most places (along the sides, inner thighs, and underarms), but the colors clash along the forehead, nose, and upper cheeks to create intricate patterns with profound social and religious significance.

Kudori reading is an ancient practice, and caste charts and diagrams have been created and revised for centuries, attaching immense prophetic and astrological significance to the slightest of details.

Despite this complexity, kudori can be categorized into three main groups and subsequent castes: ugkoy patterns (characterized by mottling and blotches, often compared to carp skin), sirena and siokoy patterns (charaterized by sharp, jagged patterns), and kataw patterns (characterized by intricate swirls and accentuating dots).

Because caste systems are determined by kudori, great attention is given to marriage. Inter-caste relationships are very taboo, but Bantay Tubig of lower castes constantly strive to marry and arrange marriages above their own station in the hope that future children will be born with a more favorable kudori. Unfortunately, mixed-caste kudori are the most common result of such efforts and carry significant shame in traditional social circles.

KU JIRA: Species of giant black and white plalomas native to the waters surrounding Ka Jiya. The ku jira are considered sacred creatures, and the Ka Jiyan kataw have long used them to transport wares and passengers to and from their isolated island home.

LAMBANOG: Type of hard alcohol distilled from coconut sap. While rice wine is the favored liquor of most Bantay Tubig, lambanog is far cheaper to produce, and therefore common among the lower castes.

LUNSOD SA DAGAT: Holy city of the kataw built on an island of the same name. Lunsod sa Dagat is an architectural wonder, built in two distinct halves that roughly mirror one another at the waterline, giving the optical illusion of a reflection along the water's surface. Because of the immense shield of blue light created by Pa Naing, the entire city is dry and watertight, even though the bottom half is submerged hundreds of meters below the surface.

The holy city was built within the collapsed caldera of an ancient volcano, and (if it weren't for Pa Naing's barrier) would be surrounded on most sides by the island's hidden lagoon. The city is composed of a complex collection of spires, towers, bridges, and buttresses, which are built out of, and into, the island's bedrock. The submerged portion of the city is supported by enormous pillars that reach the distant seafloor and skirt the great trench beyond.

Because Lunsod sa Dagat houses Pa Naing and the Temple of Light, it is the undisputed center of all religious activity among the Bantay Tubig. The conclave of monks, as well as the Sant herself, all reside in the Temple of Light. All religious artifacts (such as scrolls of the ancient hero's words, tapestries bearing his likeness, and ceremonial rice wine) are produced by the holy city's kataw. A substantial portion of all offerings collected in the many temples dotting the coast is sent to Lunsod sa Dagat to support the clergy.

NARAKA: Bantay Tubig name for hell, often associated with the deepest depths of the ocean abyss. Naraka is a place of brutal punishment for those consumed by their greed and cruelty. In legend, it is the home of the yokai, which overran the world nearly three centuries ago during the Yokai Calamity.

The kataw teach that Heaven had always intended Naraka to be nothing more than a prison for the wicked, but the greed and cruelty of the world had grown so widespread that Naraka could no longer be contained. Heaven, therefore, was powerless to stop the spread of Naraka's armies of yokai until the world had sufficiently repented of its sins, thus tipping the weighted scales of eternity back into balance. The subsequent purpose of modern kataw ceremonies, such as the Sacrament of Light, is twofold: first, to provide a sacrifice of devotion to appease Heaven, and second, to satiate the hungry jaws of Naraka with the scent of righteous blood willingly spilled.

PA NAING: Sometimes referred to as the "sea stone" or the "water gem," Pa Naing is the most sacred object in Bantay Tubig religious tradition. Legends say it was a tear shed by the Sun Goddess as she wept for the world during the Yokai Calamity.

Pa Naing has been described as an ever-flowing spiral of liquid light and glows a brilliant electric blue. It rests upon its altar of hihi'irokane, lending energy to both the shield surrounding Lunsod sa Dagat as well as the many wall etchings lighting and decorating the city.

While Pa Naing is a popular destination for religious pilgrimage, touching or interacting with the sea stone is strictly forbidden to all but the Sant herself. The conclave of monks teaches that the Sant may experience visions or revelations through communing with Pa Naing that communicate the will of Heaven.

PADMAPUTRA: Largest river on the eastern coast of the Great Sea. The Padmaputran Delta, with its surrounding system of jungle rivers, is the primary infrastructure connecting the inland and coastal Bantay Tubig settlements. The fort-city of West Muban is built along its northern banks, and Sotay Wharf is situated on the southern shore of its western delta.

PLALOMA: Aquatic mammal used extensively by the Bantay Tubig. Plalomas are the only creatures besides the Bantay Tubig themselves which have kudori: located most noticeably on the underside of their tail flukes.

There are three known species of plalomas: oceanic plalomas (which have the same blue and cream coloration as Bantay Tubig), blind river plalomas (which are mostly shades of brown to match the silty waters of the Padmaputra), and the enormous black and white ku jira (found only in the temperate, northern waters surrounding the island of Ka Jiya).

Oceanic plaloma pods are used for hauling loads and carrying ballasts in deep waters. They can also be ridden (once fitted with a saddle harness around their dorsal fin) and were used by the great plaloma bushi of the past to carry them off to battle while wearing weapons and armor too heavy for unassisted swimming.

SAMAY LAWA: Shark wrestling pool, common among siokoy bars. The samay lawas are enclosed, circular pools, about five to six meters in diameter, used to contain a single shark.

Siokoy crews use the samay lawas to test their courage and flaunt their prowess in underwater combat. The shark is starved and tormented for several days as siokoy leap in and out of the pool, narrowly escaping the creature's jaws. Fatalities are rare, but significant injuries and loss of digits are not uncommon.

SANT: Highest religious office among Bantay Tubig society. The Sant is the only female member of the conclave of monks. Regarded as an oracle, she is the only Bantay Tubig permitted to commune with Pa Naing. The Sant is also commissioned with officiating in the most sacred religious ceremonies, namely the Sacrament of Light and the confirmation of new monks.

Sant's are chosen for their exceptionally rare kudori, known as "Heaven's Hand" and are trained from youth to be Heaven's mouthpiece to discern and communicate the will of Pa Naing. The Sant in training is known as the "child of promise."

SILVER RIVER: Allegorical term used to describe Heaven, or sometimes the path to Heaven. In Bantay Tubig astrology, the Silver River is a vast conglomeration of stars that span a single stretch of the night sky, most spectacular in late summer just before monsoon. The term is common in legends about the ancient hero, and various religious figures are said to have sailed or swam up the Silver River in their attempts to reach Heaven.

SIOKOY: Male warrior caste of the Bantay Tubig. There is no cultural difference between the sirena and siokoy castes save gender. Despite this, mixed-caste crews are strictly taboo. Siokoy typically dress themselves bare-chested to flaunt their tattoos and shark tooth necklaces.

SIRENA: Female warrior caste of the Bantay Tubig. There is no cultural difference between the sirena and siokoy castes save gender. Despite this, mixed-caste crews are strictly taboo.

Because of the competition with domineering siokoy crews, sirena have developed a culture of fierce sisterhood. Young crews (sometimes referred to as "rice runners") have to work relentlessly for many seasons to build up a reputation able to compete with siokoy crews of similar experience levels.

Sirena typically dress themselves in streamlined fish-skin vests with girdles designed to hold spears and knives. Unlike siokoy, sirena never wear shark-tooth necklaces, but tattoos are not uncommon.

SOTAY WHARF: Southern trade hub along the eastern coast of the Great Sea. Sotay is the most lucrative port among all Bantay Tubig settlements and handles the distribution of all religious artifacts shipped from the holy city. Sotay is a cosmopolitan port and attracts Bantay Tubig of all castes and professions.

TORA: Reclusive and semi-mythological jungle beast, said to look a little like a giant monkey, but with devastating claws, shark-like fangs, and vibrant stripes the color of smoke and flame. Witnesses claim that it slinks around the jungle on all fours (sometimes on the ground and sometimes up in the trees) preying on creatures of all sizes, including the occasional Bantay Tubig.

UGKOY: The lowest caste of the Bantay Tubig. Commonly employed in agricultural and artisanal pursuits, especially rice farming.

UZAI: Mild expletive common among the lower castes. Denotes something as being unsavory or otherwise repulsive. Vague references to chum and other forms of ocean refuse.

WEST MUBAN: Heavily fortified city found deep in the northeastern jungle of the Bharatian Peninsula, and main trade hub for all northern Bantay Tubig civilization. The city itself spans an immense portion of the Padma River (the chilly headwaters of the Padmaputra before it merges with the Panatay) and is said to have been the ancient hero's military capital in his campaign against the yokai armies. An East Muban is rumored to have once existed, though the ancient village has long since been either eclipsed or consumed by its sprawling, western cousin.

YOKAI: Legendary devils of Bantay Tubig mythology. Thought to serve the Iron Emperor of Naraka, the Bantay Tubig teach that yokai were unleashed upon the world in a time of great greed and wickedness: a time when the violence of Naraka could no longer be contained. Said to come in all sorts of grotesque shapes and sizes, the yokai were drawn to fresh blood and killed without mercy or restraint.

Olenka and Corin's story continues in…

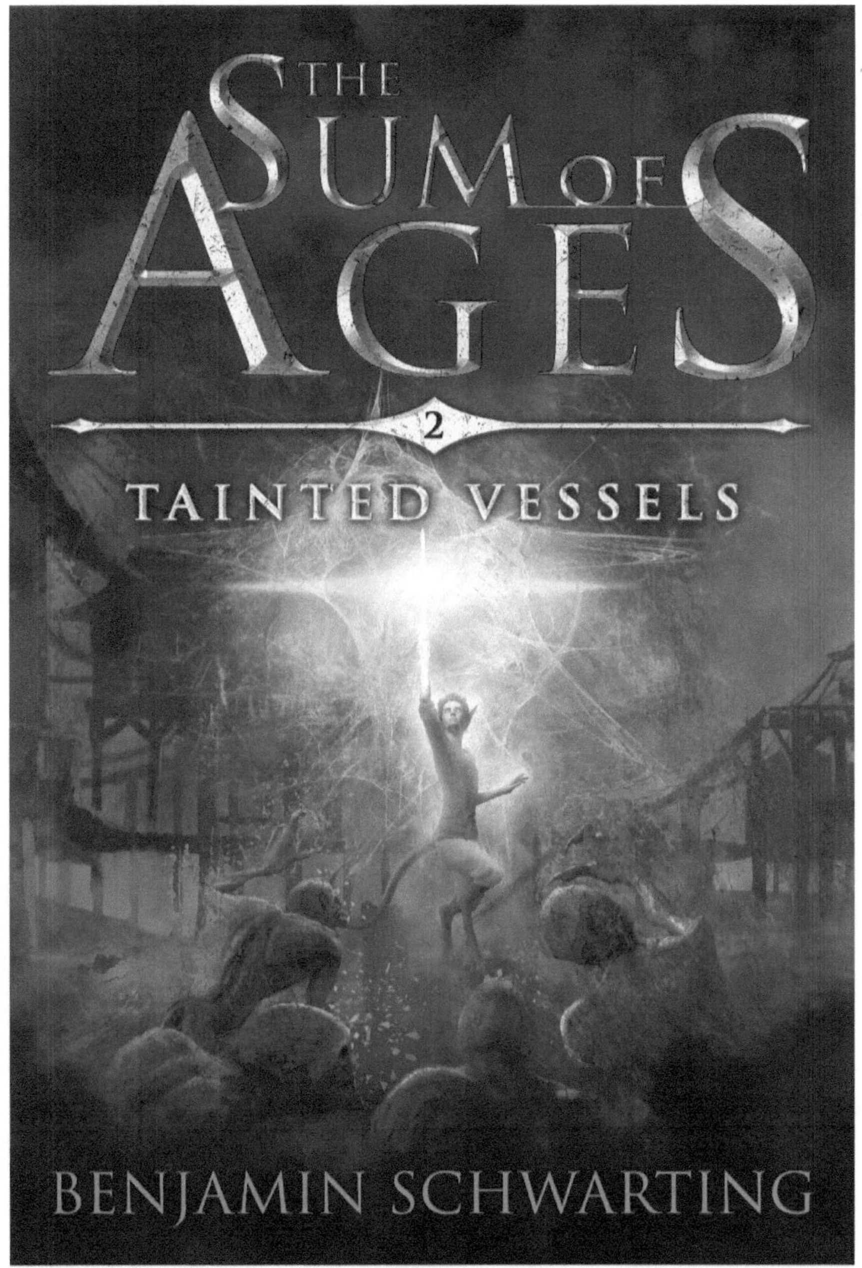

About the Author

Benjamin Schwarting is a fantasy author, high school English teacher, and co-owner of Williams & Rose Publishing. Author of *The Sum of Ages* series, Ben's work emphasizes writing complex fantasy cultures that highlight real-world issues of systemic oppression and social injustice. After earning his MAT, Ben has taught as an adjunct professor of Education at the College of Idaho and designed creative writing and young author's courses for high schoolers.

To learn more about upcoming releases, and to receive a free digital copy of *The Aetorium Anthology*, visit:

www.benjaminschwarting.com